W9-ACW-917

Ruling Destiny

ALSO BY ALYSON NOËL

STEALING INFINITY SERIES

Stealing Infinity
Ruling Destiny

THE BEAUTIFUL IDOLS SERIES

Unrivaled
Blacklist
Infamous

THE IMMORTALS SERIES

Evermore
Blue Moon
Shadowland
Dark Flame
Night Star
Everlasting

THE SOUL SEEKERS SERIES

Fated
Echo
Mystic
Horizon

THE RILEY BLOOM SERIES

Radiance
Shimmer
Dreamland
Whisper

STANDALONE NOVELS

Keeping Secrets

Forever Summer

Cruel Summer

Saving Zoë

Kiss & Blog

Laguna Cove

Art Geeks and Prom Queens

Faking 19

Fly Me to the Moon

#1 *NEW YORK TIMES* BESTSELLER

ALYSON NOËL

This book is a work of fiction. Names, characters, places, and incidents are the product of the author's imagination or are used fictitiously. Any resemblance to actual events, locales, or persons, living or dead, is coincidental.

Entangled Publishing, LLC
644 Shrewsbury Commons Ave., STE 181
Shrewsbury, PA 17361
rights@entangledpublishing.com

Entangled Teen is an imprint of Entangled Publishing, LLC.

Visit our website at www.entangledpublishing.com.

Edited by Stacy Abrams
Cover design by Bree Archer
Cover images by Alexroz/Depositphotos,
Abzee/Gettyimages, Wacomka/Shutterstock,
Remuhin/Shutterstock, EduardHarkonen/Gettyimages,
and Amado Designs/Shutterstock
Interior design by Toni Kerr

ISBN: 9-781-64937-192-8
Ebook ISBN: 9-781-64937-233-8

Manufactured in the United States of America

First Edition June 2023

10 9 8 7 6 5 4 3 2 1

For Saint, always.

At Entangled, we want our readers to be well-informed. If you would like to know if this book contains any elements that might be of concern for you, please check the back of the book for details.

Oh, when she's angry, she is keen and shrewd!
She was a vixen when she went to school.
And though she be but little, she is fierce.
—William Shakespeare
A Midsummer Night's Dream

Fact:

All of the artwork and ancient artifacts
mentioned in this novel are real.

PROLOGUE

Braxton

BASILIQUE ROYALE DE SAINT-DENIS, FRANCE

1741

I stand beside the dead man and raise my torch high, my gaze cutting from those blank, lifeless eyes to the bloodied gash in his chest where the dagger plunged deep into his heart and claimed his last breath.

I never meant for it to go this far. I never—

Desperate to block out the sight, I squeeze my eyes shut, only to find the gruesome image burned into my brain—a bleak and wretched still life destined to haunt me for the rest of my days.

"Merde." I grimace, then turn to see Killian coming to stand beside me, a cigarette tucked between his lips.

"Speak English," he says, his voice booming through the ancient space. "You can cut the act now. It's just us."

He grabs hold of my wrist and, using the flaming torch like a match, lights the tip and takes a deep drag that launches him straight into a coughing fit.

"Nothing like a good gasper." He chokes. "My pop gave me my first taste back when I was nine." Killian looks at me sideways and laughs. "Didn't realize how much I missed it. The smoke, that is. Not my pop." To illustrate the point, he blows a series of smoke rings that hover briefly over the corpse. "Sometimes I wonder if I'm not better suited for this century. You know, before all the rules and regulations and blasted surgeon general warnings."

I watch uneasily as he crouches beside the dead man and, with a tap of his finger, slides the eyelids all the way closed.

"Fuckin' giving me the creeps, the way he's half-lidded staring at me."

"Do you think it's true?" I gaze down at my boots. The toes are splattered with vomit and blood. And though my first instinct is to wipe it all off, I know that I won't.

Mainly because I can't allow myself to forget that, because of my actions, a young girl just lost her father and she'll never know why. I shake my head, shake away the thought, and return to the question. "About the Sun being a fake—what do you make of that?"

Killian flicks a length of ash onto the dead man's cheek. In that moment, I've never hated him more. *Disrespectful, despicable piece of—*

"Do you really think Arthur would send us out for a dupe?" He lets out a derisive snort.

My gaze finds the body again. *No. Not a body; a person*. A man who had a wife, a daughter. A man who, thanks to *me*—was put to a violent, premature end.

And yet, he's not just any man, but a Timekeeper. One who, even when he sensed what was coming, remained completely unshaken, accepting a fate that was not his to change.

Or at least until he heard the threat leveled against his girl. Because in that instant, he switched from loyal, oath-keeping Timekeeper to desperate father willing to do anything to save his daughter.

"Hey, Posh Spice— "

I look to Killian and frown. His constant digs at my upper-crust accent never fail to get under my skin.

He pushes himself off the ground until he's towering a good three inches above me. At fourteen, he's a bit older than me, but he's also tall for his age. Built, too. "In case you haven't noticed—" He reaches into his pocket and retrieves an engraved silver flask. "We did the damn thing. So take a load off—have a drink. Still enough time to stash the body and be on our way."

I don't want the drink, but knowing it's easier to go along, I take the flask and fake a swig. But Killian's onto me, and before I can stop him, he tips the bottom with a whack of his hand, causing a jolt of whiskey to slip down my throat, leaving a fiery trail in its wake.

"That's more like it," he grunts, reclaiming the flask, he takes a hefty swill for himself. "One Timekeeper down, another to go," he shouts, then seeing my look of confusion, he says, "I'm talking about the girl, of course."

"But that's impossible," I say. "There are no female Timekeepers."

"There are now." He shrugs. "As his first and only child, that makes his daughter a Timekeeper, too. And I, for one, can't wait to meet this miracle girl. I plan on showing her the one *true* wonder of the world before it's time to end her. Send her out with a *bang*, as they say."

My stomach rolls as I watch him thrust his hips back and forth, all the while making crude gestures with his fingers and tongue. This guy is so crass, so vulgar and obnoxious, I vow right here and now that if I should ever meet this girl, this supposed Timekeeper, I'll do whatever it takes to protect her from him.

Or, on second thought, maybe I should take care of it now. I'm pretty sure no one will miss him. Or at least not for long. Hell, people disappear all the time. What's one more?

"C'mon," he says. "Help me dump the body so we can get back to Gray Wolf and celebrate for real."

"Hide it where?" I ask, but then I see it. King Dagobert's tomb. It was left open from when the Timekeeper snatched the Sun from its centuries-old hiding spot. And though it still contains a pile of old royal bones, it can easily fit another body.

But can it fit three?

"I'll lift the shoulders—you get the feet," Killian says.

On a quick count of three, we haul the corpse to the crypt and chuck it inside. When the Timekeeper's head crashes onto King Dagobert's skull, resulting in a dull, crushing sound, my throat burns from a retch of bile I'm forced to swallow down.

That man deserved better, and if I have any hope of atoning for the part that I played, I'll need to move now, before it's too late.

I watch as Killian tosses the burning cigarette butt into the tomb like the insolent ass I know him to be. Then, retrieving the golden sphere from his pocket, he steals a moment to admire our work. "Arthur's gonna be so happy when he sees this Get!"

I stare at the back of Killian's head. "Why would he be happy?" I say, my tone gone as dark as my mood. "The Sun is a fake."

Killian whirls on me. "What the hell are you talking about?" He shoves the golden ball close to my face, but I'm quick to wave it away.

"The Timekeeper was right. The Sun is a decoy," I insist, committed to putting my new plan into place.

It's one of the worst acts a Tripper can commit against a partner, but it's the least I can do for the girl, considering all I've taken from her.

Besides, didn't Killian just brag about how he's a much better fit for this century? Well, now's his chance to find out.

Killian's eyes are ablaze. "And how the bloody fuck would you know—" he starts.

But before he can finish, I throw a punch that lands square

on his jaw.

In an instant, his head snaps hard to the side as his knees fold out from under him, and his body slumps to the ground. A quick and easy knockout. But since there's no telling how long he'll stay down, I drop to my knees, yank the leather cord with the plain silver cross from his neck, then leap to my feet and race for the portal.

With my knuckles still throbbing from the impact, and my blood- and vomit-soaked boots pounding hard against the ancient dirt floor, my mind fills with thoughts of the girl.

Is she really a Timekeeper? The first female in a centuries-long lineage of males?

A ghost of a smile forms on my lips, and I hope that someday I'll have the chance to meet her. Because that would be something to see.

She would be someone worth knowing.

Either way, at least I've managed to save her from the likes of Killian fucking du Luce.

I've just reached the glowing doorway when I glance over my shoulder to see Killian back on his feet and barreling toward me.

"You better not leave without me!" he shouts, eyes wild, face enraged. "I'll fuckin' kill you! I'll—"

I hold up the cross that doubles as a clicker, and with a single tap on its center, I soar two and a half centuries forward in time…leaving Killian far behind.

1

Natasha

Gray Wolf Academy

Present Day

A slim beam of light slips between the drapes and hits me square in the face.

But that's not why I'm awake.

It's Braxton. Caught in yet another one of his nightmares, his body thrashes against some unseen enemy as he mumbles a string of mostly indecipherable words.

I didn't… I should've… Merde…

"It's okay," I whisper, rolling to my side. I lay a hand on his chest. His skin is cool but slick with sweat, and his heart is pounding so hard I can feel the thump of it just under my palm. "It's just a nightmare. It's not real."

I watch as he sneaks an eye open. The other soon follows. And for a moment, I'm sure I catch a glimpse of something that straddles the border of fear and remorse, something that reminds me of dread. But then he wipes a hand over his face and whispers my name, and whatever I saw disappears.

"Tasha," he says. "I'm sorry. I—"

"It's okay," I tell him. "It was just another night terror—that's all." I press a kiss to his shoulder, then another to the crook of his neck. "If you want to talk about it, I'm here."

He turns his head toward me, and when his eyes meet mine, I'm sure he's about to finally reveal what's been haunting his dreams nearly every night. But then his hand finds my waist, and he pulls me down to him. Drawing me even closer, he says, "You mean the doctor is *in*?"

It's a reference to Lucy from the *Peanuts* comic strip, but also to the Gray Wolf psychiatrist who happens to be named Lucy, and it always makes me laugh.

"Speaking of..." My fingers slide to his navel, where I trace the contours with the edge of my thumb. "Today's my last day." I still my hand and arch my neck to get a clear read of his face. The confused look I find prompts me to say, "Of therapy. Today's my last day of therapy."

Braxton's jaw tightens. His brow slants with concern. And while I'm not exactly sure how I expected him to react, I know it wasn't that.

"But—are you ready? Because it hasn't been very long."

I flip onto my back and stare at the swoop of forest-green fabric hanging over our heads. "Actually, it's been nearly three weeks since my last Trip to Versailles. Or six sessions with the doctor—however you want to track it. But yeah." I shrug. "I'm as sure as I can be."

"And what does Dr. Lucy say?" Braxton slips onto his side, bunches a pillow under his head, and peers down at me.

"Don't know, don't care." I frown. "I'm free to come and go as I please. And honestly, I'm just so sick of talking about it. *How did it make you feel? How is it impacting your daily routine? Do you want to further explore the day your dad walked out of your life and never returned?*" I roll my eyes. "I mean, no, I don't want to *explore* any of it. I've said all I can, and now it's time to move on."

Braxton makes a small sound—one I can't easily pin down.

Though if I had to describe it, I'd say it's something between a gasp and a groan.

For some strange reason, talking about my dad always results in an immediate downturn in Braxton's mood. Like my dad's abandonment somehow affects him more than it does me.

"*Annnyway…*" I drag out the word. "Sometimes I wonder if all that incessant talking is just keeping the trauma alive. I mean, maybe it really is like Arthur said—that we're always writing our own stories, and it's the ones we play on repeat that determine our destiny. And if that's true, then by constantly reliving what happened in Versailles, aren't I just cementing my status as a victim of a brutal attack?"

"But you're *not* a victim." Braxton shakes his head. "You beat the hell out of that duke."

Despite the glow of pride worn plain on his face, I can't help but wish I'd kept the whole horrible story to myself. It would've been just as easy to explain my injuries by reminding him that as a female, Tripping alone to 1745 Versailles—a time in which women held little value and virtually no inherent rights—the usual time-travel dangers were only multiplied.

Which means there was no need to go on about how I was tossed in jail, assaulted, and nearly raped before I saved myself by stabbing a duke.

But at least I had the good sense not to reveal that it was Killian who stopped me from finishing my attacker.

I can still smell the putrid scent of that cell, feel the pinch of the makeshift shiv held tight in my hand as I plunged the blade into the duke's chest. I was just about to do it again when Killian walked in and saved me from myself—insisting that once I kill, I can never go back, that the course of history is not mine to change—and a bunch of bullshit like that.

Only, it's probably not actually bullshit.

There's a pretty good chance he was right.

Still, sometimes I wonder if I made a mistake by leaving that duke alive.

Either way, I'm just glad I kept the Killian stuff to myself. Because for reasons I don't fully understand, Braxton and Killian are sworn enemies. And since they're unwilling to provide any details, all I know for sure is that Killian blames Braxton for leaving him behind in eighteenth-century France, and Braxton claims Killian is pretty much a liar and a psychopath.

"Where've you gone?" The clipped lilt of Braxton's English accent draws me away from Versailles and back to Gray Wolf, Braxton's luxurious suite, and his plush canopy bed. "Because you're clearly not present."

I rise onto my elbows and return my focus to him. "I was thinking about what Arthur said."

Braxton's lips curve into a grin. "Arthur's a bit of a windbag. You'll need to be more specific."

I push a hand to my belly, and, deepening my voice, I say, "*You alone are the alchemist of the reality you create.*" It's my best impression of our…boss, leader, mentor, king? I'm still not sure how to refer to the reclusive tech trillionaire responsible for bringing me here. The man whose first initial is on the gold signet ring I wear, proclaiming me to be a member of the AAD, or Arthur's Artful Dodgers. The man who, I'm starting to suspect, is tracking our every move. And though I didn't sound anything like him, Braxton laughs, and that alone feels like a win.

"Aw, yes," Braxton says. "Amor fati."

"What did you say?" I turn onto my side, my gaze poring over his ridiculously beautiful face, moving from those ocean-blue eyes to the bit of a bend in his nose to those warm, inviting lips that really know how to kiss.

"Amor—"

"No," I cut in, "I know the phrase. It's just—how do *you* know it?"

"My dad used to say it. It's about learning to make the best of what happens—transforming the unwanted experiences into something meaningful."

I gaze at him in wonder. Our connection was undeniable from the start, no matter how hard I tried to fight it at first. But this—well, I'm not sure what to make of it. It's too strange and specific to be a coincidence.

"What?" He shoots me an inquisitive look as he cups a hand to my cheek. "Why are you looking at me like that?"

"Because my dad used to say it, too," I tell him. "And what are the chances of that?"

Braxton's gaze burns into mine. "Probably about the same chances as the two of us ending up here, in this gilded cage."

A lovely rush of warmth blooms in my chest when his fingers find the talisman that hangs from the slim gold chain at my neck. The gift he commissioned for my eighteenth birthday. The blue lapis moon and the diamond pavé star nestled inside the fine golden cage act as both a symbol of us and our lives lived inside this snow globe–like fortress, and a sort of insurance against getting lost in a Fade—lost in time, never to return.

Like what happened to Anjou, and probably Song, and once upon a time to Killian, too. The idea of it is so horrible, I instinctively shudder.

"You all right?" Braxton smooths a hand down my arm, erasing the chills. And when his eyes meet mine, his gaze is so open, so caring, I know in my heart that either Killian is lying, or he's completely mistaken.

Braxton just doesn't have it in him to ever leave anyone stranded in time.

"Of course I'm all right," I tell him. "I'm here with you, aren't I?" I look him square in the face, and the weird thing is, I don't even blush when I say it.

With Braxton, there's no need for pretending my feelings

either don't exist or, worse, that he shouldn't concern himself with them. And there's absolutely no shame in showing up as my real, flawed, totally authentic self.

As for the L word… We're not quite there yet. But, like everything else with us, there's no rush. Here at Gray Wolf, we have all the time in the world.

Braxton lets go of the talisman and watches it slide down my chest, falling beneath the deep *V* of my silk camisole. Then he slips a finger under the strap, tugs it down past my shoulder, and presses a trail of soft kisses along the ridge of my collarbone.

Despite having kissed well into the night, kissing ourselves to sleep, I can never get enough of the warmth of his lips, the electric charge of his fingers questing over my skin.

I push closer, losing my hands in his soft tousle of hair. And when his mouth finally finds mine, my lips instantly part, surrendering to his kiss—to the heated thrum that begins at my core, radiates through my skin, and straight into his.

"Do you feel it?" he whispers into the kiss. "This energy between us. This frisson."

"Always," I murmur. "Always when I'm with you."

I pull away, needing to see his beautiful bottomless gaze.

But instead of Braxton, I find the duke's hideous face staring right back.

2

My mouth falls open, but nothing comes out.

My body is frozen, my throat closing in on itself.

"Tasha—" Braxton speaks in the sort of reassuring whisper you might use with a small child or sleepwalker. "Darling." He places a careful hand on my arm. "Please—look at me."

I want to, but I can't. Not while there's a part of me that's still caught in the duke's grip.

I haul myself up against the headboard, drop my head in my hands, and fight with all I have in me to will the duke's image out of my brain.

No, I silently scold his arrogant face. *Go the fuck away. You are dead to me, and I'm done talking about you—done thinking about you…*

"It's not real," Braxton says. "You were having a flashback. He can never harm you again, never get anywhere near you. Arthur will never send you back to that timeline."

It's a few beats for my breath to grow steady and my heart to resume a more regular pace. And when I finally open my eyes to find Braxton keeping a close and careful watch over me, I've never been more determined to banish that stupid duke from my mind, whatever it takes.

"Maybe this week's session doesn't have to be your last." Braxton eyes me cautiously.

I turn away, trying to hide my humiliation. Claiming I'd been cured, only to fall into a full-blown relapse just a few moments later, leaves me feeling deeply embarrassed.

"Okay," I say, feeling even worse when I see how worried I've made him. "No quick fixes, no rushing toward a conclusion. I promise."

"Tasha—" Braxton's voice is edged with concern. "It's not about me—it's for *you*. I just want to see you feeling whole again, safe in the world. I see Dr. Lucy sometimes, too, you know. There's no shame in it."

"I guess we each have our nightmares." I sigh, hoping to put an end to it, when I'm struck by a telling sting at the back of my eyes. And I quickly lower my chin, blinking away the threat of tears until I'm sure it's passed for good.

After years of taking care of my mom and putting my own needs aside in the struggle to fill all of hers, it's been a big adjustment for me to get used to being cared for, looked after, in the way Braxton cares for and looks after me. And the truth is, while I've gotten so much better at sharing my feelings and being open to his, there are also times when his big-hearted displays knock me so sideways, I have to fight the urge to push him away.

For so many years, being alone felt safe. Even now, despite all the self-work I've done, there's still a shadowy part of me that insists I don't deserve Braxton's affections—that I'm not the sort of girl worth sticking around for.

Of course, somewhere deep down inside, I know it's not true. But it's not always enough to stop that persistent voice of gloom.

A long stretch of silence swells like an ocean between us until I finally lift my chin, level my gaze on his, and breach the quiet by saying, "I *will* feel safe again. Someday soon, I'm sure. But for now, I was hoping you could remind me just exactly where we left off."

I attempt a sexy grin, but it feels so awkward on my face,

I'm sure I've fallen short. Still, what I lack in skill I make up for in determination, and I push away from the headboard and lean closer to him until my fingers are grazing the bold curve of his biceps.

There was a time when I used to make out with random boys in a quest to escape the monotony of my life.

Am I doing that now?

Seeking physical affection as a way to avoid real emotions and a hard conversation?

Maybe.

Probably.

For me, intimate conversations always feel like a much bigger risk than an intimate act.

But I also know what I want. And right now, I want Braxton.

My fingers trail up his arm, and while I know he wants me, too, there's no mistaking the tightening of his jaw, the stiffening of his spine, or the way he holds himself in check, refusing to fully give in.

"Darling," he says, his brow slanting, lips pulling into a frown. "You don't have to—"

But I don't let him finish. I have something to prove, partly to him, but mostly to me. I need to show us both that we can enjoy a romantic moment without the duke constantly intruding.

"It's fine," I say, practically begging him to believe it so that maybe I'll believe it as well. "Really. It was just a glitch. It won't happen again."

My hands slide over his shoulders as I lay claim to his mouth. My tongue playfully nudging until he opens to me, to the kiss, to the unspoken promise to come.

A low groan sounds deep in his throat as he pulls me closer and kisses me so thoroughly that all traces of the duke are long gone. Then, he slides us both down the mattress, centers my body over his, and wastes no time reclaiming my mouth, my neck, the lobe of my ear. His lips leave a tingling trail in their wake that sets my body aflame.

"This," I whisper, conforming my body to the hard contours of his. "This is exactly what I want." I sink my teeth into his shoulder, biting playfully but still leaving a faint, crescent-shaped mark.

All this and then some more. So. Much. More. The words trill through my head, but I don't speak them. I'd much rather show than tell.

There've been so many nights when we've kissed for what feels like forever—wearing ourselves out with the searing scrape of our tongues, the sweet sweep of our fingers exploring each other. We've done all we can to take it slow—to build a solid foundation of comfort and trust. But now it feels like time to move on to... Well, everything else.

And I know he feels the same. I can feel it in the feverish roll of his hips, the urgent brush of his thumbs as they slide under my camisole, along the crook of my waist, where they pause at the curve of my breasts.

I press a palm to his chest and angle myself to his side so I can drag my gaze down the length of him, tracking my hand as it skims along the muscled valley of his abs, drawing a slow circle just south of his navel that sets his heart drumming so hard I can feel the pulse of it under his skin.

Then I inch my hand lower.

And then lower still.

Slipping past the waistband of his briefs until I find him. Laying claim to the warmest part of him. My lips curling with anticipation when I see the way he trembles under my touch, immediately ceding all power, yielding to whatever I want.

"Tasha," he groans, turning until his lips find mine, the kiss growing so heated we're forced to withdraw. "You have no idea how much I want this," he says. "How much I want *you.*"

His lips return to a crushing, fiery grind before skimming their way down my throat, all the way to where his hands are now cupping my breasts.

"Show me. Show me exactly how much," I command, and Braxton is quick to obey.

Between the push and pull of his kiss and the sweet rhythmic circling of our hips, I don't want this to end. I only want more. More of us. More of him.

I tug at his briefs, desperate to remove all barriers left standing between us. "See?" I say, gliding my tongue around the shell of his ear, watching his eyes glaze as my hand begins to move. "There's no need to worry. Clearly, I'm cured."

Braxton's mouth falls slack as he draws in a long, tortured breath. And just when I think we're going to actually, really, *finally* go there, his fingers circle my wrist, stopping my hand.

"But Tasha—are you sure?" His voice is a rasp, telling me it's taking every ounce of his strength to hold back and do the right thing. The gentlemanly thing. The Braxton thing.

Which only makes me want him more.

I sink my teeth into my lower lip. *I'm so, so ready for this.*

"Are *you* sure?" I ask. My tone is teasing, convinced I already know the answer.

He lifts his hands to my face, his gaze brimming with such unbridled reverence it simultaneously scares me and makes my heart sing.

We close the space between us, our lips finding each other once more, when, from seemingly out of nowhere, a blast of Beethoven crashes into the room.

3

Well before the first four notes of “da-da-da-dum” that mark the opening motif of Beethoven’s Fifth can sound, I know it’s a message from Arthur.

Which also explains the speed with which Braxton rolls out from under me, makes a leap for his nightstand, retrieves his Gray Wolf–issued tablet, and gives it his full attention.

I prop my head onto my elbow and release a frustrated sigh. Since everything at Gray Wolf happens by Arthur’s design, it’s no accident he chose this piece as his musical avatar. According to what Beethoven’s secretary and biographer revealed after his death, the idea behind the piece was Fate knocking at the door. Which means Arthur’s use of the symphony of fate to announce all his calls is yet another reminder that we are all here because of him.

Arthur is the ruler of all our destinies.

I stare at Braxton’s back, watching as he hunches over his tablet, his attention entirely forfeited to whatever Arthur is requesting of him.

And if it were me in his place, I’d be doing the same.

Here, on this remote outcropping of rock, a place of perpetual wind, rain, and fog, Arthur stands in for the sun, and all of us orbit around him.

My gaze moves inward to the memory of the girl I was before I came to this place. Back then, I had zero interest in anything having to do with the past. For me, it was a day-to-day struggle just to survive in the present. But here at Gray Wolf, I'm up to my eyeballs in history, since Arthur goes to great lengths to shield us from the modern world outside these walls.

At first, I was determined to rebel against everything here. But the longer I stay, the more I realize that immersing us in the cultures of previous centuries makes it easier to blend in when we're out time-traveling—or Tripping, as we call it. Which, in turn, helps keep us safe.

"Sorry." Braxton tosses a rueful look over his shoulder. "You know I have to respond." He returns to his slab, typing a reply with his thumbs.

"I also know it's Sunday," I grumble, my body still quivering in all the places Braxton touched me and all the places he was about to touch me. "Whatever Arthur wants, it can wait."

"Not sure he'd agree." Braxton pushes away from the mattress, rakes a hand through his bed-tousled hair, and lets out a sigh. "I need to shower," he says, and before I can offer to join him, he adds, "Trust me, it'll be a *very* cold shower." He grins.

I pull a pillow to my chest and make an exaggerated frowny face. But Braxton just laughs, plants a kiss on my forehead, and heads for the bathroom. "To be continued," he calls.

A moment later, I hear a spray of water coming from the shower, and I slip out of bed and head for his closet in search of something to wear so I don't have to walk through the halls in last night's dress.

Not that anyone would care. Gray Wolf operates on an entirely different set of rules than the typical school. Still, the dress is sort of skimpy, and I'm in the mood for something warmer. And if it happens to smell like Braxton, well, bonus.

Like everything in this place, Braxton's closet is pure luxury. A spacious walk-in filled with so many designer pieces, it's like wandering into an upscale men's store. I tip onto my toes, reaching for the very top shelf, and I grab a black Gray Wolf sweatshirt with the academy logo emblazoned on the front. And I can't help but wonder what the color might represent.

New arrivals at Gray Wolf always start off as Green. And honestly, I hated every moment of being a newbie. Not that being a Yellow was much better. All it really meant was that I was no longer a Green but not yet a Blue. Which also meant I was forced to eat my meals alone. If it wasn't for Braxton volunteering to share a table with me, I'm not sure how I would've made it through.

But that's all in the past. And now, after working my ass off to finally make Blue, I eat my meals with my friends and Trip to whatever timeline Arthur sees fit to send me.

At first, the idea of time travel seemed like the ultimate mind fuck. But then I made my first Trip back to 1745 Versailles, and my mind was blown open for real.

I pull the academy sweatshirt over my head, and just as I hoped, I catch a hint of Braxton's warm, spicy scent. After burying my face in the sleeve and inhaling again, I grab a pair of old sweatpants, cinch them at the waist, and am just about to go hunt down my shoes when I spot a pair of dusty black boots shoved into a far corner, and a jagged shard of memory slices right through me.

Last time I saw those boots, I joked that I should wear them, since they're obviously too small for Braxton. I was just having fun, but his reaction was so weird, the moment stuck with me.

His face turned ashen. His gaze went hollow and dark. Then he snatched the boots from my hands and tossed them into the corner where they lie now.

And seeing them again… Well, I have that same prick at the back of my neck, that same insistent twinge in my belly, when I remember the way he replied when I called him out for acting so strangely.

They remind me of a long-ago event I prefer not to dwell on, he'd said.

So why do you keep them? I asked.

Because I can't afford to forget.

A quick twist of his gold signet ring, a notable thickening of his accent—all his nervous tells were on full display.

I bite down on my lip, continuing to stare at the boots. Then, with a furtive glance over my shoulder confirming the water is still running and Braxton is nowhere in sight, I steal forward, crouch down beside them, and…release a soft sigh.

They're just boots.

Ordinary boots.

Tall, made of fine black leather, the sort of style an equestrian might wear. And though they're still as dusty as the last time I saw them, a closer look shows they also bear the stain of something crusty and dark.

Mud, perhaps?

Or something…else?

I haul the boots up by the shaft, determined to get to the bottom of this once and for all, when I catch a glimpse of my reflection in the three-way mirror and gasp.

I mean, seriously. Between my tangle of hair, my eyes smudged with last night's eyeliner, and the way my hands shake as I troll Braxton's boots like a suspicious girlfriend scrolling through her partner's phone, searching for illicit photos or texts, I'm steeped in shame that I've stooped to this level.

And yet, as ridiculous as I feel, I also can't stop. Because if there's one thing I know for sure, it's that there's a reason Braxton was so triggered by the sight of me holding these boots.

But what could it possibly be?

I lift the boots higher, inspecting the instep, the toes, trying to get a better look at the stain, when suddenly, with no warning whatsoever, the lights begin to blink on and off and the ground starts to shake.

My breath halts in my throat. But before the panic can really take hold, I remind myself there's a good chance it's not at all what I think.

It's entirely possible someone's just setting out on a Trip, since the amount of energy required to make time travel happen causes the ground to shake and the lights to blink.

But when I try to move, I find my feet are glued to the floor and my knees are locked tight, and I know it's as bad as I feared.

My heart stutters, squeezing tight as a fist, as my mind reels with the realization of what's about to take place—and how the timing couldn't be worse.

I can hear Braxton finishing up in the shower. Soon, he'll find me standing frozen in his closet, his old boots clutched in my hand, and—

I don't get a chance to finish the thought before the boots begin to heat, the walls fall away, and the floor drops out from under me.

4

I'm falling.

Tumbling through time and space—an endless abyss—and there's no way to slow down, no way to stop my descent.

My stomach vaults into my ribs, an unheard scream lodges high in my throat, and I squeeze my eyes shut, struggling to block it all out. But that's never worked before, and it's not working now.

Next thing I know, a flash of memory spins through my head.

It's just after my first Unraveling, and my dad finds me crying and shaking on the living room floor, so terrified by what I've experienced I've actually peed myself.

After helping me change, he sits me on the couch and does his best to explain the strange thing that just happened to me.

It'll probably happen again, he assures me, which is really no reassurance at all. But don't let it scare you. I have them occasionally, too. Still, there are rules you must follow whenever you find yourself in the middle of one. One of those rules is to stay calm and wait for the reveal. The other: you must promise to never tell your mother or anyone else about your ability to see through time.

I did as my dad asked. Never whispered a word of it to anyone. But unfortunately, Killian knows. And while he promised to keep my secret, I'm not entirely convinced that he will.

A moment later, the memory fades, and that's when I realize I'm no longer falling.

My eyes blink open. My vision crowds with the scene unfolding before me. And what I see sucks the air right out of me.

I'm peering into an ancient, cavernous space, lit by the glow of a single torch. It's a place of death and decay, with tombs scattered about, and in the middle of it all—

I swallow hard, struggle to keep my eyes wide, because I need a better look, I need to make sure—

No. It's not possible. There's no way.

And yet—

There he is. My father.

With his wavy brown hair and eyes the same green as mine, he's standing before me, looking exactly as he did the day he walked out the front door and never returned.

And though nothing about this makes any sense, ever since I was thrust into Arthur Blackstone's world, long-dormant memories of my dad have been rising to the surface—long-buried specters of memory refusing to be forgotten.

His obscure teachings—things that didn't make a lick of sense at the time—have all become relevant to the things we do here—all the puzzles Arthur has tasked me to solve.

I lean closer, straining to get a better look, when, from out of nowhere, a hand grabs hold of my arm, the scene disappears, and I'm left shaking, whimpering, gaping into the space where my dad recently stood.

"Tasha?" a voice says. "You okay?"

The boots fall from my fingers, landing with a thud, as my eyes shift away from the past and back to the present, where Braxton stands beside me, a towel wrapped at his hips, an unreadable look spread across his face.

"I—" My gaze skitters away. I have no idea what to say, much less how to explain.

For one thing, Braxton doesn't know about the Unraveling.

For another, this is the second time he's caught me in the middle of one, and I need to play this off better than I did the last time he found me like this.

I swallow hard, try again, but the words just won't come.

Still clutching the towel, Braxton leans down, collects the boots, and tosses them against the far wall, where they bounce off a skateboard and crash onto a bike helmet.

When he turns to face me, there's no mistaking the rapid rise and fall of his chest or the shadow of grief that darkens his gaze. And I can't help but wonder what it is about those boots that's got him acting like this.

What sort of secret is he keeping from me?

All I know for sure is that what I just experienced was only partially an Unraveling. It was also partly psychometry—a term my dad used when he told me how to access the energy field infused within objects.

Not only is everything made of energy, but objects also hold energy, he'd said. *And if you focus, listen very closely, and peer beyond the surface, you can read those vibratory messages hidden within.*

It happened once before in Versailles, just like it happened again now. But why on earth would Braxton's old boots have anything to do with my dad being stuck in some ancient necropolis?

Aside from my dad's more esoteric interests, he was an ordinary guy. A husband, a father, an accountant who bought doughnuts on Saturdays and golfed every Sunday.

When my gaze finds Braxton's, I know that even if I do press for answers, it won't get me the truth.

Just like I'd rather make up a story than confess how sometimes, when I least expect it, time shudders to a stop, the world fades, and a window flings open, allowing me a glimpse into the past.

The realization lands with a jolt.

All this time, I've gotten it wrong.

Braxton and I aren't nearly as transparent with each other as I thought.

I mean, how well can I actually know him when I haven't actually known him that long?

Everything happened so fast—my coming to Gray Wolf, us choosing to be together. And lately, when the hours slink past midnight and I wake to the sight of him tossing and turning, caught in yet another one of his nightmares, I've started to wonder if maybe we haven't quite earned this connection, this closeness, we both claim to feel.

Maybe we rushed in too quickly, spurred on by a physical attraction that was too overwhelming to fight.

I shake my head, shake the thought away, unwilling to tread down that path. Considering how this is the first time I've been serious about anyone for more than a week—I'm clearly no relationship expert.

And yet, as I stand before Braxton now, I can't help but wonder if maybe we're not nearly as special as I thought.

Maybe we're no better and no worse than anyone else on this rock.

And now that I'm starting to see us more clearly, I know in my heart that it's true.

All of us at Gray Wolf—including Braxton, and certainly me—we are all liars here.

5

Sometimes there are reasons to lie.

Good reasons.

Logical reasons.

Like the vow I made to my dad that's now forcing me to make up a story for Braxton.

Problem is, I feel terrible lying to the one person I've come to care about in this place. But with Braxton still looking at me, waiting for a reply, I need to say something fast.

I make a show of clearing my throat, then go with the first thing that pops into my head. "I thought I saw…I don't know, maybe a spider…" I swallow hard, aware of the rush of shame heating my cheeks. Deceit has never come easily to me.

I'm hoping Braxton will leave it at that—fill in the blanks however he wants. But he remains standing before me, fat droplets of water dripping off the ends of his hair, trickling onto his shoulders, before beginning a slow curve over his chest and along the taut line of his torso.

I force my gaze away, inhale a steadying breath. Then, blowing out the air in my cheeks, I try again. "And I—I just grabbed the first thing I saw and—" My voice falters; my shoulders hunch. I can't look at him. Not when we both know I'm just making it up.

Braxton glances between me and the boots. And just when I'm sure he's about to call me out on the lie, he says, "You seemed so frightened. I thought something terrible happened." He keeps his voice steady, his gaze even.

My hand drifts to my belly, my fingers nervously tracing the curved lines of the Gray Wolf logo. "Guess I've never been a fan of eight-legged creatures," I say, my voice rising so high I can't help but cringe. It's one of my tells, and I wonder if Braxton has caught on to that by now. Like I've caught on to the way he pulls at his signet ring, and how his British accent starts to sound like a character straight out of *Oliver Twist*.

"And where is it now?" he asks. "This spider you saw." He tilts his head in question, but I just press my lips together and offer a half-hearted shrug.

Braxton studies me for a nerve-racking beat. And, realizing I'm going to have to do better, I gesture vaguely toward the far side of the closet, then watch as he wanders in that direction, pretending to give a good look around.

Or maybe he's not pretending at all. I can't even tell anymore. I just want this to end, to find a way out of this ridiculous game.

"And just how deep does your dislike of eight-legged creatures go?" Braxton faces me, his mouth curving into a grin that doesn't quite reach his eyes. "Should I move out? Ask Arthur to secure another room on a higher floor? Maybe even burn the place down?"

He's approaching me now, his bare feet crossing the soft woven rug, his stormy gaze fixed firmly on mine.

"Um, no," I mumble, my heart racing so fast I can hear the thrum of it crowding my ears. "Just be on the lookout, that's all."

He stands before me, so close I can make out the individual violet flecks in his eyes, see the exact spot where his nose takes a bit of a bend, smell the shower-clean scent drifting off his damp skin.

My chin begins to quiver, my knees to shake, though I can't tell if it's because the only things left standing between us are a fluffy white towel and a shallow breath of space, or if it's because we both know I'm trapped in the center of a twisted web of my making.

Braxton lifts a finger to the underside of my chin, presses his forehead to mine, and says, "As long as you're okay, that's all that truly matters to me."

Then before I can respond, he's turning away, gathering the clothes he'll wear for the day.

I watch as he pulls a navy cashmere sweater over his head, the circular tattoo in the crook of his arm disappearing when he yanks the sleeve past his wrist.

A mistake, he'd called it that time I asked him about it. Like the boots, he was quick to brush it aside, clearly unwilling to discuss it. And while I agreed to let it go, there was so much charged energy around it, I filed it away with all the other odd things about him.

And the more I think about it, the more I realize how quickly those odd things are starting to pile up.

Just how many secrets is this boy actually keeping from me?

He steps into a pair of dark denim jeans, and when he drops onto the ottoman to pull on some socks, I find myself saying, "So, I'm guessing our beach day is cancelled?"

"Sorry," he says, and the look he gives me really does seem legit. "But I promise I'll make it up to you. You know I can't tell you anything more."

"Of course," I say, and though the words carry an unmistakable edge, it's not like I don't know the ropes. Braxton has been here longer than me, which means he's no longer a student but also not quite an instructor. He basically goes wherever Arthur needs him, and sometimes, the places where Arthur needs him are kept between them.

My eyes wander back to the boots.

What the heck was up with that vision they gave me?

I mean, how can those black leather boots possibly be connected to my dad, when my dad walked out of my life years before I even met Braxton?

"And you?" The sound of Braxton's voice draws me away from the thought. "You can still go. I'm sure Jago would be willing to teach you to surf."

I watch as he ties the laces of his sneakers, then goes in search of a belt. Jago is great, and he's become a good friend. But last time I went to Gray Wolf Cove was with Oliver and Finn. This time around, I was hoping to visit that large indoor space—an incomprehensible marriage of high-tech and nature, filled with white sand and turquoise waters with actual waves—with my boyfriend in tow. But with my plan now dashed, I'll need to come up with some other way to spend the day on my own.

Though it won't include a visit to the library. That much is sure. Ever since I returned from Versailles with the Sun—one of the missing pieces Arthur needs to restore the Antikythera Mechanism—only to learn I'd soon be heading to Renaissance Italy to go in search of the Moon, I've spent the last three weeks immersed in research. And my brain could really use a break from all the rigorous memorizing and fact-gathering I've put myself through.

"Maybe I'll stop by the spa. Followed by a visit to the stables," I say, though I'm not really interested in either of those things.

I'm about to go look for my shoes when Braxton retrieves his talisman from a drawer. And as I watch him slip the small golden compass into his pocket, I'm overcome with alarm.

"Are you—" The question stalls on my tongue. "Are you—Tripping today?" I ask.

Ever since Song disappeared, the thought of Tripping fills me with dread. Of course I know that time travel comes with its own inherent dangers and that getting stuck in the past is just one of many risks. Twice it nearly happened to me, though luckily both times I made it back safely. But clearly Song wasn't so lucky.

Braxton shrugs, rubs a hand against the back of his head. "You never know with Arthur. Better safe than sorry, right?"

My lips press tightly together, and though I try to play it cool, Braxton's by my side in an instant.

"Hey, what just happened?" He slips an arm around my waist and pulls me in close. "Is this about Song?"

I rest my forehead against his chest, feeling grateful for his support but also ridiculous for how much I need it. Tripping is what we do here, and I can't panic every time he goes back in time. Still, I say, "It's like no one cares." I bend my neck until my eyes meet his. "Or at least, no one's trying to find her."

"You don't know that." Braxton traces a hand down my hair. "We only know what Arthur wants us to know, and he goes to great lengths not to alarm us."

"But don't you think the silence is worse?" I search his gaze, wondering if he really believes what he said. "I mean, one day you're making plans with someone, and the next, they're gone, never to be seen or heard from again. What if that happens to you?" My eyes widen. "I can't even imagine what I'd do."

"It's not going to happen to me," Braxton says. "There's no reason to worry."

I take a deep breath, hoping he's right while assuring myself that Arthur would never let Braxton disappear. He's been here too long, become too important. And if the worst were to happen, he'd send someone to find him.

It's like what Jago told me on my first day here, how I should never lose sight of my value. *The more they invest in you, the more reluctant they are to lose you*, he said.

Well, not only has Arthur invested plenty in Braxton, but he also regards me as one of his most valuable assets. Mainly because he thinks I'm the only one here who can help him attain what he's after. Which means Braxton and I are both safe.

But what about everyone else—the rest of my friends?

Does Arthur really see them as easily replaced?

Desperate for a change of subject, I say, "Do you think it's too soon for me to reach out to Mason again?"

Braxton's gaze softens, but there's a twitch in his jaw that's impossible to miss. "It's never too soon to make peace with a friend," he says. "Though whether Mason wants any part of that..." He shrugs, leaving the unfinished thought hanging between us. "Give him some time. He'll come around."

"I hope you're right." I sigh.

"And now—" Braxton plants a single kiss on the top of my head. "I need to finish up. Can I see you to the door?"

It's the equivalent of ending a phone call with *I should let you go*. But I'm not offended. "No worries," I tell him. "I'll show myself out."

Braxton heads inside his bathroom as I make for the bedroom, where I find my shoes lying at the foot of the bed.

After slipping them on, I'm about to leave when I notice a small stack of leather-bound first editions piled on the table next to the door.

I study the one at the top, *Jane Eyre.* Then I smile to myself, taking it as further proof of just how much of an old-school romantic Braxton really is.

I trace a finger over the cover, then flip the book open to find it's been signed by Charlotte Brontë herself, with a personalized note for Braxton.

For Braxton,
Your will shall decide your destiny.
C.B.

My vision begins to blur.

My hand to shake.

Next thing I know, the book tumbles from my fingers, but I'm able to catch it and return it to the top of the stack.

Then I race out the door, my mind haunted by a memory of another leather-bound book I once saw. A memory so vivid, I can't believe I hadn't thought of it until now.

There are so many secrets contained in these walls, and it's time to start getting some answers to my long list of questions.

Chief among them: *What the hell is really going on in this place, and exactly how does it connect to my dad?*

6

A thrum of anticipation beats through me as I round the corner that leads to my hall. And though the hallway is empty, and I'm tempted to run, running through halls isn't done here at Gray Wolf, and the last thing I need is to draw any unwanted attention to myself.

Ever since my first day here, I've had the uncanny feeling that I'm being observed. And though no one seems willing to confirm my suspicion, they're not exactly denying it, either.

When I reach my door, I'm surprised to find Freya vacating Song's room. Sunday is the one day of the week the cleaning crew gets a break.

"Is she back?" I ask, unable to think of any other reason for why Freya would be there.

Freya turns, her coppery curls springing free of her bun, her flashing green eyes landing on mine. "Excuse me?" she says, speaking with an accent I can never quite place.

"Song," I say. "Is she back?"

A glint of comprehension darkens her gaze. A moment later, she's shaking her head. "I was sent to clear the room and make it like new," she says, unaware of the full impact of her words. The way they leave me gutted, mentally kicking myself for acting too late.

I should've checked before, but I got so caught up in my studies that—

"And her things?" I ask, hoping it's not too late, though suspecting it is. "What did you do with all her belongings?"

Freya shoots me a quizzical look. "Belongings? I am not sure she had any." Her eyes narrow on mine, and I realize she's right. All the fancy clothes, jewels, and art are merely on loan until we're…no longer here.

I imagine how the room must look now. The walls, once decorated with carefully curated pieces of modern art, now blank. The shelves empty. The space that was once so unique to Song, now returned to how my own room looked when I first arrived on this rock. Clean. Pristine. Luxurious beyond measure. And as anonymous as any five-star hotel suite.

A sort of blank canvas, ready for the next occupant to make their own mark.

But like all canvas, it takes only a fresh coat of primer to erase everything that existed before.

But what about that leather-bound book that I saw? Where did that go?

It's not until Freya clears her throat, pulling me out of my reverie, that I notice the impatient tilt of her head, the way her fingers grasp at her cart. Clearly, she's eager to go. But I can't let her leave. Not yet, anyway.

"Do you think I could…have a look around?" I nod toward the purple door.

Freya sighs, long and deep. "Natasha," she says. "You are always so…" She screws up her face, eyes squinted, nose crinkled as though searching for just the right word.

I squirm under the glare of her scrutiny, thinking of all the ways she could fill in that blank. *You are always so: Nice. Friendly. Good-natured. Annoying. Aggravating. Infuriating. Exasperating. Vexing—*

"No-nonsense," she says with a brisk dip of her head. "And while I appreciate that, I am very busy, so—"

"I'm looking for a book," I say, my voice hurried. "An old, leather-bound—"

Just then, a voice calls out from the end of the hall, and I look up to see another member of the cleaning staff.

"Freya?" he says. "They need us on the fourth floor."

Freya looks his way and holds up a hand. When she returns to me, her gaze is shrewder than I've ever seen. "We are finished here, yes?" She looks at me in a way that makes it clear it's not really a question.

"Of course," I mumble, watching her go.

As she makes her way down the hall, I notice how the tune she's humming is not from this century. It's not even from the last century. The song is much older than that. And for one fleeting moment, I have the wildest thought:

Is it possible the people who work here at Gray Wolf—the maids, the kitchen crew, pretty much all the support staff—might not actually be from this time?

Much like Arthur tasked me with finding Killian and bringing him back to Gray Wolf, did someone whisk Freya away from her own timeline?

And then another thought quickly follows—one that sends an ominous fluttering deep in my belly.

And if so, then is it also possible that disappearing works both ways?

7

First thing I do when I enter my room is kick off my heels. Second thing I do is head for the shower. And as I pass by my vanity, I notice a curious dark blue box with two intertwined snakes imprinted on the lid and the words *Niki de Saint Phalle Parfum* written beneath.

My gaze holds on those serpents. Something about that image sets my pulse drumming, as though my body has already processed something my brain is still sorting out.

Not only is Niki de Saint Phalle one of my favorite contemporary artists (I even wrote a paper on her for my freshman-year art class), but I have no idea how the box even got here.

With a racing heart and trembling fingers, I reach for that box like a tiger stalking its prey—like it might somehow sense my presence and leap out of my grasp.

When I flip open the lid, I find a bottle of perfume nestled inside. Only, this is no ordinary bottle—it's more like a mini work of art.

The base is made of cobalt blue glass. The lid is gold with two serpents rising out of the top. One of the snakes is gold, the other multicolored. Their slinky forms are intertwined, and their mouths are open as though they're about to devour each other.

I remember reading how the artist made the perfume to finance the cost of building the Tarot Garden in Italy, which served as the inspiration for the sculpture garden Arthur built just a few stories below my window. Because the sheer size and scope of the original Tarot Garden sculptures made it impossible for Arthur to snatch them from Tuscany and leave counterfeits in their place, he had his on-site artisans build similar pieces on a much smaller scale, using the plans he'd commissioned from the artist herself.

According to Arthur, it was the last project Niki de Saint Phalle ever worked on before her death in 2002.

But long before the Tarot Garden was built, there was a complicated labyrinth made of hedges. I know this because on my first day here, I stood at my window, caught in the grip of an Unraveling, as I watched a small figure clad in a red velvet cape race through the maze. Once they reached the center, they touched a crystal sphere and instantly vanished into thin air. A handful of seconds later, they reappeared. Only this time, they had a small brown object clutched in their hand—one that looked a lot like the book I later saw in Song's room.

And though I have no way to prove it, I know in my bones that none of this is a coincidence. The reveal—this perfume—they're connected somehow. But who on earth left it and why?

My first guess is Freya, mostly because she has access to my room. But it's not like I know her very well. Like most of the support staff, she goes out of her way to minimize our contact. And though Song was friendly with Freya, it still doesn't explain why Freya would leave the box for me and not Oliver or Finn, who were pretty much Song's best friends.

Also, if it was Freya, then why didn't she mention it just now in the hall?

I twist off the cap and breathe a deep inhale. The fragrance is bold, heady, and intense—much like the artist herself. But I don't remember ever smelling any of those notes on Song or anyone else.

My gaze darts back to the box, having no idea what any of this means, when my eye catches on a small square of paper I hadn't noticed before.

It's a note. A small, folded bit of cardstock bearing a wax seal of a finely detailed rose. And though I'm used to seeing the Gray Wolf wax seal, this is the first time I've ever seen a note marked with a rose, and that alone gives me pause.

I trace a finger along the edge, trying to recall everything I know about what a rose might symbolize.

There's love, of course. Passion, romance, that sort of thing.

I shake my head and frown. *There's got to be something more. Something I'm missing.*

I close my eyes, sifting through memories, when a series of images bursts across the screen in my brain.

I'm outside, in my backyard, helping my dad tend to the small garden he kept.

It's spring, our rosebush is in bloom, and I watch as he clips a bud from its stem and carefully hands it to me.

"The rose is more than just a flower—it's an important symbol," he says. "Do you remember what I taught you about symbols?"

I brush the petals against my nose, enjoying their soft, silky feel. "To always look beyond the surface. To always go for the deeper meaning of things."

My dad nods. "In addition to being a symbol of love, the rose is also a symbol of secrecy. The sort of secrets that must be kept under the strictest of confidence," he says, the words rushing out of him, as though he needs to finish the lesson before my mom can come find us. "The term 'sub rosa' literally means under the rose, which also implies secrecy. So, if you ever find yourself in a room with a rose hanging from the ceiling, whatever you learn in that room must be kept confidential. You can tell no one what happened in there."

I squinch my eyes, trying to imagine such a thing. "You mean like how some people hang mistletoe at Christmas?"

My dad grins, but there's an unmistakable sadness in his gaze that even his smile can't erase. "Yes," he says, his voice hoarse. "Kind of like that."

The images fade as quickly as they arrived, leaving me with a silent sob in my chest as I stare down at the folded square of paper and take a deep breath.

After breaking the seal, I begin to read.

8

Turns out, it's not actually a note like I thought.

It's more of a riddle. And even after reading it twice, I'm still not sure how to interpret it, so I read it once more:

O follower of fools
You stand afore the oracle
Serpent girdle at your waist
Red roses spread above and below you
It's folly that binds you to this place

Finally, after the third go, the obscure imagery clicks into place. The answer is so obvious, I can't believe I didn't see it from the start.

Of course. It's a reference to the Tarot Garden.

Between the perfume and this note, Song is pointing the way to wherever she's hidden the book.

Or at least I hope that's what this means. And if I'm right, then I'm pretty sure I know just where to start.

A tarot deck consists of seventy-eight cards—twenty-two that comprise the Major Arcana, and fifty-six that make up the Minor Arcana. And those first twenty-two cards—starting with The Fool and ending with The World—follow a specific order that also serves as an allegorical journey of life.

Just like Niki de Saint Phalle's sculptures in Tuscany, the

Tarot Garden at Gray Wolf includes pieces that represent all the cards in the Major Arcana. Which leads me to believe that the first line in Song's note, "O follower of fools," is referring to the Magician card (a card I once associated with Arthur), since that card happens to be number one, which immediately follows the Fool card, which is numbered zero.

The second line, "You stand afore the oracle," confirms that I'm right. The oracle, also known as the High Priestess, is the number two card in the deck, coming just after the number one card, the Magician.

The "Serpent girdle at your waist," along with the "Red roses spread above and below you" line, further confirms that Song is pointing me toward the *Magician* statue, since in the standard Rider-Waite tarot deck, the Magician is depicted with a snake wrapped around his middle and a bed of roses sprawling above and below him.

But I'm still not sure what she meant by: "It's folly that binds you to this place."

Is Song referring to the fact that the sculptures here are duplicates of the ones in Italy?

Or maybe it's a veiled jab at Arthur himself and this time-traveling fortress he's made?

Or is it more personal, like a reference to me and the fact that I've stopped fighting, stopped trying to find a way out of this place?

Honestly, the last phrase could mean just about anything. And since it's not like I can ask her, I'm forced to work with what I have.

With the perfume bottle and note in hand, I make for the large picture window, where I gaze out at a day that's already revealing itself to be gray, gloomy, and cold. Nothing new here.

I dip my focus downward, dropping several stories to the Tarot Garden below. When I find the silver dome that marks the top of the Magician's head, a sudden chill shudders through me, reminding me of something I'd forgotten until now.

In a traditional tarot deck, the Magician wears a red cape—much like the figure I saw racing through the maze during the Unraveling on my first day.

Is that another connection—or another coincidence?

Always look beyond the surface, my dad said. *Always go for the deeper meaning of things.*

My gaze drifts back to the sky, where dark, swollen storm clouds are crowding into one another until they double in size. Any minute now, the heavens will break and unleash a torrent of rain.

There's a voice in my head urging me to get outside while I can—before the rain has a chance to ruin my plan.

But I also know that appearances matter here, and I can't afford to draw any negative notice my way.

Setting the poem and the perfume aside, I strip off my borrowed clothes, slip into the shower, and crank the water on high.

As the shower stall fills with steam, my memory returns to the day I saw the leather-bound book in Song's room, and how it reminded me of the one I saw in an Unraveling on my first day here. But when I asked for a closer look, Song blew me off.

Some other time, she'd said. Quickly followed by a phrase I haven't been able to get out of my head: *Just so you know, magick has always been the currency of the oppressed.*

I've dissected those words more times than I can count. I even checked to see if she was quoting someone—as far as I can tell, she wasn't. And I seriously doubt she got it from one of the inspirational messages Arthur likes to send to our slabs.

No, Song was telling me something—something related to the book. And though I'm still not sure what she meant, I think I've managed to solve the riddle inside that note:

Arthur is the Magician. The rest of us are the oppressed. But we're only bound here by folly. We have defenses—by way of magick—that just might free us from this place.

There was a time when the thought of using magick for anything would've made me laugh. But now that feels like a lifetime ago.

Ever since I learned time travel is real—ever since I was vaulted several centuries into the past—virtually nothing is off the table for me.

Wasn't it Einstein who said, "That which is impenetrable to us really exists"?

And while I'm not about to argue with Einstein, I can't help but wonder if maybe I'm jumping to conclusions, getting a bit ahead of myself.

Maybe it's not nearly as bad as I think.

Maybe Song didn't disappear.

Maybe she made a choice to find Anjou, since no one else could be bothered.

As I rinse the soap from my body and wring the shampoo from my hair, I know that whatever happened to Song, the answers I seek are inside that book.

9

After slipping into a black turtleneck and a pair of dark denim jeans I wear tucked inside my boots, I hear a brisk crack of thunder, followed by a heavy downpour of rain, and I know the official window for not getting drenched is now permanently closed for what's likely to be the rest of the day.

I reach for my warmest down parka—the one with the hood—and I've just stepped into the hall, destination Tarot Garden imprinted on my mental GPS, when my slab chimes with an incoming message.

My first thought is that it's from Braxton. Arthur let him go early. And though I'm thrilled by the idea of spending the rest of the day together, for now I need to drum up an excuse—something that'll deter him long enough for me to head out into a torrential downpour so I can scour every inch of the *Magician* sculpture in search of the book.

In other words, I'm about to feed him yet another lie.

And though it'll be a harmless lie, it still makes me cringe to think just how quickly these little fabrications are starting to pile up.

Still, resolved to do whatever it takes, I'm making my way down the staircase, trying to think of the perfect response, when I glance at the screen to find the message isn't from Braxton.

It's from Killian.

And luckily, I have no problem lying to him.

Killian: Hey—I know ur boy is off with Arthur. Does that mean you're free to hang w/me? ☺

Me: Unfortunately, I

Me: Unfor

Me: Un

Me:

In the end, I don't hit send. I just choose to ignore him and delete my reply.

Not because Killian and I aren't friendly—we are.

Actually, I'm probably the closest friend Killian has in this place. Which isn't saying much, considering how, from what I can tell, he doesn't seem to have any friends.

All I really know is that Killian's been here longer than Braxton and almost as long as Elodie. But just because he was stuck in eighteenth-century France for the last four years doesn't mean his return erased all the earlier baggage nearly everyone here associates with him.

For the last three weeks, Killian's kept to himself. And there was one night when I felt so sad to see him eating alone that I nearly gave Braxton a stroke when I invited Killian to join us.

But Killian was quick to decline. And between Braxton's thinly veiled hatred and Killian's vague accusations—well, I was feeling kind of over it.

For such a small group of Blues, we are teeming with resentments. And I guess in a way I'm no better, seeing as how I've been nursing my own anger toward Elodie from the start. But at least I try to get along. At least I'm able to get through a meal, attend her in-room parties, and put in the effort required to actually have a good time.

But Braxton and Killian…forget it.

Or, as Braxton said later that night: *Never going to happen, so don't waste your time.* Followed by: *And you should seriously consider staying away from him. He's not who you think he is.*

I wish I knew what really happened between them. But those two aren't talking, and no one else will give up any details.

All I know for sure is that the whole thing makes me feel awful, which explains why I pretty much spent the rest of that dinner sneaking glances between Killian and Mason. Each of them exiled to their own tables. Each of them pretending not to care.

Even after dinner, instead of joining the rest of us in the Autumn room, Killian just wandered off on his own, just as he has every night since he returned.

For Braxton, that comes as a relief. But for me, well, I guess there's still a part of me that feels like I owe Killian a debt I can never repay.

When he found me in that cell in Versailles, I was so lost in a Fade that if it weren't for him, showing up with the talisman that I'd lost, I may have never found my way out.

Hell, I never would've made my way anywhere, seeing as how I was dangerously close to crossing my own timeline. And since the duality of existence results in nonexistence, I would've blinked out of the world as though I never was in it.

"You cannot enter the same river twice, for it's not the same river and he's not the same man."

It's a quote by Heraclitus that my dad once taught me. Which reminds me of the words engraved on the plaque that hangs over the entrance to Gray Wolf: "Panta rhei."

Translation: "Everything flows."

And while I'm still not sure exactly what it means, I do know there must be a connection between my dad teaching the eight-year-old version of me a quote and a phrase by the same ancient Greek philosopher being cited above the academy gate. It's just too specific to be a coincidence.

My dad, this place, the missing pieces Arthur expects me to find from their various hiding spots throughout the world—

throughout time—so he can finally realize his dream of restoring the Antikythera Mechanism to its original glory—it's all related, all connected.

I just don't know how.

I pass priceless pieces of art, breeze through the room where wingback chairs hang from thick silver chains. I'm about to make my way down the hall with the reclaimed-wood floors that always reminds me of a posh bowling alley when my slab chimes again.

Killian: FTR - I saw those 3 dots - u avoiding me, Shiv?

Shiv. The nickname he gave me in reference to the weapon I used on the duke that I crafted from a few pieces I pulled from my pannier. And as much as I like to pretend it annoys me, it mostly just makes me laugh. Also, if I'm being honest, it makes me feel kind of badass.

Better than my former nickname at my old school: loser.

Me: Nope. Just v busy w/v important things.

Killian: V important things = my specialty and u know how good I am at keeping secrets → ur secrets.

A furious blush spreads across my face. He's referring to the kiss. That one time we first met when I was in a Fade. And the second time when…

I shake my head, annoyed with myself for even following this particular thought trail. While Killian insists I kissed him back, I remember it differently.

I remember biting his lip so hard, I tasted blood.

I ignore the message and pause before the door when my phone chimes again.

Killian: Ur killing me, Shiv. Whatsa boy gotta do 2 grab a coffee w/u?

This is followed by a string of broken-heart and coffee emojis.

Ugh. What is wrong with this guy? What will it take for him to give up?

I shake my head and thumb a quick reply.

Me: Can't—sorry—heading to the library. Buried in research. Also, pls stop w/the emojis.

There. That should end it. I visit the Gray Wolf library nearly every day, researching stuff for my upcoming Trip to Renaissance Italy. And since I've never once seen Killian around, I figure he's not all that big on reading or books.

I pull on my gloves and tug my hood so that it falls just short of my eyes, when a voice sounds from behind me.

"Well, isn't this a wee bit of a head-scratcher. Findin' ya standin' 'ere like tis?"

I freeze. It's Killian. Speaking in one of his many fake accents. *Shit.*

"And here I thought the library was in the exact opposite direction."

Slowly, I turn. I mean, what choice do I have?

"Whatcha up to, Shiv?" His bright blue eyes shine on mine. His lips ease into a grin.

"N-nothing," I stammer. *Seriously. What is wrong with me? Pull it together already!*

"Sure looks like nothing." His grin grows wider. He offers his arm. "What do you say I save you from whatever this is, and you and I go grab a coffee somewhere?"

I glance longingly at the door, then back at Killian.

Left with no other choice, I flip my hood back and step toward him.

10

"Where are you taking me?" I ask, gesturing around the hall Killian is currently leading me down. "Because this is definitely not the way to the Spring room."

"That's because we're not going to the Spring room," he says.

I stop in my tracks. Killian takes an additional step, then turns to face me.

"Do you really think it's a good idea for us to enjoy a coffee somewhere as public as that?" he asks.

He makes a good point, but still I hesitate.

"Can you at least try to trust me?" His blue eyes plead with mine. "After all, I did save your life."

I shake my head and frown. "Not this again."

Killian laughs.

"And, while we're on the subject, stop calling me 'Shiv.'" I cross my arms against my chest, wanting him to know that I'm serious.

Killian nods and starts walking again. After he takes a few steps, I rush to catch up.

"So, let me get this straight." He turns my way, and since he's got a good seven inches on me, he's forced to dip his chin to meet my gaze. "I can't call you 'Shiv,' and we both know 'darling' is out. Discovered that one the hard way. Though I have heard a few people around here call you 'Tasha.'"

"Braxton," I say, my voice edged with annoyance. "Braxton

is the only one who calls me Tasha. Which is why it's off-limits to you."

"Fair enough." He nods. "Maybe Nat, then?"

"No." The word practically leaps off my tongue, which of course prompts him to give me an appraising once-over. Still, I won't back down. Nat reminds me of the worst version of myself, the girl I was before I came here. The apathetic, self-sabotaging loser who was failing at pretty much every aspect of life.

"Can you help me out here?" he says. "Because I'm all out of options."

"You can call me Natasha," I say. "My actual name is Natasha Antoinette Clarke. See, there's three names. You're free to choose among them."

Killian shakes his head. "Sorry," he says. "I just don't see you that way. Maybe you should make up a new name, like virtually everyone else in this place. You think your boy was always named Braxton?"

Killian glances down at me again, but I just shrug it off, not wanting to let on how much he's surprised me.

If Braxton isn't his real name, then what is it—and why did he change it—and why has he never told me?

"You think Elodie Blue is the name on her birth certificate?" Killian continues, drawing me away from my thoughts.

I shrug. Having already guessed that about Elodie, I say, "And who were you before you became Killian du Luce?" I narrow my gaze, realizing that, despite sharing the bond of a harrowing experience, I know virtually nothing about him.

Killian grins. "Nice try. But we're talking about *you*. And I gotta say, you'll always be 'Shiv' to me. Sorry, friend. It just suits you."

I breathe a frustrated sigh, but really I'm still caught on him calling me friend. I mean, I know that's the best way to describe us, but it still strikes me as sad that we're forced to hide that fact from everyone else.

And yet, I'm the only one who seems bothered. Killian doesn't give a shit what anyone thinks.

"Now tell me—" He comes to a sudden stop. "What's your favorite place on this rock? And, just a heads-up, there are no right answers, only wrong ones."

Deciding to play along, I make an exaggerated version of a thinking face—eyes squinted, finger pressed to my chin, as I stare into some unknown horizon. "Let's see…that would probably be a tie between the Moon Garden and the Glass Room," I say, though the second it's out I'm overcome with regret.

The Moon Garden is where Braxton and I almost shared our first kiss. It's also where he confided in me about what really happens here at Gray Wolf.

The Glass Room is where that first kiss finally happened—a kiss so glorious, just thinking about it makes my cheeks flush.

I should've just shrugged it off, pretended I couldn't possibly choose among all the awesomeness. The Moon Garden and the Glass Room are solely for Braxton and me. Which means I definitely don't want to visit either of those places with Killian.

"You really outdid yourself, Shiv," Killian says. "I was only expecting one wrong answer, but you showed up with two. And judging by the looks of it, they really are your favorites. Just thinkin' about 'em has put a bloom in yer cheeks." He gestures toward my face, which only makes me flush even more fiercely.

"So what is the right answer?" I ask, torn between being amused and annoyed—the usual emotional circuit when dealing with this boy.

Killian grins, and while I can objectively agree that it's an all-out heart-melter, it has zero effect on me. "Today," he says, stopping before an elevator and pushing the call button. "You're about to add a new favorite place to your list."

"That's a pretty big buildup," I say. "You sure you're not overselling it?"

"That's for you to decide." He shrugs. "But first, we need to get there. And it's a wee bit o' a journey, I warn ya." He's back to speaking in accents again, and I'm about to call him out on it when the elevator doors slide open and Killian ushers me inside.

Straightaway we're descending so quickly, I'm reminded of the time I visited the Vault with Arthur, though I'm sure that's not where we're heading now. When the car does finally stop, the doors slide open and I step into a space so plain, so dreary and austere, for a moment I wonder if we might've somehow left Gray Wolf.

I mean, clearly we're still on the rock, since the only two ways out of this place are by time travel or a terrifying ride through treacherous waters. And yet, there's no denying that with one quick elevator ride, we've managed to leave our luxurious, snow globe–like world far behind, only to arrive in a space that would best be described as industrial gloom.

The ceiling is claustrophobically low. The floor is made of the same cement as the walls. And it looks like some sort of weird indoor parking garage.

"Well, this is…" I look all around, trying to summon just the right word. There's not a single work of art, no elaborate crystal chandeliers, no expensive wall treatments to be found. Just miles of cold, gray cement harshly lit by fluorescent lights.

"Surprising?" Killian suggests.

I shake my head. "I was thinking more like *bleak*. But yeah, surprising works, too. Either way, it seems like an odd place to grab a coffee."

But not such an odd place to stash a body.

The thought comes at me from out of nowhere. And despite the warmth of my parka, a shiver courses right through me.

It's fine. You're fine, I struggle to convince myself. *You're just triggered. You're in a confined, unfamiliar space with a boy you don't really know all that well. It's a loss of control. Nothing more. Just breathe your way back to comfort and peace, like Dr. Lucy said.*

But, while I'm busy slowing my breaths, my mind continues to unspool a ribbon of thoughts so alarming I'm filled with regret for agreeing to this.

For one thing, not only does Braxton hate Killian, but I can't even count how many times he's warned me to steer clear of him.

And there's no denying how pretty much everyone else on this rock goes out of their way to avoid him.

Everyone but me, apparently.

I steal a glance at Killian. Surely I'm being irrational.

I mean, Killian is my friend.

He helped me out of a terrible jam.

And yet, he also murdered a man—a Timekeeper back in Versailles. He plunged a blade right through his belly and left him to die. And according to him, it wasn't the first time.

Doesn't matter that I still don't know what a Timekeeper is. What I do know is that Killian failed to show even the slightest hint of remorse over ending his life.

Also, isn't it odd that we've traveled all this way without running into a single other person?

Which also means that if something were to happen to me—no one will suspect Killian.

Hell, no one will even know where to look for me!

My thoughts are in a whirl. A deep sense of panic starts to take root. But I can't let on. Can't let Killian know just how anxious I'm feeling.

I drag in a slow, ragged breath as I cast a furtive glance all around, searching for an exit, a way out—

"Oh look," Killian says, seemingly unaware of just how rattled I am. "Our ride's right over there."

I glance in the direction he's pointing, only to see one of the ubiquitous Gray Wolf carts parked diagonally against a wall.

It's the same sort of golf cart Arthur used when he took me to the Vault.

The same sort of ride that whisked me to the control room both times I Tripped.

Which is to say that they're generally reserved for visits to the outer reaches of this place.

Which only begs the question: *Just how far is Killian planning to take me?*

"Ever drive one of these?" he asks, leading me toward it.

"Um...no, I—" My heart is pumping too fast, my breath rapidly sawing in and out of my lungs.

"First time for everything!" Killian hops onto the passenger seat and motions for me to take the wheel. "Hey there," he calls. "Budge up, already. I've got a craving for a cuppa that won't quit."

I swallow hard, give another anxious look around. There's nowhere to flee, and even if there was, it's not like I can outrun him.

To Killian, I say, "But I—I don't know where we're going."

Killian throws his head back and lets out a quick burst of a laugh. When he finally rights himself, my gaze sweeps across his tumble of golden blond curls, to those deep-blue eyes the same warm hue as one of David Hockney's swimming pools. His nose is strong, his cheekbones defined, his jawline a brutal sharp line—like one of Michelangelo's statues come to life. And though I hate to admit it, the mere sight of him is enough to steal the breath right out of me.

He chuckles softly. "I hav' ta say, yer lookin' a wee bit pale around the eyes there, Shiv. So, I thought maybe you might like to drive. Ya know, so you can feel more in control."

I inhale an anxious breath. *So he did notice the shift in my mood. And, if worse comes to worse, I can always crash his side of the cart and make a run for it…*

Next thing I know, I'm settled onto the driver's seat, asking Killian which way to go.

11

I steer the golf cart down a long series of hallways, following the directions Killian gives me.

"Where'd you learn to drive, Shiv?"

I shake my head, keeping a steady foot on the pedal and my hands secured on the wheel.

"Not takin' a crack at ya," he says. "Just a wee bit curious, tis all."

"Can you not— " I frown, wishing it wasn't so easy for him to get under my skin.

Killian looks at me. "Yes? You were sayin' somethin'?"

I huff out a breath and start again. "Can you just stop with the fake accent and speak in your normal voice for once?"

Killian rakes a hand through his curls and shifts so that he's facing me. "And what makes you think that's not my normal voice? Why do you assume this is the real one?"

Ugh. Why did I ever agree to this? And more importantly, why am I still agreeing?

"Sorry to annoy ya," he says. "Just trying to get to know you better tis all. Seein' as how yer pretty much my only friend 'ere."

"So, that's where you decide to land?" I say. "With a hybrid accent?"

"Just tryin' ta please us both." He shrugs.

"Mason taught me to drive," I say. "Happy now?"

Killian takes a moment to consider, then says, "And who

taught him?"

"His grandma," I say, remembering how excited Mason was when he learned to parallel park and tried to teach me. But despite giving it my best shot, I never mastered that skill.

"Well, that explains it." Killian nods.

I shoot him a sharp look. "That sounds like ageism," I snap, but Killian dismisses it with a wave of his hand.

"Not at all. Just pointing out your driving style."

"My *driving style*?"

"You go about it like a real proper lady. Yer spine straight, eyes diligently surveying the path ahead, obeying all the rules—even when there aren't any."

"That's called being a *safe driver*," I grumble. "Didn't realize it was considered a style."

"Look at your hands." Killian cocks a thumb toward the steering wheel. "From the moment you sat down, they haven't once shifted."

My first instinct is to snap back, but instead, I set my focus on the narrow aisle before me. With the low sloped ceiling and notable lack of windows, it's more like a tunnel. Where it leads is anyone's guess. Or make that *my* guess, since Killian clearly knows.

"Are you always such a stickler for the rules, Shiv?" Killian asks, and though I refuse to look at him, from his tone I can tell he's wearing one of his flirtatious grins. Charisma and charm are pretty much his default. "Don't you ever want to break one of those rules and see what might happen?"

Is he for real? I fight the urge to roll my eyes, since it'll only succeed in egging him on. Instead, I clear my throat and say, "I've broken plenty of rules. How do you think I ended up here?"

"Here with *me*?" He leans closer, practically lifting off his seat.

"Don't flatter yourself. You know exactly what I meant. In fact—"

Before I can go on to outline all the rules I used to break before I was whisked away to this place, Killian says, "Here's good. Park anywhere. It's not like we'll be returning this way."

I look at him, confused.

"We took the scenic route."

I stop the cart, leaving it in the middle of the pathway.

"Just trying to look out for you, Shiv, by making sure no one saw us together. Also, if I may be so bold, it gave me a chance to get to know you better."

"Like how I learned to drive?"

Killian laughs and climbs out of the cart.

I follow his lead, minus the laugh.

"That, along with a few other things..." He smiles mysteriously.

"Go ahead," I say. "Tell me everything your razor-sharp observation skills managed to glean about me."

"Not sure you could handle it." He grins in a way that lights up his whole face.

"Try me," I say, immune to the glowy magnetism he so naturally emits.

"Okay." He nods. "Here's one: whenever you start to feel nervous or unsafe—or, in this case, both—your voice rises higher than usual, and you take on a bit of an attitude."

Slowly, I lift my gaze to meet his. *Am I really that transparent?*

"Not to worry." He gives a quick wave of his hand. "I find it charming when you get all feisty like that. Just consider it one more secret we'll keep between us. Though, I might say, they're really starting to pile up. Still, for now, it's best if you try to relax so you'll be in the right frame of mind when you see what comes next."

Something about the way he said that gives me pause. *What exactly does come next?*

Without another word, Killian leads me down the tunnel

before stopping at a door that manages to merge so seamlessly with the wall, I could've easily walked right by it and never noticed it was there. Even the keypad beside it blends in. "Brace yourself," he says.

My belly clenches with nerves. "I'm not sure how to take that," I say.

Killian regards me from over his shoulder. "If I were you, I'd take it seriously. And, for the record, you should always take *me* seriously. Except when I'm joking, of course. But I'm sure you can tell the difference by now."

There's an undeniable charge in his voice, and there's no missing the flame in his gaze that burns brighter than ever. I have no idea how to read him; my anxiety is getting the best of me, and Killian notices immediately.

"Look," he says. "I get that you're feeling out of your depth. But I promise, you're safe. So you can stop looking at me like that." He veers so close I can feel the warmth of his breath wafting over my cheek.

"And how exactly am I looking at you?" I ask, striving for imperious and missing it by a mile.

"Like you can't decide whether you want to kiss me or whack me over the head and run for your life."

In an instant, my gaze turns to frost. He's trying to keep me as unsteady in my thinking as I am on my feet. Killian lives for moments like this. But we've played this game before, and he's not nearly as crafty of an opponent as he obviously thinks.

"Trust me," I say. "Kissing you is not on the menu. I mean, no offense, but once was more than enough."

Killian's lips pull into a grin. "Actually, you kissed me twice, Shiv. But no need to split hairs over small details."

Against my better judgment, I roll my eyes and huff under my breath.

"Oh, and one last thing—you still got yer slab?"

I nod, not sure I understand what he's getting at.

"Then you can set your mind at ease." He nods. "Nothing terrible can happen to you so long as they're able to track you." Reading the confused look on my face, he says, "You think Arthur gave you that tablet as a convenient way to send messages and read his inspirational quotes every day? He's tracking you, Shiv. Tracking all of us. Of course, this place is loaded with surveillance cameras, but the slab makes it that much easier to keep tabs on your whereabouts."

If that was meant to comfort, it pretty much did the opposite. And though Braxton once told me something similar, when he said it, it felt more like a safety precaution and less like an alarming privacy infringement.

But before I have a chance to respond, Killian presses his thumb to the keypad, the door swings open, and with a quick intake of breath, I step into a whole other world.

If life is a game of cards, we are born
without knowledge of the rules.
Yet we must play our hand.
—Niki de Saint Phalle

12

How the other half lives.

It's the first thought that springs to mind, even though I'm not entirely sure what it means, much less who this other half might be.

My gaze wanders down a wide hall with cobblestone floors and quaint, old-timey storefronts with colorful shutters and doors. In the distance, there's a cluster of cute, thatched-roof dorms, and I can't help but wonder if it's another one of Arthur's holograms.

As if reading my mind, Killian says, "It's all real. Well, except for the sky, of course."

He points toward a ceiling that's painted to mimic a nice sunny day. Just after he's said it, the hologram clouds begin to shift as a light breeze suddenly kicks into play. When those same clouds cover the beam of light standing in for the sun, the entire space dims.

I look at Killian and say, "I feel like we've just traveled back a few centuries, but we did it by golf cart instead of the launchpad."

"In a way, we have." Killian nods, looking pleased with himself. "I like to think of it as the forgotten world. Sometimes I feel like I'm the only one who remembers it's here."

I step deeper into the space. It's impossible to take it all in with one glance.

"But what exactly is this?" I ask, gesturing toward a man darting out of a pub dressed in clothes from a time long before zippers were invented. He looks like an extra who just wandered off the set of some historical drama. "Like that guy—does he live here? And why haven't I heard of this place before now?"

Killian grins. "It's the best-kept secret in all of Gray Wolf."

"So how did you find it?" I turn to him, noting how the spark in his gaze instantly snuffs.

"I used to live here," he says.

I stare at him, waiting for more. But he just places a hand on my elbow and steers me toward a pub with a sign overhead that reads *The Hideaway.*

"While I promise to answer your questions," he says. "Or at least *some* of them. The first order of business is getting me hands on some coffee and sumptin' to fill up me belly."

We enter the sort of old-fashioned tavern I've only seen in movies. The lighting is sparse, the floors are made of rough wooden planks, and the cream-colored walls look as though they were molded by hand. And there's no missing the way everyone smiles and waves the moment they see Killian.

"What are you, some kind of conquering hero?" I ask as Killian leads me to a small table situated by the far wall.

It's not until we're settled and Killian's ordered us coffees that he leans toward me and says, "You have no idea just how close you are to the truth."

The words float between us. But exactly which truth is he referring to?

The truth of him being a conquering hero?

Or something else I might've said earlier?

Before I have a chance to ask, the waitress is back. Only this time, the corseted top of her bar wench uniform is pulled so low, her abundant cleavage is precariously close to spilling out.

She plops my mug before me, sending a splash of foam

dripping over the sides. Though it's not like she's noticed. She's focused entirely on Killian, taking great care to serve him his latte as the two of them speak in a language I don't understand.

At one point, Killian pauses the conversation to say, "How do you feel about shepherd's pie?"

I shrug. "Does it make for a good breakfast?" I ask, realizing I got so sidetracked, I missed that meal entirely.

"It makes for a good everything," Killian says. When he returns to the waitress, I assume he's placing an order, but honestly, I can't say for sure. Though I do catch the lingering look she gives him as she walks away and the wink of appreciation he shoots her in return.

As soon as she's gone, I say, "Good friend of yours?"

Killian tips his mug toward me, then takes a slow sip. Using the back of his hand, he wipes a smudge of foam from his lips. "If I didn't know better, I'd think you were jealous, Shiv."

I roll my eyes, take a tentative sip of my own coffee. Then, after blowing a cooling breath across the top, I chase it with another. "What language were you speaking?"

Killian regards me with a look of amusement. "What language do you think it was?"

I shrug. "I thought I recognized a word or two, but—"

"We were speaking English. Just not the sort you're used to. Not your standard Southern California drawl." He pronounces that last part like some stereotypical surfer after one too many hits of a bong. "My friend Maisie there"—he jabs a thumb in the general direction of the bar—"she hails from Scotland." He finishes with an exaggerated brogue.

"And you—are you from Scotland, too?"

"Aye." He nods. "I'm from here, there, and everywhere."

I study him for a moment. Where Killian's concerned, the truth is always so slippery, and he works hard to keep it that way.

He settles back in his seat and savors a few sips of his drink.

Then, peering at me from over the top of his mug, he says, "And to answer your question, yes. Maisie is a good friend. Unlike the posh world where you reside, I have many friends in these parts."

I'm struck by what he just said. Though I've never visited Killian's room, I guess I assumed he occupied his own luxury suite. "What do you mean, where *I* reside?" I ask. "Don't you live there, too?"

"I'm a man between worlds." He shrugs. "I go where Arthur needs me. But, if you must know, this here's the part of Gray Wolf that'll always feel closest to home."

Something about the way he said that reminds me of Freya.

If it's possible Freya's not from this timeline, then does the same go for Killian?

I would just come out and ask him, but considering how Killian's always working an agenda, I'll need to do so in a way that doesn't alarm him.

"How about you and I make a deal?" Killian leans across the table, his fingers lightly drumming just inches from mine. "You tell me where you were really sneaking off to, and I'll fill you in on my backstory."

"First of all, I wasn't sneaking anywhere," I say. "I was about to exit through the front door, in the middle of the day. Not exactly the definition of subterfuge."

"And second of all?" Killian quirks his eyebrows at me. Then, responding to my look of confusion, he adds, "Usually, when one begins a sentence with '*first of all*,' it means there's a whole other thing lined up in the barrel, ready to shoot. So, tell me: what's part two?"

I hesitate, unsure how I'll answer, when Maisie reappears. And after serving us each a sizeable square of shepherd's pie, she leaves with a brisk nod for me and a wink for Killian.

I push the plate aside, drag my coffee in closer, and cradle the ceramic mug between my palms. Killian's right about there being a next part. Though I'm not sure I should tell him how his use of the word "backstory" only confirms my suspicion that Killian du Luce isn't just a made-up name but a made-up person as well.

Between all the accents and his seemingly infinite storehouse of secrets, sometimes I wonder if he even knows who he is behind his golden-boy facade.

Still, I just say, "No part two. I'm just waiting to hear all about this *backstory* of yours."

He shoots a quick look around the room and says, "Earlier, when you asked if I'm some sort of conquering hero… Well, please know I'm not speaking from a place of hubris when I confirm I'm exactly that."

I squint, waiting for whatever comes next. Because honestly, I was just being flippant.

"Take Maisie for instance…" Killian leans closer, fixes his gaze hard on mine. And what I find revealed in those endless pools of his eyes is not at all what I've come to expect.

The sort of flirty charm offensive he usually leads with has been stripped away, leaving a new version of Killian in its place. One that's so open and trusting, I'm taken aback. But it's what he says next that really blows my mind.

"I… Well, to put it bluntly…" He pauses a beat. "I saved her."

"Saved her from…?" I abandon my coffee, tuck my hands into my lap, eager to learn whatever he's willing to confess.

After another quick look around, Killian inhales a sharp breath, and on the exhale, he says, "I saved her from being burned at the stake."

13

I stare at Killian. No way is he serious.

"But they don't burn people at the stake anymore," I remind him.

I watch as he rubs his lips together and takes another glance around the room. When Maisie catches his eye and starts to head over, he's quick to hold up a hand and wave her away.

"Maybe not." He returns to me. "But I never claimed she was from this century, did I?" Then he digs into his food as though he's totally unaware of the impact of his words. Totally unaware of the lightning bolt striking my brain.

So there it is—the answer I was looking for. And now that it's here, what exactly am I supposed to do with it?

"And what about you?" I ask, my voice uncertain. "Are you from this timeline?"

I study him closely, catching the way his jaw clenches, the way his fingers nervously grasp at his fork. With his gaze burning brightly on mine, he says, "What do you think?"

I shrug, aware of my breath coming faster, more shallow—frantic puffs of air blowing in and out of my lungs. While I definitely have my suspicions, there's no way of knowing for sure unless he decides to confess. And even then, there's no way of knowing if it's really the truth.

He goes in for another bite, taking his time chewing, savoring, and gesturing for me to do the same. So I do. And the shepherd's pie is so delicious, another bite quickly follows.

"You probably don't know this," he says. "But my Trips aren't like yours. Arthur doesn't send me out to steal art or jewels or things of that sort—or at least, not very often. Though there have been many occasions when he's sent me out to redistribute those items among the poor. And while I thought that might shock you, going by your expression, you already know."

I nod. "Arthur told me how he does that sometimes."

"Sometimes?" Killian tips his head back and laughs. "You'd be surprised how much he gives away. Redistributing the wealth is one of his greatest joys."

"So, he really is Robin Hood," I say.

"Arthur is a lot of things," Killian replies somewhat mysteriously. "And while there's much I'm not authorized to share, I will tell you this—sometimes, when I'm out Tripping, Arthur has permitted me to free the odd prisoner now and again."

I stare at him blankly, trying to make sense of his words.

"I break them out of their cell and bring them back here." He shrugs, once again tucking into his food.

My fork slips from my fingers, clattering loudly against my plate. My mind is in a whirl, struggling to process his words.

"You mean, bring them back here like ensla—?"

Before I can finish, Killian stops me. "Good God, no." He glances over his shoulder, ensuring no one heard, then returns to me wearing an expression of horror. "Don't even think it—much less say it. It's nothing of the sort."

It's the most wound-up I've ever seen him, and yet, I refuse to let it go. "But if that's what happened with Maisie, and you brought her back here to work—"

"Shiv, *please*." Killian speaks in the sort of stage whisper intended to shush me. "Let's get one thing straight—Arthur doesn't *own* them. He doesn't own anyone. They chose to come to Gray Wolf. I'm betting it's not so different from how you ended up here."

"Oh, so you framed them for a crime before you freed them from jail?"

"No." Killian narrows his gaze. "Nothing remotely like that."

"Then it's nothing like me," I tell him, my voice edged with the sort of unmistakable bitterness I didn't expect. I truly thought I'd moved beyond all of that.

"My point is, they were given a choice," Killian says. "And I know you were, too, because that's how Arthur works. They could either stay behind and face the consequences of their purported crimes—which often meant death—or they could agree to come here, where they'd be clothed, fed, and have all their needs met."

"In exchange for their labor," I say.

"You're still not getting it." He takes another bite of his pie and washes it down with a swig of his coffee. "Look—" He pushes back a random curl that's tumbled over his forehead and into his eyes. "What I know for sure is that everyone you see here was an innocent victim of uncivilized times. They were poor, with no chance of improving their lot. And when given the choice between staring down the guillotine, being drawn and quartered, burned at the stake, or whatever punishment their executioners could dream up—versus traveling forward in time to a safe place in the new millennium—only a few didn't take the chance to escape."

I watch as he polishes off what's left of his pie, then starts eyeballing mine.

"You going to eat that?" He motions toward my plate. "Because if not—"

"Yes," I say, quick to carve another piece and angle it into my mouth.

"God, I love a girl with an appetite." Killian watches me with a look of deep appreciation.

"You were saying?" I pause my fork and shoot him a knock-it-off look.

"Yes—back to Maisie," he says. "She was training as a midwife's apprentice when the baby she was helping deliver was stillborn, and she and the midwife were convicted of witchcraft and sentenced to die. Maisie chose to flee. The midwife chose to burn. Then there was the time when..."

Killian rambles on, but my mind has traveled back to the leather-bound book I saw in Song's room. The one with the strange marking on its cover.

Magick has always been the currency of the oppressed.

Is it possible that book is some sort of spell book or grimoire?

And if so, then why did Song have it?

And what about the person in the red cape who carried it out of a maze that no longer exists in the modern day?

All I know for sure is that Song was sending a message via the perfume and the note. But did Freya put it in my room—or was it someone else?

"I've lost you," Killian says, drawing me away from my thoughts. "I can see it in your eyes. You're many timelines away."

"Sorry." I offer a thin smile that feels wrong on my face. "I guess I was just wondering..."

Killian waits.

"Do you, by any chance, happen to know Freya? She has red hair and—"

Killian's already nodding long before I can finish. "Saved her, too," he says. "They were about to put her to the swimming test."

I narrow my eyes and shake my head. I don't know the first thing about witchcraft or magick, but maybe it's time that I learn. I take another bite of shepherd's pie and settle in.

"It goes like this," Killian says. "First, they convict you of witchery. Then they haul you to the nearest, deepest body of water, where they strip you down to your undergarments, bind your arms and legs, and toss you right in to see if you sink or swim. If you're unlucky enough to float back to the top, you are confirmed a witch, in which case they pull you from the water and burn you at the stake."

"And if you sink?" I ask.

Killian shrugs. "Most likely they leave you to drown. But you and your loved ones have the honor of knowing you died with your reputation intact. Turns out you were not a witch after all. But, better safe than sorry, or so the logic goes."

"It's barbaric," I say, marveling at how easy it's always been to manipulate large crowds of people into supporting inhumane acts by appealing to their prejudice and fear.

"Misogyny in the ancient day." Killian shakes his head, causing that one stray curl to swoop over his forehead again. "Weak men have always been terrified by the innate power of strong women—of all women, really. And women who fear their own power have always supported those same weak men. Vicious cycle." He shrugs. "It's also a concept I can't wrap my head around. I love a woman who knows her own worth." His eyes spark on mine and his lips tick up at the sides, but I'm not falling for that, and I'm quick to look away. After a few silent beats, he says, "What made you ask about Freya? You two friendly?"

I shake my head, try to steer the subject in another direction. "So, this is where all the support staff live?"

"This is where they *choose* to live," Killian says. "And it's an important distinction worth noting. Of course, there are those who've tried it on your side, but no one stays very long. For them, *this* is the luxury version of the life they were living. Also, none of them actually wanted to leave their timeline, but it was their only way to survive."

"Like refugees from history," I say.

"Exactly." Killian nods.

I sigh. *Why has it always been so difficult for humans to just stop harming one another?*

"Okay," I say. "But what happens if someone comes to Gray Wolf only to decide they don't like it? Can they go back to where they came from?"

"Theoretically." He shrugs. "But why would they?"

I watch as he tilts his head back, drains what's left of his coffee, then, setting his mug aside, laces his fingers together.

"At first, it's a shock to the system. The sort of comforts we take for granted, like electricity, running water, and toilets that flush, seem like sorcery to them. And while there are those who remain convinced that Arthur's some sort of fallen angel, if not Lucifer himself—and who knows, maybe he is"—Killian laughs—"most prefer to take their chances with a potential dark overlord than return to a society that clearly has it out for them."

I take a moment to process. It's a lot to digest.

"Tell me, Shiv," Killian says. "And please be truthful, because I'm interested in hearing your answer. What would you do if you were like Arthur—if you had the same sort of unlimited access to money and technology? Would you do whatever you could to make the world a better place for as many people as possible? Or would you leave it to the hand of fate?"

I hesitate to answer. Mainly because the question is slanted in a way that portrays Arthur as the ultimate benefactor, and if I were to choose otherwise, what would that say about me?

Though it does make me wonder just how much Killian might know about Arthur's ultimate goal.

Has he seen the Antikythera Mechanism Arthur stores in its own locked room at the back of the Vault?

Does he have any idea what Arthur plans to do with that

priceless antiquity once I've collected all the missing pieces and he restores it back to its original glory?

I remember the dreamy look on Arthur's face when I asked him what he planned to do once I'd completed my task: *Why, I'm going to remake the world*, he'd said, as though stating something glaringly obvious.

And then another memory rushes in on its tail. It's what Killian said just moments before we left Versailles and jumped two and a half centuries forward in time—something about there being more to Gray Wolf than collecting trinkets and art. *Everyone in that place has a plan, darlin'. Especially Arthur. And it ain't about that.*

At the time, I got so sidetracked by him calling me *darlin'*, I missed the most important part. But now it's so clear, I can't believe I didn't see it before.

Killian knows.

Not only did he basically tell me as much, but he even sat back and watched as I reclaimed the Sun from the same Timekeeper he'd just put his blade through.

The thought alone leaves me with chills.

"You all right there?" Killian asks as I hug myself at the waist, trying to keep the shivering in check.

"I'm fine," I say. "Just..." The words fade as another thought hits me.

Is that what this is about?

Did Arthur only pretend to need Braxton so Killian could bring me here and learn just how far he can trust me?

It must be, I decide. Because how else would Killian know that Braxton was away?

I study Killian's face, trying to glean something beyond the golden-boy mask. But Killian has been playing this part for so long, the only way to peer beneath the facade is with his permission—and right now, he's denying me access.

Though one thing is sure: Arthur isn't just tracking me. He knows everything about me.

Which means if I want to get my hands on that book, I'm going to have to find a way to slip under his radar—and Killian's, too.

After way too long a pause, I return to his question. "I can't imagine having that sort of power, nor would I want to. Though you definitely come across as Arthur's number one fan. Well, next to Elodie, that is." I try to laugh, but it's such a miserable attempt, I quickly move on. "And yet, considering how he left you stranded, letting four years slip by before he finally got around to sending someone to find you, your loyalty strikes me as strange."

Because my gaze is locked on Killian's, I'm able to track the swift play of shadow that cuts across his eyes. Like a sky between seasons, I follow the shift from darkness to light before it settles into some murkier place.

"For the record," he says, his voice strained, "Arthur didn't leave me stranded. And I apologize if I didn't make myself clear the last time I told you. Or perhaps I did, but you chose not to listen. Either way, allow me to state now and for the record that the person responsible for ditching me in France isn't Arthur. It's Braxton."

14

It's not like I didn't hear him the last time Killian accused Braxton of leaving him stranded. I just don't believe him, and nothing he can say will change my mind.

Mainly because I know in my heart that Braxton would never do something like that. Unless he had a very good reason—and probably not even then.

An awkward pause passes between us, like two stop-motion figures waiting for an animator to put us into play.

"I trust that you heard me," Killian finally says. His eyes search my face, looking for signs of allegiance or betrayal, as though there's no possible place in between.

"I'm not sure what you want me to say." I cross my legs, shifting uneasily.

Killian shakes his head, tips his seat back on two legs. "I was hoping you might reconsider."

"Reconsider my relationship with Braxton?" I study him closely, trying to get a read, but Killian is as impenetrable as ever.

Killian rubs his lips together, swipes a hand through his hair. It's not the first time he's made those moves in that order, and I'm wondering if it might be some kind of tell.

I need to pay closer attention. Need to keep track of things like that.

"Look," he says, swinging his chair forward again. "I didn't set out to make you uncomfortable. But Shiv, I was in that cell with you. I saw the aftermath of all you went through. And I know firsthand just how tough, strong, determined, and gobsmackingly fierce you really are, and—"

His impassioned praise catches me off guard, and I really wish he'd just stop speaking already because I'm more than ready to go.

"—and even though you clearly don't need it, and certainly don't want it," he goes on, "I can't help feeling protective of you."

"So, you're offering your services as a bodyguard?" I cringe when I hear it. A dumb attempt at a joke that I regret the second it's out.

"No, Shiv," Killian says. "That's not at all what I'm offering."

He leans closer, nearly halfway across the table now. And his eyes are like twin blue flames, centered directly on me.

"Shiv," he starts. "I—"

Before he can say anything more, I hold up a hand, warding him off. Whatever he's about to say, I don't want to hear. The scorch of his gaze is so explosive, I need to get out of this place or risk getting burned.

I shouldn't have come here.

Despite having learned how Freya and those like her found their way to this rock, I'm no longer sure it was worth it. If Braxton ever heard about this, he'd be incredibly hurt, and I just couldn't bear that. Because despite what Killian said, despite all my qualms, I want to be with Braxton. I want us to work.

It's Braxton I've given my heart to.

"Look—" I push away from the table. "I should go. I've got loads of stuff to do and…" I make a rolling gesture with my hand but leave the sentence undone. I've told enough lies for one day. No reason to keep adding to the list.

Killian's gaze lands on my half-eaten shepherd's pie. "Well, you gave it your best shot," he says. Then, lifting my fork from my plate, he polishes off the remains, using *my* fork, not his.

Something about watching the tines slide in and out of his mouth, not long after they slid in and out of mine, feels way too intimate for two platonic friends just sharing a meal.

When he's done, he rises from his seat and moves to my side.

"So, the Gray Wolf manners are also applicable here?" My voice pitches just a little too high. Still, I'm desperate to say or do whatever it takes to put us both back on track.

Killian pulls a half grin and helps me into my parka.

"Don't worry about us," he says. "Or rather, don't worry about the two of us coming here together. No one need ever find out." His face is just inches from mine, forcing me to go to great lengths to avoid meeting his gaze.

Though he walks me to the door, that's as far as I'll let him go. I've spent enough time with Killian for one day.

"Can you point me to the shortcut?" I ask. "Earlier, you implied we took the long way."

Killian gestures to the opposite side of the street. "There's an elevator just inside that small blue gate. It'll drop you not far from where I first found you."

"Thanks," I say, turning to him. "For trusting me enough to show me this place and…and share all that you did."

My gaze meets Killian's, and I wonder if he can tell that I'm not entirely convinced of what I just said.

Was it a show of trust?

Or did Arthur put him up to it to test just how far my loyalty goes?

If Killian does know, he does a good job of not letting on. He just taps a hand to his forehead, dips his chin, and watches me go.

I've made it halfway across the cobblestone road when I chance a look over my shoulder. Though I don't know what I'm expecting to find, other than Killian bellied up to the bar, flirting with Maisie as she makes him a drink much stronger than coffee—that's not at all what I see.

Killian is standing right where I left him. His incinerator gaze centered on me. His face shadowed by the sort of thoughts I prefer not to know.

Even after I've crossed the street and made my way beyond the blue gate, I can't seem to shake the uncanny feeling that Killian is still staring after me long after I'm gone.

15

The first thing I see when I step out of the elevator is Roxanne, and from the looks of it, she's been waiting for me.

Though I'm still not sure what her actual job description is, every time I Trip, she's the one who reveals the destination along with the list of Gets.

"Good afternoon, Natasha," she says, emphasis on *afternoon.* Then, with a pointed look toward the elevator, she adds, "I trust you're enjoying your day?"

She stands before me, face grim, bright blond hair swinging just shy of her shoulders. And I remember how the first time we met I took her for a bit chilly on the outside, though I assumed she was warmer and friendlier inside. Now I'm no longer sure.

I mean, while it's not her fault that her sharp, aristocratic features lend her an expression of haughty disapproval, it's safe to say that today her face is broadcasting her true feelings loud and clear: she knows where I've been, and she does not approve.

I cringe under her glare, wondering if I should try to explain. Then, realizing there's no point, I look at her and ask, "Am I scheduled to Trip?"

Usually Tripping comes with advance warning. Then again, considering how I've only Tripped twice, I can't be sure that's always the case.

"Yes," she says. "And you better hurry so you're not the cause of any further delay."

Before I can protest, she's off, her sneakers squealing against the tiled floor, clearly expecting me to follow. Which, of course, I do. Roxanne just naturally emits an innate authority that makes you reluctant to challenge her.

"Do you know where I'm going?" I ask, hoping she'll at least offer a clue.

"I'm sure you'll discover that soon enough."

I frown at the back of her head as she picks up the pace, forcing me to race to catch up. After leading me down another hall, she stops before the electric cart and directs me to hop on.

We ride in silence. Aside from flashing my ID at the various checkpoints, I'm mostly preoccupied with the nagging worry that I might be heading off to Renaissance Italy. Because despite having spent the last three weeks up to my ears in history books, I still don't feel ready.

Last time, when Arthur sent me to Versailles to bring back the Sun, he provided clues taken from tarot cards and the symbols sketched on Christopher Columbus's map.

This time, other than the *Salvator Mundi*, he's yet to offer anything else that might help me locate the Moon.

The cart comes to an abrupt stop, and I follow Roxanne into the control room.

"They're waiting for you in wardrobe," she says, the words clipped. And before I have a chance to ask anything more, she's gone.

On my way there, I run into Keane, one of the Gray Wolf instructors, and when he smiles and gives a friendly wave, I decide to ask him.

"Is this…" I start. "I mean, am I…?"

"Are you Tripping?" He quirks a brow. "Yes. Are you Tripping to Renaissance Italy?" He shakes his head, and all my anxiety whooshes right out of me.

"But if not Italy, then where?"

I watch as he takes a quick look around, ensuring we won't be overheard. He tips his head toward me and says in a low voice, "Arthur's decided to shake up the protocol."

I stand frozen, aware of the twinge of unease clenching low in my belly as Keane draws away, acting as though that somehow explained everything.

Standing at full height, Keane is at least a foot taller than me, which forces me to crane my neck just to meet his gaze. And once I do, I'm reminded of Braxton. Not that they look anything alike, but with his gleaming brown skin, dark, tapered eyes, and perfectly sculpted body, Keane possesses the kind of good looks that seem tailor-made for the big screen. And like Braxton, he wears that star quality with a sort of bored obliviousness, like he can hardly remember the last time he bothered to look in a mirror.

"Shake up the protocol?" I search his face, having no idea what he's getting at.

"Mason's heading out," he tells me.

At first, I take that to mean that Mason won the battle. That Arthur finally grew tired of trying to break through his walls and has decided to send him back home.

But as soon as I process the thought, I know it's not true.

For one thing, Arthur would never give in so easily.

For another, the cryptic gleam in Keane's gaze tells me that *heading out* is a euphemism for something else.

"You mean he's...*Tripping*?" I ask, but even after Keane confirms it, I'm still not sure I believe him. "But Mason's a Green. He's not been properly trained, he doesn't speak any other languages, and—" I'm ready to recite the long list of reasons for why this can't happen when Keane holds up a hand, halting my words.

"You don't speak any languages, either," he says. "And that hasn't stopped you. Thing is, Mason's been an especially tough nut to crack. So Arthur's tossing him into the pool to see if he can learn to swim without any floaties."

"And if he doesn't…learn to swim?" I say, sticking with the metaphor. "If he drowns?" My voice cracks, betraying the full extent of my worry.

Keane opens his mouth, about to respond, when from across the room, another instructor, Hawke, calls out to him, effectively pulling his focus away. By the time he returns to me, his words are rushed. "That's where you come in," he says. "To ensure his safe return."

I shake my head. "You do realize Mason blames me for being sent here. It's highly unlikely he'll listen to me."

Keane's lips pull tight, but his gaze softens on mine. "Then it seems Arthur's putting you *both* to the test."

Hawke calls out again, this time gesturing impatiently for Keane to join him. But just as Keane turns away, I catch the edge of his sleeve, holding him in place. "Just—one more thing. Has Arthur ever done this before? Broken protocol like this?"

Keane gives me a long, considering look, and it's like I can see the gears spinning as he weighs just how much to reveal. Finally coming to a decision, he says, "Not since he sent Braxton out for his first Trip. Like Mason, he was nowhere close to making Yellow."

My jaw drops. I have so many questions, but there's only one that soars straight to the top. "And who—" I start, my voice so shaky, I'm forced to clear my throat and try again. "Who was there to look after Braxton—to make sure he returned?" With jangly knees and a racing heart, I wait for the answer I'm pretty sure I already know.

"It was Killian," Keane says, leaving me staring after him as he heads to where Hawke waits on the other side of the room.

16

By the time I make it to wardrobe, my head is reeling from the news.

Braxton's first Trip was with Killian.

Was that when their mutual loathing began?

And if so, why has Braxton never told me?

Why has he never said much of anything other than repeatedly insisting that Killian is an untrustworthy psychopath, while failing to provide so much as a shred of evidence as to why?

And why hasn't—

"So, you got roped into this, too, huh?"

I look up to find Elodie, and not only am I surprised to see her, but I'm happy to see her. If for no other reason than if Mason decides to go rogue, at least I'll have backup.

"Do you know where we're going?" I ask, figuring if anyone does, it's Elodie. Having been here the longest, she knows all the ins and outs of this place.

Elodie's about to speak when Charlotte, who, from what I can tell, is in charge of wardrobe, appears with a gown clutched in each hand.

Immediately recognizing the cap sleeves and empire waist, Elodie and I both say, "Regency England!" our voices overlapping.

Only Elodie claps and bounces on her toes as she says it.

My own enthusiasm is a lot more muted.

"Oh, it's my favorite!" Elodie squeals. "All those fussy manners, elaborate courtship rituals, and pent-up sexual tension." Her blue eyes glitter on mine. "It's so delightfully fun."

"I think you just summarized exactly why I love all those Jane Austen retellings," I say, watching as she takes a shimmering green satin gown from Charlotte and hands it to me before claiming the beautiful powder-blue for herself. Then, with her dress clutched to her waist, she grabs hold of my hand and twirls me about the room as she laughs.

It's been a while since I've seen her so happy, and it reminds me of the old days when the two of us would skip school to go in search of adventure, or at least something more exciting than the drudgery of the classroom. And in this moment, as the two of us dance and laugh, it's like all the old resentments and grudges have been fully washed away.

"It's going to be amazing!" Elodie exclaims. "I can't wait for you to experience it—you are in for a treat."

"You'll not be traveling anywhere if I don't get you dressed." Charlotte tries to act stern, but the twitch at the corner of her lip reveals how amused she is to see Elodie acting like this.

As Charlotte leaves to gather our stockings and shoes, Elodie leans toward me and whispers, "Can I tell you a secret?"

I look at her, startled. "Um, sure."

"I have a friend there." Her gaze glitters on mine. "A boyfriend, actually. Or should I say, *a serious male suitor*."

That last bit is pronounced in a spot-on impression of an upper-crust English accent that's like the female equivalent of Braxton's. Still, I squint, not entirely sure I understand. "In Regency England, you mean?"

She bites down on her lip and nods. "His name is Nash," she says, a flush of pink spreading across her cheeks. "He's an earl, and he's totally dreamy."

"Other than movies and books, I don't really know much about that time, but doesn't it span several years, at least?"

"Around a decade." She nods.

"So then, how can you be sure—"

"That he'll be there?" she cuts in. Then, still clutching the dress to her waist, she strikes a series of poses before the mirror. "Let's just say he's someone I've researched." She faces me then, grinning in a way that showcases the dimples on either side of her cheeks. "And depending on what timeline I arrive in, sometimes we meet for the first time, and sometimes we reconnect after a long absence. Either way, it's always super hot and totally thrilling." She wiggles her brow and breaks into a fit of giggles that's so unlike her, it's a moment before I process it all.

"And Jago?" I finally say. "He's okay with that?"

Elodie shrugs. "Jago's great—we have a good time. But we also like our freedom, and we're not interested in policing each other. When we Trip, we're free to do as we please. I know it's not the kind of arrangement that would work for everyone, but it works for us."

I watch her elegant shoulders rise and fall as I remember my first Trip to Versailles, when Elodie and Jago came along as my guides, and how amused Jago was watching her flirt her way through the Yew Ball.

"I'm sure Nash can round up a friend if you're interested?" she says, cutting into my thoughts. "It'll be like a nineteenth-century double date."

I'm quick to shake my head. "No thanks," I tell her. "Managing one boyfriend is more than enough."

Elodie, catching the unintentional inflection in my tone, turns her full attention on me. "Do I detect a hint of trouble in paradise?"

Annoyed at myself for inadvertently broadcasting my

doubts, I return the spotlight to her. "You do know this isn't exactly a party?" I say, watching Elodie roll her eyes to the crystal chandelier dripping from the ceiling above.

"Of course it's a party," she says. "Pretty much every first Trip is. Where else are you going to have access to so many fine jewels worn by so many inebriated people?"

When she laughs, that lovely, lilting sound instantly fills the room. But I'm still stuck on the first part. Wondering if her use of *pretty much* was just a figure of speech—or was she implying there'd been other first Trips that didn't take place at a party?

Like maybe Braxton's first Trip. The one he apparently took with Killian.

"And just to be clear—if you're even thinking about lecturing me on looking after Mason, then all I have to say is don't waste your breath. Seriously, Nat." She flips her long golden curls over her shoulder and, still holding the dress, plunks down onto the nearest chair. "Do you really think Mason will listen to anything I have to say?"

"He's a lot more likely to listen to you than me," I grudgingly admit.

"Listen—" Elodie crosses her legs and leans toward me. "You have no idea how many times I've seen this play out. Before you came along, I thought Song was the worst. But now Mason's proved himself to be even more rebellious than the two of you put together. And honestly, there's only so much you can do. Ultimately, it's up to him to decide how he's going to use the amazing opportunity he's been given here."

And that's when I remember how Elodie, having grown up at Gray Wolf, doesn't understand that not everyone is thrilled to have their life snatched out from under them so they can work as a time-traveling thief for Arthur.

"Is that why you and Jago ditched me on my first Trip?"

Elodie shrugs. "The only thing that matters is you found

your way back. And now you need to trust that Mason will, too."

"And if he doesn't?"

Elodie's gaze meets mine, but before she can respond, Charlotte reappears with an armful of accessories, including a custom pair of shoes for Elodie, which I can't help but envy.

"Next time," Charlotte says, clocking the covetous look on my face.

"Next time meaning my trip to Renaissance Italy?" I ask.

But Charlotte just smiles, turns her back on me, and helps Elodie into her dress.

17

By the time Elodie and I emerge from the dressing room, Mason is already on the launchpad with Oliver, Finn, and Jago beside him.

My first thought is: *What a relief*.

Since I can't trust Elodie—and probably not Jago—to help me track Mason, at least I can count on Oliver and Finn to step in if things start to go south.

My second thought is how resplendent Mason looks in his nineteenth-century finery of tailcoat, waistcoat, and breeches.

I'm about to tell him as much when he whirls on me and says, "Tell me this isn't real." He makes a sweeping gesture around the control room. "Tell me this is some sort of elaborate hoax, and you're all in on it." His dark eyes narrow on mine.

I stand before him, my gaze flicking to Oliver and then Finn, both of whom meet my look with varying degrees of alarm. Then I glance to Jago and Elodie, but their heads are bent together, paying us no mind. When I settle back on Mason, I say, "If you're referring to Tripping, it's real." I keep my voice serious, my expression solemn.

But Mason shakes his head, refusing to believe a word of it. "You, of all people, owe me the truth," he snaps, and I can't help but flinch at the bite in his words.

"It's what we do here," I say, determined to give it to him straight in hopes he'll wise up to the fact that this is no game.

"And I'm sorry I didn't tell you before, but you've been so angry with me and…" I let the word fade, no point in reliving all that. "Look," I say. "You can't tell me you didn't at least start to wonder. The classes in equestrianism and swordcraft, the lectures on the fourth-dimensional road, the constructs—it's all preparation for this. And I know you must've suspected because you're the smartest person I know. Which is probably also why you're refusing to believe it. It seems so implausible—and yet, it's totally real."

I end with a nervous grin, trying to ease the thread of tension thrumming between us, but Mason won't budge. He shoots me a look so harsh I can't help but cringe, though still I press on. If Mason keeps refusing to cooperate, he'll put us all at risk of being discovered, and the consequences of that are too grim to ponder.

"I know it sounds ridiculous," I say. "Even when it's over and you find yourself right back here, it still seems like a strange lucid dream. But it's serious business, and the cost of screwing up can sometimes prove fatal." My eyes plead with his, begging him to listen. "But we're here to guide you. You don't have to go it alone. This is how you make Blue, and once that happens your life here will drastically improve."

"Fuck Blue," Mason snaps. "I'm staying a Green until they're so sick of me they send me back home."

Normally, I'd admire his defiance. But here at Gray Wolf, I'm steeped in worry. I need to get through to him—convince him to rethink this before it's too late.

"You wouldn't be the first to try that," I say. "But failing won't get you sent home. And if you trust nothing else that I've said, at least try to trust that."

Mason squares his broad shoulders, tilts his chin imperiously high. And I immediately recognize it as his go-to defense. Whenever he starts to feel foolish or small, he reminds himself—

and everyone around him—just how much space he's capable of commanding.

"Look, I know you hate me." I shrug. "And you probably hate Arthur and Gray Wolf and pretty much everything having to do with this place..."

Mason says nothing, just waits for whatever comes next.

"And while I'm sorry to confirm that your old life is gone forever, that doesn't mean you can't build another one here. One that just might surprise you."

I search Mason's face, looking for a sign that I might've gotten through. But he may as well be wearing a mask. He gives nothing away.

Wait—wearing a mask!

I remember how Jago told me that, as a new Tripper, wearing a mask makes it easier to blend. But none of us are wearing one. And a quick look around tells me none are on offer.

I guess Arthur really is throwing Mason into the deep end. And dragging all of us along with him.

Not to mention how Arthur's not even bothering to see him off. Another look around confirms that our benefactor is nowhere in sight, but Roxanne is, and she's heading right for us with her trusty clipboard clutched to her chest.

"So," she says. "I assume everyone's ready?" On the surface, it seems like she's addressing all of us, but her gaze is centered on Mason. And though he refuses to assent, at least he doesn't lash out like I feared. "Good." She gives a curt nod, then turns to Elodie and hands her the clicker, which instantly fills me with dread.

"Why does Elodie get control of the clicker?" I ask, remembering how Elodie used it to taunt me on my first Trip, acting like she was about to leave without me as I struggled to reach the portal in time. Not exactly a moment I want to revisit.

Elodie rolls her eyes and slips the ring/clicker onto her

index finger.

"It's simply a matter of seniority." Roxanne's voice carries a notable edge. "And Elodie's been here the longest. If you have a problem with that, you're welcome to stay behind." Roxanne's gaze hardens on mine.

Stay behind and leave Mason's first Trip in Elodie's hands? No thanks.

"No…it's…it's fine," I say, watching as Roxanne doles out thick squares of paper like a blackjack dealer doling out playing cards.

I gaze down at mine and read:

Your presence is requested!

When: May 15, 1813
Where: London, England
What: The May Ball
Why: Celebration of the London Season

As usual, what's not stated is what we're expected to bring back to Arthur, which, since it's Mason's first Trip, is whatever small valuables we can manage to carry out without raising suspicions or, worse, getting caught.

Oh, and according to the contact lenses we wear, we have sixty minutes to get the job done. This is also confirmed by Roxanne.

I study Mason, wondering how he feels about all the thieving Arthur will require of him. But whatever he's thinking, he keeps it to himself. And it's not until we're just seconds from launch—just seconds before the lights flicker, the ground shakes, the wind begins to blow, and we all join hands—that Roxanne leans toward me, puts her lips to my ear, and says, "When you manage to break free from the others, check your right pocket."

18

Just as I figured, the second we arrive in a secluded spot in the garden, Elodie is off.

In a blur of blond curls and powder-blue gown, she leaves us behind without so much as a backward glance.

Oliver looks after her, shaking his head.

"I almost feel sorry for Nash." Finn laughs. "You too, Jago."

"Elodie's free to do as she wants." Jago shrugs. "As am I." With a devilish grin, he also leaves us behind.

"Um, excuse me, but is this really happening?" Mason looks between me, Oliver, and Finn, his brown eyes wide with a combination of shock, utter delight, and absolute disbelief at the situation he finds himself in.

"It's real," I say. "How do you feel?"

"Honestly?" He flattens a hand against his belly. "I think I'm going to be sick."

The second he says it, Finn takes a giant leap back, and Oliver steps forward, grasping hold of Mason's arm.

"You okay?" Oliver keeps a close watch over Mason's face as his own pinches with worry. "Did you mean like, sick in a good way, like from all the excitement, or sick like—" He nods toward Finn, who looks like he's about to be sick at the thought of Mason getting sick.

Mason places his hands on his knees and takes a series of short, ragged breaths. Once he's steadied himself, he looks around the grounds and says, "I feel like I'm dreaming." He shakes his head and returns to full height. "I mean, this is legit? Like, we've actually landed *in a whole other century*?"

Unfortunately, during that last bit, his voice rang a little too loudly, attracting the notice of a nearby couple taking a stroll.

"No." Finn laughs, plastering a tight grin onto his face. "Not *another* century. Still the same old 1813." He tips his hat to the couple, who are now openly staring, as we hold our collective breaths until they move on.

"Mason—" I lean toward him, keeping my voice to a whisper. "Are you going to be okay, because if not—"

I leave that last part unspoken, since I honestly have no idea what I'll do if he can't get it together. With Elodie and Jago gone, it's not like we can just pop back to Gray Wolf. We're stuck here for the duration, or until Elodie returns with the clicker—whichever comes first.

"I need you to answer something," Mason says, turning my way. "And it's important, so be honest."

My gaze meets his. "Always," I say.

"Am I safe here?"

I hesitate, but only because I'm not exactly sure what he means.

"As a Black, gay male, am I at risk showing up at a party in 1813 England?"

A sudden tightness seizes my core. It's something I hadn't considered, and I'm deeply ashamed at failing to recognize the risk Arthur has exposed him to.

I'm about to respond when Finn cuts in. "While it's definitely not safe to reveal that part of yourself, there are plenty of us—always have been, always will be. But unfortunately, our rights are at risk in the modern world, never mind here. As for being a Black man, Regency England was far more diverse than movies depicting that period would have you believe. Also—just look at yourself. And I mean *really* look at yourself—in all your magnificent finery."

Mason glances down at his clothes, then returns his gaze to Finn.

"You are above reproach. No one will dare mess with you. Not when you look like the wealthiest man in this whole damn place. If anything, women will throw themselves at you. You won't believe the lengths they'll go to claim your attention. And we arrived just in time."

"The trick," Oliver says, "is to slip in when the party is well underway. Drinks are flowing, inhibitions are receding—"

"In other words," Finn says, "the guests are all shit-faced."

Mason's own face pulls tight, like he's on the verge of feeling sick again. "And…that's a good thing?"

Finn breaks into a grin. "It's a wonderful thing—a splendid thing!"

"This party is the kickoff to the Season," Oliver says. "Which means all the women will be wearing their finest, trying to attract the eye of a rich gentleman like yourself. And the fact that they'll have downed a couple cocktails makes them all ripe for the picking."

"For the picking?" Mason looks confused, as well as deeply disturbed.

"They'll be so busy trying to enchant you into a proposal, they won't even notice when you relieve them of their jewels."

"Um, guys." I raise a hand, practically begging them to stop. "Can you maybe tone down the predatory vibe a level or two—actually, ten would be good."

"Sorry," Oliver says.

"Yeah, sorry," Finn echoes. "Just trying to make a point."

"Now, it's your turn to be honest." I look at Mason. "Are you going to be okay?" Having decided that if he's not, then we'll remain right here until the hour is up, the others return, and we head back to Gray Wolf. I'll deal with the aftermath when the time comes. Because this is *Mason*. I've always had his back, and he's always had mine.

What I wasn't expecting is the mischievous glint in Mason's gaze as he says, "Have I totally lost it, or is this like a real-life version of Anywhere but Here?"

I break out laughing, remembering the game we used to play during lunch when we'd pretend we were eating in glamorous locales, dressed in the sort of aspirational clothes we could then only dream about.

"It's even better," I say. "Because it's real." I bite down on my lip, hoping he'll see the amazing opportunities afforded in this. "So, are you ready to meet the nineteenth century?"

"We just go in there and…and fill our pockets?" he says.

"That's the idea. Just try to keep the talking to a minimum," I say. "And, when you do speak, avoid slang, keep it formal, follow their lead, that sort of thing."

"And most importantly, don't get caught," Oliver says.

"Whatever you do, don't get caught," Finn repeats. "It puts us all at risk. Once we're inside, it's every person for themselves."

"Oh, and don't be late," Oliver adds. "Just blink three times in quick succession, and your contacts will display the amount of time left and direct you back here. And if you're not back before the hour is up…" He leaves the threat unspoken, prompting Mason to turn to me in alarm.

"The portal waits for no one," I tell him.

19

The space is a dazzling sight to behold.

A vast and vibrant ballroom, dripping with what must amount to thousands of candles and even more flowers, and it's not long before Mason, enthralled by the opulence and grandeur, takes off, leaving me with a view of his back before he's lost in the crowd.

I'm about to go after him when Oliver pulls me right back. "Let him go," he says.

"You're not serious?" I whirl on him, trying to appear refined and genteel on the outside, but inside, I'm a five-alarm bell. "He has no idea what he's doing, and—" I gesture toward the party, my heart banging out a frantic beat at the thought of Mason getting lost, caught, left behind, or any of the terrible things that can happen when Tripping. "He doesn't have a talisman, and I seriously doubt anyone warned him about the dangers of falling into a Fade." I try to jerk free, but Oliver is surprisingly strong.

"And whose fault is that?" Oliver says. "Believe me, we tried. But you were buried in library books. You never got to witness his one-man revolt. So maybe Arthur's right. Maybe this is the only way to get through to him. Because honestly, Natasha, nothing else worked."

He lets go of me then, but I remain rooted in place. "I thought you guys were supposed to be his friends?" I snap, spending equal time glaring at each of them.

"We are," Finn says. "Which is why we tried to warn him. Even

Elodie did what she could. But he refused to play along, and—"

"And now's his chance to use whatever he might've retained and find his own way," Oliver cuts in.

My gaze scans the crowd, hoping to catch a glimpse of my friend, but it's a blur of bright shiny faces, sparkling jewels, and dazzling gowns.

"It's sink or swim," Finn says, and my heart flails at the thought.

Partly because I know that they're right. And, if it were anyone else, I might go along.

But this is Mason. My best friend in the world. And the very fact that he's here is completely my fault.

"And now…" I turn, watching as Oliver blinks three times in rapid succession before centering his gaze on me. "We're down to fifty-two minutes, so…"

Finn is the first to leave, winding through the crowd until I can no longer see him.

Oliver hangs back, but only long enough to say, "No one's going to leave Mason behind, so just focus on the job and don't worry."

Before I can ask him for a promise, a guarantee, a solemnly sworn vow that he really, truly won't let that happen, Oliver is walking away.

So I use the moment to go in search of a quiet, secluded space so I can check my pocket and see what Roxanne might've put there.

I edge my way through the room, hoping to avoid getting caught up in the crowd, or worse, pulled onto the dance floor. Then, spotting an opening that leads to a long hall with a partially open door, I hurry toward it, duck inside, and shut the door behind me.

At first glance, it seems I've found my way into a library. Or at least what passed for a library in Regency times. The space is large, with high vaulted ceilings and dark emerald walls studded with portraits of finely dressed, sober-faced people, staring out from fancy gold frames. And of course, there's an impressive bookcase overflowing with leather-bound editions.

As I make for the window that looks out at the gardens below, I realize how quickly I've grown used to opulent spaces like this. How my time spent at Gray Wolf has nearly erased the memory of what it was like to live in a house where half the electrical outlets didn't work and it took an entire bucket of water to get one of the toilets to flush. And yet, if I have any hope of getting back to Gray Wolf, I need to stop wasting time and get to the task set before me.

I slip a hand into my pocket, surprised to find that, unlike last time, it's not a copy of Christopher Columbus's map. Nor is it a tarot card. It's a small square note with a tiny golden star sketched at the center.

That's it. A single gold star, and absolutely no clue as to where I might find it.

Though I think it's safe to assume it has to do with the Antikythera Mechanism, since the star on this paper is depicted with eight rays. And, from what I recall, the Star card in both the modern and ancient tarot decks Arthur uses is portrayed the same way.

Also, the Star is yet another missing piece Arthur needs me to find so that he can restore his ancient relic and remake the world as he claims.

Problem is, I've been so busy prepping for Renaissance Italy, I know virtually nothing about this Regency timeline.

I blink three times, curious to know how many minutes are left on the clock, only to see the number forty-six projected before me. Then I shoot a frantic look all around, wondering what the hell Arthur expects me to do. There's no way I can solve this thing—no way I can even hope to return with the Star.

Is he setting me up to fail? Because the task is impossible.

And yet, I can't keep thinking like that. So, I close my eyes and recenter my focus.

Okay, let's see… What else do I know about the Star? In the Visconti-Sforza deck…

I struggle to summon an image from the cobweb-filled attic otherwise known as my brain, trying to locate a clip from that long-ago time when my dad taught me all about the twenty-two cards that comprise the Major Arcana.

In my mind's eye, I flip through the deck until…

That's it. The Star is number seventeen on the journey. Which means it shares a numerological link to the eighth card, which is Strength, since one plus seven equals eight. And in numerology, you always reduce a double digit down to a single digit.

Okay, good. I'm finally onto something. All that's left now is to remember some of the other details. In particular, what exactly do the cards look like, and…

In the ancient deck, there's a woman holding the star. A woman who… A woman with blond hair, wearing a blue dress, and…

And a red cape! Just like the person I watched disappear, then reappear, in the labyrinth that once existed below my window at Gray Wolf.

But it can't be, can it? I mean, is there really a connection between the card and the strange vision I saw?

And, if so, is Arthur really sending me to look for the Star?

Or maybe this has nothing to do with Arthur. Maybe it's about something else…something to do with magick, the strange leather-bound book, and…

I'm so lost in thought, I fail to notice the sound of the door opening and closing, of the soft thud of footsteps finding their way across the room, all the way to where I now stand.

20

"I'm sorry I've kept you waiting," a male voice calls. "I was—" He reaches for me at the same time I turn, and the second he notes the startled look on my face, he steps back.

"My apologies," he says. "I'm afraid I mistook you for another."

His eyes meet mine, and though the room is dim, lit only by the muted glow of an early spring moon and the flickering candles scattered about, I can still make out a mane of dark curls, a finely chiseled face, a set of broad shoulders, and a lean waist. This man is pretty much the definition of what Elodie would refer to as dreamy, even though he is kind of old, probably somewhere in his mid-thirties.

"No need to apologize," I say, discreetly tucking the square of paper back into my pocket. "I was merely..." The words stall on my tongue, and I mentally kick myself for not preparing an excuse for a situation like this.

"You were perhaps taking a break from dancing?" he offers, his deep-blue gaze lighting on mine.

I nod, relieved to slip out of this so easily. "But now I must take my leave, so..." I start to move past when I'm struck by the sight of the pocket watch he now holds in his hand.

"It's an unusual piece," he says, reading my expression. "Would you like a closer look?"

There's a notable shift in the air, like a switch has been

flipped, transforming this handsome nineteenth-century gentleman into someone who's clearly his opposite.

I avert my gaze, aware of the kick of my heart, the frantic clang of my pulse filling my ears. "That's quite all right. I really must—"

"You really must—" He steps before me, blocking my way. And it's only now that I notice the sickly sweet grin glued to his face.

My breath grows ragged, coming so quickly I struggle to steady myself.

I can't let him see my fear. I can't—

"You're not afraid of being alone with me, are you?" He tips his head toward mine, and for one horrifying moment, when my gaze meets his, I swear I see the duke's hideous face staring right back.

But it can't be. It'll never be the duke again. But that doesn't mean this stranger's intentions aren't just as bad.

I narrow my gaze, and in the most imperious voice I can summon, I say, "This is most improper. Now if you'll please step aside—" Before I can finish, he's cutting me off.

"You're right," he says, blue eyes glimmering on mine. "There's nothing proper about any of this. So tell me, little Time Jumper: What exactly is it you seek?"

My face has gone white. I know this because I can literally feel the blood draining away, pooling down to my feet, leaving them heavy, leaden, unable to flee.

"I spotted you the moment you arrived," he tells me.

And that's when I remember—he was in the garden. He was one half of the couple that overheard our conversation.

"Your friends are in the ballroom." He makes a vague gesture toward the door I'd do anything to be on the other side of. "Dancing, drinking. *Thieving.*" He emphasizes that word. "They do appear to be enjoying themselves. Last I saw of the fair one—Elodie is her name?"

He looks to me for confirmation, but I give nothing away. "She's run off with her gentleman friend. I've seen her on many occasions. And yet, her only interest is a bit of light thieving and the boy—mainly the boy." He lifts a brow, chuckling softly. "Unlike you, Elodie poses no threat. But *you* are on a mission. Which I suppose is why you've captured my interest."

"You are gravely mistaken," I say. "And now I must insist you step out of my way." I square my shoulders and lift my chin, hoping to come off as indignant, deeply offended, but the man remains firmly in place, completely unmoved by my display.

"Look—" He directs my gaze to the pocket watch he's balanced on the center of his palm, bidding me to watch as he spins it in a way that never once falters.

On one side is a clock face.

On the other, an engraving of a familiar circular design.

And before I can stop it, I'm mesmerized, locked into place. Watching as those circles appear, then disappear, only to reappear once more. Only vaguely aware of the man before me, regarding me with a look of bemusement as he waits for me to wear myself out and finally come to terms with my fate.

Unfortunately, it doesn't take long.

21

I'm not sure how long it takes for me to snap out of it, but once I do, I glare at the man before me and say, "Are you going to let me go? Or shall I scream for help?"

His lips curve slightly upward as he folds the pocket watch into his fist. "Though it's likely the orchestra will prevent anyone from hearing your cries, please, do not hold back on my account."

Not only is he not wrong, but he also knows I've issued a challenge I'm unwilling to meet. Mainly because I can't afford to draw that sort of attention to myself.

"Then perhaps you could let me go and spare us both the trouble," I suggest, only to watch as he takes another step toward me, standing so close now that if I wanted, I could reach out and snatch that golden pocket watch right out of his hand. Then take it back to Gray Wolf and turn it over to Arthur as one of my Gets.

If only this man wasn't nearly twice my height and double my weight, I'd do exactly that.

Though surely, it's safer to try to talk my way out of this mess. Or at least that's what I think until I blink three times and see the clock is quickly running down.

Only thirty-one minutes left.

"Perhaps a deal can be made?" he says. "You give me this enchanting charm"—he dips his free hand toward my neck, pinching my talisman between his forefinger and thumb—"and in exchange, I grant you this pocket watch." He dangles the piece before me.

Dangles it in the same way Jago once dangled a pocket watch he'd used to hypnotize me.

The realization comes too late, and before I can act, my head has gone woozy as my mind reels backward in time, conjuring a dizzying collection of nonsensical images that seem more like a fever dream than anything real.

Clocks melting down walls—a torch singer wearing an antler crown—and a spectacular boy with a bend in his nose and eyes like a storm-ridden sea—

And I know the boy—he told me his name, it's—

Braxton!

I didn't realize I voiced the name out loud, until the soft bump of my talisman falling back into place knocks me out of the vision, leaving me gaping into the face of the blue-eyed man now looming before me.

"What did you say?" He leans so close I can see the individual flecks of copper in his irises, the light smattering of freckles sprinkled across his forehead and nose.

My knees start to crumble. My body sags toward the floor, as though I'm yet another delicate female, overcome by the heat, or exhaustion, or the scandal of being alone in a room with a virile male and no chaperone to safeguard my virtue.

But the man is on to me and he watches my descent with a pitiless gaze.

It's only after I slip a hand under my hem, only after I spring back to my feet and wield my dagger before him—only after all that is done does it even occur to him to register a look of concern.

The look deepens when I wave my blade before him and say, "Now kindly move out of my way, or I swear I will cut you."

22

For a handful of seconds, it feels so empowering to act like that, talk like that.

But that doesn't mean I get what I want.

Because the blue-eyed man takes one look at my dagger and another at me, then breaks into a fit of unrestrained laughter.

Seriously, he stands right there before me and laughs in my face.

So, I do the only thing I can think of—I lunge.

Here, before the rows of dour-faced nobles encased in gilt frames—before the towering bookshelves overflowing with Captain Cooks, Jane Austens, and Sir Walter Scotts—I aim the lethal tip of my dagger straight for my enemy's heart.

Only to be confronted by the gleaming blade of his much larger sword—a broadsword, it turns out—that I'd failed to notice until now.

"Seems you're not as well trained, nor as well prepared, as you think," he says, voice edged with the conviction of one who has all the proof that he needs.

My arm is stretched as far as it will extend, and still, there's a notable gap between my blade and his chest.

While his own arm is casually, comfortably bent, his hand secured in the basket hilt, as the tip of his double-edged blade comes perilously close to piercing my throat.

I've made a terrible mistake. All this time, I've been worried about Mason when it's clearly me who needs saving.

I stand before my nameless opponent, knees shaking as I force down the scream building at the back of my throat, knowing I need to keep quiet, keep a clear head. I can't afford to let on just how terrified I really am.

If you're going to pull your dagger, you must be willing to use it, Braxton once said.

Well, I *was* willing to use it. Still am, now more than ever. But seeing as how I can't even reach my target, it's become glaringly apparent that's no longer an option.

So, I try another approach.

Dropping all pretense, I say, "So this is it? You slash my neck and leave me for dead in the study?"

His face breaks into a grin. But, more importantly, his blade remains pressed to my skin. "There it is," he says. "Your true face. Tell me, Time Jumper. What year are you from?"

"I'm from 1813," I say. "Just like you."

"Lies," he growls, prodding his blade deeper, poking a small hole in my flesh.

"What makes you say that?" I choke out the words, knowing I'm taking a risk by calling his bluff, but the more I can convince him to talk, the more time I'll have to plan my next move.

"You don't fit, you don't blend, and you clearly don't belong in this century," he says.

Before I have a chance to respond, his eyes spark on mine as the tip of his blade slides clean across my throat.

23

In an instant, my flesh turns to fire.

And it's only when I watch his fingers close around my talisman that I realize not only has he cut me, but he's managed to separate me from my one and only connection to Braxton, to Gray Wolf, to my memories of my proper place and time.

No.

No!

Without even thinking, I attack.

Swinging my blade for real, for keeps, without any care to the spilling of blood soon to come.

I attack in spite of Killian's warning that once I kill, I can never go back to who I once was.

And though my blade is too small to cross the distance between my hand and his chest, I aim for a target I can reach and slice straight into his wrist.

The man staggers backward, those blue eyes filled with shock and—and something else. Something so dark and menacing it leaves me wishing I'd never set foot in this study.

I track the spill of blood, but the wound is superficial at best and does nothing to weaken his grip.

Cursing under his breath, he regains his footing and sets my talisman and the pocket watch on a table beside him. "You are a brazen one," he says, eyes locked on mine as he brandishes his blade. "But you're in over your head. So, why not spare yourself, little Time Jumper, and be on your way."

He tips his head toward the door—a door I'd do anything to make my way through. But not without my talisman—the one thing that connects me to everything that matters in my world.

A shot of dread courses through me as I cut a nervous glance between his blade and mine.

How am I supposed to compete when I've clearly brought a box cutter to a sword fight?

My mind reels back to my first lesson in swordcraft. Braxton had a sword, I had a dagger, and it ended with me pinned against the wall, begging for mercy.

Focus, Braxton had coached. *Stay in the moment, quiet your mind, and use your intuition to anticipate your opponent's next move.*

My mind wandered that night, but tonight I'm sharp, laser-focused, and the stakes have never been higher.

"Give me my charm," I say, my voice hoarse but sure. "And I'll gladly be on my way."

The man regards me from under his brow. "It's yours for the taking," he says. "If you can get past me, that is."

I'm out-armed—out of my league—but Braxton trained me for moments like this. It's why he always fought with a sword, and I with a dagger. Never wanting me to forget that, as a woman traveling through the past, the odds would rarely be in my favor.

I stand before my opponent, expertly tossing my dagger from hand to hand and twirling it around my thumb in the way I was taught, but it only succeeds in making him laugh.

"Nice of you to demonstrate the limits of your skill," he says. "But do not make the mistake of thinking I'll go easy on you. The best way to learn—"

"Is by facing an opponent who's better than you," I finish the thought for him, quoting the very thing Braxton once said to me.

"Though your theory is solid," the man says, "your form

leaves much to be desired. Allow me to show you how it's done."

Next thing I know, he sets his blade swinging as his feet slide along the carpeted floor, moving with such speed and grace it's all I can do to keep up without growing dizzy.

I know this game. He's trying to distract me—make me spend all my energy on keeping track of his placement.

Luckily, I've been trained in this, too. So when he arcs his sword toward me, I'm quick to angle my dagger so it stops him on the downward slope of his swing. Filling the space with the screech of metal meeting metal, I force my blade against the tip of his and successfully push him away.

"Impressive," he grunts. "For a novice, that is."

I blink three times, wanting to check in on the clock, only to watch in horror as he rebounds quicker than I foresaw.

With his blade arced high above his head, he swings it down so quickly I have no chance of meeting it—no chance of stopping it—without running the risk of being split right in half.

So I do the only thing I can: I duck out from under it, watching wide-eyed as that sharp, double-edged broadsword misses my head by less than an inch.

I won't win this.

Can't win this.

I'm totally and completely outmatched.

All I can do now is play a game of perpetual defense until the time on the portal runs out or he slices me to ribbons—whichever comes first.

There's got to be a better way—there's got to be—

"You can always surrender," he says, coming at me again. Forcing me to leap, spin, swerve out of his reach, as his blade continues to carve up the air.

I duck around tables, crash into chairs, send a priceless vase smashing to shards, as I run for my life.

Still, I run with purpose. And when I find myself back beside the table where he left my talisman along with that gold pocket watch, I make a grab for them both. Only to nearly lose my arm when he clears the table with a hard swing of his blade.

As the talisman and pocket watch soar toward the ground, I instinctively follow. Diving to the floor, I crash hard on my belly, scramble to my knees, and just when the prize is well within reach, the man tips his broadsword toward my face and says, "Pick one, Time Jumper. And only one."

I run a wary glance up the length of him, and the way his gaze darkens on mine, it's clear he's fully committed to ridding me of an eye.

"Your time is running out." He angles his blade precariously close to my face. "So, pick one and be on your way."

The pocket watch glimmers before me, and as I grip the rounded edge, my fingers grazing over that intricate circular design, the golden case warms as a vision streaks across the screen in my head.

It's a boy.

A young, happy boy, and he's laughing so hard his eyes are squinched closed. But when he opens them, when he lowers his chin and stares directly before him, a sudden coldness seizes my core, leaving my skin tingling, my heart racing.

"Choose, Time Jumper!" The man's voice snaps me out of the vision and back to the present, where his blade veers dangerously close to my eye. "Choose!" he repeats.

But I won't choose. Can't choose. I need that watch as much as I need my talisman.

And that's when I see a way out.

That's when I duck my head, and with his blade hovering above me, I reach for my talisman with one hand as the other plunges my dagger straight into the tender spot where his knee meets his boot.

Slicing through fabric, flesh, ligament, it's only when I reach bone—only when the man cries out in shock, staggers backward, and falters to the ground—that I scoop both the pocket watch and my talisman into my hand and race for the door.

The last thing I see when I glance over my shoulder is the unspoken threat in his glinting blue eyes as he watches me go.

24

It's only once I've managed to escape with my talisman and pocket watch secured, my dagger returned to its sheath, that I can finally process the hell I just went through.

Who was that man? And how did he know that I'm a… Time Jumper, as he called me?

I shake my head, ridding myself of the thoughts, then blink three times only to find there are less than fifteen minutes left on the clock.

I race for the end of the hall, nearly reaching the ballroom when Elodie appears from the other side of a door, her cheeks flushed, hair mussed, with a ridiculously handsome boy trailing behind her.

"Natasha!" she calls. "How wonderful to see you. You must meet my friend, Nash."

Like any well-bred gentleman of his time, Nash steps forward and bows. While I, like any awkward Gen Z forced into a social ritual she's not at all used to, dip into a nervous curtsy.

"Elodie speaks very highly of you," he says, and when he grins, it's clear why she's so taken with him.

With his thick, dark curls, piercing green eyes, and blunt, masculine features, Nash emits the sort of natural magnetism that's hard to resist. But, when he smiles, he lights up the sky as bright as Christmas Day and Fourth of July combined.

"Oh, dear." Elodie frowns and gestures toward my neck. "It

appears you've been scratched." And though her tone effectively hides her alarm, the look she shoots me is brimming with dread.

I run an idle finger along the scrape left by that angry man's sword. *Was he a Timekeeper? Is that how he recognized me as a girl out of time?*

"Oh, I'd almost forgotten." I laugh, as though it's all just an amusing bit of whimsy. "I came across a cat, and you know me—I couldn't resist. Though the cat had other ideas."

I laugh again, and it's not long before Elodie joins in. And though her own laughter rings false to my ears, Nash remains unaware.

"Dearest Nash," she says, placing a hand on his shoulder. She blinks three times and shoots me a look of alarm. "Would you mind terribly if I help Natasha attend to her—" She gestures to her own neck to indicate my neck, and the way Nash regards her, he's clearly besotted with her. And despite what Elodie claims about her heart having wings—fluttering freely to whomever it fancies—it's obvious she feels the same.

"You will save the last dance for me?" he asks.

"Always." She grins, her gaze glittering on his. Then she tips onto her toes and right there, in front of me and well within view of the crowded ballroom, Elodie kisses Nash full on the lips, without a care in the world. Just like a girl from the twenty-first century would.

Then, grasping hold of my hand, the two of us break into an all-out run.

"Fuck," Elodie whispers as we move through the crowd, scanning for Mason. "I mean, what the absolute fuck?" she repeats, her gaze turned to me as I search the dancers, the wallflowers, and coming up empty. "Seriously, Nat—what the fuck happened to you?"

"Nothing," I say, trying to keep my expression pleasant as I pull her along. "All I care about now is finding Mason."

"Screw Mason," she says. "Forget that ungrateful little shit. It's *you* I'm worried about. I mean, where is your talisman? Do you even know who you are?"

"It's in my pocket," I tell her. "The clasp broke, and—"

"Oh, so your clasp broke." She shakes her head. "Just how stupid do you think I am?"

I release a lungful of air I didn't realize I'd been holding. "Honestly?" I say. "You're one of the least stupid people I know."

She gives a satisfied nod, then narrows her gaze. "Then why are you lying to me?"

I take a moment to decide on an answer. "Because I can't risk sharing the truth."

Elodie considers me for an agonizing beat. "So," she finally says. "What do you think of Nash?"

Classic Elodie. We have less than twelve minutes left on the clock, no sign of Mason, and Elodie wants to discuss her Regency crush. If the situation wasn't so dire, it would strike me as hilarious. But who am I kidding—it still does.

"You did not overhype him. He's totally dreamy," I tell her. And while I'm glad she had a nice Trip, I've got bigger issues at hand. "But you do realize Mason doesn't have a talisman," I say. "*And* apparently no one saw fit to warn him about Fade. *And*—"

"So, why didn't you warn him?" she asks. "Is it because you were so caught up in Renaissance Italy you couldn't be bothered?"

The words cut right to the core. Mainly because I know that she's right. I could've done better, tried harder.

"Look," she says. "All we can do now is make sure we find that rebellious little fucker before the clock runs out, which—"

I watch as she blinks three times, then I do the same.

Nine minutes and twenty-nine seconds left.

We exchange a worried look. Or rather, I'm worried. Elodie remains as unruffled as ever.

She points toward the door and the portal beyond. "For his sake, I hope he's somewhere between here and there. Otherwise, I will leave without him."

With that, she's gone. And as I watch her make a beeline for the portal, it occurs to me that if Mason is in this ballroom, considering how much taller he is than most of the men here, he should be easy to find.

I move through the well-heeled crowd, keeping my gaze high so I'll have a better shot at spotting him. Which is why I fail to notice a woman barreling straight into me until she's nearly knocked me over.

First, the back of her heel crunches down on my toe. Then the point of her elbow slams into my belly so hard it sends me staggering, gasping for breath, as my heels skid out from under me. And just as the ground rises up to meet me, someone swoops in from behind, catches me in his arms, and settles me back on my feet.

The whole thing is over in a matter of seconds. Still, those are precious seconds I cannot afford. And though I'm eager to move on, the woman insists on dragging it out—alternately blaming me, then apologizing to me, only to blame me again. A tedious cycle, and I desperately want it to end.

"Pay her no mind," a voice sounds in my ear. "All that matters is that you are okay."

I turn to find the one who saved me from falling in front of a ballroom full of people—none of whom I know or will ever see again, and yet I'm grateful to be spared that indignity.

"Thank you," I murmur, brushing my hands down the front of my gown. "No broken limbs from what I can tell."

"But perhaps a bit of broken pride?"

I lift my gaze to meet his and nearly laugh at the sight.

This boy is adorably, foppishly handsome—the closest thing the nineteenth century has to the young Hugh Grant of old

British rom-coms. If I was Elodie, I'd take full advantage of this moment and consider it the meet-cute that kicked off my own Jane Austen experience.

But I'm not Elodie, and, more importantly, I'm dangerously short on time.

"Might I—" the boy starts, but whatever might've followed, I'm afraid I'll never know. And as I move past the woman who nearly knocked me to the ground, I casually reach out and pluck the pearl-and-diamond pin from her hair.

I may have failed at finding—never mind claiming—the Star, but I'll be damned if I return to Gray Wolf empty-handed.

I've just made it halfway across the room when I spot Mason on the dance floor, happily engaging in a quadrille. And while I'm relieved to see he looks none the worse for wear, I need to find a way to intercede without making a scene.

The second Mason circles back to my side of the room, I'm about to step in, when, from out of nowhere, someone grabs hold of my arm, and a harsh male voice says, "Is this the one?"

I turn to find a stern-faced man glaring at me, and beside him, the woman who plowed into me.

The same woman who is one jeweled hairpin short of those she arrived with.

"What is the meaning of this?" I look between the scowling man and the place on the dance floor where Mason just stood.

Only he's no longer there.

My gaze scans the long line of revelers, desperately searching, hoping, but Mason is nowhere in sight.

"Come with me." The man's fingers clamp down on my arm, squeezing mercilessly hard. And though I've been trained to always maintain my composure, I can't afford to waste another second dealing with this nonsense.

"I will not." My voice thunders. My gaze locks on his. "Now kindly release me."

But he doesn't. Not even close. If anything, he just squeezes harder.

"This woman claims you've stolen her hairpin," he says. The woman nods indignantly, and the man deepens his frown.

"And exactly where do you suppose I've hidden it?" I gesture down the length of my gown.

It's a challenge he can't win. Not without risking the sort of impropriety I'm sure he'd prefer to avoid. Besides, Charlotte is a genius when it comes to hidden pockets. There's no way he'll find it.

In an instant, the man removes his hand from my arm, but the woman refuses to fold.

"I am certain it was her," she says. Her face, like her voice, is all rage and fury.

As she continues to hurl accusations, I conduct another quick sweep of the dance floor, only to confirm that Mason really is gone. And I can only hope that Elodie managed to find him, because after what I'm about to do next, staying behind is no longer an option.

25

People are starting to notice.

They're pointing, staring, looking over their shoulders as they whisper in a way that threatens to go viral if I don't do something quick.

Deciding to go with the fainting ruse, my knees begin to buckle, my hands fumble under my dress in search of my dagger, when Elodie steps in.

"Please," she says, "give her some space." She immediately drops to my side, fanning me with the back of her hand as she whispers into my ear, "Don't even think about pulling your blade."

The man looks on in confusion. The woman squints with obvious skepticism.

My lids fall heavy, my mouth slack, and as Elodie circles an arm at my waist and hauls me to my feet, my body slumps onto her like a sack of dead weight. "My friend is unwell and in need of rest," she says. "So please— "

She gestures in a way that instantly clears the space, and the second we've made it outside, I push Elodie away and say, "I'm not leaving without Mason!" I start to head back in, but Elodie pulls me back to her side.

"Mason is waiting on you," she says. "Everyone is. Turns out, you're the one we should've been worried about."

I've barely had a chance to digest that when the numbers

switch from green to red, and when they begin to blink, I know the final countdown is on. We're down to the last ninety seconds before the portal closes for good.

Elodie must've clocked it as well, because the next thing I know, she hitches her dress to her knees and starts running.

Less than a second later, I set off behind her, frantically chasing the flashing green arrow projected before me as the number above steadily drops.

We race across a meticulously kept lawn and down a gravel pathway.

We cut through a flower bed and skirt around a fountain.

Before me, Elodie is a vision—a streak of powder-blue lightning blazing a path I dutifully follow. Her long-legged gait is powerful, sure-footed, and seemingly tireless compared to my own gasping, reckless plodding and plunder.

With all pretenses of breeding and comportment abandoned, we run like the wind, run for our lives, ignoring the spectacle we leave in our wake. Both of us spurred on by the horror of being stuck here forever, with no money, no resources, no good way to explain our outlandish behavior.

Elodie shoots me a look from over her shoulder, and I could swear I catch a ghost of a smile, a gleam in her gaze.

My God—she's actually enjoying this!

As much as I wish I could find the fun in this nerve-fraying race against time, I don't expect that to happen until much later, if it even happens at all.

Because the truth is, Elodie's right. I really did make a fucking mess of this Trip.

With fifty-seven seconds left on the clock, I'm starting to panic, which does nothing to help my overtaxed lungs. And in the midst of this frantic, sweaty event, I swear to myself that if—no, correction: *when—when* I make it back to Gray Wolf, I will hit the gym, I will run track, I will take the fitness part of the

Gray Wolf curriculum a lot more seriously than I have.

But first, I need to make my way back. And with forty-four seconds left on the clock, it's not looking good.

Elodie is way ahead of me, and I wonder what it will be like for her, seeing me, red-cheeked and desperate, gasping my way toward the finish line, only to fall tragically short.

Then again, it'll hardly be the first time.

Back in Versailles, Elodie watched from the safety of that circle of light as I fought off my attacker—the groundskeeper, she called him, though later, after Killian killed him, he referred to him as a Timekeeper. Either way, I clearly recall Elodie standing at the portal's edge, clicker in hand, more than willing to leave me stranded in time should it come to that.

But would she really do that again?

Would she really risk her own safety by coming to find me if she'd planned to leave me behind?

But then I remember that ghost of a grin—that unmistakable gleam in her eye—and the fact that Elodie's never met a risk she didn't want to kiss, or make out with, or have sex with. That's just who she is.

And this way, she can prove to all the others she tried.

They'll give her a cape, a crown, hail her as a hero whom no one can blame.

Thirty seconds.

I'm not going to make it. I'm not—

"Run!" Elodie shouts at me. "We're almost there, Nat! Almost—"

Twenty-seven seconds.

I push my legs harder, faster, trying to look past the trees to the clearing ahead. And that's when I see them—Jago, Finn, Oliver, and Mason—all of them frantically waving.

"Hurry," they call, with Mason's voice rising above all the rest.

Eighteen seconds.

Elodie is nearly there—a few more steps and she's free.

As for me—the news isn't nearly as good.

"Run!" Finn screams.

"Hurry!" Jago and Oliver chime in.

While Mason yells, "Dammit, Clarke, get your butt off the bench and *run* that track!"

Twelve seconds.

If my lungs weren't on fire, if a flaming spear of blazing hot agony wasn't currently tunneling its way through my insides, I'd be reeling with laughter at Mason's spot-on imitation of our junior year gym coach—the one we both detested as much as she detested us.

"You think you're too good to sweat like the rest of us, Clarke?" Mason shouts, continuing to recite the entire litany of soccer field, baseball diamond, volleyball court taunts.

And it must work. Because between that and the sight of Elodie leaping through the glowing doorway, my adrenaline spikes, fueling me through the home stretch.

Oliver extends an arm, shouting encouragements. And with my lungs about to explode, I watch the green arrow shrink, watch the amount of time left on the clock tick dangerously close to the dreaded zero.

The portal is so close, but with time dwindling down, it could go either way.

Six seconds.

Elodie's face is red, dripping with exhaustion and sweat, and yet she still manages to look annoyingly radiant. "Fucking move, Nat!" she shouts, and to her credit, she truly looks worried.

"You're almost there!" Oliver shouts.

"So close!" Jago echoes.

"You can't give up now!" Finn looks frantic.

But it's Mason who sends me over the edge. "Clarke," he

shouts. "I swear, you run even slower than you drive!"

When I'm down to the very last second, my right foot shoots forward, extending uncomfortably, excruciatingly far, and the second it lands and my toes make contact, I leap.

With no time to spare and everything to lose, I hurl my body through the air—soaring, plummeting, desperately clawing for the finish, only to fall tragically, infinitesimally, short.

That's it.

I'm done.

My epitaph streaks across the screen in my head. Just a handful of words etched onto a boring gray stone:

So close, and yet…

It's the last thing I see, the last thing I think, before a hand reaches down, grabs hold of the back of my gown, and drags me right over the line.

"Don't think I'll ever let you forget this," Elodie says, letting go of my dress. She grasps hold of my hand, pulls me to my feet, and the next thing I know, the six of us soar forward in time.

26

Just like he wasn't there to see us off, Arthur is also not there to greet us.

So instead of the usual debriefing, we give our Gets to Roxanne as Keane takes inventory.

Apparently, Mason did well. Not only did he bring back two rings and a ruby-and-diamond pin, but despite having no talisman, he also avoided falling into a Fade.

When it comes to logging my own stash, the reception I receive isn't nearly as warm.

"Where's the rest?" Roxanne looks me over.

"I, um, I'm afraid that's it." I gnaw the inside of my cheek as she studies the unremarkable pearl-and-diamond hairpin I've plopped onto the table, while the pocket watch remains tucked away. After what it revealed—the vision of the young boy I saw when I touched it—I have no intention of handing it over. Not until I understand what it might mean—and probably not even then.

Roxanne's lips pull tight as she maintains a steady watch over me, prolonging the look for the sheer pleasure of watching me squirm. And just when I'm sure I can't take another second, she calls, "Next!" And I move out of line to see that it's Elodie's turn.

I need to thank her for saving my life when I'd convinced myself she was set on leaving me behind.

But when Elodie's gaze meets mine, she waves a hand in dismissal, then, shifting her focus to Roxanne, goes about emptying her own pockets. And when I see the pile of loot she brought back, I realize Elodie was truly made for life here at Gray Wolf.

In just one hour, she managed to filch from a host of unsuspecting nobles, hook up with her crush, get Mason to the portal, and then come back to save me from my very worst instincts.

Which leaves me to wonder why Arthur insists I'm the only one here who can help him restore his precious Antikythera, when clearly Elodie is much better suited for the job.

By the time I make it back to my room, there's a message on my slab. And as exhausted as I am, my heart still leaps, certain it's from Braxton, only to discover it's from Killian again.

Killian: Thanks for today. Delete after reading if you must. Just needed to say it.

The fact that he used full sentences, correct spelling, and not a single emoji leaves me so unsettled I have no idea how to reply.

So, after several deleted attempts, I break my own no-emoji rule and send him a thumbs-up. Then, determined to put Killian out of my mind, I toss the phone aside and wander to the windowsill where I left the perfume bottle along with Song's note.

Well, that was a mistake.

Just because the doors are biometric doesn't mean plenty of people don't have access. Like the maids for starters. Braxton, too. And obviously Arthur has control over everything here. There's no telling how many people can slip in and out without my ever knowing.

You think Arthur gave you that tablet as a convenient way to send messages and read his inspirational quotes every day? He's tracking you…tracking all of us.

A sudden chill pricks at my skin as Killian's warning sounds in my head. A moment later, a burst of lightning scorches the sky, and the heavens break open, drenching the statues below.

I push closer to the window, the ledge digging into my belly, the pads of my fingers pressing hard against the pane, as my gaze fixes on the collection of sculptures marking the center. *The Magician*, *The High Priestess*, and *The Wheel of Fortune*, all arranged the same as the Tarot Garden in Tuscany.

In my mind's eye I replace *The Magician* sculpture with an image of Arthur.

One statue down is *The Wheel of Fortune*—the card I drew at Arcana that set this whole thing in motion—so I picture myself in its place.

But what about everyone else? What cards did Finn, Oliver, and Jago draw?

According to Elodie, Arthur rescued her from an abusive children's home when she was a kid. So while her journey differs from mine, is it possible she also represents one of the Major Arcana?

If so, my guess would be the High Priestess—Elodie is deeply intuitive, but she's also harboring some very dark secrets. Also, that sculpture just happens to stand between *The Wheel of Fortune* and *The Magician*. Or, to put it another way, between me and Arthur, which may sound weird, but it certainly fits.

I remember how I once said to Braxton that living here at Gray Wolf feels like a game, like I'm living on a chessboard of Arthur's design. At the time, I wasn't entirely sure what I meant, but what if it turns out I was closer to the truth than I ever could've guessed?

The sculptures below, just like the cards in the deck, are basically archetypes that represent the various stops on the journey of life.

But what if the same could be said of us all?

What if Arthur has specifically chosen us as representatives of each of these cards?

In the world of tarot, the journey ends with the World card. And it comes as no surprise that Arthur's personal journey ends there as well.

Why, I'm going to remake the world, he once said when I asked him what he planned to do once the Antikythera Mechanism was restored.

And since Arthur always means what he says, I was a fool not to take him at his word.

But what about what Braxton said when he told me how he ended up here? *Just like you, I drew the Wheel of Fortune card, too.*

Does that mean our destinies—or at least our destinies here at Gray Wolf—are somehow intertwined?

Or am I being ridiculous—seeing conspiracies wherever I look?

I huff out a breath that fogs up the glass as my gaze follows the ribbons of water that sluice down the pane. If the book really is hidden out there, then I hope it's tucked away in a place that stays dry.

I turn away from the window, thinking I'll order some food and run a bath, when my chime sounds again—and this time, it really is Braxton.

Braxton: Done for the day. Exhausted but still want to see you. I have a surprise.

Me: Always up for a surprise.

Braxton: Great. But first, I need a quick nap. I'm knackered.

I reread his message. Every time he needs a nap after a secret mission with Arthur, it means that he Tripped. And though, depending on the level of confidentiality involved, I may never know where he might've gone, I'm just relieved he made it back safely. That, this time at least, neither of us will join the growing list of lost ones.

Braxton: Can you be ready by 8?

I respond with the thumbs-up emoji.

Braxton: I'll send directions. See you then.

After reading his last message, my gaze flips back to the one I sent just before, and I'm instantly overcome by a guilty pang in my gut.

It's thc same message I sent to Killian. Different context but still the same.

Nothing happened, I'm quick to remind myself.

But that doesn't stop me from scrolling to Killian's message and deleting the entire thread.

While I can't erase the time we spent at the Hideaway Tavern, I will do whatever it takes to ensure that Braxton never learns I spent a good part of the day hanging out with the enemy he's sworn himself against.

27

The moment I reach the spiral staircase, I know exactly where Braxton's arranged for us to meet.

The Moon Garden is his favorite spot in all of Gray Wolf, and it's one of mine, too.

When I push through the door, I'm met with the faint strains of classical music and the sight of Braxton waiting for me.

"Buona sera," he says, and though I'm struck once again by how beautiful he is, Braxton pays so little notice to his looks, I'd be tempted to think he's stopped caring about such things, if it wasn't for the portrait of Narcissus that hangs in his room.

While I'm not exactly sure what might've occurred in his past, I'm guessing his taste in art, along with his determination to always be bettering himself, most likely stems from the sort of regretful deeds he'd prefer to forget.

He grasps my hand in his, presses a soft kiss to my cheek, then leads me to a table set with a crisp white tablecloth, etched crystal wine goblets, and gleaming silverware—all of it lit by the flickering glow of the candelabra that sits at the center. And I can't believe how far I've traveled from the girl who used to eat lunch beside the recycle bin in the school cafeteria.

Unlike my last visit here, there's a glass roof over our heads, effectively shielding us from the late-winter storm that continues to rage. And though the stars I remember as being so abundant are now hidden by a cover of clouds, the air is still infused with a heady mix of sea brine and night-blooming jasmine.

"If this is an attempt to make up for ditching our surf lesson," I say, watching as Braxton fills my goblet from a carafe of red wine, "it'll probably work. You've outdone yourself."

"Well, that's a relief." He grins. "I was afraid I wouldn't be able to compete with how you spent your day."

My gaze lights on his. "Wh—what does that mean?" I stammer, wondering if he might've heard something, and if so, what has he heard, and from whom?

Is this about the time I spent with Killian?

Braxton leans back in his seat and tips his goblet toward me. "Rumor has it, you Tripped," he says, then takes his first drink.

I take a sip of my own wine, trying to appear as though everything's perfectly normal on this side of the table. Then, setting my glass aside, I say, "We Tripped to Regency England. A blur of a Trip—over in a blink."

Braxton nods, and just as my shoulders sink with relief, I realize I left a large portion of the day totally unaccounted for, which does not go unnoticed.

"And before you Tripped? Did Jago give you that surf lesson?" The way Braxton looks at me, his face flickering under the glow of candlelight, makes it hard to determine if there's more to the question than there seems on the surface. And the longer the silence drags on, the more certain I become.

Braxton knows.

He knows I spent the bulk of the morning with Killian.

I don't know how—I don't know who told him, but he definitely...

I pull an uneasy breath, force my gaze to meet his as a

loaded silence continues to build. Desperate to break it, I say, "Braxton, I—"

Before I can continue, a strange man appears by our table from seemingly out of nowhere. And I guess I was so shocked by his sudden appearance, it's a moment before I realize he's actually a waiter here to serve the first course.

Once he's disappeared behind a walled fountain, I lean toward Braxton and say, "Has he been hiding there that whole time?"

Braxton looks at me in surprise. "I'm not sure he was *hiding*. There's a small kitchen in the back. I meant to show it to you last time, but I guess I got distracted." His eyes glint on mine, and I know exactly the distraction he's referring to—our almost-kiss that was delayed another day but, as it turns out, was totally worth the wait. "Arthur likes to eat here on the few days the sun dares to shine."

"So this was Arthur's idea?" My belly pangs with suspicion. And though I'm not exactly sure what I'm suspicious of, it's a feeling I know better than to ignore.

"Not exactly," Braxton says. Then, with a laugh, he adds, "Or maybe I'm just reluctant to hand off the credit. I think Arthur felt bad about interfering with our plans. So, he offered to cater a private dinner in the place of my choosing, and I chose here." He grins. "So anyway, back to you. Sounds like you had an eventful day."

Back to me. Awesome.

I make a show of pushing my salad around on my plate, trying to decide what to say. Any mention of Killian will only upset him, and yet, I owe him some semblance of truth.

I angle a forkful of salad into my mouth, delaying a beat, before I say, "Well, I think I might've made some progress with Mason."

"That's great!" Braxton's eyes spark in a way that tells me

he means it.

"Yeah, well..." I start to backtrack, worried I might've overstated it. "It's a start, anyway."

"Still great." Braxton nods. Then, abandoning his own salad, he settles back in his seat and sips from his wine. "Anything else?"

Seriously—he needs more? Like my small breakthrough wasn't enough?

"Well, before that, I went for a bit of a...walk."

"Around Gray Wolf?" He cocks his head in study. "I would've thought it too cold to visit the gardens."

"Yeah, um, it was, but..." I swallow hard and let the words fade. I hate lying. And I especially hate lying to him.

"Tasha, is everything okay?" Braxton asks, and though the question seems casual on the surface, the way he continues to study me leads me to think there's nothing casual about any of this. Probably because we both know I'm acting guarded and cagey. And the only time people ever act that way is when they have something to hide.

Sick of this game, I inhale a steadying breath and take a chance on telling him straight.

"I—I was thinking about Song and this strange leather-bound book I once saw in her room. Do you know anything about it?"

Braxton shakes his head, playing it cool. And though I want to tell him everything—about the perfume, the note, my suspicions about Freya—when I see how quickly he abandons his goblet so he can use his free hand to spin that gold signet ring around and around, that small, insistent voice in my head warns me to stop.

Instead, I just say, "I guess I keep putting myself in Song's place, and if it were me who went missing, I hope someone would at least try to find me."

There's a flicker in Braxton's eyes, but I'm not sure if it originated with him or if it's a result of the candlelight. "It's never going to happen to you," he says. "But, for the sake of this conversation, if it did happen, I'd dedicate the rest of my life to bringing you back."

Before I can stop myself, I say, "But would you?"

Braxton jerks back, like I just threw my drink in his face. "Tasha—" he says, his voice strained, his gaze as turbulent as I've ever seen. "You're not serious—are you?"

I rub my lips together, drop my gaze to my lap. *Here it is—the port of now or never. And since I'm the one who steered us into this harbor, I may as well throw down an anchor.*

"I guess I'm just wondering..." My fingers nervously pick at the edge of my napkin. "How would you even go about it? I mean, unless you and I were on the same Trip, you wouldn't even know where to look. And even then—"

My breath catches. Braxton leans back in his seat, as though needing to put some distance between us. "*Even then?*" His features pinch tight, his shoulders tense, and when he starts to reach for his gold signet ring, he catches my eye and tugs on his shirtsleeves instead.

I shake my head, lift a hand to my talisman, pressing my finger into the bend. I'm being ridiculous. Killian's gotten into my head. Managing to sway me just enough to drive a wedge between Braxton and me, which is clearly what Killian intended.

It's not like Braxton and I haven't danced this waltz before. And yet, here I am, dragging him out for another spin around the dance floor, hoping that this time when he denies leaving Killian behind, I can believe him—that I can know in my heart he's telling the truth.

"Maybe I'm just being paranoid," I say. "Now that I actually know people it's happened to—it's freaking me out."

I cast a cautious gaze Braxton's way, trying to gauge his reaction. Only to watch as his brow slants and his lips press together so tightly, they practically vanish.

"*People?*" he says, his fingers returning to his gold signet ring. "Don't you mean *person*?" There's a twitch in his jaw that's impossible to miss. "Unless, of course, in addition to Song, you were referring to Killian."

28

The words hang so heavy between us, I can't bring myself to reply.

"Every Trip is a risk," Braxton says. Abandoning his ring, he reaches for his goblet again. "And I'm afraid I know this firsthand, having once taken a Trip where things went so sideways, I had no choice but to return on my own."

A shot of adrenaline races through me. A film of sweat spreads over my skin. My mind is a whirl of thoughts that sound as insistently as my own heartbeat. *He's admitting it! It really is his fault that Killian was stranded in time.*

"I'm sorry I didn't tell you before," Braxton says. "It's something I don't like to talk about..." He runs his index finger along the rim of his wineglass. "And yet, I know in my heart I was left with no choice."

I gape at him wide-eyed, struggling not to voice the first thing that pops into my mind: *Oh, but there's always a choice, isn't there?*

"It's one of the reasons I still visit Dr. Lucy." He shoots me a look that practically begs my forgiveness. "And, as you've probably guessed, it's the subject of all my nightmares. I was with a new Tripper, and—"

"Wait—" I say, unable to contain my surprise. "A *new* Tripper?"

Then it can't be Killian. He's older than Braxton, and he's been at Gray Wolf longer.

Braxton dips his chin as though he can't bear for me to look at him. "Things went off the rails, and..." He sighs, rakes a quick hand through his hair. "Sometimes you have no choice but to do the wrong thing for all the right reasons."

He's visibly shaken. Like when he wakes from one of his night terrors. And my chest tightens, my shoulders tense, when I realize I'm responsible for leading him here.

"I'm sorry," I say, hoping he hears the regret in my voice, sees the remorse in my eyes. "I can't even imagine how hard that must've been."

Braxton dismisses it and takes another sip of his wine.

A moment later, the waiter reappears, and the way he studies my face as he goes about exchanging our plates leaves me to wonder if he lives over on Killian's preferred side of Gray Wolf. And if so, is it possible he saw me at the Hideaway Tavern?

By the time he's gone, I've worked myself into such a panicked state that Braxton leans across the table and asks, "Hey there—you okay?"

I glance at the fountain, wondering just how much the waiter might know. Then I turn my gaze away, force a curt nod, and dig into my food.

By the time I've polished off my tiramisu and the waiter has finally bid us good night, Braxton leans toward me and says, "I'm wondering if you noticed a theme to our dinner?"

The rain is still falling, pattering softly against the glass canopy, as my mind reels back to when he greeted me with "buona sera," then on to the wine he poured, which happened to be a chianti. The salad I barely touched was topped with fresh ricotta cheese and homemade Italian dressing, and it was soon followed by a delicious bowl of pasta. And the music that's been playing in the background all along is Vivaldi's *The Four Seasons*.

A slow smile spreads across my face. "Is this some kind of immersion experience to prepare me for Renaissance Italy?"

Braxton grins. "But is it your Trip or *our* Trip?" His gaze glints on mine, and though it takes a moment to register, the second it does, I'm so excited I can barely contain it.

"You're serious?" I say, hoping with all my heart that he is.

"Dead serious." He nods. "I think it's Arthur's way of rewarding me for today's Get."

"That must've been some Get," I say, noting how it's the first time he confirmed that he Tripped.

"I brought back the *Salvator Mundi*," he says. "And Arthur was so pleased that—"

"Wait—" I hold up a hand and lean toward him. "You brought back Leonardo da Vinci's *Salvator Mundi*?"

"You know it?" He leans toward me, though he doesn't seem all that surprised.

"Yeah, thanks to my high school art teacher," I tell him.

But what I don't mention is how Arthur thinks the *Salvator Mundi* holds the clue I'll need to locate the Moon in Renaissance Italy.

"The *Salvator Mundi* is thought to be one of da Vinci's long-lost works," I say. "It was purchased for less than two thousand dollars, then ultimately sold at auction for over four hundred million. Though some are convinced the whole thing's a fraud."

"Well, I guess they'll have to take that up with Leonardo." Braxton shrugs. "Because while I can't vouch for the one sold at auction, the one I brought back is definitely his, seeing as how I got it from the artist himself."

"The artist—" I shake my head, needing a moment to process. I mean, I get that as Trippers we often mix with the legends of long-ago times, but that doesn't mean I've grown used to it. And it certainly never occurred to me that Braxton might've—

I clear my throat and start again. "By that you mean you

actually spoke to Leonardo da Vinci? *Today?*"

Braxton grins. "I stopped by his workshop. We shared a meal. I told him all about you, in fact."

Um, what? There's no way. He can't actually mean that.

"You. Told Leonardo da Vinci. About *me*?" I eke out the words.

Braxton nods like it's no big thing.

"But why? And I'm being serious. Why would you do that? Why would he even care?" I can't even imagine how a conversation like that might've gone.

"He asked if there was anyone special in my life, and you're the first person I thought of. Well, the only person, if you must know. He said he hopes to meet you someday. And now, if our timing is right, he will."

"I can't believe this." I shake my head. "It's like..." My voice falters. I search Braxton's face. "So, what's the catch?" I ask, not wanting to dampen the mood but sure that there is one.

Braxton shrugs. "None that I'm aware of."

But that's where he's wrong. There is a catch. And it's a big one. Since Braxton doesn't know about the Moon, and since I've sworn to Arthur not to tell anyone about the Antikythera Mechanism, I'll be forced to lie to him in Renaissance Italy, too.

The train of deceit will continue to roll, and it's starting to feel like there's no end in sight.

And yet...Killian knows. I'm as sure of that as I've ever been.

So does that mean Arthur lied when he claimed I was the only one at Gray Wolf who knew about the Antikythera?

But now that I think about it, Arthur actually said: *Few at Gray Wolf have seen what I'm about to show you. And certainly none of the Blues...*

Few is a long way off from *none.* And considering how neither Braxton nor Killian are Blues, is it possible they already know?

This time, when I focus on Braxton, it's as though I'm seeing him through a new lens. There are so many secrets between us, but it's time to blow this one out into the open.

I lean toward him. My voice lowered to a whisper, I say, "Did Arthur tell you why he wants the *Salvator Mundi*?"

Braxton squints in confusion. But is it real confusion or feigned? The way the flickering candles illuminate one half of his face while obscuring the other makes it impossible to tell.

"I'm not sure what you mean," he says, fingers tracing the base of a wine goblet he's long since drained.

I bite down on my lip, wishing I could just get it over with, tell him everything I know. And yet, there's a good chance I've got this all wrong. I mean, just because Braxton and I both chose the Wheel of Fortune card—just because we both live at Gray Wolf, Tripping and thieving for Arthur—doesn't mean our destinies are fated or even intertwined.

And if Arthur's tracking our moves, then by suggesting we dine here, does that mean he's found a way to listen in, too?

Or maybe he's been listening all along, via our slabs?

I look at Braxton, filled with so much anxiety I can't bring myself to explain. So, instead, I say, "I was just wondering if Arthur might've told you what kind of Gets he has in mind."

Braxton shrugs. "The Renaissance era is ripe for the taking. There's no telling what he wants. The important thing is, we'll be there together."

I gaze down at a splotch of red wine on the tablecloth, and I know I need to stop these paranoid thoughts, pull myself together, and return to the moment on offer.

I mean, here I am, in one of the most stunning spots in Gray Wolf, with this beautiful boy, and all I've done so far is shut down my heart so that my head can spin out conspiracies.

Once we're safely in Italy, I'll tell him everything. But for now, the bank of clouds overhead has shifted, revealing a sprinkling of stars and a sliver of moon. It's a scene set for romance if there ever was one.

Returning to Braxton, I say, "So, what should we do between now and curfew?"

A slow smile spreads across his face. Like a person rearranging a room by moving a lamp from one corner to another, it effectively brightens the mood.

In one fluid move, he's standing before me, offering his hand.

A moment later, I'm wrapped in his arms as Braxton sweeps me across the stone floor, our bodies swirling in perfect time with the concerto, until he twirls me into a darkened corner lit by a single flickering torch.

"I brought these back for you," he says, slipping a hand into his jacket. He retrieves a pair of beautiful emerald-and-pearl earrings.

"How?" I gape at them. "And—I mean, where?"

"I didn't steal them off a noble—if that's what you're thinking." He laughs. "I thought you might like to wear something on your Trip that wasn't borrowed from Wardrobe."

"Other than my talisman, you mean?"

Braxton grins. "May I?" He gestures toward my ears.

I slip out my small golden hoops and insert the new earrings. "What do you think?" I ask, wishing there was a mirror nearby.

"I think I'm the luckiest guy in the world," he says.

My cheeks instantly flush, and the moment I'm back in his arms, his lips parting for mine, I can't believe I wasted so much of this night hunting for lies and cooking up intrigue, when this—right here, secure in Braxton's warmth—is the only place I want to be.

His lips find my neck, trailing a path of sweet, fevered kisses down to my collarbone. "What happened here?" he asks, tracing a finger along the scratch on my throat.

"It's nothing," I say, trying to silence him with a kiss. But unfortunately, he's also noticed the finger-shaped bruises marking my arm.

"Natasha, did something happen today?"

The question almost makes me laugh—so many things happened. But Braxton's gaze is brimming with worry, so I do what I can to ease his concern.

"I'm fine," I say. "Better than fine, because I'm right here with you." I burrow back into his arms, returning to where we left off.

"Your scent reminds me of springtime and sunshine and laughter and joy." He kisses me with a wanting that matches my own. "And you taste like faith and hope and promises kept." He groans low and deep as his hands trail down to my waist and his lips find their way back to mine. "What have I done to deserve a girl like you?" He kisses me until I'm dizzy with it, until I'm forced to pull away, drag in a breath, before I go back for more. "Tasha," he says, his voice barely a whisper. "I need you to know, I've never felt this way before."

We kiss frantically, hungrily, taking all that we can. I slide a hand under his jacket, my fingers making quick work of the row of buttons lining his dress shirt.

"I've never felt this way about anyone, ever." He presses the words into my flesh.

Not even Elodie.

The thought is like a sticky lyric now stuck in my head. But I force myself to tune it out and focus on the feel of Braxton instead.

Like the way his fingers trace along the seams of my dress, moving up and over my rib cage before pausing at the undercurve of my breasts.

I arch into his touch, wishing we could immerse ourselves in each other until we are one, intertwined, no clear boundaries between his body and mine.

And all the while we kiss like we're starved for it—our lips eternally seeking—our hands greedily exploring.

We are hooked. Addicted. Completely and utterly lost in each other.

And the best part is, we've only just gotten started.

When Braxton lifts me off my feet and places my back against the wall, my legs instinctively fold around his hips, tethering our bodies so tightly, a low, sexy grumble sounds deep in his throat.

With a wash of stars glimmering above and a wide splash of ocean breaking below, my palms skate over the muscled curve of his chest, then down along the taut valley of his torso, and then down lower still.

"Tasha..." he breathes, his own hands skimming past my knees, under my dress. His fingers move gently, reverently, pausing in question when his thumbs edge against the flimsy strip of lace—a barrier so easily breached with a simple nod of my head.

I shutter my eyes, marveling at the relentless scorch of his touch.

"Tasha, I—" His lips retreat; he presses his forehead to mine. And as my eyes slide open and our gazes lock, I know he's on the verge of telling me something—when a new symphony suddenly blares from out of nowhere, drowning out the vibrant chords of Vivaldi.

29

"Ignore it," Braxton whispers. "Arthur's letting us skip curfew tonight."

"Remind me to thank him later." I grin, eager to get back to kissing when Braxton's hands circle my waist, and he lowers me back to the ground.

"Listen—" He lifts a hand to my face and traces the edge of his thumb over my cheek. "I was wondering if maybe we should…wait."

"Wait for what?" I press closer, eager to shed my clothes and his clothes and—

"For Italy," he says. "You know, make it more special."

I pull him back to me, my lips nipping at the soft lobe of his ear, making my way to that sweet hollow space at the crook of his neck.

Braxton groans, slides a hand around my hip while the other holds fast to my waist. "I just thought that if we waited, it could be really special. Or rather, even more special," he says.

I study his expression, unsure if he's serious or just trying to do the right thing. And honestly, while I appreciate the sentiment, right now, when there's so much heat passing between us, I can't see the point of waiting for anything.

"You do know it's not my first time," I tell him, pretty sure I told him about that regrettable night back when I was a sophomore.

"Nor is it mine," he says. "But it will be our first time together, and I thought it might be nice if we waited to share that moment in some place more memorable."

His eyes shine with so much sincerity, I'm tempted to go along, but not before saying, "You do realize that to the outside world, Gray Wolf would qualify as pretty memorable."

"True," he agrees. "But I have to say, Renaissance Italy is truly outstanding."

"So, does this mean you've done some location scouting?"

His lips curve into a grin. "I have the perfect place in mind. Not that the safe house isn't nice, because—"

"Safe house?" I frown. "That sounds…kinda dodgy."

Braxton laughs. "Then you're definitely in for a treat. It's a very grand, very old palazzo. Of course, it's not so old in its timeline, but you know what I mean. The person who runs it is from Gray Wolf."

"Seriously?" I gape, surprised to hear that's even a thing.

Braxton nods. "Some people choose to live in another time. And, in certain cases, Arthur provides the housing and funds, in exchange for their hosting us Trippers and introducing us to the sort of people it's helpful to know."

Well, look at that. Not only do Trippers disappear, but some choose to leave their own timelines so they can live here, while others forgo the modern world so they can experience life in an ancient one.

"Anyway," he goes on. "Though the palazzo is pretty special, Arthur agreed to let us spend our first night in Venice."

"Venice." I blink. "Like, the *real* Venice. Not a hologram like last time?"

"Definitely not a hologram." Braxton laughs. "And I can't wait to share it with you."

I gaze at this beautiful boy, and I can hardly believe how lucky I am—how my life is so much better than I ever allowed myself to imagine. And it's all because of Braxton, and Arthur, and yeah, even Elodie.

Then I lean closer, thread my arms around Braxton's neck, and press a kiss to that place where his nose takes a bit of a bend. "I'm in," I say, pulling away. "I guess all good things are worth waiting for, right?"

Braxton grasps hold of my hand, entwining my fingers with his. "There are so many places I can't wait to share with you," he says. "And so many people I want you to meet."

"Like Leonardo?" I tease.

"For starters." He laughs.

As we make our way to the door, I pause a moment to lift my face to the sky, wishing for one last look at this glorious space before we call it a night.

The storm clouds have gathered again, hanging so low the moon is no longer visible and most of the stars are obscured. So, I lower my gaze and cast another look around the garden, and that's when I notice something I don't remember from before.

"What's that?" I gesture toward a large marble frieze set before a stone wall that's otherwise covered in flowering vines.

Braxton looks from me to the carved stone medallion with its hollow eyes, prominent nose, and gaping maw of a mouth.

"That's the *Bocca della Verità*," he says in what sounds to my ears like perfect Italian.

"Translation?" I move closer to the frieze to get a better look.

I've stopped just before it when Braxton says, "The Mouth of Truth."

I glance over my shoulder, waiting for more.

"It's a medieval lie detector," he says. "Would you like to try it?"

I glance between Braxton and the creepy face carved into the marble slab.

"What do you mean *medieval lie detector*?" I ask.

Braxton comes to stand beside me. "According to legend, it bites off the hands of liars."

I gape, sure that he's joking. Though nothing about his expression is leaning that way.

"It's said that if you were to stick your hand inside the mouth and tell a lie, it would chomp your hand right off."

"But that's impossible." I let out an unsteady bark of a laugh. "I mean, why would anyone believe that?"

Braxton shrugs. "Superstition is a powerful force. Still, there's only one way to find out." He motions toward the stone disc.

He can't be serious. I study Braxton's face, wondering if he can sense the wave of panic rising inside me.

"Seeing is believing, right?" He slings an arm around my shoulders and says, "Or, in this case, maybe it's more like believing is seeing? How about I go first."

After pressing a kiss to my cheek, he approaches the creepy medallion and plunges his hand deep into that gaping maw. "Go ahead," he says. "Ask me anything."

Of course, the first question that springs to mind is the most obvious—the one thing I've been wondering all along. And yet, how can I possibly ask him if he's been lying about leaving Killian behind when this is meant to be fun?

I purse my lips as though I need a moment to think. "Okay," I finally say. "I have a question."

"Lay it on me." Braxton grins.

"Did you really tell Leonardo about me?" I ask. "Or was that just a thinly veiled attempt at flattery?"

Braxton gives a solemn nod; then, with his free hand pressed to his heart and the other pushing deeper inside the mouth, he says, "I, Braxton Huntley, do hereby solemnly swear that I told the great Leonardo da Vinci all about the super-smart, incredibly hot, absolutely amazing girl that I cannot stop thinking about."

Then he shuts his eyes tight and waits. When enough time has passed, he pulls his surviving hand free. "Looks like I'm clear." His eyes light on mine. "But now that it's your turn, I should warn you—I only play hardball."

I stare at Braxton, trying to figure out what the hell that even means.

Okay, I know what it means—that he won't go easy on me. But just how hard of a ball is he planning to pitch?

Since I'm in no mood to find out, I say, "This is silly. We should head back."

I shoot an anxious glance between Braxton and the creepy frieze otherwise known as the Mouth of Truth, fully aware of just how ridiculous I'm being. Clearly there's no way some ancient chunk of marble can really have a go at removing my hand.

And yet that doesn't stop the chill from crawling over my skin.

Doesn't stop my heart from practically banging right out of my chest.

"C'mon," Braxton coaxes. "There's nothing to fear. Just slip your hand inside, answer the question, then wait for the *Bocca della Verità* to sort it from there."

I gnaw the inside of my cheek, seriously regretting having steered myself here. Still, the longer I delay, the more Braxton will think I've got something to hide.

"Fine," I say, trying to put on a game face. "But just so you know, this whole thing is creeping me out. But yeah, go ahead, take your best shot."

The moment I shove my hand inside that mouth, Braxton's gaze locks on mine, and I'm surprised to find that playful glint suddenly replaced by something I can't readily identify.

A loud blast of thunder explodes overhead.

"Ready when you are," I say, only it doesn't come out nearly as light as I'd hoped. If anything, I sound nervous, anxious, my voice pitching several octaves too high as my entire arm starts to shake.

Next thing I know, a bolt of lightning incinerates the sky, causing Braxton's face to flash in and out of focus, flickering from dark to light to dark again, as he looks at me and says, "So tell me, Tasha—what did you really get up to today?"

Wait—what?

Did he really ask that, or is my head playing games?

Another earsplitting crack of thunder roars through the night sky.

"Any day now," Braxton says, but his voice is soon overtaken by a screeching howl of wind.

"I'm sorry—what?" My tongue's gone so dry the words come out slurred. A moment later, the heavens burst open, releasing a deluge of rain that hammers the glass roof.

Braxton moves in, closing the distance between us. With his gaze fixed on mine, he says, "So tell me, Tasha—do you really like the earrings, or was that just a thinly veiled attempt at flattery?"

In an instant, all the tension whooshes right out of me, and my shoulders sag in relief. "Yes," I say, returning his gaze. "I truly do like them."

We both wait. Wait for the jaws of truth to play judge and jury.

When enough time passes, I step away from the frieze, and Braxton pulls me into his arms.

"You know it's not real, right?" He smooths a hand down my back.

"I think I'm just tired," I murmur, pressing fast to his chest. "Tripping has that effect."

"For a moment there, you looked truly frightened. What was it you thought I said?"

I draw away, making quick study of the hard line of his jaw, the sharp angle of his cheekbones, the bottomless depths of his ocean-blue gaze.

"Nothing," I say. "Just a trick of the wind, that's all."

With his arm slung loosely around me, he walks me back to my room. And though physically I feel as close to him as ever, mentally we are a thousand miles apart, barely exchanging so much as a word.

"Should I come in?" he asks once we've reached my door.

I shake my head. "If you do, I'll never be able to hold out until Venice."

Braxton grins, but the tension at the edge of his mouth hints at his mood from before.

Eager to erase it, I tip onto my toes and press a kiss to his lips. But well before it takes hold, I pull away, press my thumb to the keypad, and say, "See you tomorrow?"

"And every day after," he calls, making his way down the hall.

Once I'm inside with the door closed behind me, I sink down to the floor.

Outside these walls, a fierce storm continues to rage.

Inside my head, I recreate the scene in the Moon Garden, until I can clearly see Braxton, his gaze locked on mine, his voice so low and deep it's like he's right here before me.

"So tell me, Tasha," he says. "What did you really get up to today?"

30

The storm raged all night.

And since I wasn't about to sneak outside and scale the *Magician* statue in eighty-plus-mile-an-hour winds to search for a book that may or may not be hidden in there, I opted for sleep instead, telling myself I could always wake up early and try again.

Only, I didn't wake up early. I slept straight through my alarm.

And then, I continued to sleep right through the chiming of my slab announcing the inspirational quote of the day.

It's not until the phone in my room starts ringing that I'm finally cut loose from my dreams.

Since we rely on our slabs for pretty much everything, the phone is an emergency-only device. And I guess I've gotten so used to ignoring its presence on my nightstand, I've forgotten it even existed.

"You okay there?" a voice barks before I have a chance to eke out a greeting. And right away, I recognize that voice as belonging to Arthur. "I had breakfast sent to your room," he says, and as if on cue, there's a knock at my door.

"I think they're here now," I tell him, already bolting from bed.

"Good. When you're ready, head downstairs. Directions will be sent to your tablet."

I'm about to ask him what this is about when Arthur hangs up.

The knock sounds again, and I race for the door. When I see the delivery guy standing in an otherwise empty hallway, I motion for the tray and tell him I can take it from here.

After helping myself to some coffee and a wedge of croissant, I pull my hair into a ponytail, slip on a pair of black leggings and the first pair of sneakers I see. Then after tugging on the blue Gray Wolf Academy sweatshirt that's pretty much mandatory on school days, I sling my Gray Wolf logo tote onto my shoulder and am about to head out when I remember the perfume bottle and note sitting on the window ledge and the golden pocket watch I left on my nightstand.

Knowing I can't leave them out in plain sight, I toss it all in my bag, and as I'm on my way out the door, I check my slab for today's inspirational quote:

Fortune favors the bold. – Virgil

Here's hoping it's true.

The second I hit the bottom of the stairs, a green arrow appears on my screen, and I follow it down a series of unfamiliar halls before ending at a door I don't remember seeing before. Then again, Gray Wolf is so big, I doubt I'll ever truly know my way around.

Since there's nothing on the door to indicate what this might be, I lift a hand and give a tentative knock. A moment later, an electronic click sounds, the door springs open, and after taking an initial step through the entry, I pause.

I'm not sure why I'm feeling so edgy. I mean, it's hardly the first time I've been summoned by Arthur, and so far, it's never gone badly.

Then again, I did fail to bring back the Star, and I'm starting to worry that this might be the Gray Wolf equivalent of a visit to the principal's office.

I force my legs forward, stepping deeper into the room. The walls are black as midnight, while the floor—a mosaic of gleaming white marble and mother-of-pearl—shines as bright as the moon.

There's a tapestry on a far wall that might've been lifted straight from the palace of King Henry VIII. On another wall hangs a gilt-framed master I don't immediately recognize. And though most of the furniture is modern and sleek, it manages to blend seamlessly with the other pieces that are clearly antiques.

There's an enormous fireplace with a blazing fire crackling inside, and a quick glance at the mural that covers the domed section of the ceiling has me wondering if Michelangelo might've painted the Sistine Chapel as practice for this.

And of course, there, poised behind a huge carved wooden desk, sits Arthur himself.

"Welcome to the inner sanctum." He motions for me to take a seat just opposite him.

Because my earliest impression of Arthur was shaped by all the magazine covers I saw long before we first met, I always expect him to appear much bigger than he actually is.

In person, he's average in height, with the sort of lean body of a dedicated runner. His hair is dark, his features simultaneously blunt and fine, as though his face was carefully whittled from a soft piece of wood using a very sharp knife. His clothes lean toward casual—mostly high-end cashmere sweaters, dark, slim-cut jeans, and designer loafers, lately tending toward Gucci.

At first glance, he seems like any other standard-issue rich guy. Just another lump of meticulously maintained flesh who somehow managed to surpass nearly everyone else in the game of success.

That is, until you take in his eyes, which always remind me of shattered obsidian.

"So," he says, watching me gaze around the space. "What do you think?"

"Is it possible your office is even more amazing than a trip to the Vault?"

As expected, Arthur laughs.

"Do you have a favorite?" I ask, remembering how closely he watched me choose a piece from the Vault, like he was getting a glimpsc into a part of me I might otherwise try to keep hidden.

And if that's the case, then what does Arthur's favorite piece say about him?

He leads me toward a display cabinet containing what looks to be an ancient manuscript. "*Meditations*," he says. "A collection of essays written by Marcus Aurelius. A great Roman emperor. Are you familiar?"

I cringe, embarrassed to admit my one and only connection to him. "It's not exactly the timeline I've been researching," I say. "But I do remember him from the movie *Gladiator*."

Arthur lets out a short bark of a laugh, which comes as a relief. "If we ever manage to stretch our time-travel abilities back to his day, he's the first person I plan to meet. If you've never read *Meditations*, you should at least take a look. There are several copies in the library in various translations, and his writings are still relevant to this day. One of the wisest men on earth, and he had an absolute shit for a son—the dreadful Commodus." He shakes his head. "Which just goes to prove that the apple doesn't always fall close to the tree."

The way his gaze catches on mine makes me wonder if he's referring to me and my parents—and if so, which one?

"And that?" I motion toward an easel draped with a cloth cover. "Is it what I think it is?"

Arthur shoots me a quizzical look. "I suppose that depends on what you think it is."

My belly instantly clenches, like it knows I've made a terrible mistake well before the realization can take hold in my brain.

I thought it might be the *Salvator Mundi*—that Arthur summoned me here to show it to me. But now I realize I've made a mistake.

Not to mention how there's a really good chance Braxton wasn't authorized to tell me about his recent Trip to Renaissance Italy. In which case, now we're both screwed.

"I—I don't know," I mumble, followed by an awkward pause. "I just—"

I watch as Arthur grasps the edge of the cloth, and in one swift motion that reminds me of how my mom used to rip off my Band-Aids when I was a kid, he whips it right off.

"Not what you thought?" Arthur cocks his head, responding to my look of confusion as I study the painting.

It's of a beautiful, sleeping woman with wavy blond hair dressed in a filmy white nightgown. Her body is draped across a bed as though she's lost in a dream so deep, she's unaware of the demon crouched on her chest while another horse-faced demon looks on.

"It's by Henry Fuseli, an eighteenth-century Swiss artist," Arthur says. "It's called—"

"*The Nightmare*," I whisper, unable to tear my gaze away.

"It was quite controversial in its day. And though I do admire it, it's much too macabre for my personal tastes. It's only here temporarily. Soon, it'll be installed in Braxton's room."

I turn to Arthur in shock, and when I catch the way his gaze narrows on mine, I wish I'd kept my reaction in check.

"Braxton did me a great favor yesterday," Arthur says. "And this is the reward that he chose."

I nod, swallow past the lump in my throat, and force another look at the ominous painting before me.

"Are you really so surprised?" Arthur says. "Are you not aware of the darkness Braxton carries inside?"

31

Of course I'm aware of Braxton's tendency toward darkness.

And yet, after our conversation last night, this painting feels like a nod to something deeper than just having a taste for melancholy art.

By choosing to hang this in his room, he's ensuring he'll never get past his own nightmare. Which makes me wonder if he doesn't actually want to—if he prefers to torture himself for something that wasn't his fault.

Unless, of course, it *was* his fault.

Like keeping those old, stained boots in his closet. Boots he must've been wearing on the Trip that went sideways. It's the only way to explain why he insists on keeping them.

Between the boots and this nightmare of a painting, one thing is sure: Braxton is determined to keep the story alive by surrounding himself with so many reminders, he'll never have a chance to forget.

And yet, none of that explains why, when I touched those boots, I saw a vision of my dad, all alone, inside some ancient necropolis.

What is the connection between my dad and those boots?

A whirl of possible explanations spins through my head, but none of them make any sense. I'm so lost in my thoughts, it's not until Arthur clears his throat that I realize he's been observing me this whole time.

I turn away from the easel and make for my chair. "What is it you wanted to see me about?" I ask, sure I'm about to be dragged on my failure to bring back the Star.

Instead, I watch as he returns to his desk, reaches for a carved jade box, and retrieves three rectangular cards he then slides toward me.

"You're familiar with these?" He leans back in his seat.

I cast a quick glance over the three vintage tarot cards that look a lot like the ones my dad used to have. Though, of course, my dad's cards were replicas. These are the real ancient deal.

To Arthur, I say, "The High Priestess, the Moon, and the Hermit card."

He nods. "Though, of course, these are from the Visconti-Sforza tarocchi deck. The images differ from the more common Rider-Waite cards. But I'm pleased you recognize them."

Um, yeah, I was raised on these cards. But I keep that bit to myself.

I start to reach for the Moon, wanting to study it closer, when Arthur hands me a pair of white cotton gloves. "The cards are very old and rather fragile," he explains, watching as I tug the gloves past my fingers. "I bought them at auction, long before I built Gray Wolf. Of course, plenty of decks have been brought back by Trippers since then, but I have a fondness for these. They mark the start of my journey."

Which journey? The journey to finding the missing pieces of the Antikythera Mechanism, or—

As though reading my mind, Arthur says, "The journey into occultism." My startled gaze meets his, but he's quick to dismiss it. "The word has gotten a negative connotation over the years. All it really refers to is secret knowledge. It's derived from the Latin word 'occultus,' which translates to clandestine, hidden secret, knowledge of the hidden—that sort of thing. You are aware of my interest in alchemy, yes?" He studies me closely. "After all, it is the very foundation that Gray Wolf was built upon."

I look to the cards again, noting that the Magician is missing. Only, that's not exactly true; he's sitting right here before me.

"I guess transcending the boundaries of time is the ultimate alchemy," I say.

Arthur grants me an enigmatic smile. "I prefer you glean whatever you need from these cards here and now. I can't risk you losing them in Renaissance Italy."

I'm struck by the way he says *Renaissance Italy*, like it's Maui or Berlin—just another destination as opposed to a whole other timeline. Though, in the scheme of things, I guess it is. Seeing as how the past is just a continuous echo looping through time.

Or, as Nietzsche said, *Time is a flat circle.*

I also know that bit about losing the cards was meant to remind me how I returned from my first trip to Versailles without the cards Arthur gave me. And though he didn't seem to care at the time, I suspect he wants to remind me to not get too ahead of myself. That while he's pleased with my performance so far, his standards are, and will remain, incredibly high.

"I'm guessing these hold clues that'll lead me to the Moon?" I look between the cards and him.

"With any luck." He shrugs.

While luck is certainly part of any Trip, it has nothing to do with why Arthur has summoned me here. Out of everyone else in this place, he's pegged me as the one who will help him fulfill his biggest dream. And I have no idea why.

"I'm looking for a brief overview of the numerological, astrological, and elemental connections. But don't overthink it. Often, it's the surprise component that leads one to the prize."

I study the cards. "Since the Hermit helped me locate

the Sun, I'll start here," I say, taking a moment to collect my thoughts before I go on. "As the ninth card in the deck, the Hermit is numerologically linked to the Moon card, which is the eighteenth card, since one plus eight equals nine." I lift my gaze to meet Arthur's. He nods for me to continue. "Its element is earth, its astrological link is Virgo, and the meaning behind the card is basically that of healing and self-exploration."

"Good." Arthur nods. "And the others?"

With a gloved index finger, I gently slide the Popess, known in contemporary decks as the High Priestess, card before me—a card that I've come to associate with Elodie.

"She comes in at number two, which links her to both Justice, the eleventh card in modern decks, since one plus one equals two, and Judgment, which is the twentieth card, as, of course, two plus zero also amounts to two. Her astrological sign is the Moon, her element is water, and she stands for secrets, wisdom, and things of a spiritual nature."

I lift my gaze again. "Does this mean the Moon is hidden in a church or cathedral, or a place where judicial decisions are made?"

Arthur shrugs, but his mouth wears the hint of a grin. "That's for you to discover," he says.

I rub my gloved hands together and move on to the next. "As for the Moon card—" I pause, noticing how Arthur leans in. "As the eighteenth card, it's connected to number nine, the Hermit, since one plus eight equals nine. Like the High Priestess, its element is water, and it's astrologically linked to Pisces, the fish, which again points to water. As for its meaning, it's basically all about illusions, dreams, that sort of thing."

Arthur nods, though whatever he's thinking remains hidden from me. An uncomfortable silence stretches between us. Or maybe I'm the only one who's uncomfortable; Arthur seems perfectly at ease. "And?" he finally says, his gaze darting between the cards and me.

I glance down at the three cards splayed before me. "Maybe I should look at the map again?"

Arthur reaches into a drawer, retrieves a folder, and slides it toward me. "A copy," he says. "As you know, the original is kept in the Vault."

I shift forward on my seat and study the same map Christopher Columbus used to chart his way across the Atlantic. Since that historic journey, a slew of symbols were added. Symbols that, from what I can tell, mimic the images used on the tarot cards.

The first thing I do after locating Italy is search for an image that's the closest to Florence.

And there they are—a crown, an hourglass, and an archer's bow. Only one of those objects is placed upside down, and another is knocked on its side.

"Reversed meaning." I slide the map toward Arthur and tap the hourglass with my gloved finger. "It's an important distinction, indicating that this hourglass isn't heavy on time, but rather, it's running out of time."

Arthur is nearly halfway across his desk now, his fingers pulling at a ring that once belonged to Edward the Black Prince.

I focus back on the cards. "See the difference?" I push the card toward him. "On the Hermit card, the hourglass is heavy on available time. On the map, the sand is running out."

Arthur says nothing but motions for me to continue.

"Of course, there are plenty of tarot experts who ignore upside-down cards. But since the symbols are purposely drawn this way, it seems like a mistake to dismiss it."

Arthur nods. "What else?" he says.

I point toward the bow. "While the Rider-Waite tarot deck portrays an entirely different image, the female on this card is said to represent Diana the Huntress. And since she carries a bow, I think you're correct to relate the symbol on this map to the Moon card."

Arthur makes a thorough study of the card and the map. "And," he says, his voice edged with excitement. *Or is it impatience?* "Anything else? What about the crown?"

I gaze at the map again. Though the crown isn't quite upside down, it's clearly been sketched to show it lying on its side. And just thinking about the reversed meaning of the High Priestess card fills my belly with dread. Still, Arthur is waiting, so I have no choice but to say it.

"The upside-down High Priestess points toward secrets—the kind that can possibly cause trouble or harm. It can also mean that someone is listening to bad advice, following the wrong path or even the wrong teacher."

"And?" Arthur asks, always looking for more.

And making the grave mistake of ignoring your own intuition—it can also mean that.

But I don't say it. Instead, I say, "Maybe I'm missing something. But that's all I've got."

Arthur leans back in his seat. "Tell me," he says. "How's your prep work coming?"

I shrug. "My equestrian skills have improved, and I'm feeling more confident with swordcraft. Though, admittedly, I'm far from an expert in any of those things. As for languages..." I make a sheepish face. "It's like my tongue refuses to speak anything other than Southern Californian."

Arthur runs a hand along the edge of his desk. "Then I suppose it's a good thing you'll be Tripping with a fluent speaker."

"About that—" I lean toward him. "This whole thing with the Antikythera and you sending me to Florence to bring back the Moon—it's still confidential, right? Which means I'll have to slip away and secure the piece on my own?"

"Will that be a problem?" he asks.

Of course it'll be a problem! Braxton thinks we're going to spend every waking moment together!

But since Arthur doesn't like excuses or the people who make them, I simply say, "Well, it might prove a bit difficult, but—"

"But not impossible." His gaze narrows on me.

I shake my head, return my own gaze to the map.

"When do you think you'll be ready?" he says.

My head jerks up. *Is he serious? Is it actually up to me to decide?*

"Or, should I say, what more do you need to be ready?"

Ah, yes, that's more like it.

I take a moment to think. Then, remembering today's inspirational quote, "Fortune favors the bold," I look at Arthur and say, "Two things."

Arthur nods, waiting.

"One, if possible, I'd really like to see the *Salvator Mundi* in person."

"And two?" Arthur places his elbows on the desk and steeples his fingers together.

"I'm really hoping you can explain just what the heck a Timekeeper is."

32

A moment passes between us. It feels charged, dangerous. Like a live wire stretched to its limit, ready to snap any second.

And just when I'm about to breach the silence, Arthur does the strangest, most unexpected thing—he throws his head back and laughs—a deep, hearty howl of a sound—as I sit just opposite him, having no idea why that struck him as funny.

"My apologies." He shakes his head. "I assumed you'd figured it out by now."

My first instinct is to slump in embarrassment, but, reluctant to do anything that risks diminishing me even further in his eyes, I square my shoulders and say, "I'm guessing they're some sort of enemy?"

Arthur centers his gaze on mine. "And what makes you think that?" His fingers idly pick at the cuffed sleeves of his sweater.

"Well, the man who went after me in Versailles—twice—according to Killian, he was a Timekeeper."

Arthur nods. "I suppose Killian would know."

"Because he lived there?" I ask. When Arthur fails to respond, I go on. "All I know is Killian claimed he was a threat and he left him for dead."

"Sounds like Killian was looking to protect you."

I shrug, but what I don't say is that I didn't need protecting. And even if Killian believed that I did, he could've just injured the man. He didn't have to kill him.

"Don't make the mistake of mourning your enemies," Arthur says. "Do you really believe that Timekeeper wouldn't have killed you, given the chance?"

I think back to both Versailles encounters. That man I initially mistook for a groundskeeper—mainly because that's how Elodie referred to him—was menacing, enraged. But he mostly seemed focused on stopping me from claiming the Sun—and on the second visit, stopping me from bringing it back. And while I readily admit to being scared out of my wits, in retrospect, I'm not convinced he was the murdering type.

But what about the guy in England? The one who found me in the library—was he a Timekeeper, too?

Probably. If for no other reason, he instantly recognized me for what I am—a Time Jumper. And the way he pulled his sword…

I can still see the malicious glint in his eyes, the flash of his blade. And though he seemed reluctant to kill me, if pushed, I've no doubt he would've left me for dead.

Though of course I don't share any of that. Instead, I say, "I think they're the ones who hid the pieces and will stop at nothing to ensure they stay hidden."

Arthur's expression is guarded, giving nothing away.

"And so…what I'm wondering is—just how many Timekeepers are out there? Are they in every timeline or just a few?"

I watch as he leans back in his seat, rubs a hand over his chin as though weighing just how much he should share. "There are many," he finally says. "You'll find them throughout history. Their roots extend all the way back to the Great Mystery Schools of Egypt."

I suck in a breath. I have no idea what that means, but something about it sounds occult-like and dangerous.

"I don't—" I start, but Arthur's quick to cut in.

"It's an ancient society with access to great wisdom. The Timekeepers have sworn an oath to keep that knowledge secret, forbidding access to the rest of us."

"But why?" I ask. "And what sort of secrets?" I imagine clandestine meetings, complicated handshakes, and men dressed in masks and long robes. All of them gathered into a room lit by torches, attempting to conjure some powerful entity from the great beyond.

Arthur pulls at the ring that once belonged to the Black Prince. "Why, the secret of time, of course. That, and the true nature of reality." Responding to my confusion, he adds, "By which I mean the power that exists within all of us but has so far been accessed by only a few."

I stare at him, hoping he'll elaborate, because honestly, I'm totally perplexed.

"As for the *why*..." Arthur's voice fades, and his gaze wanders to the far side of the room. "I suppose it's because they believe the common man can't handle that sort of power—that it would only result in tragic misuse—that the very nature of man bends toward destruction. And because of that, we're not fit to create our own world."

My breath comes a little too quickly, leaving me feeling hollowed out, queasy.

"And do you know these secrets?" I ask, wondering if he's a descendant from a long line of Mystery School initiates. *Is that how he became who he is, built all that he has?*

As though reading my mind, Arthur says, "I've been called many things, but I'm no Timekeeper. If it were up to me, I'd share the knowledge, allow everyone a chance to create a better experience. It's the foundation my company was built upon—providing access to great knowledge and the world's greatest teachers with only a few taps on a keyboard."

"So, the man who hoards art wants to share knowledge with

the world?" I shouldn't have said it, and the moment it's out, I'd do anything to reel the words back into my mouth. But if Arthur is annoyed, he doesn't show it.

"I believe humans have reached this current miserable state because intuitively they know they were created for more. That they're here to do better—to be better. But they've gotten so sidetracked by false messaging, they've descended into a shadow world and have no idea how to claw their way out. Think about your own life." He gestures toward me. "The person you were before you came to Gray Wolf, and how eagerly you participated in your own downward spiral. You certainly weren't born that way. You came into this world eager and bright-eyed.

"It's the constant barrage of toxic messaging you received through the years, the ones that told you all the things that were wrong with you, all the instincts you had to curb to fit into that miserable box we call a society—a box of people so afraid of their own power, they want you to be afraid of yours, too. But it's the outliers, the ones who resist the noise and tune in to their inner compass and voice—they're the ones who pave a new way. Throughout history, it's the nonconformists who are the true wayfinders of their day."

"I get what you're saying," I tell him. "But I'm not sure I get how the Timekeepers are responsible for the state of our modern-day world. I mean, aren't we each responsible for who and what we become? Aren't we the ones who decide whether we rule our own destinies?"

"Perhaps," Arthur says. "But I've always believed great knowledge should be shared. And the Timekeepers believe that sharing their knowledge will lead to our doom."

While the conversation does hold a certain appeal, I feel like we've veered way off track. I wasn't looking to start a philosophical discourse. I was mostly looking for answers.

"I guess what I really need to know," I say, "is that, if these

Timekeepers are everywhere, scattered throughout the centuries, tasked with guarding the missing pieces, then that must mean there's a Timekeeper in Florence, just like there was in Versailles." *Versailles and London*, though I keep that last bit to myself.

Arthur nods, which I take as both good and bad news. It's always good to be right, but it's not so good to confirm there's an enemy in the sixteenth century waiting for me to arrive.

"Okay, and so, what exactly am I supposed to do about that? Do I wait for a Timekeeper to come after me? Or is there some easier way to head them off before they can get very far? I mean, how will I even know? Is there a way to tell them apart? And one more thing—" I'm on a roll. There's no stopping me. "Why is it always so easy for them to find me? Is it because I happen to be in just the right place at just the wrong time? Or is it something more? And—"

Arthur flashes a palm, bringing my questions to a grinding halt. "As for how they find you—while I can't confirm it, it's said there are many who came out of those Mystery Schools with a sort of heightened psychic ability—a gift that's been passed down through their lineage, and—"

I have no idea what Arthur says next because my mind is stuck on the words *heightened psychic ability* and *passed down through their lineage.*

That sounds an awful lot like the Unraveling. *But it can't be that—can it?*

I shake my head, sure I've misunderstood. "You mean like—like a psychic or a medium?" I say, my voice gone noticeably shaky.

Arthur shrugs, flicks a piece of lint from his sleeve. "I'm not up on the details, but yes, they can access scenes from both the future and the past. As for how to spot them—" He pauses, centers his gaze on mine. "I suppose you could always look for the mark."

33

My jaw drops. My limbs start to shake.

Look for the mark, Arthur said.

If this were a movie, the sound of a record scratch would screech through the room, the action would halt, and the main character would be catapulted into an awkward scene from the past.

But this isn't a movie. And while Arthur continues to study me like I'm a bug under a powerful lens, an image bursts onto the screen in my brain.

The man is lying before me, bleeding from a knife wound to his belly, as I focus on the strange round symbol tattooed on his arm. An intricate series of interlinking circles—a design that seemed so familiar, though I couldn't place it at the time—

It was only later that I realized my dad bore a similar mark—and it's the same mark that was engraved on the back of that gold pocket watch.

A wave of dread hits me so fast, I clutch the arms of my chair to steady myself.

It can't be.

It's ridiculous to even think such a thing.

Not to mention how it doesn't make the slightest bit of sense.

But while my brain trots out a long list of arguments against it, it fails to convince my heart to play along.

All my dad's long-forgotten teachings that I started

remembering from the moment I entered Arcana…

Our shared gift for Unravelings…

But no.

There's no way.

Absolutely not.

Because if my dad were a descendant from the Great Mystery Schools, if he really was a—a Timekeeper—then wouldn't that make *me* a Timekeeper, too?

And yet, how can I be a Timekeeper when I'm working for Arthur, and Timekeepers, according to what Arthur just told me and what my own experience has taught me, are my sworn enemy?

My hand shoots to my throat, holding back the sob before it has a chance to slip out.

Breathe, you fool. Just calm the hell down.

You don't have a mark.

And yeah, maybe your dad had a tattoo, but big deal, lots of dads do.

Not only are you being ridiculous, but you are seriously on the verge of becoming one of those paranoid weirdos who see conspiracies wherever they look.

You need to stop this.

You need to—

"Natasha." The sound of Arthur's voice snaps me out of the trance. "Are you okay?" His lips are flatlined, but his eyes brim with concern.

I force a nod. Force my hand back to my lap. "I'm fine. Just…a bit nauseous, that's all."

"Stop by the Spring room," Arthur says. "Get yourself a proper lunch. Something more than coffee and a third of a croissant."

Recognizing my cue to leave, I rise from my seat and start to head for the door, when I freeze.

A third of a croissant? How the hell would he even know about that?

I'm about to call him out, demand to know why he's keeping tabs on my breakfast, when my gaze catches on the stretch of ceiling just over his head.

There, among the collection of frescoes, is one of the most recognizable images in the world, aside from the *Mona Lisa*, of course—*The Creation of Adam*.

Michelangelo's masterwork, meant to depict the biblical narrative of the moment God gives life to man.

The original can be found on the ceiling of the Sistine Chapel.

In this version, the hand standing in for God's clearly belongs to Arthur. I can tell by the ring the artist included on his finger.

"I am not in the right place, and I am not a painter."

I turn to Arthur, unsure what he means.

"It's a translation of part of the poem Michelangelo wrote about the hardships of painting the Sistine Chapel. Four years of agonizing labor that resulted in one of the most masterful works of all time. And yet, he wrote those words believing he was not suited for the job."

So even Michelangelo suffered from imposter syndrome. To Arthur, I say, "And this version?" I gesture toward the fresco.

"A private commission from the artist himself."

On the outside, I nod. On the inside, I'm feeling really on edge.

"And be prepared to Trip by the end of this week," Arthur says. "If not sooner."

"But that's only a few days away," I say. "And I'm not sure—"

"I had the *Salvator Mundi* sent to your room," Arthur says, ignoring my protest. "So you can study as needed. Though try to keep any direct contact to a minimum, of course."

I blink. Once. Twice. Struggling to grasp the reality of what he just said. "You had an original Leonardo da Vinci *sent to my room*?" Despite having grown used to being surrounded by priceless works of art, the thought of sharing a space with an original da Vinci still feels fantastical.

Arthur nods like it's no big thing. "And don't worry about the Star," he says. "You'll have another chance soon enough." Then, with a brisk wave of his hand, the meeting is over.

It's only as I'm making my way down the hall that I realize how easy it was for him to outmaneuver me, outplay me, effectively using a legendary piece of art to sidetrack me from what I really wanted to ask.

What about the mark?

What does it look like?

Not to mention—why the hell are you tracking my breakfast?

Then again, maybe that's all for the best. Because the thoughts now spinning through my head are making me second-guess everything I once thought I knew about my dad, about myself, and even about Braxton.

34

It's not until I've left the Spring room after wolfing down a quick lunch—partly to appease Arthur, and partly because I really was hungry—that I realize this is the perfect time to go look for Song's book.

But just as I start heading that way, a sudden burst of cheers sounds from one of the rooms. Curious, I crack open the door and peek inside, only to find they're in the middle of a construct—a detailed hologram of some fancy masquerade ball—with Mason at center stage, holding a jeweled hair comb he must've just nicked from Elodie's wig.

Seeing him like that, glowing in his success, fills me with relief. Though, that relief is soon followed by a hit of sadness over the undeniable fact that Mason is here because of me.

As though sensing me watching, Mason turns my way, but not wanting to distract from his moment, I slip out and race through the stairways and halls until I've made it outside, where I'm greeted with the rare sight of a clear and beautiful day.

But just because it's not raining doesn't mean it's not cold. So, I clutch my tote to my chest, tug my sleeves past my knuckles, and follow the winding stone path that leads me to *The Magician.*

Though the design was conceived from the brilliant mind of Niki de Saint Phalle, the way the sculptures fit so seamlessly together with *The Magician*'s silver head perched directly on top of *The High Priestess*, whose gaping, blue-tiled mouth opens to a steep flight of steps that lead straight to *The Wheel of Fortune*, feels destined, fated, and even somewhat eerie.

Like an allegory of Arthur, Elodie, and me—it all begins with Arthur, but in this scenario, it ends with me. Elodie is merely caught in the middle.

Luckily, Arthur decided against the water element found in the original Tarot Garden. Which means all I need to do is climb those steps, scale *The High Priestess*, and peer inside *The Magician*'s mouth, where, hopefully, I'll find the book.

I take a quick look around, ensuring I'm still alone. Then, leaving my bag at the foot of *The Wheel of Fortune*, I make my ascent. And just when I've managed to haul myself up the ledge of *The High Priestess*'s lip, a voice calls out, saying, "What the hell are you up to, Nat?"

I ignore her and keep climbing. Since she's already seen me, there's no point in stopping.

"Whatever you think you're looking for, you won't find it there," Elodie calls.

I glance over my shoulder and, seeing she's still wearing the costume from the construct, I say, "Your wig's crooked." I jab a thumb toward the towering black wig that's now veering to the left like the Leaning Tower of Pisa. Then heave myself up the sculpture until I'm peering into *The Magician*'s gaping mouth, only to find that Elodie's right. It's completely empty inside.

Great.

With nothing left to do and nowhere else to go, I begin the humiliating task of finding my way to the ground, painfully aware of Elodie gleefully bearing witness to my clumsy descent.

When I finally reach the bottom, I say, "Why are you following me?"

Elodie nods toward my tote, and that's when I notice the straps have fallen open, revealing the contents inside.

My slab, the perfume box, and the note with the waxy red

rose are sitting right at the top. Luckily, the pocket watch has sunk to the bottom.

"C'mon," she says, her voice laced with false cheer. Or maybe it's real cheer; it's hard to know with her. "Let's go inside where it's nice and warm, so you can tell me what you're looking for, and I can explain why you're never going to find it anywhere near that *Magician*."

The only reason I go along is because it's freezing, not because I owe her an explanation. We settle into the room just past the entry where a collection of cushy wingback chairs hangs from a white coffered ceiling. Elodie chooses the purple velvet one, and with her billowing blue dress and collection of glittering jewels, she looks like a descendant from a long line of royals.

I watch as she yanks off her wig, drops it to the floor, then frees her hair from a complicated threadwork of pins until it tumbles in soft golden waves that spiral to her waist.

Figures. I fight the urge to roll my eyes. Every time I remove a wig, I'm left with a rat's nest. Elodie, of course, is left with the sort of gleaming mermaid hair I can't even manage on a good day.

Her fingers grip the thick silver chains, and as she sets the chair swinging, she says, "Has anyone ever told you what existed in that space before the Tarot Garden was built?" She speaks in a tone that strikes me as deceptively casual.

A labyrinth, I want to say. But not wanting her to know how I know that, I just shrug.

"It was a maze." She nods, seemingly pleased to share that with me. "One that was meticulously carved from rows of tall hedges."

I tip farther back in my blue velvet chair. But unlike Elodie, I don't swing. Instead, I use the toes of my sneakers to gently rock back and forth.

"And at the center of that maze," she continues, "was a single crystal sphere."

"You act like you were here back then." I keep a close watch on her face, looking for clues, signs of deception, anything that might slip past her carefully crafted facade.

She laughs. "Arthur keeps an archive of all the changes he's made since he took ownership of the island. There's a whole section of the library devoted just to that. I'm surprised you haven't seen it, considering all the time you've been spending in there. Not to mention your newfound interest in that part of the garden."

Her gaze locks on mine, but I just continue to rock my chair back and forth like a person who has nothing to hide. But Elodie is nearly impossible to fool, and she's not fooled by me.

"You're lucky I showed up to save you," she says.

"And how exactly did you save me?" I ask, annoyed at myself for taking her bait. Still, something tells me I do need to know.

I watch as her entire face brightens. Having expertly led me to this point, now's her chance to reveal something she's convinced I don't know, and Elodie loves nothing more. "That exact area, where the crystal sphere once stood and where *The Magician* now stands—" Her gaze hardens on mine. "It's where the first time portal was discovered."

"I thought that was the light—" I start, but Elodie's already shaking her head.

"The lighthouse was the *second* portal they found."

My gaze wanders to the far side of the room as I remember how Braxton told me about the missing lighthouse keepers, and how the local authorities, left with no clues and not wanting to alarm anyone, concluded they all jumped to their deaths as the result of loneliness, the cold, and the general austerity of living alone on the rock. Never mind that none of them left a note and not a single body ever washed ashore. It's how Arthur purchased the island for so cheap. No one wanted anything to do with a place that was cursed.

The problem was, while the energy needed for Tripping was there, they had no way to control where and when you went, much less how to find your way back. So Arthur and his team set to work, determined to harness that energy so they could use it for their own gain.

"The energy was too erratic," Elodie continues. "And Arthur, not wanting to risk anyone else getting lost, decided to tear it down and had the garden built in its place."

"But wasn't that dangerous, too?" I ask. "I mean, what about the workers who constructed it, and—"

"What about them?" Elodie shrugs. "It's only on certain days that those lighthouse keepers disappeared. The conditions have to be just right. And, lucky for you, they weren't the right conditions today, or else you wouldn't be sitting here now."

I stare at Elodie. Part of me wants to believe she's just being her usual theatrical self, while the other part fears she might be telling the truth.

Still, I say, "If it's really that dangerous, then why doesn't Arthur fence it off?"

Elodie laughs. "That *is* Arthur's version of fencing it off. It's not like he expected anyone to go crawling about a piece of treasured art. I mean, seriously, Nat. It's so disrespectful." She shakes her head, clicks her tongue against the roof of her mouth. "Anyway," she goes on. "Do you remember what the artist, Niki de Saint Phalle, said about the Magician?"

"She called him the great Trickster," I say, remembering a book I once read. "The card of God, the creator of the universe, that sort of thing."

Elodie gives an excited nod. Our shared love of art was the one thing we had in common—other than our love of fashion and ditching school. "It's the card of active intelligence, pure light, pure energy, mischief, and creation." Elodie grins. "And yet, as I watched you trying to climb inside *The Magician*'s mouth, I wondered if maybe you knew, and that you wanted to disappear."

"I wasn't *climbing inside.*" I roll my eyes. "I was trying to—"

Elodie lifts a hand, cutting me off. "Whatever it is you think you're looking for, you'll never find it in there. Nothing stays inside *The Magician* for long."

And that's when it hits me—either the book was there but I missed my chance, or that note wasn't leading me to the book at all—it was leading me to the gateway that'll fling me right out of this place to God knows where.

Is that what happened to Song?

Did she know about The Magician *and so she chose to disappear?*

Or was she led there, in the same way someone tried to lead me?

When my gaze meets Elodie's, my blood runs ice-cold.

"Be careful where you wander," she says. "And who you wander with. You may not find your way back."

A look passes between us. And deciding to finally just get it out in the open, I say, "Which leaves me to wonder why you showed up to stop me."

Elodie blinks. Once. Twice. A little too rapidly, though her expression stays locked in neutral, giving nothing away.

"It would've been so easy, right?" I rock my chair forward. "No one would ever know, and they'd never think to blame you."

Elodie clings to the quiet for a painfully long beat. Finally breaking the silence, she says, "After all we've been through—and you still think the worst of me." She shakes her head as though saddened by the thought. And yeah, maybe she did save me yesterday—twice, actually. But I can't afford to forget how she framed me for a crime I didn't commit, which resulted in me getting tossed in jail and ending up here.

"Did you ever stop and think that maybe it's *because* of everything we've been through—everything *you* put me through—that it's hard for me to trust you?"

She huffs a dramatic sigh, and for a moment, the arrogant roll of her eyes reminds me of the Elodie I knew back in our old school. Or rather, *my* old school. Elodie was always more of a tourist, an interloper, some glittering star shooting through campus long enough to dazzle us commoners before blasting off to better horizons.

"While I get that you have a low opinion of me," Elodie starts, "and while there's not much I can do to change that, please know this much at least: yes, sometimes I get jealous of the attention Arthur lavishes on you. He's like a dad to me, and maybe I've enjoyed favorite-child status for too long, which has made it hard to share." Her gaze holds on mine. And while it's a heartfelt admission, it's nothing I didn't already know. "But that doesn't mean I'm actively trying to sabotage you."

"So…you're *passively* trying to sabotage me?" I shouldn't have said it. It was a childish, knee-jerk reaction. And when she shakes her head and frowns, it's not like I blame her.

"Look," she says. "You said it yourself. If I truly wanted to get rid of you, then I would've just left you on the ground yesterday. But I didn't."

But is that because you had an audience? What if it had been just us?

"And even now," she continues, "I could've easily sat back and watched you climb inside. Not that you would've gone anywhere, seeing as how the conditions weren't right, but not only did I stop you, but I rushed out of that construct because I could tell you were up to no good. And now that I've told you, my conscience is clear. So tell me, Nat, are we good? Have I managed to redeem some small part of myself?"

I want to believe her. Mainly because being able to trust

Elodie would make my life here at Gray Wolf a helluva lot easier. So I take a deep breath and say, "Thank you. For saving me yesterday."

She nods, brings her chair to a stop, and collects her wig from the floor, flopping it over her arm in a way that makes it look like she's cradling some sort of strange, faceless dog.

"You might want to take a closer look at whoever sent you out there." She runs a hand down the bodice of her dress as she stands. "Because clearly, they can't be trusted."

As she's making her way up the stairs, I call out to her. "You mentioned something about it needing to be just the right conditions."

Gripping the banister, she turns to face me.

"What did you mean?" I try to get a good read on her, but the way the chandelier reflects off her features makes it nearly impossible to catch her expression.

So, all I can do is take her at her word when she says, "It follows the cycles of the moon."

I nod, sensing there's more.

"And the conditions for disappearing are right when the moon is in its waxing phase."

I blink. Swallow. Incapable of moving, speaking, doing much of anything other than open-mouthed staring.

"The waxing phase," she repeats. "Just like it was yesterday."

35

By the time I make it back to my room, I'm so distracted by what Elodie said, it's a moment before I notice there's a freaking Leonardo da Vinci painting casually propped in the corner.

Or at least I assume it's the *Salvator Mundi*, because it's not like I check.

Because right now, it's just one big *whatever*.

Right now, all I can think about is how Freya might've directed me to *The Magician* during the waxing phase on purpose—that she might've actually set out to *make me disappear*. And the worst part is, she has access to my room during the times I'm not here.

I flip the switch next to the hearth and warm my hands before the fire, trying to think of the best way to handle her, when there's a knock at my door.

My first instinct is to ignore it. If it's Freya, I can't risk speaking to her until I've sorted it out. But then the knock sounds again, followed by: "I know you're in there." And I immediately recognized the voice as Mason's.

"Do you want to sit?" I usher him through the door and gesture nervously toward the velvet settee. It's the first time he's been in my room—the first time we've spoken since yesterday's Trip—and I'm not entirely sure where I stand with him.

Mason ignores the offer and wanders the space. Pausing

before the Salvador Dalí, he says, "*The Persistence of Memory*?" He shoots a squinty look over his shoulder, his eyes slowly taking me in. "Do I want to know what you stole to get your hands on that?"

"Probably not." I sink onto a chair and watch as he continues his inspection.

After taking a moment to study *Vanitas*, he heads back toward me. "I'm sensing a theme," he says. "Time, memories, vanities..." He nods toward the easel. "And that one?"

I shake my head. "It's not mine." Then, desperate to change the subject, I say, "I hear you did good today."

"You heard or you saw?" Mason cocks a brow.

"Both," I admit, my belly clenching when he wanders over to the easel, lifts the cloth, and flings it aside.

Other than the crackling of flames in the hearth, the room is quiet enough that I can hear his quick intake of breath when he takes in the sight of the da Vinci masterpiece.

"It's real," I tell him before he can ask. But by now, he's probably already guessed that.

"So—" He turns away from the painting and settles onto the velvet settee. "Is there a reason you didn't at least try to warn me?"

I study him for a long moment, my eyes grazing over his green Gray Wolf sweatshirt, his dark slim-cut jeans, and the colorful designer high tops he would've drooled over back home. "I didn't think you'd believe me," I say.

"Oh, I definitely wouldn't have," he agrees. "But you could've at least tried."

"I know." I sigh. "You're right. But there's a whole protocol in place, and since I'm not authorized—"

"Authorized?" Mason balks. "Since when do you give a shit about authorization? Since when has *not* being *authorized* ever stopped you from doing whatever you want?"

He makes a good point. Back at school, I pretty much broke every rule.

"According to Finn," he says, "I'm well on my way to Yellow, and I need you to explain what that means."

"Finn didn't tell you?"

"He did. Told me about the Vault, too. But that doesn't mean I don't want to hear it from you."

"It's basically the step before Blue." I shrug. "It means you've stopped fighting the system, and—"

"And have you stopped fighting the system?" he asks.

I close my eyes, and though it's only a brief respite, it does buy me some time before having to admit that I like it here. That I'm happy. That I've finally found a place where I truly belong.

"I know you may not understand it," I finally say, my gaze meeting his. "But unlike you, I have nothing to return to."

"You sure about that?"

His words give me pause. Has he really forgotten how every day was a slog, a grind, a terrible drudge with no hope in sight? And yet, the tightened lines of his mouth and the clench of his jaw seem to suggest that my own remembered experience is somehow flawed, if not outright wrong.

"Nostalgia is a fun house mirror," I say. "A distorted view of what was."

"But maybe that works both ways," he shoots back. "Maybe you're choosing to remember only the bad stuff and none of the good."

The last thing I want is to argue with him, but I'm no longer the girl he once knew. "I don't miss it," I say. "I like the life I've built here."

He takes a moment to consider, then casts another look around my room. "So, it's really that easy, then. A nice room, fancy clothes, a hot boyfriend—I mean, what more could a girl want?"

It's a low blow, and I'm sure there was a time when he knew me better than that. When he knew I couldn't be bought.

But then it hits me—maybe I always had a price and I'm the only one who couldn't see it?

I mean, in a way, isn't that what connected me to Elodie—my willingness to engage in self-sabotage in exchange for shopping sprees and hanging out at VIP clubs?

The realization hits hard, and yet, it's not as simple as that. Deep down inside, I was never that shallow. And I won't allow Mason to distort my own memory of what it was like to live my experience.

"I never wanted a cookie-cutter life," I remind him. "And Gray Wolf offers so much more than I ever could've hoped for back home." I frown, wanting him to know that if he came here to judge me, then maybe it's better if he goes. Maybe the ties that once bound us no longer hold. "Thanks to Arthur, my mom is financially secure for the first time since my dad disappeared, and—" My voice halts.

Disappeared?

Where the hell did that come from?

Usually, I think of my dad as having *left*, or as *the day he walked out on us and never returned*. I can't remember ever referring to him as *disappeared*, like he's Anjou or Song.

"You were saying?" Mason prompts.

Shaking my head, I return my focus to him. "Look, all I know is that if I ever did find a way to leave this place—not that I want to, mind you—but if I did, then all that financial support would go away, and my mom would be back to struggling again. It's the deal we agreed to. By signing those papers, my mom willingly signed me into Arthur's care. She knew exactly what she was doing, and from what I saw, she had zero regrets."

A brief image flashes into my head—my last glimpse of my mom, standing outside our house, looking the happiest I'd ever seen her as she took in the sight of her shiny new car.

To Mason, I say, "Trust me, we're all better off."

Mason regards me for a long, steady beat. "The reason I stopped by," he says, "is because I have something for you." He reaches into his pocket and pulls out a battered envelope that's creased in the middle where it's been folded in half. "I've been carrying this around in my backpack, and honestly, I don't even know why, except maybe it felt like a connection to you. But now I think you should have it."

He places the envelope on the table between us, and the second I catch sight of the writing, my entire body goes numb.

"What—" I start. "I mean, how—"

Mason nods. "I think you should read it. It's a letter from your mom."

36

I flip the letter over in my palm and trace a finger across my mom's familiar tight scrawl.

"But—it's addressed to you," I say. "It's a letter for you, not me."

Mason shrugs. "She had no way to reach you. So, I guess she decided to reach out to me."

I slip my finger under the flap and retrieve the note tucked inside.

Dear Mason— it begins, and already my hands are shaking. Already my mouth has gone dry. And still, I force my gaze down the page.

I know you probably miss her. I miss her, too.

I also know you're probably confused, wondering what might've happened to her. My hope is this letter will help ease your mind. And perhaps mine as well...

I frown. I can't read this. I'm not ready. With trembling fingers, I stuff the note back inside.

I mean, now that I've finally managed to tuck her memory away in a box, do I really want to risk unpacking all that?

Do I really want to face all those emotional triggers again?

"You don't have to read it now," Mason says. "I just wanted you to have it because—well, I think once you do read it, you'll know it was written for you all along."

I set the letter on the cushion beside me, and when I raise

my gaze to meet his, I release a soft sigh. "I'm sorry I didn't tell you," I say. "If I'd known Arthur was going to spring it on you…" I shrug, hoping he can find a way to forgive me for that, along with everything else.

"I thought you were sent to some kind of reform school," he says. "I had no idea you were living in luxury and traveling through time."

I laugh awkwardly. I've missed our friendship so much, but I also know we're on delicate ground, and I don't want to do anything to mess this up.

"So, where was your first Trip?" he asks.

"Eighteenth-century Versailles," I say. "Up until yesterday, it was the only place I'd Tripped."

"And I'm guessing that's where you got the diamond hair clip you sent me?"

I remember the drunken noblewoman I stole it from and nod. "Except I didn't send it. I still don't know who did."

Mason stares down at his hands, and we fall into a silence that's closer to companionable than fraught.

"So," he says, lifting his chin. "Arthur really is grooming me to be part of his international time-traveling theft ring."

When I nod, Mason shakes his head, a quiet whistle escaping his lips.

"We sort of liken it to *Oliver Twist*," I say. "Arthur is Fagin, and we're his artful dodgers. Or rather, Arthur's Artful Dodgers." My fingers instinctively fidget with my gold AAD ring. "But please don't let on that you know. You need to act surprised when you're initiated."

His gaze wanders my room before settling back on me. "I feel like a traitor to myself," he says. "But I have to admit—yesterday was amazing."

I grin. "Care to kiss and tell?"

He laughs, leans in, and spills all. And when it's my turn, I do the same. Minus the sword fight in the library, of course. And while I don't try to pretend that Tripping isn't dangerous, I do gloss over some of the scarier bits.

It's not until Mason's on his way out that he says, "You know he was a vegetarian, right?"

I follow his gaze to the *Salvator Mundi*. "Who—Jesus?" I joke, but Mason is serious.

"Leonardo," he says. "If you ever meet him, you should tell him about the vegan café where we used to work."

I laugh, watching as Mason takes a closer look.

"What do you think that hand gesture means?" He glances over his shoulder at me. "You know, the way his right hand is raised with the fingers slightly crossed."

I take a moment to consider. "I always assumed he was making a cross," I say. "I mean, it is a portrait of Jesus, and Leonardo was known for putting hands into motion—pointing, grasping. Like his painting *Saint John the Baptist*, or even *The Last Supper*, where pretty much everyone's hands are reacting. I'm not sure it means much of anything."

"Maybe," Mason says, though the slant of his brow and set of his jaw tell me he's far from convinced. "But Leonardo always created with intention. I'm not sure you should make assumptions about any of his works."

"What are you saying?" I ask, aware of the hair starting to rise on the back of my neck.

"Well, maybe he's making the sign of the cross, or even making a gesture of fingers crossed for good luck. But that gesture is also used when someone is lying, no?"

I'm frozen, my breath stalled in my lungs.

"You know, like, crossing your fingers behind your back when you lie."

I glance between Mason and the painting. "But isn't that more of a modern-day theater or TV trope?"

Mason shrugs. "You don't think they had theater back then? And what better way to send a message than to create a portrait that carries a double meaning? Don't forget, Leonardo was as much of a storyteller as he was an artist and engineer. Anyway, just a thought."

As I stand at my door, watching him leave, I can't help but wonder if maybe there's more to his being here than I originally thought. If Arthur was somehow aware of his talent for peering past the surface of things.

Is it possible Mason is the one they were originally after?

I remember the way Elodie approached him first. How she walked right up to him and complimented him on his look. But Mason wanted nothing to do with her, so she shifted her focus to me. And I was so flattered to be noticed by someone like her that I ignored every flashing red light, every alarm bell going off in my head.

All this time, were they just using me to get to him?

But no, that's impossible. Arthur has tasked me with restoring the Antikythera.

After closing the door, I return to the painting. If Mason's right about the crossed fingers, then does that mean there's more to the crystal sphere beyond it being a symbol for the Moon?

It's well known that Leonardo was deeply curious and sharply observant—that nothing he created was by accident. Which means those three white dots he added to the crystal—the very markings that most scholars view as Leonardo's effort to portray how a real crystal might look—might be something else entirely.

Because despite that bit of accuracy, the view through the crystal shows none of the distortion one might expect.

Since Christ's robe isn't touching the orb, the view through the sphere should be magnified or even reversed.

But it's not. It's perfectly clear, as though that crystal was nothing more than a thin sheet of glass.

But why?

Why did Leonardo choose to include the occlusions only to portray the view through the crystal in such an unnatural way?

Is it some sort of spiritual message—that nothing could distort the perfection of Christ?

Or was it intended as a nod toward the location of the Moon?

And then I remember the reversed symbol on Arthur's map—the sideways crown and the upside-down hourglass—illustrations that were added a century after Leonardo painted this.

They're connected. I know it all the way down to my bones.

Problem is, I have no idea what it might mean.

But there's no doubt that, thanks to Mason, I'm now able to see this painting in a whole new way.

37

The next two days race by in a blur of classes, library cram sessions, a final session with Dr. Lucy, and what feels like endless fittings for the clothes I'll bring to Renaissance Italy. And with Braxton's schedule being equally busy, we've barely had a chance to catch up.

So by the time I get to Halcyon, Gray Wolf's version of a speakeasy, wearing a roaring twenties–style dress for Elodie's party, Braxton's the last person I'm expecting to see.

"What are you doing here?" I ask, my heart kicking up a few beats as I watch him cross the room to meet me.

"I missed you," he says. "So I arranged for some alone time, before everyone arrives."

I squint in confusion. "But Elodie texted. She asked me to get here early, so..."

"I wanted to surprise you," he says. And when he grins, I can't help but feel a twinge of discomfort. I mean, while it was nice of Elodie to help Braxton arrange this, the idea of them plotting together makes me feel weird. Especially considering their history. Not to mention my own complicated history with her.

"You make an amazing flapper," he says, giving me an appreciative once-over.

"And you make a really great Gatsby." I gesture toward his white flannel suit. "Maybe we can visit the roaring twenties together someday?" I smile at the thought.

"At the moment," Braxton says, "I'm far more interested in this timeline, in this"—he makes a wide sweep of his arm—"very odd space."

It's a fever dream of a room. Decorated with strange and random objects Trippers have brought back from various times. There's a death mask said to be cast from the face of Dante Alighieri, a battle-torn Viking shield, and of course, the creepy jewel-encrusted skeleton in the glass case that, according to Elodie, is one of Braxton's more illustrious finds.

I jab a thumb toward the piece. "Rumor has it that's one of your donations."

Braxton laughs. "Why would you ever believe such a thing?"

"Maybe it's your taste for the macabre, or at least when it comes to art."

"Only when it comes to art." He hooks my arm in his and leads me toward the dance floor that, with a brisk wave of his hand, transforms into a blanket of fluffy white hologram clouds as the ceiling glimmers and glows like the sun.

"I can't remember the last time I felt the warmth of the sun," I say, but then I do. It was just after Braxton bailed me out of jail. I was standing on the sidewalk, feeling warm, free, and completely ignorant of everything soon to come.

Being from California, it's weird how I don't miss the sun nearly as much as I would've thought. But what's even weirder is how easily I've let go of pretty much everything else.

The music swells through the room, pulling me away from my thoughts as Braxton circles an arm at my waist. "Do you recognize it?" His eyes fix on mine as the two of us swirl through a hologram sky.

"It's an old one," I say, knowing he's referring to the song, a beautiful string-quartet version of "Brighter than Sunshine."

"I'm just surprised you know it, considering how it's from the new millennium and all."

Braxton laughs. "I'm not all Mozart all the time, you know."

As we continue to dance, I hear the song's lyrics play in my head, and when it reaches the part about history and destiny, I get why Braxton chose it. It seems so specifically about us, I know without a doubt that, from this moment on, I'll never listen to it the same way again.

Tipping his lips to my ear, Braxton says, "The moment I first saw you, it was like a switch had been flipped. Suddenly all the darkness that engulfed me—a darkness so familiar I no longer noticed it—was illuminated by a light so warm and bright, I knew right then it was you I'd been seeking all along."

My heart swells as I take in his beautiful face. The hard angles of his jaw, the finely sculpted cheekbones, that irresistible bend in his nose, the lock of wavy brown hair that spills into those deep, ocean-blue eyes that sear into mine.

He lifts a hand to my cheek and touches me so tenderly it's all I can do to breathe.

"Tasha, I—"

No.

Absolutely not.

I'm not ready—I'm not—

A wave of panic rolls through me. I have to stop him—stop him from speaking those three life-changing words.

Before he can finish, I lift my heels and kiss him into silence.

Kiss him until his arms tighten around me, drawing me closer.

Kiss him until he's forgotten his words and I can no longer recall why I ever doubted this wonderful, sexy, magical boy.

And it's during this kiss that I make a silent promise to us both.

As soon as we're in Italy, away from Arthur's watch, I will tell him everything, and he'll do the same, until we are cleansed, free of our lies, with no more secrets between us.

Maybe then I'll let him finish that thought.

Maybe then I'll be ready to say it right back.

38

Not long after the song ends, everyone starts spilling through the door. And with a quick wave of his hand, the hologram disappears, and Braxton presses a kiss to my cheek. "To be continued." He winks. "Elodie's put me on bar duty."

He slips behind the green marble-topped bar and starts popping champagne corks and filling drink orders, as I move through the crowd, checking out the variety of costumes everyone's chosen to wear.

Keane has gone with a 1970s roller-disco theme, wearing a pair of surprisingly short track shorts, a tight T-shirt, striped knee socks, and a pair of glittery sky-blue roller skates that, going by the way he glides through the space, he really knows how to work.

Hawke looks like he's arrived straight off a three-day bender at Woodstock. His beat-up suede jacket hangs open to reveal a pile of beaded necklaces that fall halfway down his bare chest. The hems of his faded denim bell-bottoms are crusted with mud, which strikes me as a nicely authentic touch. Beside him stands Roxanne, and with her early 1960s Jackie Kennedy pastel suit and pillbox hat, they're like a visual nod to opposite ends of a turbulent decade.

Finn and Oliver are wearing togas, with gold headbands and gladiator sandals that wrap around their legs, all the way to their knees.

Jago and Elodie also match, going with a couple's theme of Antony and Cleopatra.

But Mason's costume outshines them all. With his long curly wig, lacy cravat, and elaborate purple tailcoat and matching breeches, he's clearly channeling Louis XIV's brother, Philippe I, the Duke of Orléans, who was known for his colorful, outlandish attire. And as he saunters into the room with his head held imperiously high, it's obvious he's enjoying this part that he plays.

I'm just about to approach him when Elodie pulls me aside. "I decided to switch things up. Do something different from my usual room parties," she says, her voice forced to compete with the sudden burst of applause when Keane takes to the dance floor and shows off some serious roller-disco moves.

I glance around the crowded space. "Looks like it's working." I motion toward Keane, who's convinced Roxanne to join him, and the sight of her dancing to a seventies disco song is so funny that Elodie and I can't help but laugh.

"You know me." She grins. "I can never resist a chance to play dress-up." She holds my gaze. "Also, I thought you and Braxton deserved a proper send-off."

Something about that gives me pause. "You do know we're coming right back? It's not like we're *moving* to Renaissance Italy," I say. Then, as an afterthought, I add, "Unless you know something I don't?"

"Don't be ridiculous." She waves it away. "It's just that it's been a while since a Blue set out on a Trip that lasted more than a few hours."

Except for the Blues who never returned.

"Anyway." Elodie gestures toward my dress. "I like the look."

"And I like yours." I take in her filmy blue dress with gold trim that rolls over her body like oil on water. "It suits you," I say. "You definitely have a certain Cleopatra quality."

"So I'm a legendary seductress?" She quirks a brow.

"Definitely." I laugh. "But, more importantly, you're resourceful, astute, and one step ahead of everyone else."

Elodie pats her black wig, looking equally surprised and pleased by my words. "It was Jago's idea. I think he wanted to go as Mark Antony just so he could show off his legs." She rolls her eyes, but in a playful way.

I watch as her fingers creep toward the gold snake medallion she's taken to wearing. And I'm reminded of how Song warned me about Elodie, that I should treat her like any venomous snake—*try not to agitate her and do what you can to stay out of her way*.

Is there a connection between Elodie's pendant, Song's warning, and the serpent perfume bottle I found in my room?

In the Tarot Garden, both the one in Tuscany and the one at Gray Wolf, the steps leading from *The Wheel of Fortune* to *The High Priestess* are flanked by a snake. *Is there hidden meaning there, too?*

I shake the thought away and return my focus to Elodie.

"I mean, Jago's cute, right?" She casts a glance to the other side of the room, where he's talking with Hawke. "Oh, who am I kidding? He's hot as hell." She laughs. "And don't get me started on that accent." She adopts a swooning pose and makes a dramatic fanning motion with her hand. "But honestly, he's so much more than that. He's super smart, too. Which is good because it keeps me in check. There's no getting anything over on him."

I study her. "Sounds like a love match."

Elodie smirks. "Let's just say, it's good for right here and right now. If anything, my heart belongs to the nineteenth century."

"To the nineteenth century or to Nash?" I ask, curious as to just how serious she is about him.

Elodie hesitates as though weighing just how forthright she can be. Then, with a slight lifting of her shoulders, she says, "Honestly, I'm not sure I believe in one love, or one true love, or twin flames, or whatever. I'm mostly convinced those fluttery feelings are nothing more than amped-up hormones and lust. I mean, Jago's fun, and Nash is, too. I just don't see why I should have to choose when I can have the best of both worlds."

I smile. Mostly because it seems like it's what I'm supposed to do.

"And what about you?" Elodie says. "Do you honestly believe in all that fairy-tale, soulmate stuff?"

My gaze instinctively searches for Braxton. When I find him by the bar, deep in conversation with Oliver and Finn, I turn to Elodie and say, "It's nice to think that it's possible."

Elodie studies me closely. "Well, belief *is* half the battle," she says. Then, her voice gone suddenly serious, she adds, "Anyway, a word of advice?"

I hesitate. If this is about my relationship with Braxton, I'm pretty sure I don't want to hear it. I'm still dealing with the fact that the two of them were once a couple.

"Honestly," I tell her, "I'm not sure."

I expect her to laugh or at the very least crack a grin. But instead, she leans closer and says, "If you're going to delve into magick, you need to be sure of one thing—"

"Wait—magick?" I balk. This conversation has taken a detour I wasn't expecting.

Elodie shoots me an impatient look. "Are you seriously going to pretend you're surprised?"

Her gaze locks on mine as my mind spins back to Arthur's office, when he told me about how the Timekeepers want to guard the secret of the true nature of our reality—the real power that exists within all of us but has so far been accessed by only a few.

Was Arthur talking about a kind of magick then, too?

"To be clear," Elodie says, "I'm talking magick with a *K*. Not the stage magic of rabbits being pulled out of hats. But rather *real* magick. The magick of the natural world—the invisible force that exists all around us. A force we encounter and interact with every day whether we know it or not. A force that exists independently of our acknowledgment. The sort of magick that blurs the line between fantasy and science. I'm sure you're familiar with manifesting?"

This is getting weird. Still, I just look at her and say, "The idea that our thoughts create our reality?"

Elodie nods. "Some would consider that a type of magick. Alchemy, too, for that matter."

So, Arthur really is the Magician—using his vision and his knowledge of alchemy to fulfill his dream of changing the world.

"And this naturally occurring portal that allows us to time travel—you don't think that's a sort of magick as well?" Elodie says.

I nod, wanting to tell her what Song said about magick being the currency of the oppressed, but Elodie starts talking again.

"Everything you perceive as solid matter is really just vibrating energy. And those who are attuned can manipulate that energy and bend it to their will."

Kind of like how I can read the energy of objects by using psychometry.

"Magick is the most natural thing in the world." Elodie drags the snake medallion across its gold chain. "You engage with it every day with the thoughts you generate. The only real difference between you and a true sorcerer is intent."

She pauses to make sure I'm listening, but it's totally unnecessary. I'm glomming on to every last word.

"When it comes to magick, your intention is everything. More than crystals, rituals, and whatever spells you might find in a book—while they do hold a certain energy—it's your intent that serves as the fuel. So, until you're crystal clear on exactly what your intention is, it's best to stay away from all that. Otherwise, you risk falling victim to one whose intentions are far stronger than yours."

There's an uneasy twinge in my belly as I absorb the deeper meaning of her words. "Why do I feel like you're trying to tell me something while at the same time avoiding what you actually mean to say?"

Elodie's kohl-rimmed eyes lock onto mine. "It's all right there, Natasha. No riddles, no subterfuge. As your friend, I just thought I should warn you."

"Am I right to think you're speaking from personal experience?" There's a tremor in my voice, and I'm hoping she won't notice. But who am I kidding? Nothing ever slips past her.

Her fingers pick at the thick gold bangle she wears just north of her elbow. "Do you know how they cultivate a rose?" Her gaze locks on mine. "It's an acquired skill that takes lots of practice. Ideally, you'd start in early spring and begin at the base, cutting away all that's died over the winter. You even cut away some of the tender new bits, which only seems cruel until you understand that the point is to shape the rose, to train it to stop growing inward toward its base and to grow outward instead. The rose is a powerful symbol of so many things. The original wild rose has five petals, which some relate to a pentagram or five-pointed star. It's also a symbol for both life and death."

"I have no idea where you're going with this."

"I know," she says. "Which is why I'm telling you. You wouldn't be the first at Gray Wolf to chase after the magick of the rose, but I'm hoping you won't end up like the last."

My stomach churns. My pulse pounds so hard, it makes my ears throb. "Elodie—do you know something about what happened to Song, or even Anjou?" I ask.

Elodie just looks at me, not blinking, not flinching—just a steady, blunt gaze.

"And…do you happen to know something about Freya?"

"What I know is this: be careful who you choose to align yourself with. And if I were you, I'd tread a little more carefully than you have so far."

"You're freaking me out," I say. "But then, I get the feeling that's *your* intent."

"Maybe." She shrugs. "But feel free to add this to the number of times I've gone out of my way to help you in just a handful of days."

Her words take me aback. "Sounds like you're keeping score." I study her face.

"Look, I get that I have a lot to make up for. But while I'm willing to do what it takes to get you to change your mind about me, I can't do it alone. In order for a peace treaty to work, there needs to be compromise. It can't be one-sided."

I'm about to reply when her gaze flits away from mine, landing in the vicinity of the doors that lead into the club. "I wonder who invited him?" she says. "Because it certainly wasn't me."

I follow her gaze to find Killian has just entered the room—and he's heading straight for me.

39

Long before Killian can reach me, Elodie is gone.

"I have a theory," he says, his gaze trailing after her. "That girl is secretly in love with me, and the fact that it's unrequited brings her so much pain she can't bear to be around me."

"Another astonishing display of deeply penetrating insight." I laugh.

Killian takes a bow, and when he rises, his swimming-pool eyes fix right on mine.

"So, is this your costume?" I gesture toward his loose-fitting white linen shirt, faded jeans with a hole in the left knee, and black velvet slip-ons with skulls and crossbones embroidered on the toes. "Louche playboy enjoying cocktails on the French Riviera?"

Killian balks. "Is that how you see me—as some disreputable, indolent, ne'er-do-well dilettante?" He clutches dramatically at his heart. "That hurts, Shiv. Truly. Thing is, I saw no need for a costume when my preferred timeline is standing right here, right now, next to you."

"You need to stop," I tell him, my cheeks growing heated. "You know I have a boyfriend, and still you insist."

"What—I'm not allowed to tell you how much I enjoy being around you? That you're the only one I like talking to in this whole bloody place?"

I roll my eyes. "Please," I say. "Save it for Maisie."

Killian laughs and takes a quick look around. "Is your boy here?" he asks.

I glance to where Braxton is still talking with Oliver and Finn—except now, they're all looking our way.

Great.

Killian follows my gaze, then turns back to me. "Well, I guess that rules out a dance. Which is a shame because this happens to be one of my favorite songs."

I cock an ear, trying to determine the score that's playing in the background. "The Halcyon club remix of Beethoven's Symphony No. 3 is one of your favorites?"

Killian nods. "Turns out, I'm not quite the philistine you pegged me for. Though I do like surprising you. That look you get on your face when—"

I lift a hand to stop him. "Can you just—"

"What?" He squints. "You don't want me to point out how the dimple in your right cheek—"

"Is this really why you're here?" I cut in. "To study my varied expressions?"

"Well, it's definitely one of the reasons." He gives a playful wiggle of his brow. "But you're right. We shouldn't flaunt this vibe that's happening between us."

It just never stops with this guy.

"You know, the vibe where you pretend not to notice how I'm like a thousand times more fun than your gloomy boy Braxton. And, I don't want to brag, but there are those who might also point out that I'm actually better-looking as well. Though that bang in his nose does make for a certain bad-boy effect, and—"

"That's it. I'm out." I turn on my heel and start to walk away, only to have Killian call after me.

"Shiv—*please*," he says, and even though I know better, something about the way he says *please* has me turning back toward him.

"Killian, what?" I say. "What do you want? Just spit it out already, and make it quick, because I am literally timing you and the clock is not in your favor."

I watch as his face transforms from the arrogant tease I know him to be to this earnestly sincere new version I'm not sure is real. "I just wanted to say goodbye." His voice is quiet, his gaze so heated, I go out of my way to avoid it.

"Are you going somewhere?" I try to keep my voice steady, as though I don't really care either way.

Killian rakes a hand through his golden tumble of curls and shoots a look around the room. Returning to me, he says, "No. But you are. And though I know you don't need my protection, I can't help worrying about you, and…" His voice trails off, and I stare down at my shoes, pretty sure I know what comes next. "I just need to know you're okay. Or at least in a good place—a good headspace."

"Dr. Lucy gave me the all-clear," I tell him, lifting my chin in a way that I hope makes me appear more confident than I currently feel.

"Well, that's great." He rubs his lips together, takes another swipe through his hair, confirming what I've already guessed—those two moves done in succession are Killian's tell.

"*But…*" I say, sensing there's more.

"Let's not forget, Dr. Lucy is on Arthur's payroll."

"Meaning?"

"Look—I'm sure she knows her stuff, but I'm less interested in what she has to say and more interested in how *you* feel about going away."

Again, with that burning gaze.

Again, I stare down at my shoes.

"So—you okay, Shiv? Are you ready to kick some Renaissance ass?"

"Actually—" I lift my gaze to meet his. "I was hoping it wouldn't come to that."

He takes a beat to consider. "Good," he finally says. "A much better, healthier approach."

I take a deep inhale, cast a glance across the room, only to see Braxton making his way toward us.

"Look—" I turn to Killian. "I appreciate your concern, but—" I give a subtle nod toward Braxton. "I think it's best if you go."

Killian shoots a look past my shoulder; then, grasping hold of my hand, he slips something small and cool into my palm. "Not a talisman," he whispers. "You already have one. Consider this a reminder. A sort of good-luck charm, if you will."

I sneak a glance over my shoulder, expecting to find Braxton looming behind, only to see Hawke has stepped in. And as the two of them get to talking, I straighten my fingers and take a quick peek.

It's a small shiv, carved from black stone and made to resemble the one I used to defend myself back in that cell in Versailles. When my gaze meets Killian's, those blue eyes of his are so unfathomably deep, I force myself to look away, unwilling to see the unspoken message he's trying to send me.

"It's made of onyx," he says, his voice thick with some unnamed emotion. "A stone of protection and strength. It helps you to keep your own counsel and master your own destiny. It's said it holds memories, too."

I trace a finger over the lines that delineate the three separate pieces of metal used to craft the weapon. The level of detail that went into this is impressive.

"Did—did you make this?" I ask, my voice tight.

Killian nods. "You didn't take me for the creative type?"

"Nor the magickal rock type." I shrug.

"I'm betting you carry a lot of misconceptions when it comes to me." His gaze bores deeper. "Maybe someday I'll have a chance to prove them all wrong. Or at least the bad ones."

I shoot a covert look across the room. Braxton is still talking to Hawke, but it looks like they're close to wrapping up.

Sensing my unease, Killian speaks quickly. "Put it in your pocket or the bottom of your shoe. Or, if it makes you feel bad, leave it behind. I just know that whenever I Trip, I like to keep a reminder of the one time it went terribly sideways."

The one time. And by that you mean the *time—the one where you claim Braxton left you behind.*

"Why would you carry a reminder of a bad Trip?" I ask, and though I know I shouldn't do this—if anything, I should be encouraging him to move on—I truly am curious.

Killian leans closer. So close I can feel his breath on my cheek. "Because I can't afford to forget," he says.

A rush of chills sprints down my spine. It's the exact same thing Braxton said about keeping the boots.

"You all right, Shiv?" Killian draws away. "You've gone a wee bit pale." He's back to his fake accent again. But I know he's only trying to lighten the mood.

"I guess I'm just surprised by all the talismans, good-luck charms, and superstitions that go along with Tripping," I say, my voice wavering in a telling way.

"Venturing into the unknown has always been daunting," he says. "And many of those superstitions have been carried through time. For instance, you should never sail on a boat with no name—you've heard that one, right? And throwing a coin into the Trevi Fountain in Rome ensures you'll return. And, if ye find yerself in Ireland, lass, you best be kissin' the Blarney Stone to ensure yerself some good fortune and luck."

"Thank you," I say. "For the charm and…" My gaze wanders toward Braxton, who's now just a few feet away. "You should go."

Killian doesn't check to see what we both already know. That in a handful of steps, Braxton will join us.

"For the record," he says, "I would hug you goodbye, but I didn't much like the feel of Braxton's fist on my jaw the last time around, so I see no point in courting that now."

I shoot him a questioning look. *What the heck is he even talking about?*

But Killian just shakes his head. "Godspeed, Shiv," he says, managing to slip away just seconds before Braxton reaches my side.

40

"Everything okay?" Braxton slips an arm around my waist and presses a kiss somewhere north of my ear.

"Of course," I say. "Why wouldn't it be?" Then, realizing how defensive that sounded, I soften my tone. "He was just wishing me good luck on our Trip."

Braxton's mouth flattens like he doesn't believe it. But who he doesn't believe is the question—is it Killian or me?

"Don't forget he was there when the last Trip went bad," I say. "And if it wasn't for him—" I stop, deciding to end it right there. No point in going over it again.

"But you were cleared by Dr. Lucy, right?" Braxton studies my face.

I nod, but when my gaze meets his, it's Killian's voice that sounds in my head.

Killian put more trust in me than the doctor. But Braxton clearly doesn't.

I'm about to call him out on it when the music stops and Elodie takes to the stage.

"Hey, everyone!" She gives a little wave. "Just a quick thanks for showing up and putting some serious effort into your outfits—and I'm looking at you, Keane!" Everyone laughs. "Since Braxton and Natasha have an early morning tomorrow, I'll make this quick. You two"—she points our way—"buon viaggio! And Mason..." She squints around the room until she locates him. “Congrats on making Yellow!” The room erupts into cheers and applause. “And also, Mason, just so you know, you got off way easy this time, and you can thank your friend Natasha for that. She absolutely forbade me from putting you through the usual hazing. So, if you’re still grudging hard against her, you might reconsider.” From across the room, Mason shoots me a look. I shrug in return. “Oh, and one more thing.” Elodie pins her focus on me. “Not that I’m keeping score, but Nat, feel free to count that as number five. And with that— ” She lifts her champagne flute and drains what little is left. “I bid you good night!”

As Elodie leaves with Jago by her side, Braxton turns to me. “Number five?” he asks.

“The number of times she’s done a good deed on my behalf.” I shrug. “She’s determined to prove herself, and she wants me to notice.”

All around us, I watch as some people leave while others make for the dance floor.

“Should we head out?” Braxton asks.

I shake my head. “I’m going to hang back a bit,” I tell him, noting the way his eyes widen with surprise. *But is it only surprise? Or is there a shade of suspicion as well?* “I have something for Mason,” I add.

Braxton hesitates. Then, leaning toward me, he plants a soft kiss on my cheek. With his lips lingering next to my ear, he whispers, “Just think—tomorrow night, we’ll be in Venice.”

The moment he says it, everything inside me that felt rigid and tight instantly melts. Like I’ve finally rid myself of all the doubt that Killian managed to raise.

Why is it so easy for him to get in my head, when Braxton’s the only one I truly want to be with?

In Venice, we’ll finally be free of Elodie, Killian, and all the cloaked secrets concealed in these walls. To Braxton, I say, “I truly can't wait." And I hope he can see the truth of it—know in his heart that I mean every word.

Then I thread my arms around his neck and kiss him until his is the only face, the only body, the only voice that exists outside of my own.

After parting with the promise of meeting up on the launchpad tomorrow, I watch him go, and I can't help but grin in anticipation of all the good things to come.

41

By the time Mason, Oliver, Finn, and I are heading back to our rooms, Mason takes my arm in his and says, "What was that about you saving me from hazing?"

I shoot a quick glance at Oliver and Finn, noting how deeply uncomfortable they look. Probably because they remember the role they played in my own brutal initiation.

"It's nothing," I say. Seeing no point in reliving it, I continue down the hall.

But Oliver won't let it go. "Not so," he says. "What she did on your behalf *is* a big deal."

"Natasha is the only one to ever stand up to Elodie," Finn adds.

Mason frowns. "That girl is toxic. And the only reason she gets away with it is because you all let her. An autocrat is only as strong as the people who support them."

"Maybe so," Oliver says. "But it's not quite as simple as you make it sound."

"You sure about that?" Mason asks. "I mean, why is everyone so afraid of her? What can she possibly do to you?"

"She's been here the longest," Finn says. "She has access to all sorts of things, and…" His voice fades as though he fears even talking about it.

"Sometimes it's just easier to go along than risk facing her wrath," Oliver adds.

"Look," Finn says. "For as long as I've been here, Elodie's been Arthur's favorite."

"True." Oliver's quick to confirm. "Though I'm not sure that's still the case anymore."

They all turn to me.

"What?" I stare back at them. "You think I'm the new favorite?"

"Sure seems that way," Finn says.

"I'm pretty sure Arthur is Arthur's favorite," I tell him. "Also, why not start calling Elodie on her bullshit? What's the worst that can happen?"

Oliver and Finn exchange a guarded look.

"Apparently, you've forgotten what happened to Song," Finn says, only to be shushed by Oliver.

But now that he's opened that door, I insist on kicking it all the way down. The fact that they don't want to talk about it only confirms there's more to Song's absence than anyone's willing to let on.

"What exactly *did* happen to Song?" I ask. "Because it seems like you know a lot more than you claim."

"Who's Song?" Mason glances between us, prompting Oliver to shoot a quick look over his shoulder, afraid of being overheard, while Finn jumps in to explain.

"She used to live here," Finn says as he picks up the pace, as though trying to outrun this conversation.

"Used to?" Mason looks from Finn to me, his face a mask of confusion.

"But then she…left," Oliver says, his voice merely a whisper.

"Left. Sure," Finn says under his breath, which pretty much proves he knows something—or at least suspects something.

"But I thought—" Mason starts, only to have Oliver cut in.

"Look," he says. "All we know for sure is that one day she was here, and the next—" He makes a rolling gesture with his hand. "And now, all we're left with are theories."

"And what exactly are those theories?" I ask, but neither of them acknowledges my question.

We walk in silence for a while before finally stopping in front of their door, which is right across from my own. And I know if I have any hope of getting the truth, I need to act now.

"Look," I say. "I know you don't like to talk about it, but do you actually think Elodie's responsible for what happened to Song?"

"Not...directly," Finn says. "I can't say that."

"Then what are you saying?" I ask. "Because last we spoke of it, you guys were sure Song never made it back from her Trip."

"Excuse me?" Mason's eyes go wide, and while I realize this is probably not the best conversation to be having in front of someone who's still new at all this, it's not like he didn't witness what nearly became of me in Regency England. "Does that actually happen?"

"It absolutely happens," Oliver says. "Not everyone is lucky enough to get rescued."

I'm not sure if Oliver was referring to me, Killian, or all the other nameless people I don't even know about. But when he turns toward the door, I know I need to get whatever answers I can while I still can.

I have so many questions—about the note, the bottle of perfume, the small leather-bound book—but before I can so much as open my mouth, Oliver says, "Look, here's what we know for sure: Song missed Anjou. And because of it, she no longer wanted to be here at Gray Wolf, so she made a choice to go. Whether she purposely got lost in time or found some other way, I can't say for sure. But she's gone now, and I seriously doubt we'll ever see her again."

"But Killian returned," Mason says.

"Only because Natasha dragged him back," Finn says. "Or

so the story goes." The way Finn slides a gaze over me makes me think he doesn't quite believe the story I told.

Which, I have to admit, is pretty perceptive, considering how I hardly dragged Killian anywhere. He was all too willing to make his return.

"*Any*way," Oliver says, in the way of a person who's desperate to end a conversation. "It's late, everyone's tired, and this isn't exactly the best place to talk about this. So, Natasha, good luck tomorrow." He leans in with a hug.

"Yes," Finn says. "Safe Tripping." When he joins the hug, I catch a whiff of something familiar, but a moment later, they're gone, leaving Mason and me standing alone in the hall.

Knowing how on edge Mason must be after hearing all that, I give a nod toward his outfit and say, "I really hope Arthur sends you to the court of Louis XIV someday."

Mason gazes down at himself, tugs on his ruffled shirtsleeves, and grins. "He'd be a fool not to, right?" Then his eyes meet mine, and he says, "So, your friend Song—what do you think really happened to her?"

I sigh. "No idea. But I hope to find out."

His eyes meet mine, and I wish I had more time to share some of my thoughts, if for no other reason than Mason's probably the only one here with an unbiased perspective.

But the truth is, I'm exhausted. So, I get right to the point and say, "I have something for you." I reach into my bag and hand him a small velvet pouch.

Mason loosens the drawstring, slips a finger inside, and, finding the golden ring, he holds it up before him.

"It's a talisman," I say. "For when you Trip. It's a sort of insurance against getting lost in a Fade, which is when you forget your own identity and what timeline you belong in. Not that you seemed to have a problem with that, but…" I'm rambling. I need to get to the point. "Anyway, do you remember?" I ask, my voice betraying my nervousness.

"How could I forget?" His face lights up at the memory of the time the two of us spent a rainy afternoon watching *Breakfast at Tiffany's* on repeat, before we decided to head out to the nearest dollar store and recreate a scene from the movie. "I wore the Marilyn Monroe mask."

"And mine was a masquerade one." I nod, my eyes pricking with tears.

"You stole a glittering tiara for me, and I gave you—" He holds up the crown-shaped ring I had made using the gold from the ring I'd stolen from the duke who attacked me.

Taking something horrible and turning it into something beautiful, meaningful—it's the perfect symbol for the sort of alchemy I've learned at this school.

"The only difference is mine was pink," I remind him.

"And made of plastic," Mason says.

"Do you like it?" I watch as he slides it onto his finger—it's a perfect fit, just as I'd hoped. "I would've given you a tiara, but a talisman needs to be a little more discreet."

Mason glances between the ring and me. "It's perfect. I'll wear it every day."

"The important thing is that you bring it with you when you Trip."

"Yes, Mom." Mason laughs.

I grin in return, but it's quick to fade. As excited as I am to be heading off to Italy, it's shadowed by the truth that every Trip carries its own inherent risk—every goodbye here at Gray Wolf could well be the last.

"I know this isn't the life you chose." My gaze locks on his. "And if there was any way I could get you back home, I would. But I just wanted you to know that you're still my best friend. For me, that was never in question."

Mason pauses, and honestly, I'm not sure what to expect.

But when he leans in and hugs me, for a handful of seconds, it feels like all is forgiven.

"Arrivederci," he whispers into my ear.

"Buona notte," I whisper back, erasing the tears from my cheek.

It's not until I'm inside my room that I realize I should probably find a place to stash the perfume, the note, and the gold pocket watch while I'm gone.

Not that there's a good hiding place, because if someone is determined to find it, they will. Still, there's no point leaving it out in the open. I can at least make them work for it.

So, after slipping the note inside a pair of boots, I hide the perfume and the pocket watch on top of the canopy of fabric that hangs over my bed, positioning it close to the post so that the dip in the fabric is kept to a minimum.

It's not until I'm washing my face and getting ready for bed that I notice the lingering scent of perfume still on my fingers.

And that's when I realize it's the exact same scent I smelled on Finn.

42

Surprisingly, I must've slept well, because it's not until I hear the incoming chime of Mozart's "Turkish March" that I finally rouse myself from bed.

I thought for sure I'd spend the bulk of the night tossing and turning with the usual nerves that come before any Trip. Never mind all the nagging worries about Finn's possible connection to the Niki de Saint Phalle perfume.

But when my slab chimes with the inspirational quote of the day, I know that particular mystery, and all the others as well, will have to hold until my return.

I reach toward my nightstand and squint at my slab.

> Accept the things to which fate binds you, and
> love the people with whom fate brings you together,
> but do so with all your heart. – Marcus Aurelius

Wise words from Arthur's favorite Roman emperor.

A moment later, there's a knock at my door. Knowing my breakfast is being delivered, as per usual on Trip days, I rush to open it, only to find Freya standing there, coppery curls twisted into a bun, her uniform freshly starched and pressed. She holds a silver tray in her hands.

My stomach drops. She's pretty much the last person I want to see.

"What're you doing?" I ask.

She nods toward the tray. "I was told to bring you your breakfast."

"By whom?" I squint past her shoulder into the empty hall, and then back at her.

"Sorry?" she says, the words slightly strangled. She looks as confused as she does hurt.

"Normally, it's a boy who delivers my tray on Trip days." My voice is scratchy but indignant all the same. And though I inwardly cringe at myself, it's not enough to keep my gaze from dragging over her face, noting the way her brow furrows, her mouth flatlines, as my mind reels with questions I can't bring myself to voice.

Did you leave the perfume and note in my room?

And if so, were you actually trying to make me disappear?

To Freya, I say, "Did something happen to him—the boy? I mean, why did they send you in his place?" I squint past her shoulder again, only to find the hall is still empty.

Is that a good thing? Or a bad thing?

I mean, if there's no one around to witness…

"Natasha—" Freya cuts into my thoughts. "Are you okay?"

My attention snaps back to her face. Her complexion is whiter than usual, her eyes rimmed red with fatigue, and I'm overcome with shame for having acted like this.

This place is making me paranoid—making me turn everyone into a suspect.

"I'm sorry." I scrub a hand through my tangle of hair. "I guess I'm just—" Frustrated, I shake my head and reach for the tray, hoping to unburden her, but Freya holds firm.

"Truly," she says. "Are you okay?" She grips the tray with such force, her knuckles go white.

My gaze lands on hers, and though I'm far from dropping my suspicions, I also know I haven't a shred of evidence to support them.

In fact, it's entirely possible she didn't leave the perfume. And if she did, it's entirely possible someone put her up to it, and she was just following orders.

Besides, hasn't this girl been through enough? According to Killian, she was nearly put to death after being falsely accused of being a witch.

Only Killian didn't say she was *falsely* accused, did he?

He only mentioned saving her from the swimming test.

When I look at Freya again, I've never wanted to get to Renaissance Italy more than I do in this moment.

Life here at Gray Wolf is starting to feel far more perilous than any Trip to the past ever could.

"Sorry," I repeat, and this time when I reach for the tray, Freya allows me to take it. And honestly, my stomach is such a jumble of nerves, I'm pretty sure I won't be able to eat any of it. "I'm just nervous," I say. "I'm Tripping today, and—" I shake my head. I'm wasting time I don't actually have.

"Good luck," she says, dipping into a curtsy. Then, just as I'm closing the door, I swear she whispers, "Buon viaggio." And just like that, my blood turns to ice and my belly bottoms out.

Why would Freya say that when I never told her I'm heading for Italy?

43

On Trip days, simplicity is key. Any prep beyond showering and brushing my teeth will be handled down in hair and makeup. Which makes getting ready quick and easy.

On my way out the door, I grab my Gray Wolf tote, and, after tossing in my talisman and the earrings Braxton gave me, I include the small onyx shiv that Killian made. But when I see the note from my mom that I still haven't read, I run back to my closet to stash the envelope on the underside of a drawer. Then I head out to where the man in the electric cart is waiting.

As he whisks me through a series of long, meandering hallways, I idly thumb through the messages Braxton has sent to my slab.

He must've gotten up much earlier than me. The messages start at the crack of dawn.

Braxton: Are you up?

Braxton: I hope your silence means you slept better than me. Guess my excitement kept me awake.

Braxton: Arthur just summoned me, so I'm heading down early. I'll see you there.

Considering how the last message was sent around the time the inspirational quote came through, it's strange that I'm just now seeing them.

Did I somehow click something that pushed them into the background?

After cruising through several security checkpoints that require both the driver and me to show our slabs and prove our identities, I'm left outside a door where I find Keane waiting.

"What, no skates?" I shoot a pointed look at his sneaker-clad feet.

And while I admit it's not the funniest joke I've ever made, Keane's expression is so serious, I wish I hadn't said anything.

"You okay?" I ask as he whisks me inside.

"Are you?" He regards me with an intensity that leaves me feeling uneasy.

I nod, wondering if it's just me or if something weird is going on. Keane is usually much friendlier than this.

"Good." He nods. "Now let's get you over to Charlotte."

"Can I see Braxton first?" My stomach is in such a tangle, and Braxton always has a calming effect.

Keane shakes his head, though there's no missing the troubled glint in his eyes as he hurries me along.

After Keane's tense and edgy energy, Charlotte's sweet enthusiasm is a welcome relief.

"I have a surprise," she says, her eyes lighting up, and I watch as she rushes to the rack and brings back a dress I don't remember being fitted for.

My gaze pores over the fabric—a beautiful, dark blue brocade with a sparkly thread woven throughout that makes the whole thing shimmer as though it's woven from stardust.

"A surprise travel dress for good luck." She clasps her hands at her waist and grins.

After she helps me into the filmy silk undergown, I slip into the sparkling dress, followed by an equally beautiful giornea and my custom-made shoes. Then, once my hair is done and some light makeup applied, I stand before the mirror, and I can't help but gasp at the sight.

With a quick change of clothing and a new way of wearing

my hair, I've truly transformed into a vision of Renaissance nobility.

"I think this is my favorite look yet," I tell her. "And even better, there's no awkward hoops or pannier."

Charlotte's cheeks flush. "It is a very good look." She nods, as pleased with her work as she is with my appreciation of her skills.

"And the other dresses?" I ask.

"The trunk is packed and waiting for you on the launchpad," she says. When she catches me eyeing my tote bag, she adds, "If there is something more you'd like to bring, might I suggest you stow it in one of your pockets?"

The hidden pockets—of course. Since this isn't the usual thieving Trip—or rather, it is, but with only one small Get I'm expected to bring back—I'd forgotten all about them. And as soon as Charlotte turns away, busying herself with gathering my clothes and my slab to be returned to my room, I slip the onyx shiv into a small pocket hidden inside my giornea.

Once I'm ready, I head for the launchpad, excited to see how Braxton might look in sixteenth-century attire. But instead, I find Arthur surrounded by a bunch of tech guys who make their leave as soon as I approach.

"Have you narrowed down a location?" Arthur asks.

"I have some ideas," I tell him. "But I won't know for sure until I get there."

"Do you need anything from me?"

"A copy of the map and the tarot cards might help."

"You'll find both inside your trunk."

I nod.

"And the painting—the *Salvator Mundi*—was it helpful?"

"It made me realize there's more to that portrait than I first thought," I say. *Thanks to Mason, that is*. "But again, I won't know for sure until I'm immersed."

I say it like I'm an expert, when the fact is, just because I managed to score the Sun doesn't mean I actually know what I'm doing. But Arthur appreciates a good show of confidence, so I do what I can to appease him.

"Good." He nods, but I can tell by his faraway look that he's ready to move on to the other million things that occupy his mind. "The portal will stay open for two hours, on the off chance you should need to make a speedy return. Of course, I expect it will take much longer, which is why I'll be sending another portal after forty-eight hours. If you should finish early, you are free to hang around until then. It should be more than enough time, so there's no reason to worry about getting stuck. You are far too important to me to allow that to happen."

I stare at Arthur, only partially relieved by his assurances. *I mean, what about Song and Anjou—were they not important enough? Why isn't this standard procedure for everyone?*

I shake away the thought well before it has a chance to really take root and, more importantly, before Arthur can clock it on my face. "Thanks," I say. "I appreciate the opportunity. I only hope I don't disappoint."

"Just make sure that you don't," he says. Then, looking past my shoulder, he adds, "Looks like your Tripping partner is here."

My heart somersaults in my chest, and I turn, grinning with excitement and the heady anticipation of all that awaits us. The moment we've been waiting for has finally come.

Only it's not Braxton I find.

And my stomach roils, my heart stutters to a stop, when I see Killian standing on the launchpad instead.

44

There's been a mistake.

A horrible, dreadful, terrible mistake.

That's the only way to explain it. The only way—

In a fit of fury, I turn away from Killian and whirl on Arthur.

"I don't understand." My voice rises embarrassingly high. "*Braxton's* coming with me—it's all been arranged. We're starting in Venice, and—" The words fade as I become painfully aware of Arthur shaking his head.

"Braxton was needed elsewhere," he says. "Killian is taking his place." He speaks simply, plainly, as though it's as easy as that. And, for him, I guess it is. But for me, there's nothing simple about it.

"But I need to see him," I say. "I—"

"He's already gone," Arthur tells me.

Gone? What the hell does that even mean?

"Braxton is Tripping. But I'll make sure he's here to greet you when you return."

My eardrums throb from the frantic pounding of my own heart. "Did you do this?" I glare at Killian, already convinced that he did.

Killian stares down at his shoes as Arthur cuts in. "I assure you he did not." His tone is so sharp, I flinch at the sound. "When it comes to Tripping, I am the first, last, and only word around here."

But why Killian—of all people? I'd be better off with Elodie. I'd be—

"It was my understanding that you and Killian are friends." Arthur's gaze slices right through me with laser-like precision.

I sneak a glance at Killian, who still refuses to look at me. "It's just—" I shake my head. *Shit. I mean, seriously—this is the worst. I can't go to Italy with this guy. I just can't—*

"Killian is loyal to me." Arthur's voice crowds out my thoughts. "I trust him implicitly. And I think he's proven his willingness to protect you, no?"

Sure, by killing the Timekeeper. But neither of us says it—neither of us needs to.

"So, are you ready to accept the things to which fate binds you, and love the people with whom fate brings you together, so that we can move past all this and prepare for launch?" He's paraphrasing the Marcus Aurelius quote he sent to my slab, and I realize I should've known then.

Nothing with Arthur ever happens by chance.

I shoot another glance at Killian, and when he finally lifts his chin and his eyes square on mine, they are filled with apology, along with a glint of something else I can't easily identify. Then I lift my shoulders and reluctantly nod my consent. Because while my heart is in pieces, my brain has worked hard for this moment, so that's where I focus.

I'm heading for the launchpad when Arthur calls, "Oh, and Natasha—"

With my heart ripped to shreds and the anger only just beginning to fade from my cheeks, I turn toward him, wondering what he could possibly say that would make up for any of this.

The lines around his mouth deepen. His obsidian gaze glints hard on mine. "I believe in you," he says.

A moment passes between us before I nod, press my hands

together in thanks.

And as I turn back toward the launchpad where Killian waits, my head swirls with the question: *But do I still believe in you?*

45

"I don't think you've ever been so happy to see me," Killian says.

"Don't," I snap, barely able to control my anger. "Don't make jokes. Don't even talk to me."

"Fair enough." He nods. "But first, can you tell me how long I'm to take this vow of silence?"

"For the duration." I glare.

He scratches his chin and squints until those swimming-pool eyes practically vanish. "That might be a bit hard to pull off," he says.

"Well, give it your best shot." I bite off the words, aware that I'm being unfair, but at this point, I'm too angry to care.

"Look—" He bends toward me. "While I won't pretend that I'm sorry this happened, I take none of the credit. I got a message on my slab telling me to meet Arthur here, and the rest unfolded from there. None of this is on me."

"All I heard was the first part," I say.

"Then you are seriously overestimating me if you think I wield that sort of power around here. Though I am flattered."

"Don't be."

Killian regards me for a long, uncomfortable beat. "I get that you're mad," he says. "I get that you probably had fanciful visions of you and your boy swooning around in Renaissance times. I get that—in your eyes, anyway—I am one sorry replacement and probably the last person you ever wanted to Trip with. But I'm hoping you can at least try to find a way to get through this, because the whole point of us traveling together is we're supposed to make people believe we're a couple."

"Couples fight," I say. "We just happen to be one that fights all the time."

Killian is about to reply when Roxanne appears by our side. Looking so pristine and efficient with her trusty clipboard in hand, you'd never know she spent the previous night swigging champagne and burning up the dance floor.

"So," she says. "I understand there's been a change of plans. But you both look well rested and ready, so I'm sure you'll find a way to move past the drama and get the job done."

That last bit was for me. And I know this because her gaze fixes on mine when she speaks.

"Is there an envelope?" I rise onto my toes, trying to get a peek at whatever's attached to her clipboard, but she drops it to her side before I can see.

"No envelope." Her gaze is flat, her lips pulling into the world's stingiest grin. "Though I'm told you already know you're going to Renaissance Florence and exactly what Arthur expects once you arrive."

Well, I know what not to expect—a magical night in Venice with Braxton.

I take a deep breath and nod.

Roxanne gives her own brisk nod and goes on. "Then I suppose there's nothing left to say but safe travels." That grin of hers pulls so wide and tight, I expect to see her lips crack and bleed. And I can't help but wonder how I could've been so wrong about her. Just because she was nice the first time we met doesn't mean she's not working an agenda.

As Killian once said, *Everyone on that rock should be on your radar.*

But was he included in that?

Once Roxanne is gone, Killian leans toward me and says, "Shiv, will you look at me, please?"

I don't want to. But I also know I can't delay this forever. Eventually I'll have to look at him, talk to him, like a normal person. So I take a deep breath and force my gaze to meet his. What I find makes me feel bad for taking my disappointment out on him. He looks almost as unhappy as I am.

"I know you're upset and hurt and angry and…" He shrugs. "I also know you're looking for someone to blame, and while I'm willing to absorb the brunt of your anger, I swear to you, Shiv, I did not arrange this, nor did I ask for it. Like you, I go wherever Arthur sees fit to send me. And, for whatever reason, he sees fit to send me to Italy with you."

I watch him closely, waiting for him to rub his lips together, swipe a hand through his hair. But he remains steady before me, hands by his sides, gaze openly pleading with mine.

"What we're about to do is dead serious work. So before *I* feel safe enough to set out with *you*, I'm going to need some assurances."

I look at him. Swallow past the lump in my throat.

"I need you to take a breath. I need you to center yourself, and I need you to remember what this is really about. My job in Italy is to help you when needed and protect you if things go south. And I promise you this—I will willingly risk my own life to ensure your safety. But for me to do that effectively, I need you to take my life seriously, too. When this is over and done and we're safely back at Gray Wolf, you can go back to hating me for as long as you wish."

"Promise?" I say.

Killian's lips tug into a half grin. "I give you my word. Now…" He slides a silver ring from his pinky finger and offers it to me.

"What're you doing?" I glance between the silver ring and him.

"It's the clicker," he says. "I think you should have it."

I stare at the ring, but my hands remain by my sides. "I don't need it," I tell him.

Killian's brows press together. His head cocks to the side in a way that causes a renegade curl to spill into his eyes.

"None of this is about me not trusting you," I say. "It's just—"

"You're upset. I know. And that I can deal with. But I also know you don't entirely trust me. And since trust is essential in our line of business, I'm going to insist that you take control of the clicker. You determine when you're ready to return."

"And what if I leave you behind?" The words tumble out of my mouth before I can stop them. It's a terrible thing to say to someone who's already suffered that fate, but the trust he's putting in me, the way he's looking at me, willingly accepting my anger, leaves me feeling strangely unsteady.

He shrugs. "You won't do that."

"How can you be so sure?" I challenge.

"Because I know you better than you think, and it's not in your nature." Gently, he grabs hold of my wrist, deposits the ring in the center of my palm, and folds my fingers around it.

"It's only good for a few hours," I say.

"And it will be good again in forty-eight hours. But hopefully I'll have proved myself by then." His eyes roam my face, searching for an opening, a way back to the friendly banter we once shared. "I don't know if you've noticed, but I haven't used a single accent during this entire conversation. That's got to count for something, at least?"

There's a burning in my throat, a sting at the back of my eyes, and though I do what I can to quell the emotional turmoil waging within, I'm pretty sure Killian has already mapped that terrain.

"So, we good?" he asks. "You and me—we ready to do this thing?"

He offers his hands, and since this is what I came for, I reach down and take them. They're warm, strong, and so large, they practically swallow mine whole.

"Are you ready, Shiv?" His blue eyes meet mine.

I fill my lungs with air. On the exhale, I say, "Fine. Let's do this. Let's go."

I watch as he signals to the control room, and the next thing I know, there's a sharp blast of sulfur—a vaporous cloud—as a thunderous buzz explodes through the room.

"Don't let go." Killian's fingers squeeze mine as a flash of dazzling light races toward the gaseous cloud, freezes on contact, and instantly transforms into a glittering doorway.

The last thing I see before the wall drops and gravity fails is the determined look on Arthur's face as he watches from the control room.

Then Killian and I lift high off our heels as a great rush of wind thrusts us through the portal, rocketing us right out of this century and back into another.

History is a set of lies agreed upon.

—Napoleon Bonaparte

46

I glance around the narrow alleyway.

Going by the dim light and chilled air, I'm guessing we arrived sometime in the late afternoon, early evening hours. But honestly, it could just as easily be early morning as well.

I pull my giornea tighter around me, trying to ward off the cold. "Where are we?" I look to Killian, hoping he knows, because I haven't a clue.

He squints into the distance. In a voice as tight as his expression, he says, "All I know is we need to memorize this place, because this is where they'll send the next portal. And without the aid of contacts or masks, it's our only hope of returning to Gray Wolf."

"So…you don't actually know where we are." I let go of his hand. This is ridiculous. Braxton would know his way around. So why did Arthur send Killian, who's already lost?

Killian shoots me a look from over his shoulder. "Don't do that," he says.

"You're lost. Admit it." I cross my arms over my chest, partly to conserve whatever body heat I still have, partly to ensure my hands remain completely inaccessible to him.

"How can I be lost when I just arrived?" Killian rubs his hands together and blows the air out of his cheeks as he shifts his weight between his feet. "Can you at least try to trust me? And if you can't manage that, then can you at least pretend like you trust me? Tripping is all about playing a part, and it's time for you to start playing yours."

He's not wrong. But that doesn't mean that I like it.

"I'm not holding your hand," I say.

Killian frowns. "Well, it's going to be hard to convince people we're a couple if you don't at least try to show some sign of affection toward me."

"See, that's where you're wrong." I narrow my gaze. "Nobles didn't marry for love. It was all about politics, position, power, and a sizeable dowry."

"Maybe so." He shrugs. "But like it or not, your twenty-first century mindset will only land us in trouble. These women are nothing like you. Their life choices are limited to marriage, domestic service, a nunnery, or to work as a courtesan. And you, Shiv, are now cast in the role of one who chose marriage. Which means you need to start acting like your Renaissance sisters—completely dependent on the men in your life for your very survival."

Gross. I want to roll my eyes, but I know better. I also know that none of that is Killian's fault.

"Fine." I huff. "But I won't pretend to adore you."

Killian sighs. "Fair enough." He starts making his way down the alley.

"Where are you going?" I call.

"Good God." He turns to face me. "Is the whole Trip going to be like this?" He swipes a hand through his hair, rakes a harsh gaze over me. "Just tell me now, so I can prepare."

I narrow my eyes, noting the way his jaw clenches, the way the veins in his neck seem to pop, like it's taking all his will just to keep himself in check. Which only confirms that, if I wanted, I could push him right over the edge with a few well-chosen words.

"Guess we won't know for sure until you manage to get us successfully *un*lost," I say, watching as he throws his hands up in frustration and storms down the alleyway.

"Hey!" I yell after him. "What am I supposed to do with this thing?" I gesture toward the oversize trunk that made the Trip with us.

"You're strong." Killian tosses the words over his shoulder. "You want to exert your independence—figure it out."

I watch as he continues down the alley, leaving me with an ancient version of a suitcase that weighs more than all the clothing inside. I scowl at the monstrous thing, half tempted to just abandon it, since there's no way I can lug it on my own.

"Enjoy your anger while you can," he calls. "Because your mind is about to be blown."

I sink down onto the trunk. Feeling defeated, deflated, wondering how it's come to this and how much worse it can get.

So much for Venice. So much for being with Braxton.

At the sound of a loud, sharp whistle, I look up to see a coach at the end of the alley. A moment later, a man leaps from the driver's seat, heaves the trunk onto his shoulders, and hauls it onto the back of our ride.

"What is this?" I ask, making my way toward Killian. "An ancient Uber?"

"While I don't get the reference, I take that to mean all is forgiven?" Killian opens the door to the carriage.

"Don't push it," I say, brushing right past him and climbing inside.

"Cosimo sent this." Killian settles onto the opposite seat and taps the roof twice, sending the carriage on its way.

"Who's Cosimo?" I ask, squinting at him.

"You're about to find out." He grins, his deep blue gaze gleaming on mine. "As for now, let the adventure begin."

47

As the coach sets off through the streets, I start to get my bearings.

Judging by the location of the sun in the sky, it's late afternoon. And when I catch a glimpse of that spectacular red dome that can only be the famous Duomo that sits atop the Florence Cathedral, my heart skips a beat. According to my research, there's a good chance the Moon is tied to that spot.

I tap the roof, but the coach keeps rolling.

"What're you doing?" Killian regards me with a trace of amusement.

"How do you get this thing to stop?" I ask.

"Why would you want it to stop?"

"Because I need to check out the cathedral." I jab a thumb in the general direction of the landmark now receding into the distance.

"There'll be plenty of time to play tourist and check out the sights, Shiv." Killian laughs. "Right now, you and I have much bigger fish to fry, as they say."

"Is that a Renaissance saying?"

"Certainly not." He grins.

"Well, don't you think we should at least try to get in character and speak in the colloquial way to each other?"

"Trust me, when it's just us, this is easier."

"Fine," I say. "But I really need to get inside that cathedral—

the sooner the better. And, by the way, I'm hardly a tourist. It has to do with the—" I pause, wishing I'd taken the time to better rehearse this part. "With the Get Arthur has tasked me to find."

Killian's gaze locks onto mine. "I promise, you'll see the Duomo," he says. "And you'll get your…Get. Just not today."

"And why not today?" I ask, unable to think of a single reason for why I should delay.

Killian gestures toward the window. "Because it's getting late, and we need to come up with a plan before you go wandering about and get us both into trouble."

"Why do you assume *I'll* get us into trouble?" I ask, lifting a brow.

"Because you have little grasp on the language, and you're impulsive as hell."

His words land like a slap. And though I know he's not wrong, I waste no time in punching right back. "Did you ever consider that maybe you bring out the worst in me?"

It was meant to be caustic, scathing. But the way Killian regards me—like he's peering through layers of flesh and bone, all the way to my fluttering belly and quickening heart—leaves me feeling so exposed, I wish I'd just let it go.

"Well, if that's your worst," he says, his voice thick, "then I'd argue I'm actually a good influence. At least I bring out the fighter in you. Better that than to make you all soft and compliant like you are with Braxton. Your willingness to believe him seems so contradictory to everything I know about you."

He shoots me a probing look, and I'm about to tell him he doesn't know the first thing about Braxton and me, but I realize there's no point. So I steer us back to our original topic. "But what if the cathedral can't wait? What if I have a hunch and I need to act while I can?"

"What if the cathedral can't wait—or *you* can't wait?"

Killian's eyes glint. A ghost of a smile tugs at his lips.

"Maybe it's both." I shrug. "Why does it matter? I came to do a job, and the sooner I've done it, the better, no?"

"Look," he says, "while I get that you're eager to return to your boy, this is how it's going to go: first, we're going to get ourselves settled. Then, we're going to attend a very fancy dinner that our host has gone to the trouble of arranging for us."

My gaze locks on Killian's. "But I thought you didn't know you were Tripping with me until the very last minute," I say.

Killian freezes. And I watch as he swallows, nods, drums his fingers on his knee, like a mouse who's realized too late that by going after the cheese, he's stepped into a trap.

"So," I say. "How could you possibly know about a fancy dinner if you didn't even know you were Tripping with me?"

Killian rubs his lips together and rakes a hand through his hair. And the second I clock it, I'm on high alert for whatever comes next.

"Fine," he says. "Here's the truth—when I saw you at Halcyon, I had no idea. I swear."

I tilt my head in study, trying not to let on to the whirl of anger churning inside me. "So, when exactly *did* you know?" I ask.

He drops his gaze to his knees, takes a deep breath, then returns his focus to me. "Just after we said goodbye, Arthur messaged me, asking to meet. That's when he told me."

"So, all that time in between, you let me believe I was going with Braxton?" I glare at him. "I mean, don't you think you should've warned me? I thought we were friends?"

Killian huffs under his breath, mumbling something I can't quite make out.

"You owe me an explanation," I say.

"You're right." He sighs. "But Shiv, you can't pull the friend card whenever it suits you, then serve me a boatload of shit the second I prove I'm a human who needs a moment to determine my whereabouts. Look, I get that you're angry and probably a bit nervous about the task ahead, but do you think you can maybe cut me a break?"

"I'm sorry," I say, knowing he's right. "I'm sorry I was a brat back in that alleyway. But that doesn't get you off the hook for not warning me. I could've—"

"You could've *what*?" His gaze narrows on mine, and the intensity is so strong, I shift my focus outside the carriage, watching a smear of creamy stone buildings stream by.

I could've spent the night with Braxton.

I could've been wrapped in his arms, kissing until we were drunk with it, and…

And so much more.

I chance a look at Killian, only to find he's still staring at me. Who knows how long he'll try to drag this Trip out? And since Arthur claimed Braxton left on an earlier Trip, who even knows if I'll see him when I return?

Every time we say goodbye, there's no way of knowing if it might be the last.

But I can't afford to think like that. I need to stay strong, get the job done, then deal with everything else as soon as I'm back.

"I just wish you'd told me," I say, my anger starting to dissipate.

"Believe me," Killian says. "I wish I had, too. But the choice wasn't mine."

"Do you always do what Arthur says?" I run a critical gaze over his face, but Killian doesn't flinch or look away.

"Don't you?" His brow lifts.

I shrug but keep my lips sealed. Mainly because we both know that at Gray Wolf, all of us are under Arthur's rule.

"Look," Killian says. "All I ask of you tonight is that you play the part. Tomorrow, you're free to roam as you please—so long as you do so with an escort in tow."

"And let me guess—that escort is you?"

"Beautiful and clever," Killian says. "My favorite combination."

"You know this is ridiculous." I glare at him.

"Maybe so." He shrugs. "But this is Tripping. And I don't make the rules, Shiv. I just try to live by them so I don't get myself killed."

"Easy for you to say."

He shoots me a curious look.

"I mean, you must love Tripping back to these times."

"I thought you did, too." He squints. "And while I realize that enthusiasm took a hit the second you realized you'd be Tripping with me, it's still pretty fucking brilliant to be here. So don't let your disappointment spoil what could turn out to be an amazing experience."

"What I meant was, you must love traveling into the past, because for a man of your means, with your good looks, it's the ancient equivalent of being a rock star. The whole world is yours. You can do whatever you want, whenever you want…" My gaze fixes on his. "With whomever you want."

"Clearly not *whomever.*" He shoots a pointed look at me that leaves me wishing I hadn't said anything. "Though I am chuffed to know you think I'm good-looking. I was beginning to worry you didn't see me the same way as everyone else." With a satisfied grin, he sinks deeper into his seat and spreads his arms against the backrest, allowing for the full, glorious view of him.

"Always so humble." I shake my head and cast a glance out the window, marveling at the passing scenery as the carriage slowly rolls through a series of streets that are far more deserted than I expected them to be.

After a stretch of silence I was beginning to enjoy, Killian says, "I wonder if something's going on. He's taking the long route."

"Should I be worried?" I ask.

He shifts his focus to me. "Most definitely," he says. "But probably not about that."

"Then what should I be worried about?"

His mouth pulls tight. He crosses his legs at the knees; then, leaning toward me, he says, "There'll be a lot of attention paid to us. Not only are we new in town, but in these fancy clothes"—he gestures toward his gleaming jacket and my own shimmering gown—"we're a striking pair, which is both a blessing and a curse. A blessing because it'll open a lot of doors."

"And the curse?" I ask.

"Because standing out makes it harder to sneak about."

"So…do you have a way around that?"

He nods. "We sneak out under the cover of night. Which is why you're not going to kick up a fuss about sharing a room. You're going to take it in stride, like a good little Tripper."

"You can't be serious." I glare so hard I risk getting a headache.

Killian meets me straight on. "I would never lie about that."

I shake my head and gaze out the window again. "Then you better hope that room comes with a couch," I say. "Because there's no way in hell we're sharing a bed."

Before Killian can respond, the coach comes to a stop, and the driver announces that we have arrived.

48

"Let me take the lead," Killian says as I follow him to the door.

"Why? I thought this place belonged to a fellow AAD?" I shoot back, reluctant to give him control. It sets the sort of precedent I cannot afford.

A uniformed guard opens the door, and after a quick exchange in rapid-fire Italian I can barely keep up with, we're ushered inside where it's warmer, but only marginally so.

While the exterior of the palazzo struck me as plain, inside it's really quite beautiful. With high ceilings and shiny marble floors, the entryway is covered in frescoes, and it's built around a pretty courtyard rife with olive trees and bubbling fountains.

"Benvenuto!"

I look up to see a man descending a wide staircase. From this distance, he appears much shorter than Killian, and much wider, too. His gait is purposeful if not heavy, and he walks in a way that seems to lead with his belly.

He has a dark complexion, a wild mane of black curls that spiral just past his shoulders, and features so coarse, they look like they were drawn by a child using a very dull crayon. But his eyes are a warm velvety brown, and when he grins, it's like watching a sunrise: the whole space seems to brighten.

Killian makes the introductions, speaking in such quick and fluent Italian that the only thing I grasp is that our host's name is

Cosimo, which I already knew. But once he's led us to our room, which is really more like a suite of rooms with an expansive bedchamber and another, even larger, sitting room with a door that leads out to the garden, Cosimo resumes the conversation in English.

"I expected you days ago," he says. "Your timing couldn't be worse."

"What do you mean?" I ask, trying to contain my alarm.

"Today's February sixth, 1497," he says.

Killian briefly shuts his eyes and lets out a low whistle as Cosimo glances between us.

I guess I've been so focused on finding the Moon, it takes a moment to process the news. "So...we're in the fifteenth century, not the sixteenth," I say, cringing when they both look at me like I've just stated something glaringly obvious, which, I realize, I have. And yet all this time I was sure we'd be traveling to the early fifteen-hundreds. Mainly because I'm using the *Salvator Mundi* as a clue, and it's reputed to have been completed around 1510. But clearly, I should've known better than to ever assume anything to do with Arthur, or Gray Wolf, or Tripping, or—

"I nearly gave up on you," Cosimo says. "I've sent a carriage every day for weeks now."

Killian shrugs. "You know Arthur," he says, and Cosimo nods, but I'm not sure I get it.

"Can you unpack that for me?" I look between them, but it's Cosimo who speaks.

"Arthur likes to keep us on our toes—it prevents us from getting too comfortable. Anyway, if you're looking for art, you'll need to move fast."

"Because it's the Bonfire of the Vanities." I look between them, noting how Cosimo shoots me a withering look while Killian wearily shakes his head.

"We are one day out from that sad bit of history." Cosimo's

tone is irritated and sharp. "Most of my staff have already fled. The ones who haven't left to follow that fanatical preacher, that is." He openly grimaces. "But the rest have set off for Venice, where I'm planning to go until the trouble dies down."

"So," I say, my belly clenching at the full implication of that. "We're to stay on without you. Just—" I jab a thumb toward Killian. "Just the two of us—all alone—in this giant palazzo?"

Cosimo regards me with a look of such open scorn it makes the withering gaze from before seem almost fond. "You're new, I take it," he says.

I give a nervous laugh. "What gave it away?"

"Your obvious lack of training." His scathing gaze runs the length of me.

"She was fast-tracked," Killian jumps in. "But not to worry—she's trained well enough."

"Let's hope you're right," Cosimo says. "Because her Italian is shit."

"Hi. Hello. Ciao." I wave a hand in his face. "I'm right here."

"I can see that." Cosimo frowns. "And you'd do well to remember *when* you are and tone down your…" He tilts his head as though searching for just the right word. "Your *confidence*." He speaks as though it left a bad taste on his tongue. "This is not the time to exert your new-millennium fourth-wave feminism."

"My apologies," I say, my voice edged with anger. "I thought it was safe to be my authentic self in front of a fellow AAD *when there's no one else around*."

Cosimo is starting to respond when Killian places a hand on his shoulder. "Brother," he says. "I'm beginning to think you've been immersed in your timeline too long. And believe me, I can relate, having been stuck the last four years in eighteenth-century France. But not only did Natasha rescue me, she also coached me on how to conduct myself in the modern-day world."

Cosimo gives me a considering look. Like now that I've met

with Killian's approval, he's willing to view me from a fresher perspective. "Perhaps you're right," he finally says. "And perhaps I've grown paranoid. But this is not the Florence it once was. The city is shaken, ruled by the hand of fear. There's a war on art, beauty, luxury—all things that once drew me here. And though I knew this day would come, watching it unfold has been distressing in a way I can't quite explain. These are serious times, with serious consequences for those who dare step out of line. Good people are being accused, punished, and put to gruesome, violent ends for all manner of made-up atrocities. So please, be on guard, keep your head down, and never forget that as a female in this timeline, you have no inherent rights."

A sudden chill courses through me, but I refuse to let on just how much those words have gotten to me.

"If you're smart," Cosimo continues, "you'll switch out your fancy dress for something more subdued."

I glance down at my gown, wondering why on earth Charlotte—no, make that Arthur, since, as he said himself, he's the first, last, and only word when it comes to Tripping—why Arthur would send us here, dressed in such finery, during a time when so many are following a fanatical preacher who speaks against the very things Arthur cherishes.

"They're raiding homes," Cosimo says. "Of course, I've made plenty of fakes and willingly handed them over. Being the philistines they are, they can't tell the difference."

"Wait— " I say. "You painted the fakes?"

Cosimo nods.

"So, you're not a Blue."

He tosses his head back and laughs, and the sight is so unexpected, I'm taken aback. "I was a Blue before I became a Red. Do you know what that is?"

Killian looks at me, apparently as interested in hearing the answer as Cosimo.

"You meet with the artists," I say, remembering what Arthur once told me. "Commission pieces, serve as a benefactor, and you also paint copies of all the great works."

Cosimo lifts a brow. "Do you know how many of my pieces hang in the Uffizi and the Louvre?"

I gaze at him in wonder.

"Let's just say I lost count." He laughs again, but this time it's an odd, hollow sound. "Listen," he says. "I'm sorry for my earlier coarseness. These are dangerous times, but I know you wouldn't be here if Arthur didn't trust you. Which means I need to trust you as well. But you do understand what's going to happen tomorrow?"

"I do," I tell him.

"The Savonarola fever burns so hot, many of the rich are ridding themselves of their jewels, furniture, mirrors, cosmetics, and—most tragically of all—heaps of priceless and irreplaceable manuscripts, books, and master works of art—all of which will be tossed into the flames."

I shake my head sadly. I can hardly imagine it, and I certainly don't want to watch it. "I read that Sandro Botticelli was so caught up, he burned several of his own paintings—ones that stemmed back to his earlier, more secular works."

"The only reason *Primavera* and *The Birth of Venus* survived is because both paintings were secured elsewhere." Cosimo sighs. "And now, of course, we all know they're both kept back at Gray Wolf."

What a colossal shame. Yet another despairing example of how slow humanity is to change—how history keeps repeating itself, spurred on by the masses who refuse to see just how closely their current behaviors mirror the irrational ones of the past.

"In the late fifteenth century, we had the Bonfire of the Vanities," I say. "In the new millennium, we're still dealing with book banners."

"Once again, the past is prologue." Cosimo regards me in the way of a fellow conspirator, which is a welcome change from the derision of earlier. "For now…" Cosimo rubs his hands together. "You'll find your trunk in your rooms, minus a few supplies Arthur intended for me. You have a bit of time until our guests arrive. I've planned one last extravagant feast before the darkness descends. And trust me when I say you won't want to miss it."

When he's gone, Killian turns to me and, in a lowered voice, says, "Fuckin' Savonarola. How's that for shit timing?" He shakes his head, huffs under his breath. "I suggest you grab yourself a nice power nap, because we'll definitely want to head out tonight. And you'll need to be rested if we have any hope of getting past the night police and their damned curfew."

He turns away and heads for a daybed, where he plops himself down without first removing his boots.

"Killian?" I say, my voice quiet. "Do you—" The words stall on my tongue. I lick my lips and start again. "Do you happen to know the real reason why Arthur sent us here—sent me here?"

I hold my breath, keeping close watch over his face, when he peeks an eye open and says, "We're here for the Moon, Shiv." Then, turning onto his side, he drifts off to sleep.

49

Killian knows.

And if he knows about the Moon, then he probably knows about the Antikythera Mechanism and Arthur's plan to remake the world.

But then why didn't Arthur just send him on his own? Why does he insist I'm the only one who can fulfill his dream?

Once I'm sure he's in a deep sleep, I head into the bedroom, retrieve the map and the tarot cards from our trunk, then pilfer through another trunk of old clothes until I've assembled an outfit that'll help me blend in—as a boy.

I dress quickly, then, after tucking my hair under a brimless cap, I study myself in the mirror. Though my disguise is far from perfect, the hooded cloak hides my face just enough that I doubt anyone will take notice. Then, I sneak through the garden, slip out the gate, and head in the direction where I saw the cathedral.

Considering how close it is to nightfall, the streets are busier than I would've thought, but it's not the lively Florence I'm used to seeing in movies.

By this point, Lorenzo de' Medici, also known as Lorenzo the Magnificent, is five years in the grave. His son Piero—ultimately to be known as Piero the Unfortunate—is exiled, and there's a palpable feeling of fear in the air. Like Cosimo said, a war on beauty and art has been declared.

I hurry through the streets, one hand clasping the front of

my cloak, the other shoved deep in my pocket, clutching my talisman. When I spot the red dome in the distance—the most famous and enduring symbol of Florence and the Renaissance—I pause a moment to take in the sight.

According to my research, the Duomo is actually comprised of two domes, one internal and one external, with a golden copper ball and cross situated at the top, put there by Andrea del Verrocchio in 1471. And since Leonardo da Vinci was working as an apprentice for Verrocchio at the time, it's thought that the difficult task of getting the two-thousand-pound orb on top of the dome was what spawned the legendary genius's interest in engineering.

It's said that the walk to the top is not for the faint of heart—that claustrophobia and a fear of heights should be considered before making the trek. And though I'm no fan of tight spaces or high places, I have every intention of climbing those steps. But I'm not in it for the sort of view most tourists are after. I'm hoping to either cement or destroy a theory I've been working on.

The first thing I notice when the cathedral itself pops into view is the unruly crowd that's gathered out front. Like Cosimo warned, this is the Florence of Girolamo Savonarola, the Dominican-friar-turned-puritan-fanatic who seized control of the city after the Medicis were driven out. This hellfire-and-brimstone preacher has denounced everything the Renaissance was founded upon—poetry, luxury, innovation, and all manner of sensuous pleasures, especially the sort of sex enjoyed by those he refers to as sodomites. The joyous festivals Florentines used to enjoy have been replaced with strict religious observance, as Savonarola insists that the only way to avoid an eternity burning in hell is to give up their love of beauty.

Though he's not without opponents, most of whom refer to him and his followers as Snivellers. And he's managed to make many enemies during his reign, like the Borgia pope who will ultimately excommunicate him and condemn him to hang.

At this point, though, as I watch his followers dump their belongings onto an ever-growing pile of treasures, all of it soon to burn, it's weird to think how in just over a year, when Savonarola is forty-five, he, along with two of his most ardent supporters, will be arrested, tortured, condemned to death, and hanged in the Piazza della Signoria before being set aflame. What little remains will be tossed into the Arno. His quest to erase the Medici family from history and reverse the Renaissance will not see fruition. But at the moment, he's so lost in his own sense of righteousness, he can't see how he's actually cast himself as the villain.

I keep my head down as I pass, all too aware that if any of these people caught wind of who I am, I'd be burned at the stake, no questions asked. When a young boy—one of Savonarola's street urchins, no doubt—appears out of nowhere and tugs at my cloak, I try to shake him off and brush past. But he's so small and quick, his hand slips inside my pocket well before I have a chance to register that it's happened.

With his grubby face, ragged clothes, and greasy hair, he reminds me of a character in a Dickens novel—one of the Artful Dodgers out thieving for Fagin. A boy who's not so unlike me.

Only this boy has convinced himself he's stealing for God, while I…

Well, I'm beginning to think I might be thieving for a man who wants to play God.

Either way, this poor child has no way of knowing that I'm not just another terrified Florentine. I'm willing to fight with everything I have in me.

"Che cosa?" he shouts, his eyes narrowing on mine, his lips curling into a sneer as his hand slides free of my pocket and he dangles my talisman before me.

Shit.

My belly plummets, my mouth goes dry, as I watch the delicate golden cage swinging before me.

I mean, seriously, what the hell?

I chance a quick glance around, ensuring the boy is working alone, then I arc my arm toward him, determined to claim it, but he quickly snatches it out of my reach.

I can't let him get away with this. I won't—

"What is this you hide?" His Italian comes at me in a pitch so high, it would be heartbreaking if it weren't for the fact that he's gotten hold of the one thing I can't afford to lose. "Give up your vanities," he yells, "or risk an eternity burning in hell!"

Though the boy is only a child, his eyes bear the fevered glaze of a zealot who's convinced he's an essential part of God's army, and that alone makes him dangerous.

"Give it back," I hiss in my own version of Italian that comes out so disjointed, the boy screws up his face and leans closer.

"Scusa?" His voice rises above the noise, causing a few passersby to slowdown and watch.

Damn. I can't afford this kind of attention. But I also can't afford to lose my talisman.

My hand clamps down on the boy's wrist, and though he tries to jerk free, I squeeze my fingers so hard he lets out a yelp and the charm falls from his grasp.

His eyes blaze on mine, and just when I'm sure he's about to attack, a piercing scream cuts through the square, the boy whips his head around, and I seize the moment to push him away as I spin on my heel and lose myself in the crowd.

50

With my head ducked low, I drive my legs forward, hoping to appear as just another street person in search of solace, sanctuary, refuge. And aside from a few random fanatics screaming in my face about eternal damnation, I'm able to enter the cathedral mostly unscathed, relieved to find I'm the only one here.

I linger by the door, needing a moment to settle my nerves. Then, lifting my gaze to the painted clock above the entry, I remember reading how it runs in accordance with Italian time, or ora italica, where the clock hand runs backward, and the twenty-fourth hour of the day ends at sunset. Five hundred years from this day, that clock will still be in that same place, still tracking the hours that pass.

There's a dome on the other side of the room displaying a mural of the Last Judgment. And as I cross a mosaic floor with a design so elaborate it resembles a rug, I wonder if the Moon might be hiding in here.

There were three tarot symbols on that map—the Hermit, the High Priestess, and the Moon.

Last time around, the Hermit card helped me find the Sun, because of its association with the Roman god Saturn. This time, the connection is different. As the ninth card in the deck, it shares a numerological link to the Moon, which, as the eighteenth card, reduces to nine after you add the one and the eight together.

The Hermit's astrological link is to Virgo, and since this place is clearly all about the virgin birth, it seems as good a place as any to begin my search. The Hermit is also a card with a message of healing, which also works.

The High Priestess, being a number two card, links to both Justice, the eleventh card, since one plus one equals two, and Judgment, the twentieth card, because that number also reduces to two.

I gaze up at the interior of the dome and take in the Last Judgment once more, hoping it's proof that I really am onto something.

The High Priestess's astrological sign is the Moon, her element is water, and she stands for secrets, wisdom, and things of a spiritual nature, which also fits for this place.

And then there's the Moon card itself. As the eighteenth card, it's directly connected to number nine, the Hermit, and, like the High Priestess, its element is water. Astrologically, the Moon is linked to Pisces, the fish, which just so happened to be used as an ancient secret symbol for Christianity, which also makes a pretty good case for this cathedral being the right place.

The symbols etched onto that map were a crown, an hourglass, and an archer's bow. But one of those objects was placed upside down, and another was sideways, and while I'm not entirely sure why, seeing as how it's a treasure map of sorts, it's got to mean something.

But does it point to the traditional reverse meaning, like I've assumed?

And if so, what exactly does it mean that the hourglass was flipped upside down to show time running out?

Is it a nod toward this time right now—the end of the Renaissance?

And if so, then what about the crown?

In the tarocchi deck, the High Priestess is portrayed as a woman sitting on a gold bench, wearing a crown over a wimple. In one hand, she holds a scepter; in the other, she balances a book on her knee. On the map, the crown is tilted sideways, and assuming it was portrayed that way on purpose, the question is why—what could it possibly mean?

I shake my head, start to wander about the space, delighted to have it all to myself while just outside those doors, the streets are erupting into chaos.

Okay, let's see... the crown is a circle, symbolizing immortality, eternity...the coronation itself signifying a union with the divine, which again assures me I'm in the right place. But why it's depicted that way, I have no idea.

As for the hourglass, it marks the passage of time and the inevitability of death. And yet, the hourglass also resembles the number eight, which placed on its side is also the sign of infinity. Also, the hourglass can restart time, allowing for a sort of rebirth, merely by flipping it over and starting again.

And what about that crystal on the *Salvator Mundi*?

I told Arthur it represented the Moon, and I still believe that to be true. But it also resembles a crystal ball—the sort of tool used by psychics, mediums, and other adepts—allowing one to see into the future or gaze into the past.

Did Leonardo da Vinci know about the location of the Moon?

And if so, is he sending a message through that painting that the Moon I'm looking for is hidden somewhere that'll soon be lost from the world if I don't find it quickly?

I close my eyes and summon an image of that painting, focusing on those three points of white on the crystal that, according to most scholars, are meant to represent the sort of occlusions that are normally found on rock crystal. Just another sign of Leonardo's devotion to getting the details just right.

Others claim they represent a constellation.

But the more I think about it, the more convinced I am that those three dots point to something else entirely.

After all, Leonardo was also known for his passion for creating and solving puzzles. So is it possible that those three dots are a message of some kind?

There's definitely a connection. I can feel it in my bones. I just don't know what or how, but I'm determined to figure it out.

I've made my way to the pulpit when the door suddenly bangs open and a roaring crowd rushes into the space. And when I turn, I find myself locking eyes with Savonarola himself.

A man who's so sure he's the one and only human conduit to God, and yet, he has no way of knowing that soon, these same people will become so disillusioned with him, they'll cheer as they watch him burn.

I try to duck my head and turn away, but it's too late.

"You there!" Savonarola shouts, pointing at me. "Have you given up your vanities? Or have you chosen eternal damnation?"

As the crowd turns on me, hundreds of fevered gazes directed my way, my fingers instinctively reach for my dagger. But who am I kidding? I'm completely outnumbered.

Knowing my shaky Italian will only put me at risk, I bend my head in feigned reverence and pray to whoever might be listening that this zealot will soon remove his focus from me.

"Come!" he shouts, voice cracking like thunder. "Come join us, child, and let us repent for our sins."

Savonarola takes his place at the pulpit, launching into a hellfire sermon. And as the crowd surges forward, I start to edge my way back when, from out of nowhere, a hand clamps over my mouth, an arm clutches hard at my waist, and I'm hauled backward, heels dragging, as I'm lugged out of the cathedral and onto the street.

51

"First things first—do you know who you are, or even *when* you are?"

Killian whispers into my ear, but with his hand clamped over my mouth, I can only manage a nod.

"Good." He breathes a sigh of relief. "Good," he says again. "So, now that you've proved you're not in a Fade—have you gone completely mad?" He grips my waist so tightly, I struggle for breath. "Seriously, Shiv—have you lost your fucking mind? What the hell do you think you're doing getting caught up in this mess? Or perhaps you've decided to join Savonarola's army of zealots—is that it?"

He pulls me into an alleyway and pins me up against a wall. And though he lifts his hand from my mouth, his grip is so tight, there's little chance of freeing myself.

"I knew it wouldn't be easy Tripping with you." His gaze cuts right through me. "But this is ridiculous. I don't know if you're poorly trained, or just wildly impulsive, or both. But you cannot—absolutely cannot, under any circumstances—pull a stunt like this again." He shakes his head. "Do you have any idea what could've happened to you?"

"So, which is it?" I snap. "Are you angry or worried?"

Killian loosens his grip. "Can't I be both?" His voice is thick in a way that has me averting my gaze. "If something were to happen to you—"

"Arthur would never forgive you. I know." I grind out the words.

"No, Shiv," Killian says, looking at me in a way I'd rather not see. "It's me who'd never forgive myself." I try to jerk free, but he tightens his hold. "Look at me," he says, but I shake my head and keep my focus on the road. "Shiv, please."

So I do. I take a deep breath and force my gaze to meet his. And the look I find leaves me wishing I hadn't. I don't want to see what he's feeling, and I certainly don't want to know.

I start to turn away when Killian lifts a hand to my cheek. "What are you so afraid of?" he whispers.

"Nothing," I say. "It's just—I'm with Braxton. And you know that. So, why do you insist on—"

"Why do I insist on what? Going after the one thing I want more than anything else?" He tilts his head closer to mine, until his lips are just a heartbeat away. "Last I checked, you and Braxton were neither married nor engaged. Hell, you haven't even been together that long. And I'm willing to bet you don't know each other nearly as well as you think."

"You don't know that. You don't know anything about us," I say.

"Maybe not." He shrugs. "But I know you don't know the most important part."

I swallow past the lump in my throat. "This again?" I say. "The same old story about how Braxton ditched you in Versailles—is that the best you can do?"

"That's just the prologue." He frowns. "There's an entire story still to follow."

"Then why not just tell me? I mean, it's not like I can go anywhere—not with you holding me hostage."

In an instant, he loosens his grip. "You're not a hostage," he says. "And, for the record, I *will* tell you someday. I'll tell you the whole bloody story so you can decide for yourself just exactly whose version you're willing to trust."

"So, why not now? Why not just get it over with and quit playing around? You're hardly the first person to hint at whatever this is." My mind reels back to what Song once said—how I don't really know Braxton; how I don't really know any of them. *You haven't been around long enough to hear all the stories.*

Killian looks surprised but is quick to contain it. "I refuse to win your favor by default. I prefer to win you over by my own merits. But that'll require you giving me a chance. You like me, Shiv. There's no point denying it. That's why you're so afraid to even meet me halfway. You're afraid of the feelings I stir up inside you. You're afraid of this—"

His face looms closer, so close his lips are just a whisper from mine.

My breath catches, refuses to come. There's an infinity of choices passing between us but only one that I'm willing to make.

"Tell me," he says. "Do you love him?"

"That's none of your business," I say, the words barbed on my tongue.

"And I acknowledge that." Killian gives a curt nod. "You're under no obligation to answer to me. Though I am wondering if you can answer for yourself. Do you love Braxton, Shiv?"

Do I love Braxton?

I want to love Braxton.

Sometimes I think for sure I love Braxton.

But then I remember last night on the dance floor, how I was sure he was about to say those three words to me, and how unprepared I felt to face a moment like that. And so I kissed him. Kissed the words right off his lips to ensure that he didn't, *couldn't*, speak them to me.

Do I love Braxton?

How is that possible when I'm not even sure I really know

who Braxton is?

"I'm no mind reader," Killian says. "But I do know how to read a face. And what I see in yours points heavily toward undecided. And I'm telling you, it shouldn't be that hard. It's an answer that lives in your heart, not in your head."

"Oh, and now you're an expert on love?" I bite off the words.

Killian scoffs. "Hardly," he says. "Though I do know what it feels like to be completely besotted by someone."

He looks at me in a way that doesn't quite match his words. That glaze in his eyes is much closer to lust than anything resembling lovestruck. And I really wish he'd just stop.

"You're so terrified of the heat," he says, "that you insist on hiding yourself away in the cold. But I offer you this—here in Florence, it's just you and me. So, why not give your undecided heart a chance to see what it truly wants? If it's not me, I'll back off, and no one will ever be the wiser. I do know how to keep a secret, Shiv. Trust me on that. Also, I'm an adult. I know how to deal with a broken heart should you decide against me. So, what do you say—won't you give us a chance?"

He cups a hand to my cheek, tracing a tender line around the slope of my ear, all the way down to my jaw.

His touch is warm—the warmest thing I've felt all day. But I don't like what he's asking, and I have no intention of cheating on Braxton.

I'm about to tell him as much when a gang of street urchins appears, and though it would've been bad enough to be caught in what probably seems like a public embrace in a time that's waging a war on pleasure and romance, considering that I'm dressed as a boy, this situation is a hundred times worse—and a thousand times more dangerous.

52

"Sodomites!" one of the boys cries out.

His gaze fevered, face enraged, he points at us and shouts it again.

In a matter of seconds, the others join in. Forming a circle around us, they chant, "Sodomites—burn in hell!"

Their filthy hands grasp at Killian, plucking at his gold rings, his silk cloak. And it's only now that I realize just how big a risk Killian has taken by setting out to find me. He must've woken from his nap, realized I was gone, and rushed out without bothering to change into something plainer. And now, because of it, because of me, he's being targeted by a gang of baby-faced crusaders.

"Bugger off!" Killian shouts, forgoing his Italian.

He pushes back at their grasping hands, but they keep at him, the chants growing louder. And when one of them goes after me, Killian curses under his breath and pulls out his dagger.

"I said, bugger off!" He brandishes the blade, and though they do back away, it's not far enough. These boys are brazen, completely brainwashed, and I fear that violence, or at least the threat of it, is all they'll respond to.

I pull my blade as well, and together, Killian and I walk backward, waving our weapons before us and managing to hold them off just enough for us to spin on our heels and break into an all-out, gut-busting run.

At first the kids start to follow, shouting, calling us heretics, heathens, and threatening the eternal damnation to come. But luckily, our legs are longer, we're faster, and we soon outpace them until they give up the chase and go in search of other sinners. Still, the chill of their taunts trails us all the way back to the villa.

Once we're safely inside the palazzo walls, Killian yanks down my hood. And as my hat tumbles to the ground, he grasps my face in his hands, his palms hot and damp against my heated cheeks.

"Don't," he says, his voice shaking in a way I never expected to hear. "Don't *ever* do that again." His gaze burns fiercely on mine as my body trembles from the terror of what nearly happened and the uncaged look in his eyes. "Promise me, Shiv, you'll never sneak out like that again."

"I won't," I say, though I'm not entirely sure that I mean it. I just want this to end. To put some much-needed distance between us.

"Okay," he mumbles, catching his breath. "Okay, then." Reluctantly, he lets go of my face, swipes a hand through his hair. "I'll call for someone to prepare you a bath."

The words take me by surprise, and I gaze down at myself. I know I need to change, but am I really that bad?

"And wear something nice," Killian says. "After all, you're going to meet Leonardo da Vinci tonight."

I stare at him in confusion. "But Leonardo left Florence in 1482 to go to Milan. He's busy painting *The Last Supper* as we speak." I follow Killian to our suite of rooms.

He glances over his shoulder at me. "Who told you that, Shiv?"

"Um, countless sources. It's a known fact."

"A known fact." Killian laughs. "Perhaps Napoleon was right when he said *history is a set of lies agreed upon*. Either way, you can take it up with Leonardo. I'm sure he'd love nothing more than to listen to you dispute his current whereabouts. Because despite what your history books say, here, in this current space-time continuum, he's left Milan to spend a few days in Florence, in the interest of ensuring his work isn't burned. He arrived not long after you snuck out. Shame you missed it. But, like I said, you'll meet him at dinner."

"Have you met him before?" I ask, relieved to have returned to a friendlier banter. "Before this, I mean."

"Of course."

"And—does he remember you?"

"Why? Do you consider me someone who's easily forgettable?"

I look at him. Even red-cheeked, sweaty, and short of breath, Killian is so resplendent, there's no chance of that. "I just meant that if you met him in the future, then he wouldn't know you when you meet him in the past, as it hasn't had a chance to happen yet."

Killian shrugs. "Not sure it matters. Like most people say, Leonardo's on a whole other level—doesn't perceive much of anything in the usual way. But now, dear Shiv"—he ushers me into the bedchamber, where a tub is being filled—"your bath awaits."

As he starts to leave, closing the door behind him, I say, "Killian—"

He looks at me.

"Thanks for…for showing up when you did."

"It's like I told you—I'll risk my life to protect you, but you need to take my life seriously, too." He holds my gaze for just a little too long, then takes his bow and leaves me to bathe.

53

Once I've changed into one of the gowns Charlotte made, I reach for the emerald-and-pearl earrings Braxton gave me, and the sting of his absence hits me again.

I miss him.

Miss him so much my heart aches for the loss of all that we'd planned.

And I can't help but wonder why Arthur chose to send Killian instead.

Was it to keep me on my toes, like Cosimo said?

Or was it because Arthur doesn't want us alone in a place where he can't watch us like he can back at Gray Wolf?

Since there's no use dwelling on what's already done, I take one last glance in the mirror, then head into the dining room, where a beautiful table is set for a feast. And though the room is crowded with artists and nobles, my gaze instinctively veers to the far side of the room and the unmistakable sight of Leonardo da Vinci himself.

My jaw drops. A hand clutches my chest, ready to catch hold of my heart should it actually pound its way right out of my flesh.

This is no dream. This is really happening.

I reach for my talisman, my fingers curling around that small golden cage. Just because I was told he'd be here doesn't make the reality of it any easier to take.

I mean, it's *freaking Leonardo da Vinci*! One of the greatest talents and minds of all time—and he's standing just a few feet away.

"Hey there, Shiv." Killian sidles up beside me. "Didn't anyone ever tell you it's not polite to openly gawk at the guests? Or at anyone, for that matter."

Just as he says it, Leonardo glances across the room, his gaze briefly locking on mine. And it's enough to cause a flame of embarrassment to redden my cheeks, and I quickly look away, staring down at my feet.

"Subtle." Killian laughs, nudging his elbow into my side. "You know, I'm more than happy to introduce you. But first, you need to pull it together. Think you can manage that?"

"Stop it," I whisper, my face so hot I can't make myself look at him, either. "It's not every day you get to meet one of your heroes." *Especially one who's been dead for over five centuries.*

"Here. Have some wine. Take the edge off." Killian thrusts a goblet into my hand, then tips his glass to mine. "What should we toast to, Shiv?"

I lift my chin, look Killian square in the face, and say, "To all the art and beauty that will continue to exist long after Savonarola's dark reign."

"Couldn't have said it better myself." Killian raises his glass, then takes a deep swig.

A moment later, Cosimo calls us to the table. The meal is about to be served.

Though I have no idea how it happened, I'm as amazed as I am intimidated to find myself sitting with Leonardo da Vinci on one side and Cesare Borgia, the infamous son of the current pope, Alexander VI, on the other. Luckily, Killian is seated directly across from me, since my Italian is so poor that I'm in desperate need of a translator.

Not that I'm called on to talk all that much. The conversation mostly centers around the current state of Florence, the tense relations between Savonarola and the Borgia pope, and the event that's set for tomorrow, along with everyone's predictions for how it all might play out.

The discussion is lively, robust. And though I don't understand most of it, as the night presses on, it becomes easier to catch more and more. But, when it comes to my own ability to join in, there's only a marginal improvement between now and my very first Italian lesson.

Which isn't such a bad thing, since it keeps me from saying something I shouldn't. Like assuring them all that there's no reason to worry—that in just over a year from now, Savonarola will be reduced to a memory.

As the conversation continues, I set my focus on the food, and the sheer quantity alone makes my head spin.

There are ceramic tureens of rich soups, heaping platters of pheasant and beef, and great mounds of fish, their glazed eyeballs staring at me. There are plates of pork jelly, a variety of pastas and breads. There are fritters, pastries, and more. Cosimo has gone all out, spared no expense. And when I'm sure I can't take another bite, I lean back in my seat, and Leonardo turns to me and says something I translate to mean, "I recognize your earrings."

I inhale a quick breath, remembering how Braxton brought them back from the Trip where he procured the *Salvator Mundi.*

A painting which Leonardo has yet to paint.

A painting that is still a few years away.

"So then," Leonardo says, intently studying my face. "Is this to mean that you are well acquainted with the boy out of time?"

I stare at Leonardo, wondering if he means what I think, or if my nerves caused me to misinterpret his words.

Needing to make sure, I lean toward him and say, "Scusa?"

Leonardo laughs, his mouth opening wide, eyes crinkling at the sides. "The boy out of time showed them to me." He tips a hand toward my earrings and, with the slightest touch, sets them swinging. "He appeared to be very lovestruck by you."

I nod, make some sort of indecipherable sound in my throat, which instantly makes my cheeks flush. I've had loads of training in swordcraft and equestrianism, but nothing to prepare me for moments like this.

"So, tell me—" Leonardo runs a gaze over my face. "How does history view me and my work?"

He knows.

Somehow, Leonardo knows that I am not from this time.

I mean, it's not like I'm fool enough to believe I've done a perfect job of blending in, but still, it's not like that's the next logical conclusion a person might jump to.

Someone must've told him. Cosimo, maybe? Even Braxton? Or maybe he just knows because, well, he's Leonardo da Vinci, which means he doesn't view the world through the same lens as the rest of us mortals.

Like Arthur, his vision is elevated, limitless, always with an eye to the future.

Realizing he's still waiting for an answer, I clear my throat, about to tell him he's bigger than any A-list actor, any rock star or world leader. But, not sure he'll appreciate those references, I say, "You are viewed as an absolute wonder. A genius. Five centuries from now, they're still writing about you, celebrating you, trying to figure you out."

"What we do now echoes in eternity," he says. Then, looking at me, he adds, "A quote from Marcus Aurelius."

The moment he says it, my mind turns to Arthur.

"And my friend here?" Leonardo nods toward Cesare Borgia. "How does history view him?"

That must've caught Killian's attention, because he turns away from the beautiful noblewoman sitting beside him and glances nervously between Cesare and me.

Cesare shoots me a curious look, his intense dark eyes poring over my face, causing me to pause, unsure what to say. The news isn't nearly as good where he's concerned.

"What is this?" Cesare looks to Leonardo. "Have you stumbled upon yet another one of your time travelers?" He laughs.

I laugh, too. A dreadful, high-pitched sound I regret the second it's out.

Leonardo shrugs. To Cesare, he says, "All the best oracles are time travelers of sorts."

Cesare gives me a long, considering once-over, thrusts his palm toward me, and says, "My friend here has the most inquisitive—often infuriatingly so—mind. And he will not stop until you spill all. So tell me, oracle: What do you see?"

Or at least that's how Killian translates it to me.

But Killian also looks worried. Like, really, gravely worried.

He gives me a subtle shake of his head that's meant to deter me. And when Cosimo catches on, he tries to distract both Cesare and Leonardo with offers of more food and wine.

But Cesare holds his focus on me, waiting for the verdict.

So I do the only thing I can. Tracing a light finger over the lines of his palm, I say, "You are a very complex man."

He looks to Leonardo, smiles smugly, then says, "Continue."

I lick my lips, unsure how to navigate this. I sneak a peek at Killian, who is clearly on edge, so I move on to Cosimo, who's so panic-stricken he's practically falling out of his chair. Then, focusing back on Cesare, I say, "And because you're so complex, you're often misunderstood. But mostly— " I pause, painfully aware of how Killian and Cosimo are both bracing for the moment when I explain to Cesare Borgia how five hundred years from this day, people will still be debating what exactly might've occurred between him and his sister, and how the word *sociopath* is often used in conjunction with his name. But of course, I have no intention of revealing any of that. Instead, I say, "You are primarily known for your achievements—the various roles you inhabit, from cardinal to condottiero."

Cesare jerks his head back. His shoulders stiffen. "Condottiero?" His dark brown eyes make a thorough study of my face, as though trying to determine whether to believe me.

And that's when I remember that, on this day, Cesare is still a cardinal, still a few years away from becoming a captain in charge of a mercenary army. Though according to the shine in his eyes, that particular dream already has roots.

Cesare grins, folds my hand in his, and lifts it to his lips. "I like this girl," he says. "Does she belong to anyone here?"

Belong? It's all I can do to bite back the scathing reply that pops into my head.

Luckily, Killian jumps in to rescue me from both myself and from the infamous Borgia. "Sorry," he says. "But the girl belongs to me."

Cesare nods, releases my hand. "Never mind, then," he says.

54

As Killian returns his attention to the beautiful woman beside him, Leonardo leans toward me and says, "So, you are not with the boy out of time? Or this is a game that you and Killian play?" Before I can respond, he nods toward Killian and adds, "He is very beautiful, no?"

I glance briefly at Killian. "Sì," I say, aware of the flush that rises to my cheeks. Still, there's no point in denying what's so plain to see.

"But I would like to do a quick sketch of you," Leonardo says. "If you are agreeable."

"Me? Seriously?" I gape, unaware I'd answered in English until I see the amused look on his face. "Um, certo," I tell him, struggling to keep my cool, which, let's face it, I lost long ago.

With a square of parchment and a stub of red chalk, Leonardo positions me so I'm looking directly at Killian. "It is very complicated between you," he says, his left hand deftly moving across the page. "It is this that I am determined to capture."

I turn to him then. "Wait—what?" I ask, sure I misunderstood. "I mean, che?"

But Leonardo doesn't respond. He just continues sketching as I watch Killian ramp up the full extent of his charm for the beautiful noblewoman's benefit.

There are so many things I want to say—so many questions I

need answered. But how can I possibly ask Leonardo to explain the choices he made in a painting he's yet to begin?

Even if he did tease me about being an oracle and Braxton a boy out of time, I still can't bring myself to go through with it.

For one thing, it might risk introducing one of those pesky time-travel issues, like a causal loop or bootstrap paradox. If I were to so much as mention a painting Leonardo has yet to conceive of, then whose idea is it, really?

Still, if there's one thing I've learned in our short time together, it's that Leonardo is deliberate, deeply observant, and undoubtedly the smartest person in any room. He's also incredibly charismatic. And I'm left with the unmistakable feeling that nothing he does is ever by chance.

"You enjoy your studies?" he asks, the question seeming to come out of nowhere.

I turn to him, trying to get a better grasp of what he might mean. Was he referring to my Italian-language studies, or does he somehow know about Gray Wolf?

I'm about to ask him outright, but before I can summon the words, he gives a curt nod and directs my attention back to looking at Killian.

"Sì," I reply, not knowing what else to say. "My studies are... buono." *Or is it buona, or even bene?* Suddenly, whatever flimsy grasp I had on the language eludes me completely.

As Leonardo continues to draw, I watch as Killian fills the noblewoman's goblet with wine. Or, should I say, even more wine.

When he returns the carafe to the table, his eye catches mine, and though I have no idea how it might look from Leonardo's vantage, I swear I hear the legendary artist mumble something that sounds a lot like "perfetto."

With a few more strokes of his chalk, Leonardo is done. "Enjoy your studies," he says. "But remember: poor is the pupil who does not surpass his master."

His gaze locks on mine as he slides the sketch toward me. "I would very much like to see your eyes when you look upon the boy out of time," he says. "Maybe someday, yes?"

I give a tentative nod, then stare down at my portrait.

"What do you think?" he asks.

My gaze greedily devours every line, every contour and curve, marveling at the way he's managed to capture the tilt of my chin, the way my hair spills over my shoulders, the question in my eyes as they reflect upon Killian.

"It's so…honest," I say, the wonder of being sketched by Leonardo ringing clear in my voice.

Leonardo nods, seemingly pleased.

"Will you sign it?" I ask, remembering how he never signed the *Mona Lisa*—a painting that, as of this day, he's not yet had a chance to paint—but hoping he'll agree to sign this.

He shoots me a curious look.

"Just so I won't forget who sketched it." I grin.

Luckily, he finds that as amusing as I'd hoped, and I watch as he signs the bottom right corner using the left-to-right style he's known for.

"I will treasure this always," I tell him, about to tuck it away when I notice the small interlocking circle design he's added just below it. But before I can ask what it means, Cosimo announces the coaches are packed and ready to take him to Venice. Dinner is officially over.

55

"Tell me something."

Killian looks at me, amused. "Okay," he says. "What would you like to know?"

I hesitate, unsure if it's because I've just said good night to both Leonardo da Vinci and Cesare Borgia after a lovely, multi-course meal that I'm so brash, or the one and a half goblets of wine in my belly, but I boldly press forward and say, "Why does everyone hate you?"

Killian flinches, runs a slow, deliberate hand over his jaw, looking truly perplexed. "I wasn't aware that they did," he says.

"Perhaps *hate* is too harsh," I say. "But you must notice how they all go out of their way to avoid you."

Killian leans toward me with interest. "And exactly who is *they*?"

My fingers find their way to his sleeve, where I tug at it playfully. "I don't think it's a secret that, after a four-year absence, not a single person at Gray Wolf celebrated your return. And I'm curious to know why. What exactly have you done?"

"Oh," he says, feigning relief. "For a minute there, I thought you were talking about Cesare Borgia. I saw the two of you earlier, with your heads bent together, whispering like coconspirators, and it got me worried. He's exactly the type of enemy I prefer not to have. You do know he's the subject of Machiavelli's *The Prince*?"

"So I hear. And don't change the subject. You said so yourself. Everyone at Gray Wolf dislikes you, but you never said why."

"I don't recall ever admitting such a thing." Killian slides back in his seat.

"At the Hideaway Tavern. You said that while practically everyone on that side of the rock worships you, I'm your only friend on the other side of Gray Wolf."

"Just because no one threw me a welcome-back party doesn't mean Arthur wasn't pleased by my return," he says. "And as far as I'm concerned, he's the only one who matters."

"Stop trying to dance around it." I frown. "You know exactly what I mean."

"Fine," he concedes. "But that doesn't mean I can give you a reason. You should probably go straight to the source and ask them."

"And what if they're unwilling to tell me?"

"Ah." He tilts his seat back on two legs and regards me from under a slanted brow. "So you have asked around." His head bobs. "Good to know you've been inquiring about me."

"Don't flatter yourself." I roll my eyes. "I'm a curious person, that's all."

"Look." He sets his chair forward again. "I don't know what you want from me, Shiv. But have you ever heard that old saying, 'What other people think about me is none of my business'? Well, that's pretty much my motto. I don't give a shit what people whisper about me in your gilded hallways. It's all projection—more about the opinion holder than the subject in question. Which, in this case, is me. And if I'm not worried, then you shouldn't be, either."

"It's just—" I stall for a moment, then decide to push on. "There are so many secrets at Gray Wolf, and it's impossible to unravel them all. It's even harder to know who to trust."

"If I were you, I'd trust no one," he says. "As for those

secrets—maybe they're not for you to unravel."

"But I'm tired of it," I protest. "I mean, why won't anyone just say what they mean and be straight with me?"

Killian's gaze locks onto mine. "And what about you, Shiv? Exactly how straight have you been? Seems to me, you've been holding on to a few secrets of your own."

"Me?" I balk. "Sorry to disappoint, but I got nothing." I force a laugh, but I can see from the angle of Killian's brow that he's not buying a word of it.

"It's a wonder to watch just how easily the lie spills from those beautiful lips." He slides to the edge of his chair, his hand reaching for my face but stopping just shy of making contact. "Do you remember the night we met?"

His gaze holds on mine, and just like that, the high I was riding a few moments earlier has taken a turn toward something that feels like a warning of sorts.

"Yes," I reply in a tremulous voice. "I was in a Fade."

"And yet still you remember." He veers toward me in a way that leaves me regretting the part I played in bringing us here.

I was only looking for some truths—hoping that, as my friend, Killian might finally be honest with me. But I should've known better. Considering the proposal he made earlier, when he basically asked me to cheat on Braxton, Killian wants far more than I'm willing to give.

I swallow hard, start to look away, when he dips a hand toward my chest and lifts the talisman that hangs from my neck.

"And are you in a Fade now?" he asks, studying the small golden cage that Braxton had made.

Not trusting my voice to speak, I shake my head.

"Then you have no convenient excuse for the way you're looking at me, do you?"

56

"Killian…" I start, having no idea what will follow. I just know that I have to say something, anything, to stop this—whatever this is—from progressing any further. But Killian cuts in before I can finish.

"Outside the shelter of these walls," he says, voice barely a whisper, "the heart and soul of this city will soon be ablaze. But here, it's just you and me, where no one can harm us, observe us, judge us. Doesn't that strike you as remarkable? That we should find ourselves here, all alone, at this dark time in history?"

My heart is pounding so hard, I fear he can hear it, see the beat of it under my skin. I pull away, watching the talisman fall from his fingers. "It was supposed to be Braxton," I say, my voice a choked whisper. "You're here by default."

I hold my breath in my cheeks, waiting to see how my words land. And from the way his lips tighten and his eyes pinch at the sides, it's the equivalent of tossing a pail of freezing cold water over his head.

Good. Maybe now we can get back on track.

"And what I really want to know," I say, determined to finally get some answers, "is the truth of what happened between you and Braxton back in France. I want every detail—leave nothing out. And I'll know if you're lying, so don't even try."

Killian considers me for an agonizingly long beat. Then, coming to a decision, he tops off his wine, settles back in his seat, and launches into a story that stretches all the way back to the eighteenth century.

The year 1741, to be exact, when Braxton and Killian Tripped to the Basilique Royale de Saint-Denis in France, a necropolis where many French royals are buried.

I lean toward him, on the lookout for signs of duplicity. But so far, everything checks and his voice rings with sincerity.

According to Killian, there were three of them in that ancient Necropolis. Himself, Braxton, and another man who goes unnamed. But, in the end, only Braxton returned to Gray Wolf. The man was left for dead, and Killian was left to fend for himself in a time that wasn't his.

"It's a miracle you found me," he says.

"No." I shake my head, lower my gaze. "Not a miracle." I sigh, alarmed by the way my heart has gone numb, as my mind whirls with the glaring disparities between Braxton's version and Killian's.

But who to believe?

During Braxton's telling, he acted cagey, like he hated every moment of being forced to talk about it.

But is that because the memory really did pain him, like he claimed?

Or is it because he hadn't had a chance to fully hone his story and polish the lie—to sell it in a more believable way.

While Killian, on the other hand... Well, he seemed so eager to spill it. And yet, why wouldn't he be?

In his version, he's cast as the victim.

In Braxton's version, it never actually happened.

And while it feels like a terrible betrayal of the boy I thought I'd given my heart to, something about Killian's story bears the ring of truth.

I don't know how I know, but I do. I can see it worn plain on his face. I can feel it deep in my bones. And now, all I can think is: *How could I have been so wrong?*

How could I have fallen for all the lies Braxton told me?

"Not a miracle," I repeat, my voice robotic, monotonous, stating a fact with zero emotion attached. "Arthur specifically sent me to find you. You were just another Get."

"I'm talking about the first time," Killian says. "Think about it, Shiv. Your very first Trip, and you run into me? What are the chances of that?"

It wasn't long ago when Braxton said the same thing. Both of our fathers taught us the meaning of "amor fati," and we took that to mean we were some sort of miracle, destined to find each other.

But now I know that was just magical thinking. Because the truth is, Braxton was in pursuit of me. He was sent by Arthur.

Not so different from Killian approaching me at the Yew Ball, having recognized me as a girl out of time.

I take a steadying breath, lift my gaze to meet his, and remind him of that truth.

"Doesn't make it any less of a miracle," he says. "And I'm sorry to say it, Shiv, but I can't help but wonder what might've happened had you met me first and not Braxton."

I study his face. His gaze is even. His lips slightly parted.

But all I can think is: *if Killian's telling the truth—then that also means Braxton's been feeding me lies.*

I look at Killian, my stomach roiling in protest, as a voice in my head insists there is safety in keeping this next part to myself, protecting my heart from the sort of things that might prove too hurtful to know. But I ignore that voice and press on.

"Braxton keeps a pair of old boots," I say. "They're covered in—"

"Blood and vomit." Killian nods.

With those three little words, he's knocked the breath right out of me.

It's proof. Absolute, irrefutable proof.

I mean, how could he possibly know about that unless he was there?

"He was wearing them on that Trip. Breaking in a new pair, when—"

I hold up my hand to ward off the words. I've heard more than enough. I can't take any more.

"I'm sorry," Killian says, his voice dripping with sincerity, but I'm not sure I believe him.

My eyes meet his. "You say that, but I'm not convinced that you are."

"Maybe you're right." He rubs a hand along his jaw. "Maybe it's more accurate to say that while I'm not sorry you know the truth, I also feel badly about the way it's made you feel. I can only imagine what a betrayal this must be. To know that the boy you trusted, the one you've grown close to, has been lying to you."

The last thing I want is Killian's sympathy. And I certainly don't want to discuss the burning sting of Braxton's betrayal. But there is something more I need to know, and Killian is clearly the only one who's willing to tell.

"Who was the man?" I ask. "The one who didn't make it back. Was it a fellow Blue—a Tripper?"

"Neither a Blue nor a Tripper," Killian says.

"And this person—this man—you're saying *Braxton* left him for dead?"

A shadow of memory darkens Killian's gaze. "The man took a blade to the back, and then another to the heart," he says. "I'm afraid there was no hope after that."

"Was he—" The words stall on my tongue, forcing me to clear my throat and begin again. "That man—was he a...a Timekeeper?"

Killian's gaze narrows on mine. "Do you know what a

Timekeeper is, Shiv?"

"They're the enemy," I say, remembering my conversation with Arthur—the man that Killian left for dead in Versailles, the one that confronted me in the library in England.

"Yeah." He nods, traces the rim of his wine goblet with his index finger. "That's exactly what they are. The enemy."

He shoots me a lopsided half grin, and in an instant, I'm up and out of my chair.

"Where are you going?" Killian asks.

But I'm already gone, racing into the dark.

57

By the time Killian finds me by the fountain, I'm shivering from the cold.

Only it's not entirely due to the weather.

It's the chill of realizing the colossal mistake that I've made.

"Shiv." Killian places a tentative hand on my arm. "Please, come back inside."

I lift my gaze to meet his. His eyes are blue liquid, his lips tinged with wine. And with his shock of golden curls falling over his forehead, his prominent nose jutting from beneath a strong brow, and the near brutal line of his jaw, he's exactly the sort of boy I used to dream about when I watched all those romantic movies that took place in long-ago times.

The dashing, capable, strong-willed though tender-hearted hero who bore little patience for simpering girls trained in the art of landing a husband.

No, this particular hero only had eyes for the equally headstrong girl who rose to every challenge the world threw at her.

Standing before me now, under the glow of a torch, Killian seems perfectly cast for that role.

And yet, right on the heels of that thought, I remember how I once felt the same way about Braxton.

Once felt.

Is it truly over, then—just like that?

Has my heart really turned to stone against him?

Are my feelings for Braxton so easily dismissed just because Killian's story differed from the one Braxton shared?

After all that we've been through, it hardly seems fair. I mean, shouldn't Braxton at least get a shot at defending himself?

"Shiv," Killian says, "talk to me, please. What is it you're thinking—feeling?"

Other than the burn of betrayal, I'm feeling angry. Angry at having been lied to. Angry at myself for being such an easy target. So easily manipulated into believing Braxton and I shared something special—that we were somehow, miraculously, bound and destined to be together.

This energy between us, Braxton once said, calling out the electric charge that always sparks from our nearness.

But did I really feel it?

Or was I so caught up in the moment that I just wanted to feel it, so I convinced myself that I had?

Like Killian, Braxton also referred to our meeting as a miracle. But now I know better—there are no miracles here.

Arthur's been in charge all along. We are merely what results from the choices he makes.

"Shiv, you're shaking." Killian places a hand on my arms, moving them briskly, trying to warm me. "Please, be sensible and come back inside."

But I stay rooted in place—as immune to his touch as I am to his attempt to talk sense.

Inside, I am gutted, a hollowed-out core.

I crane my neck back and gaze up at the sky, trying in vain to locate a moon in a cloud-dense night.

"What are you doing?" Killian grips my arms, his voice barely so much as a whisper.

"I want you to swear it on the moon," I say.

"Which moon?" Killian asks. "The one hidden behind the clouds, or the one Arthur has tasked you to find?"

My skin pricks with chills, and for a moment, I wonder if that's why Arthur made the last-minute swap.

Was it because he knew I was worried about having to sneak away from Braxton, so he sent Killian to alleviate that problem?

I lower my chin and level my gaze on Killian's. "How do you know about that?"

"About Arthur's Antikythera?" He raises his brows. "He sent me to get the Sun when… Well, let's just say, that's the Trip that went south."

"Then he sent me to find it."

"And you did. You scored major points with Arthur that day."

I shrug like I don't care either way. "Aren't you worried about what Arthur plans to do with the Antikythera Mechanism once it's complete?" I ask.

"Why would I be worried?" Killian squints. "Arthur's been very good to me, and I trust him implicitly. And you shouldn't worry, either, Shiv. It's clear how much he values you."

"What makes you say that?"

"Well, just think about it. Out of everyone at Gray Wolf, he chose you to go after the Sun and the Moon. Not Hawke, not Keane, not Roxanne—not even Elodie. Hell, he didn't even send Braxton to give him a chance to make up for the royal fuckup from last time. Out of all those people with their years of experience, you're the one he sent. I think it's obvious, Shiv."

"Who else knows?" I ask. "About the Antikythera?"

"I think what you're really asking is if Braxton knows."

I give a tentative nod.

"Seems to me that if your relationship is as close as you think, then you wouldn't be looking to me for the answer."

There's no denying that's true.

He holds my gaze for a long, steady beat, then, lifting his face to the sky, he says, "I found it. It's right there."

I follow the direction of his finger, all the way to where the clouds have parted to reveal a slice of pale Tuscan moon.

"And now that I've located your moon, what is it you want me to do?"

"I want you to swear on it," I say, my voice shaky. "I know it seems like a child's game, but I'm serious. I need you to swear that everything you told me tonight is true."

"You are aware of the Shakespeare quote?" His narrowed eyes fix on mine.

I stare at him blankly. Arthur has sent loads of Shakespeare quotes to my slab, but I have no idea which one Killian's referring to.

"O, swear not by the moon, the inconstant moon," he says, his voice quiet, eloquent, blending into the night.

"All I want is the truth," I tell him, my own voice indignant. "No more games, no more lies. I need you to promise you've been honest with me."

Without hesitation, Killian presses a hand to his heart and, in a solemn voice, says, "I swear to you, Shiv. I swear on the moon to every last word."

As my eyes lock on his, these are the words that spin through my head: *I am Natasha Antoinette Clarke. This is not my time, this is not my place, this is not my boyfriend, and I am most definitely not in a Fade. So whatever comes next is entirely on me…*

Then I take a deep breath and place my hand over Killian's. And though there are too many layers to feel the actual beat of his heart, I can see it in every blink of his eyes, can feel it in the way his hand eagerly conforms against mine.

"Shiv," he says. "Don't do this if you don't mean it. Don't do this if you're going to regret it later and blame it on wine or a Fade or end up angry with me. And please, definitely don't do this if you're only searching for a quick fix to heal your broken heart."

"What exactly is it you think I'm going to do?" I ask.

"You're going to kiss me," he says, as though it's an indisputable fact.

58

It's true what he says.

There is a part of me that's thinking about kissing him.

But my heart is scorched, my mind is confused, and I'm well aware of what a mistake that would be.

Still, I play along when I say, "If that were true, then why do you propose I do it, if not because I'm in a Fade or drank too much wine?"

"If you do decide to kiss me," Killian says, his voice thick. "It should be because you want this kiss as much as I do. Because you want to celebrate beauty and pleasure and life and spirit and adventure in a city gone so mad it's turned its back on everything that makes life worth living—everything that reminds us that God is real, and good, and not searching for ways to damn us. We don't need God for that—we humans do a fine job of it all on our own."

"And if it's a mistake? If we end up regretting the kiss?"

"That won't happen for me." His gaze glitters on mine. "I've wanted to kiss you, really, truly kiss you—not a Fade kiss, not a fake-it-to-avoid-getting-caught-by-palace-guards kiss, but a real kiss—a desperate-for-it sort of kiss—from the moment I met you. This is what keeps me up at night. As for your own regrets, I'm afraid I can't comment on that. That's for you to weigh the risk versus the benefit."

As Killian's words fade, I remember back to the first night

I almost kissed Braxton. And then the second night, when the kiss finally happened, how I tipped onto my toes and kissed him under a star-filled sky with a wink of moon hanging high overhead.

A kiss so memorable, so meaningful, he took those very symbols and used them for the talisman that now hangs from my neck.

Only now I know we were built on a lie.

But is it possible to erase the sting of that lie by kissing this golden boy under that very same moon from a long-ago time?

Of course not.

It's never as easy as that.

But I also know that if I don't kiss Killian, if I don't allow myself this one small indulgence, it's the type of thing I'll always wonder about.

What could have been? It's the sort of thing that haunts people at the end.

So what's the harm in finding out now, while I still have the chance?

There's an ease in being with Killian. Unlike Braxton, he doesn't feel like it's his job to carry the weight of the world on his shoulders.

But now I know it's not really the weight of the world Braxton's been carrying, but rather the weight of his lies.

I look at Killian again. His gaze is open, deep, and filled with unfiltered longing for me.

It's just a kiss.

It doesn't have to mean anything.

Besides, it's not like I haven't kissed him before—

And yet…

I can't bring myself to do it.

Not now.

Not when my heart is in shreds.

It's not fair to me, and it's not fair to him.

So, I do the next best thing. I press a finger to his lips and tell him my truth. "I can't." I stop. Shake my head. "Or rather, I won't. Not like this. Not tonight. I need to get my head sorted out."

He grasps hold of my finger, traces a hand over my cheek. "I'm not going anywhere," he says. "I'll be here if, and when, you decide that you're ready."

I nod, and, not trusting myself to hold true to my word, I take a step back.

"For now"—he slings an arm around my shoulders—"what do you say we get you to bed?"

I look at him in alarm.

"Alone. I'll take the daybed."

I nod, relaxing again.

"Because tomorrow, Shiv, while Florence is burning, we've got ourselves a Moon to go find."

59

I stand on the other side of the door, waiting until I hear soft, even snores sounding from Killian's bed. Then I slip into the boy's clothes I wore earlier, grab a few additional items along with a torch, and steal into the night.

Though I have no idea what time it might be, I'm guessing it's close to predawn. Early enough that the streets are quiet, which means there's little chance of getting caught.

Or at least that's what I hope, since, according to Killian, there are patrols of night police who are all too eager to enforce Savonarola's new curfew.

And while I guess I could've, maybe even should've, waited for Killian to wake up and join me, when I think of what almost happened between us, how close I came to kissing him, Killian feels more like a guilty distraction.

I mean, yes, sometimes I'm impulsive. But I'm not the type who hops from one boyfriend to the next. And until I settle things with Braxton, I can't be thinking of Killian like that.

Also, I've got a job to do, and getting sidetracked by a bunch of relationship drama will only put me at risk.

The streets are dark, but I navigate easily enough. When I see the cathedral, I dart quickly toward it, skirting around the pile of treasures that are set to burn later today, wishing I could save them all, especially the paintings and books, but that's not what I'm here for.

Once I'm inside the cathedral, I head for the stairs and begin climbing all 463 of them. With my flickering torch my only source of light, I try not to think about the all-too-real threat of falling to my death or being claimed by claustrophobia.

When I've finally made it to the top, I gaze out at the view beyond. But since it's too dark to see much of anything, I find a place to sit and settle in.

I have a theory. And after meeting Leonardo, I'm more convinced than ever that he paints with intention, that every drop of color is placed for a reason. Like the collection of words that comprise a book, every stroke of Leonardo's brush is part of the story he's chosen to tell.

And, in this case, those three dots he placed on that crystal sphere in the *Salvator Mundi* aren't just random splotches he included to mimic the sort of occlusions that naturally occur.

No, Leonardo was pointing at something. Telling us something.

And if my theory is right, it should direct me straight to the Moon.

When the first rays of sun steal past this ancient horizon, my heart fills with gratitude for the chance to experience such a wonder, while trying not to think about the cost of such a Trip—of every Trip.

Still, the nagging questions continue to spin through my head.

What is Arthur really planning to do once the Antikythera Mechanism is restored?

And should I really be so complicit in helping him get there?

When the sun edges higher, painting the city in a warm and glittering shade of Florentine gold, I close my eyes and summon the image of the *Salvator Mundi* in my mind's eye, centering my focus on those three white dots. And when I see them so clearly it's as though the painting manifested before me, I open my eyes and gaze once more at the view, delighted to find it's right there, plain as day, just as I'd hoped.

The white dot on the far left of Leonardo's painting stands in for the Basilica di San Lorenzo.

The dot to the right symbolizes the Palazzo Medici.

And the dot Leonardo placed at the bottom represents the Duomo, where I stand now.

And yet, when I consider the tarot cards and the symbols etched onto the map—the sideways crown, the upside-down hourglass, the archer's bow—I'm still not convinced I'll find the Moon here.

I close my eyes, summon the image again and...*yes!*

Suddenly it seems so obvious, I can't believe I hadn't seen it before.

So much has been made of the fact that Leonardo chose to paint Jesus's robe without distorting the image, which is not how it would normally appear when viewed through an orb.

If Leonardo was so intent on getting the crystal right by adding occlusions, then why wouldn't he take it all the way and paint the robe in an inverted image?

Some claim it's because Leonardo chose to be polite to the viewer—to not distract or confuse them or upset the visual continuity of the picture.

Others say he did it to show the perfection of Christ—that even his robe couldn't be marred.

But now I know it's neither of those things.

Leonardo placed those three dots to represent three specific landmarks.

And he left the crystal clear because that one prominent white streak, which is made to look like a fold in the robe Jesus wears—that one streak that cuts straight through the center dot and ends just shy of Christ's middle finger—is like an arrow pointing me directly to where the Moon hides.

And as I look out at the city again, the sun lifting higher into the sky, a burst of adrenaline shoots through me as I line up those three dots, noting how that arrow points straight to the Baptistery of San Giovanni—the octagon-shaped building that's right across the street from where I now stand.

Since this will probably be my last chance to see Florence like this, I steal another moment to soak in the view of this magnificent landscape, determined to imprint the image onto my brain so I can carry it with me long after I return to Gray Wolf.

In my studies leading up to this Trip, I learned about Stendhal syndrome—a condition specific to Florence, where people fall ill after witnessing the stunning Renaissance-era art displayed throughout the city. The symptoms include dizziness, heart palpitations, disorientation, and more. It's said that a man once had a heart attack while looking at Botticelli's masterpiece, *The Birth of Venus.*

I take it as more proof of the power great art has to touch our very souls.

And maybe that's what Savonarola's so afraid of. He wants our souls to be touched only through God—his version of God, anyway. But what he's failed to realize is that great art is the direct byproduct of artists connecting to the divine.

When I take in the golden sphere that rises from the top of the dome with a cross placed just above, something about that particular view gives me pause.

Though I'm certain the *Salvator Mundi* is pointing to the location that'll lead me to the Moon, seeing the golden ball glinting in the early-morning sun reminds me of something else I recently learned. How, just five years before, in 1492, a bolt of lightning struck this red dome, causing damage to the lantern.

In just over a century from now, the dome will be struck once again. Only this time, the lightning will cause that same gilded sphere to break away from the structure, topple down the side of the dome, and smash onto the street below.

Thankfully, because of the storm, the streets will be empty, and no one will be hurt. A year later, a new ball will be put in its place, and a marble plaque will be set in the exact location where that first ball landed.

As I take another look at the golden orb, my skin pricks with chills—and I know in that moment that Arthur got it wrong when he matched those three symbols on the map to their corresponding tarot cards.

While I'm sure he's right about the Moon and the Hermit cards, the crown is where he took a wrong turn.

Had he asked me, I never would've picked the High Priestess to represent the crown. Especially considering the way it was drawn on Columbus's map as though it had fallen onto its side.

No, I would've reached for one of the most dreaded cards in the deck.

The card that's right up there with Death and the Devil when it comes to bad news, the Tower is almost always viewed as a portent of doom.

While both modern and traditional decks portray the High Priestess as a woman wearing a crown, and while all the other elements seem to line up as well, if I'd known back at Gray Wolf that Arthur was sending me to Florence during the Bonfire of the Vanities, I would've told him right then that the Tower is the card that brings the whole thing together.

Like the modern and traditional versions of the High Priestess card, the Tower also bears a crown. Only the crown on the Tower card is portrayed as being blown sideways off the top of the building after suffering a terrible blow from nature—or an act of God.

I pull the map from my pocket, and there it is—the crown on the map, just like the crown on the Tower card, is sideways.

Leaving me more convinced than ever that the Tower will provide the ultimate clue.

As for all the other links… *Let's see, let's see*… The Tower shares an astrological link with Mars, which fits, since according to my studies the place where the baptistery stands was once an ancient Roman temple for Mars.

Okay, and… Its element is fire, which corresponds to the event later today, when the Bonfire of the Vanities is set to take place.

And, while the card is considered a portent of darkness, which doesn't necessarily bring a baptistery to mind, it also holds the promise of the enlightenment that awaits on the other side.

Also, isn't the whole point of a baptism to save one's soul from that very brand of darkness?

And lastly, and more personally, just like the Wheel of Fortune card, the Tower is also a card of fate.

Though I'm not sure how to interpret that last part, I still make a point to tuck it away.

Once the sun is fully risen, I make my way back down the stairs, out the cathedral doors, and onto the street of a city that's just beginning to wake. Which means if I have any hope of getting this done, I'll need to move quickly.

60

Though there are three doors through which I could enter the Baptistery of San Giovanni, I head straight for the gilded bronze eastern doors, which Michelangelo famously likened to "the Gates of Paradise." And I'm delighted to find they're just as stunning as they're rumored to be.

If I ever get the chance to visit Florence in the modern day, I'll have to view these doors in the Duomo Museum. But for now, I steal a moment to study the series of reliefs that represent the life of Saint John the Baptist, the patron saint of the city.

Once inside, I find a spectacular display of Byzantine-style mosaics spread across the dome, telling the stories of the Last Judgment, scenes from the life of Saint John the Baptist, and more. But nothing that points to the location of the Get I'm looking for, even though I'm sure I'm in the right place.

Slowly, I move through the space, poring over the clues in my head.

An upside-down hourglass that represents time running out.

A sideways crown, which I'm convinced points to the Tower, which also points to an ending of sorts.

Is it because this is considered the end of the Renaissance era?

Or is it something else—something I still can't quite grasp?

Though the various connections to water, virgins, fish, healing, and spirituality have also landed me here, I can't forget the painting that started it all—the *Salvator Mundi.*

Leonardo da Vinci pointed the way, and…

I stop in my tracks, silently repeating that phrase in my head.

Leonardo pointed the way, and…

Leonardo pointed.

My mind reels back to my conversation with Mason about all the ways those crossed fingers could be interpreted and how so many of Leonardo's works portray active hands.

A rush of chills races over my skin, a sure sign that I'm onto something—but as to what that might be, I'm not entirely sure.

Okay, okay, just think, put the pieces together…

Jesus's fingers were depicted in the *Salvator Mundi* as both raised and crossed, and…

And what?

Outside, it's getting lighter. It won't be long before someone comes in and finds me. And I'm not sure what would be worse—to be caught by one of Savonarola's followers or by a Timekeeper. Either way, I prefer not to find out.

I blow out a frustrated breath and stare up at the dome once again. When my eyes catch on the mosaic of Saint John the Baptist, I remember the portrait Leonardo also painted of him.

Or, according to this timeline, the painting he will one day paint of him, sometime in the early sixteenth century.

Saint John the Baptist is the patron saint of Florence.

This baptistery is named after him.

The story of his life plays out on the eastern doors and the ceiling above.

In Leonardo's painting, Saint John is radiant. His hair a mane of cascading curls, his expression serene as he points toward the sky with his right hand, while his left, mostly painted in shadow, bends toward his heart.

I snap my eyes open, and with a cautious glance over my shoulder, ensuring I'm still alone, I make for the baptismal font where the Medici family and Dante Alighieri himself were once fully immersed.

My pulse races, my footsteps echo hollow and light, but once I'm standing before it, I'm disappointed to find it just doesn't feel right.

Yes, it's water, which bears a connection to the Moon. And it's also a Christian ritual, which corresponds to the fish.

But how does the Tower fit in, other than its connection to Mars and the fact that this baptistery was once a Roman temple for Mars?

I step away from the font and take another look around. Lifting my torch, I focus on the gleaming golden tiles above. Starting at the left, I move through the various tales until my gaze wanders to the section reserved for hell and the terrifying horned creature with snakes coming out of his ears and a pair of human legs dangling from his mouth.

Satan is making a meal of the doomed, while the others are all left to burn.

The depiction is brutal—terrifying, even. And I can only imagine the urgency those fifteenth-century parents must've felt, in a time when so many children didn't make it through childhood. Among the devout, the rush to baptize must've been serious.

It also calls to mind Francisco Goya's *Saturn Devouring His Son*, a painting I once came across during a Venetian construct with Elodie.

Back then, I never imagined I'd one day find myself here, tasked with finding a priceless piece that's been hidden for centuries.

Back then, it was the clues left in that collection of paintings that led me to claiming the true prize—the one only I could see.

And now...well, it's not so different, considering how it's Arthur's choice of the High Priestess that led me to this place of holy waters. But it's the flames of doom depicted on the Tower card, along with Leonardo's penchant for pointing fingers, that are about to lead me straight to the Moon.

With an image of those fingers fixed in my mind—both in the *Salvator Mundi* and the portrait of John the Baptist—I focus once more on the scene of damnation that plays out above, then drop my gaze downward.

All the way to the altar where a holy relic sits on display.

I remember reading about this very thing. At the time, it seemed so unbelievable I was quick to dismiss it and move on to what I thought were more relevant topics. But now, standing before this elaborate glass case with its fancy gold lid, I know in my heart that the Moon is hidden somewhere inside it.

I lean closer, peering through the glass and making a thorough study of the finger. Or rather, the skeletal remains of an index finger that's said to belong to Saint John the Baptist himself.

A holy relic that's spawned countless pilgrimages to Florence for hundreds of years.

Normally, the reliquary is put on display once a year, on June 24, also known as the Feast Day of Saint John. But I guess, with all that's going on, Savonarola wanted to display it today, in honor of the Bonfire of the Vanities.

Time is running out.

The metaphorical crown will soon fall, marking the end of the Renaissance, and—

My breath halts, a rush of chills shudders through me, and I can't believe I didn't see it before. Leonardo da Vinci left nothing to chance. Everything about the *Salvator Mundi* is a clue, including the robe—that anachronistic blue-and-gold robe he depicted Jesus as wearing—which is probably the most obvious clue that time is running out.

In just over a decade from when I now stand, Leonardo will paint the *Salvator Mundi* and purposely put Jesus in a Renaissance-style robe—as opposed to the sort of robe Christ might've worn during his own time—as a hint toward the urgency required for this task.

If I have any chance of finding the Moon, it needs to happen now, before Savonarola hides it away once again.

With no time to waste, I grab hold of the reliquary and examine it from all sides. But no matter how hard I look, I don't see a single thing that resembles the Moon.

Outside these walls, I hear footsteps, shouting—the sounds of once-dormant streets coming to life.

It won't be long before someone comes in to find me.

Should I take this thing and run?

Shove it under my arm and escape through one of the side doors?

Maybe. I mean, there is a small chance I'd get away with it.

But there's just as good a chance that I won't.

With frantic eyes, I study the reliquary again. I even shake it to see if something comes loose, but nothing.

Nothing until…

In my mind's eye, I see those pointing fingers again—see the beatific look on Saint John the Baptist's face, his finger pointing toward the heavens.

His finger.

The same finger that's inside this glass case.

And that's when I know.

With a racing heart and trembling hands, I screw off the lid, and, following the direction in which Saint John is pointing, I peek underneath the cap to find the small silver ball.

With a single twist, the ball comes loose, and my breath rushes right out of me as I stare at the glimmering sphere now held in my hand.

The Moon.

I did it! I really did it, and now—

Before I can finish the thought, the world caves in all around me.

61

The world as I know it falls away, only to be replaced by another.

And I watch from the sidelines, balanced on the scantest strip of mosaic-tiled floor, as a small group of people begin to gather. And from the looks of it, it's taking place in a time long before mine.

A man with long white hair and a matching beard stands before them. And though there's no sign of a rose hanging from the ceiling, I instinctively know this is one of those secret meetings my dad told me about.

These people are seekers—initiates who've traveled the globe to delve into the greatest mysteries of the universe. But first, they must undergo a sort of personal alchemy—a complete transformation of their physical, moral, and spiritual selves. If the transformation is successful, they'll transcend into a higher state. But along with the great power that's soon to be theirs also comes great responsibility.

I watch as a young boy kneels before the elder and offers his arm. After the old man asks him a question I can't quite make out, he dips something sharp into a pot of dark liquid, then slowly, meticulously, marks a small circle into the boy's arm.

With one circle complete, the elder is about to begin another when he suddenly stops, lifts his head, and even though it doesn't make the slightest bit of sense, I swear he's peering through centuries of time until his gaze lands directly on mine.

The moment our eyes meet, he raises a hand, extends a finger, and directs the others to see what he sees.

Come, they gesture to me. *Come join us.* Their call reverberates throughout time, throughout me.

Instinctively, I try to move forward, but I'm stopped by a sudden shift in the atmosphere. And I watch as the elder's gaze darkens as he points toward something just beyond my right shoulder.

I'm about to turn, eager to see what he sees, when the vision explodes into millions of tiny, glittering shards that scatter like stardust before disappearing into the ether.

Next thing I know, I'm jolted backward.

Tossed right out of the vision and back into the baptistery, where I stand shaking, gasping for breath, and failing to notice until it's far too late the sound of footsteps echoing behind me as a low voice says, "So, it appears you did manage to find it."

Though the smartest option would be either flight or fight, I choose freeze.

With my feet glued to the floor and my spine gone rigid and tight, on the outside I must appear as solid and still as one of Michelangelo's statues.

On the inside, it's a whole other story.

My breath frantically saws in and out of my lungs as my brain scrambles to make sense of the unfathomable truth that a phantom from the past has come back to find me.

The duke.

In my mind's eye, I can see his hideous leering face, looming just a few steps away.

I don't know how he managed it, but he definitely…

A wave of anxiety crashes over me, dragging me down until I'm swept away by the undertow of the past.

The duke is…

No.

The duke is in France—existing in a time that's nearly two and a half centuries from where I currently stand.

Just breathe, Dr. Lucy once coached me. Whenever I find myself gripped by a panic like this, I'm to take a slow, deep breath, followed by another, and then another, until—

Slow, steady, and deep... Her soothing voice replays in my head. *The duke is no longer a threat. He will never, ever, find you again.*

Gradually, my pulse settles, and I realize it's true.

But if not the duke, then who?

If it's a Timekeeper, I know exactly what I must do.

Slowly, I edge my free hand into my pocket, wrap my fingers around the hilt of my dagger, then turn, weapon ready. I stare him square in the face, willing to fight till the end if that's what it takes.

But the shocking sight that awaits me leaves me convinced my eyes must be playing some kind of trick. And for a fleeting moment, I'm sure it's all part of the Unraveling/psychometry phenomenon. *Maybe it hasn't quite ended. Maybe—*

But then I blink.

Once.

Twice.

And still, Braxton remains rooted in place.

62

My heart lurches at the sight of him.

My limbs ache to move toward him.

But my head is in charge, and it's quick to remind me that Braxton is not the person I once thought he was.

I drag a slow gaze over his plain muslin shirt, the loose-fitting brown breeches he wears tucked into boots. Unlike the way Killian and I arrived, Braxton is dressed plainly, less like a noble and more like a commoner. A look that's far safer for this particular timeline. A look that's nearly identical to mine.

And yet, he wasn't fooled by my boy's disguise. Even before I turned to face him, he knew it was me.

But is that because he was expecting me—because he knew where to find me?

Considering how he lied about leaving Killian behind, I can only imagine what other secrets he might be hiding.

The silence grows, and I'm so torn between my head and my heart I can't seem to find the right words, so Braxton speaks first.

"May I ask what you're planning to do with that now that you've claimed it?" He nods toward the small silver ball I hold in my hand.

I swallow hard, my gaze narrowing on his. Worried he might make a grab for the Moon, I take what I hope to be an imperceptible step back. But the way Braxton's jaw grinds, the way his mouth tugs down at the sides, I'm sure that he's noticed.

"What are you doing here?" I ask.

But Braxton ignores the question. With another nod toward the ball, he says, "Seriously, Tasha. What now—what will you do with it?"

I shrug, aiming for casual, but he sees right through the facade. Unfortunately, I've made the mistake of letting him know me too well. So, I decide to lead with the truth. "I'm bringing it back to Gray Wolf," I say. "It's the only reason I'm here. But I suspect you already know that. You've known all along, haven't you?"

The second the words leave my mouth, I know it's the truth.

He hasn't just lied about Killian—he's lied about everything.

Braxton cocks his head, drawing his gaze from my head to my feet. And there's something so strange, so unreadable, on his face that it prompts me to take another step away.

"Are you sure you should do that?" he asks. "Do you know what Arthur has planned?"

"Do you?" With another step back, I leave the question suspended between us.

Neither of us willing to answer, to move this thing forward.

Neither of us willing to lay it all on the line.

"You shouldn't trust him," he says.

"Are we still talking about Arthur?" I ask, trying to get a better read on him, but his eyes are like the bottom of the ocean, dark and unknowable.

"Sure." He shrugs in the casual way of one who's convinced they're in full control of the situation. "But I'm also talking about Killian. Tasha, darling, please hear me. You've got it all wrong. I'm not your enemy, and Killian isn't your friend. He's not the person you think he is."

Darling. Does he really believe that endearment still works?

I roll my eyes and shake my head. "Funny how he said the same thing about you," I snap.

There's a crease in Braxton's brow as he lifts a hand to rub at his chin. "I've no doubt he did," he finally says, the words hollow, his voice dull.

"You still haven't answered my question." I tighten my grip on my dagger, trying to summon the courage to use it on him if that's what it comes to. "What are you doing here?"

With one look at my blade, Braxton raises his hands to prove he's unarmed.

But I know better. Because somewhere in one, maybe even two, of his pockets, he's stashed his own weapon.

I also know that he's far more proficient than me when it comes to wielding a blade.

"I'm here because I missed you," he says, slowly lowering his hands. "I was beside myself with worry when I learned Arthur paired you with Killian. And I thought you might be missing me, too. But I see I was wrong. You don't look the least bit happy to see me."

Braxton stands before me, looking strong, capable, and ridiculously beautiful as his ocean-blue eyes fix on mine. The sight of him looking like that is enough to make my heart literally melt in my chest.

God, I miss him.

Or rather, I miss the idea of him, the dream of him. Because now that I know he's been feeding me lies—it casts everything he's ever said under a veil of suspicion.

Including his feelings for me.

"Today's the Bonfire of the Vanities," he says, the words a hushed echo through the ancient, hallowed space.

"I saw a Botticelli out there on the pile." I flick my blade toward the door. "You should try to save it before it's too late."

Braxton ignores the crack and takes a step toward me. "Come back with me, Tasha," he pleads. "Leave the Moon behind and come back to Gray Wolf."

"And return empty-handed?" I scoff. I mean, what the hell is he thinking? Is he actually trying to sabotage me? "You can't be serious."

Braxton sighs, the sound deep and resigned.

"You really think it's that easy? That Arthur will just shrug it off?" I shake my head. "He'll either send me right back, or he'll send someone else in my place."

"Doubtful," Braxton says. "Only you can bring it back—and Arthur's well aware of that."

"What difference does it make if it's me or someone else?" I frown. "Arthur gets what he wants. And right now, he wants the Moon. If I don't bring it to him, someone else will."

"My God." Braxton runs a startled gaze over my face. "You really don't know, do you?"

He holds the look for an agonizing beat, forcing me to fight every bodily impulse to erase my brain of all that I know and rush into his arms, in search of his warmth, his touch, his comfort, his love. But Braxton can't be trusted, and there's no going back to what we once had.

Or, rather, what I thought we once had.

Breaching the silence, I say, "All I know is that if I don't bring this back to Arthur— " I hold the Moon before him. "If I decide to rebel and stop playing his game, then he'll drop me, lose me in time. Just like he did with Anjou and Song and whoever else became too big of a burden and not worth keeping around."

I watch as a shadow of some unnameable emotion flits across Braxton's face. "I'm not sure that's what happened to Anjou and Song," he says.

"Oh, so now you claim to know, when all this time you acted like you didn't even care?" I breathe a sigh of frustration.

"I've always cared, Tasha. I'm just not sure they weren't more in control of their disappearance than you might think."

"What are you saying?" I glare at him. "Seriously. For once, just spit it out and tell me the truth. Enough with all your evading, maneuvering, and veiled statements. Enough with all your lies. Just get to the point, already."

"My God—is that how you see me?" He looks gutted by the news, but I merely shrug, having recently been gutted by him, too.

"Okay," he says. "You want the truth. Here it is—sometimes, people grow tired of life at Gray Wolf, and they take their own way out."

"By purposely getting lost in time?" I roll my eyes, but inside I can't help but wonder if it's the one thing he's said that isn't a lie.

"Are they really lost if they choose it?" He pauses as though waiting for me to respond. When I don't, he goes on. "I'm sure you saw how Cosimo prefers to live in this timeline. So don't you think it's possible that Song and Anjou chose the same?"

"Cosimo is living in luxury. He has Arthur's full support. Whereas Anjou and Song are just…gone." I frown.

"But you don't really know that they're lost," he says, leaving me to wonder why he's being so stubborn.

Does he know something more that he's refusing to share?

"Well, if you're so convinced they're not, then maybe you should come clean with the truth—at least try to redeem yourself." I practically spit the words.

Braxton's head jerks back as though he'd been slapped. "I wasn't aware I was in need of redeeming," he says, his voice nearly a whisper, his gaze tinged with deep sadness.

I shake my head, show him the Moon one last time. "I'm bringing this to Arthur," I say, slipping the silver ball into my pocket to safeguard it from him. "If I don't play the game, Arthur will stop helping my mom, and I can't be responsible for that. I have no choice but to do whatever it takes to ensure she's looked after."

"At what price?" Braxton asks.

I stand before him, unsure what he's getting at.

"At what sacrifice to yourself—and quite possibly the world?"

I swallow hard but keep my thoughts to myself.

"Tasha, please," he says. "You need to rethink your plans for that Moon. Because you're wrong about one thing, darling—you're the only one at Gray Wolf who can bring it to him. Other than—"

"Step away from the girl."

At the sound of his voice, Braxton and I both whirl around to find Killian storming straight toward us, eyes blazing, hands clenched into fists.

63

Braxton glances nervously between me and Killian. "Tasha," he says. "You have to believe me—you can't trust him."

"Maybe it's *you* she can't trust, mate." Killian comes to stand beside me. "Don't you think it's time you fessed up? Tell her what you did to me."

Braxton works his jaw but says nothing.

"Figured as much." Killian nods. "Not that it matters, seeing as how I already told her all about how you knocked me out cold, left me alone. She knows everything now."

"Everything?" Braxton scoffs. "Somehow I doubt that. Did you tell her how you—"

He doesn't get to finish before Killian lunges, aiming a fist at Braxton's jaw that lands with such force, it sends him spinning, reeling, rocking back on his heels. Leaving me to watch in horror as Braxton's body twists, his knees crumpling out from under him as he crashes to the floor, and his head smacks so hard against the stone tiles, I can't help but cry out.

"What've you done?" Fueled by a rush of fury and rage, I whirl on Killian, demanding an answer.

"Nothing he hasn't already done to me." Killian towers over Braxton. Flexing his fingers, he blows on the place where his knuckles have gone red.

I curse under my breath and race for Braxton's side, horrified to find a small pool of blood spilling from the back of his head. I press a hand to his brow, his temple, then down to his neck, overcome with grief when I fail to detect even the faintest trace of a pulse.

Omigod—omigod—omigod—

With Killian still standing over me, not bothering to help, I push up Braxton's sleeve, press my fingers to his wrist, and desperately search for a pulse.

Please, I silently beg, hope resonating like beating wings in my heart.

But it's a dandelion wish—a wisp of a dream with no real consequence.

Still, I pray, *Please, let him be okay…*

A handful of agonizing beats later, I feel it. The faintest tremor of a vein throbbing ever so slightly against the pad of my fingers.

In an instant, my shoulders sink in relief. My heart swells with gratitude. *Oh, thank you—thank you—thank—*

I'm returning his wrist to his side when I remember the faint tracings of a tattoo in the crook of his arm. Needing to be sure, to confirm my worst suspicion, I push his sleeve higher until I find those two circular lines joining together.

A mistake, he'd called it.

And yet, to my eyes, it looks a lot like the vision I just saw from that long-ago time.

It also looks a lot like the scaled-back version of the tattoo I saw on the Timekeeper in Versailles—and on the pocket watch I took from the Timekeeper in London—and the mark Leonardo sketched just beneath his autograph.

And since Timekeepers are the enemy, is that why Braxton doesn't want me to bring back the Moon?

And is that also why no Timekeeper showed up to try to stop me from claiming it?

Is Braxton a Timekeeper, living at Gray Wolf, pretending to

be my boyfriend, and hiding in plain sight all along?

My God. It's even worse than I thought.

A wave of nausea rolls through me as I stare at that damn tattoo as though I'm incapable of doing anything else.

"You lied," I whisper, and though I'm not sure he can hear me, it's not enough to silence me. "You were the one person I trusted, and..." I swallow past the sob lodged in my throat. "And now all I can do is regret you."

"So, now you know." Killian gazes down at me, his face darkened by a long shadow of pity.

I release Braxton's arm, but when I try to rise to my feet, eager to put some distance between us, my knees refuse to cooperate.

All this time, I've been sleeping with the enemy.

I look at Braxton again, still out cold, his breath coming in shallow, uneven gasps.

"Come on." Killian reaches for my sleeve, but I'm quick to brush him away.

I can't stay here. But I also can't leave—not like this.

Just because Braxton and I are history, just because there's no chance of us ever going back to what we once had—or, correction, what he fooled me into thinking we had—I can't just leave him here to bleed all over the baptistery floor.

I grab the hem of my shirt, tear off a strip of fabric, and prop it under his head. Then I tear off another piece and go about wrapping his wound. All the while torn between what my mind knows and the stockpile of antiquated feelings my heart stubbornly clings to.

Vaguely aware of Killian grumbling, *Are ya fuckin' kiddin' me, Shiv? Let the bastard bleed, already! He lied to you. He doesn't deserve you. He—*

"Does Arthur know?" I cut into Killian's tirade as I watch over my former boyfriend, wondering who he really is, this boy

I'd given my heart to. "About Braxton," I clarify. "Does Arthur know who—or rather, *what*—he is?"

"Pretty sure Arthur knows everything," Killian says. "You know the old saying, 'Keep your friends close and your enemies closer.' But right now, it's you I'm worried about. You okay?"

I gaze up at him, my vision as bleary as the thoughts that swirl through my head. "Why didn't you tell me?" I ask. "Why'd you keep it all to yourself?"

"Figured it was better you learn the truth on your own, without me leading you to it." He rubs at his chin. "It was selfish. I know. But I didn't want you to resent the messenger. I was afraid you might think—" He stops, presses his lips tightly together as though holding back whatever was about to come next. "Look, none of that matters now. All I care about is—"

Just then, a sharp cry rings out in the square.

Killian looks at me. "You still have the Moon?"

I nod.

"Then let's get the hell out of here."

Killian reaches for my hand, but I can't leave Braxton like this. He may be the enemy, a Timekeeper, but it turns out Killian was right—unless it's self-defense, I just don't have it in me to leave someone for dead.

Braxton lies sprawled on the floor, still out cold, with a growing pool of blood seeping from his wound.

"We can't," I say. "It's not right. Arthur trained us better than that." But a quick glance at Killian makes it clear he's not buying it.

"He's a fuckin' Timekeeper, Shiv." He shoots a dismissive look Braxton's way. "I shoulda killed him. And yet, leaving him behind seems like its own poetic justice, no?"

I'm about to reply when the door to the baptistery bangs open, a gang of Savonarola's crazed followers rush in, and they immediately spot Braxton out cold on the ground and me kneeling beside him.

"Fuck this," Killian mutters under his breath. "We need to get out of here—now!"

Before I can stop him, Killian hauls me up by the arm and tosses me over his shoulder.

I pound my fists into his back, kick my legs against his hips, and call him every curse word I can think of in both Italian and English. But Killian is determined, and he races out the side door and onto the street.

Refusing to stop, refusing to let me go no matter how much I fight, no matter how much I protest, until we've made it all the way back to the palazzo.

64

My ex-boyfriend is a Timekeeper.

With every pound of Killian's boots, the words replay in my head. All along I suspected Braxton was lying, but this—this is far more horrible than I ever imagined.

How could I have been so wrong?

And yet, how can I still be worrying about him, hoping someone will take pity and help him?

Even after all that he's done, I still find it hard to switch off my heart.

At the very least, I don't want him to die.

When we reach the palazzo, Killian rushes inside, settles me onto a chair, and thrusts a mug of water into my hands. "Drink up," he says.

Though the water provides some relief, it's a pleasure I barely recognize. My mind is caught in the past, gathering and assembling clues, which only makes me feel worse. Because the truth is, it was right there all along. If I'd only been willing to look.

And what about the brown-haired boy I saw in that vision back in Versailles, just after claiming the Sun—the one who looked like a younger version of Braxton?

Is it possible the boy really was him?

Was it Braxton who hid the Sun all those years ago?

Is it possible Braxton's not from the modern-day timeline?

"Hey there." Killian pulls up a chair next to mine, takes the mug from my hands, and sets it on the table beside me. "You okay?" He studies my face.

I shrug. I'm not exactly sure what I am. But *okay* is definitely not in the running.

"I wish you'd told me." I shoot him a reproachful look as my fingers nervously pick at the ragged place on my shirt where I tore away the fabric in an attempt to save Braxton, or relieve my guilt over Braxton, or… I'm no longer certain of my own motivation. All I know for sure is that it wasn't enough.

I left him to bleed. I—

"Shiv—" Killian's voice breaks into my thoughts. "I did try to tell you." He speaks softly, gently, as though wanting to defuse whatever argument I might try to start.

"Never mind." I sniff, scrub a hand over my face. "I know now, and—" I close my eyes, struggling to hold back the tears I refuse to cry. Not in front of him, not over this.

"Hey now." Killian takes my hand and clasps it between both of his. Rising to his feet, he helps me to mine until the two of us are so close, there's only a whisper of space left between us.

I run my gaze over him, noting the uncertain look in his gaze, the rigid line of his shoulders. And I know I've trained him so well, there's no way he'll make the first move. If something is going to happen, it's up to me to initiate.

And while I'm not exactly sure that's what I want, I could use a hug—something to ease the sting of this night. So, I take a deep breath and ask him for one.

In an instant, Killian's arms are sliding around me, pulling me close, as I bury my face in his chest. He's as warm and strong as I remember him being, and I'm not going to lie, it feels good to be comforted like this.

With one arm circling my waist, he lifts the other to smooth a hand down my back. "I'm sorry," he says, his voice soft and soothing. "I'm sorry I didn't tell you before."

I press closer, as close as I can possibly go, until our bodies conform to each other.

And now?

I squeeze my eyes shut, reminding myself that I have no one to answer to. No need to feel guilty or ashamed of whatever comes next. I'm sick of playing it safe, of always being so cautious. I gave my heart to Braxton, and look where it got me. Maybe it's time to take a leap and see where I land.

"Killian," I whisper. Drawing away, I lift my chin until my gaze finds his.

"Yes, Shiv?" he says, his voice hoarse but edged with the faintest trace of something that reminds me of hope.

"I was wondering if you still want to kiss me?" I ask.

I watch as his eyes blink closed. When they open again, they shine brighter and bluer than I've ever seen them.

"I can hardly remember a time when I didn't want to kiss you," he says.

"That's good." I nod, clutching fast to his arms. "Because I'm pretty sure I've run out of reasons for why you shouldn't." A burst of butterflies takes flight in my belly as I wait—wait for whatever comes next.

Killian takes it slow. Bringing his hands to my cheeks, he cradles my face with such reverence, any thoughts of dissent I might have instantly flee. And when he lowers his mouth onto mine, the skillful push of his lips, the expert slide and press of his tongue, remind me of the way we kissed the first night we met.

It's a blue-ribbon kiss from a boy who's clearly elevated kissing into an art form.

"Shiv—" He pulls away, tilts his head to the side, causing a riot of golden curls to fall across his brow. "You okay with us—with this?"

I nod—it's all I can do. He's robbed me of breath, of my

ability to form words.

"May I?" he asks, motioning toward the boy-style cap I'd forgotten I was wearing.

With my consent, Killian frees the collection of pins, tosses the hat to the ground, and spears his fingers through my hair until it tumbles into a cascade of soft waves that fall to my waist.

"My God," he says. "Look at you, standing here before me. Tell me I'm not dreaming." The way he speaks—the hitch in his voice, the soft reverence of his tone—sends a flush to my cheeks that has me wanting to look away. Until he tips a finger to the underside of my chin and says, "You'll tell me if you change your mind—about this, about me?"

I nod again and pull him back to me, if only to prove I was right.

Killian is gorgeous. Sexy. And while kissing him is an absolute pleasure, while it's everything a kiss should technically be—

Killian is not Braxton.

He's not the boy I gave my heart to.

65

Though it's clear that Killian isn't Braxton, I'm quick to remind myself that Braxton is no longer an option. And what chance does Killian have when I insist on comparing them?

I thread my arms around Killian's neck, run my fingers through his soft silky strands, aware of the chill racing over my skin, as a low groan sounds deep in his throat.

"You are the most amazing girl I've ever met." With a sigh, his hands move from my cheeks to my waist as he pulls me in closer, hauls me up against him, and devours me with his kiss once again.

A kiss I return with equal ardor and hunger. But it's merely a physical hunger. The hunger of seeking warmth, of wanting to be comforted and held close. Because the heart—or at least my heart—it beats for somebody else.

And when I open my eyes and draw away for a breath, I'm surprised to find it's not the duke's hideous face that haunts me. It's Braxton's, with his ocean-blue eyes, that bend in his nose, the way he looked, gaze shadowed with shock and defeat, just seconds before Killian's fist met his jaw.

Still, I slide my hands to Killian's shoulders and tug off his jacket. Convinced that if I can just kiss him enough, I'll forget about Braxton.

I left him to bleed, right there on the baptistery floor.

And yet, he lied to me. I have every right to do this. He's been playing me all along—

Killian's jacket drops to the floor. And as he yanks his shirt over his head, my eyes greedily take in the sight. He is tanned, strong, made of the sort of masculine beauty that would make Michelangelo weep. Killian is a sight to behold.

After my own jacket is shed, Killian watches as I undo the ties that bind my top closed. My fingers are trembling, and I wonder if he's noticed, or if he's too caught up in the anticipation of the reveal soon to come.

Once the ties are undone and all that's left is to pull this thing over my head and allow our bodies to collide once again, he clasps my hands together in his. "Shiv," he says. "Are you sure—of me—of what we're about to do?"

Though I'm not at all sure, though I'm riddled with doubts, that doesn't stop me from lifting my shirt over my head, revealing the thin cotton tank top I wear underneath. A modern piece I found in the trunk that I'm glad I took the risk of wearing. It gives me one extra layer to decide if I really want to move forward.

"You're like a Russian doll." Killian grins. "So many delightful layers to uncover."

I return the grin and reach for the small leather pouch tied at his waist. It contains something hard and round, and for the briefest moment I wonder if he somehow managed to get hold of the Moon.

"What's this?" I dip a finger inside, startled to find it's a small golden sphere.

Killian freezes, his gaze darting from me to the small golden ball I now hold in the center of my palm.

"It's…the Sun," he finally says.

My gaze lands on his. "But that's impossible. I brought the Sun back from Versailles and gave it to Arthur."

Killian nods. "Turns out this one's a dupe—a decoy."

"But I don't understand," I mumble, partly to him but mostly to myself. Because the truth is, I don't understand much of anything right now. All I know is that my blood has gone to ice and there's a notable shift in my mood.

"I told you how I like to carry a charm that reminds me of a Trip that went sideways? Well, this one is from 1741. When I foolishly fell for a fake and Braxton left me behind."

Killian reaches for it, but for some reason, I'm reluctant to let him have it. And yet, it's clearly not mine to keep, so I let him take it, watching as he places it onto the table, then eagerly turns back to me.

He's just pulling me into his arms when I release an exaggerated yawn. "I'm sorry," I say. "I think this time lag is starting to kick in."

"No need to apologize." Killian trails a soft hand along the line of my neck. "I realize this is a lot. Besides, we've got plenty of time to figure things out. What do you say we both grab a nap, then we'll see what happens from there?"

There's an awkward moment as we head for our rooms when I worry that Killian might want to nap with me.

But he surprises me by making straight for the daybed in the next room.

"Turns out, I'm a bit knackered myself," he says. And just before I close the door between us, he calls, "And Shiv—sweet dreams."

66

I don't dream.

Hell, I don't even sleep.

Instead, I quietly sneak back into the dining room, where he left that golden decoy sitting on the table.

I'm not even sure what it is I'm expecting to find, but my intuition is urging me to get to that ball. It's a feeling so insistent, it's like I have no choice but to follow through. So I fold it into my palm…and wait.

Wait for the energetic message to come.

Wait for the phenomenon of psychometry to kick in, much like my dad once taught me.

Because while it may be true that Braxton is a Timekeeper, I can't let go of the fact that my dad bore a similar mark to both Braxton and the Timekeeper Killian killed in Versailles. And I know it's not a coincidence.

And yet—

I close my eyes, steady my breath, and try to clear a space for the message to come.

For what feels like the longest time, nothing happens. And I'm about to give up when the ground begins to shake, and I peek an eye open, only to realize that the reason the lights aren't blinking on and off is because there's no electricity in the late fifteenth century.

Besides, this isn't just an Unraveling.

It's also psychometry.

The next thing I know, the golden ball warms in my palm, and before I can so much as form another thought, I'm instantly hurled out of this world and into that same ancient necropolis I saw when I held Braxton's boots.

The air is dank and stale. The space is cavernous, the light dim. Yet, much like the last time I viewed it, I can clearly make out the sight of my father standing before me.

This is a message from him.

Though I don't know how or why—though it doesn't make the slightest lick of sense—somehow, I know in my heart, in my soul, that my dad purposely infused this golden sphere with a message for me.

I can feel his energetic imprint as clearly as I can feel the slick surface of the decoy Sun I now hold in my palm.

My stomach churns. My knees fold out from under me, and I sink to the floor, where I sit gasping for breath as I watch the message left by my dad.

It begins with an apology.

A long list of regrets for all that he failed to accomplish—all the things I'll be forced to face without the benefit of his guidance.

He's sorry he ran out of time, didn't have a chance to properly train me for everything still to come.

Didn't have a chance to explain all that will be expected of me to fulfill my destiny, my legacy, as the youngest Timekeeper in our vast family tree.

Wait—what?

This is a mistake.

I mean, how can that possibly be?

My breath comes too quickly. My heart beats too fast. Afraid of waking Killian, I clasp a hand to my mouth. Silencing the involuntary sob that slips from my lips, I force my focus away from my thoughts and concentrate hard on my dad.

According to him, we are descendants of a long line of Timekeepers. Which means it's our job to ensure the missing pieces remain hidden forever so that the Antikythera Mechanism is never restored.

There are so many things he wants to tell me, about the tarot, about Christopher Columbus's map, about psychometry, and about the Unraveling—my gift for seeing into the past. There are ways to control it, direct it, he says. And someday I'll be called upon to do just that. But now, it's up to me to figure it out.

My dad, it seems, is not long for this world.

He's running now.

All too aware of the futility of such a move, he's chosen to use what little time he has left to explain how his apparent desertion was never by choice.

He was grabbed off the street, kept under sedation, then flung back in time.

The missing pieces are enchanted. Even the decoys. It's only the worthy, the Timekeepers, who are able to find them and carry them into the future.

The words crash into me, leaving me hollow, lightheaded, while I watch through bleary eyes as my dad continues to run.

Inside, I'm shouting, cheering him on. He's just hit his stride when he suddenly staggers, and a sharp burning pain pierces his back—my back—slamming us both between the shoulder blades and robbing us of breath.

I pitch forward, desperately trying to fill up my lungs as my eyes stream with tears. And that's when I realize that, just like the vision of the boy I saw in Versailles, whatever's happening to my dad is now happening to me as well.

I am fully immersed in his world.

These last precious seconds are all he has left, and it's not nearly enough time to tell all that he needs me to know.

I struggle to peer deeper into his mind, to uncover the teachings he was unable to share. But with his life force rapidly slipping away, he's narrowed his focus, his vision, down to one single point. And I know in my heart that whatever comes next is what he most needs me to see.

A torrent of tears rolls down my cheeks, but my dad remains calm, steadfast in his determination to not waste a single shred of energy waging a war he has no chance of winning.

Instead, he meets the inevitable with the sort of resigned acceptance of one who has spent a lifetime knowing this day would come.

In the very definition of "amor fati," my father has accepted his fate, and he's chosen to dedicate these last few moments to me. The daughter he loves more than anything in the world.

The daughter he never intended to leave.

His face now a twisted grimace of pain, he lurches forward, taking me with him, only to have his knees fail, causing his body to tip. And I watch through his eyes as the ground races right up to meet him.

No.

No!

An involuntary gasp sounds from my lips, as my vision, still tangled with his, reveals a pair of tall black boots striding out of the darkness and coming to stand just beside him.

Oh, God.

Oh, no.

My body recoils. I don't want to see.

But I've come this far, and there's no point now in looking away.

This is the moment when Braxton lays waste to the Timekeeper, otherwise known as my father.

And while I don't know why he'd choose to kill one of his own, I do know this is the truth I've sought all along.

I watch as those shiny black boots come to a stop beside my father's body as he—we—lie prone and bleeding on the ground. And I can't help but wince as I watch, as I *feel*, a hand pull the blade from his back as the small golden sphere is ripped from his hands.

My father's story is soon to be over, but not before he reveals to me the face of the blue-eyed enemy I know all too well.

67

It's the worst thing I've ever seen.

And though my father's side of the story ended the moment the ball was snatched from his grip, jolting me out of his perspective and tossing me headfirst into another, it's not long before a new story begins to unfold.

This one belonging to the one now in possession of the small golden ball.

The shift in energy is a shock to the system. So shadowy, fragmented, and bleak, I can't help but wonder how I didn't notice until now.

How could I have possibly missed that level of darkness?

Was I really so shortsighted?

Or is he really that good at hiding his true self?

I steer away from my thoughts and focus on the shiny black boots as they kick hard against my father's side, effectively flipping him onto his back.

"Were you fool enough to think you'd get away, old man?" a scathing voice says as the blue-eyed boy stands over him, his gaze glittering with malice, the thrill of the kill, as his mouth stretches into a wide, mocking grin.

I watch, stomach rolling, as the boy raises the bloodied dagger high and, without a moment's hesitation, swings it down hard, plunging the blade straight through my father's dying heart.

"No!" I shout, unable to hold myself back. I'm overcome

with all that I've witnessed, all that I've lost. "*Nonononono!*" I whimper, shaking with sobs, with the hollowness of my grief, with my absolute inability to intervene.

More than anything, I want to drop this ball, end the story right here. But I know that I can't. My father intended for me to see it all, so I honor him by watching it to the end.

As a stream of blood pumps from his chest, my father's gaze narrows, his face glazed with pain, and he uses his last breath to say, "Are you fool enough to believe you're holding the real one?"

The blue-eyed boy stands frozen in shock. "What the fuck did you say?" he shouts at my dad. But the answer never comes, and the boy watches, face etched with fury, as my dad exits the world.

A moment later, another boy steps out of the shadows and rushes to my father's side. His face stricken with grief, he drops to his knees, tries in vain to stop the flow of blood and revive him. Then, realizing it's too late for any of that, he rises to his feet, staggers backward, and hurls until he's empty.

My God.

My body folds into itself as I rock back and forth, my mind exploding with all that I've seen—all that I know.

Oh my God—what have I done?

Before me, the scene continues, and I can hardly believe what I see.

The blue-eyed boy is sneering, jeering, boasting of all the dreadful things he'll one day do to me.

My vision grows blurry. My stomach plummets with dread.

The spell is finally broken when the ball drops from my fingers, rolls across the tiled floor, to where it stops just shy of the feet of the same golden-haired, blue-eyed enemy my dad showed to me.

68

I leap to my feet.

Killian has woken, and he's standing before me.

I reach into my pocket and grab hold of my dagger, but Killian is too quick and too smart, and he immediately clocks the move.

"I have no plans to harm you," he says. "And I know you don't want to harm me." Flashing his palms in surrender, he continues to advance.

"Why—because once I kill, I can never go back?" I repeat the very thing he once said to me when he stopped me from ending the duke.

"Something like that." Killian nods.

"You lied," I say.

He stops. Closes his eyes for a beat and blows out a breath. When he opens them again, he says, "Shiv, *please* at least hear me out."

He takes a step forward, but when I flash my blade between us, he's smart enough to stay put.

"Don't," I say. "Don't take another step, because I swear, I will cut you. I will jam this blade into your heart so fast you won't know what hit you. *Just like you did to my dad*."

I watch as the air whooshes right out of him. His shoulders sink, his spine slackens, and this fake, plastic boy deflates right before me. "So, you know," he says, not even trying to deny it.

"May I ask how?"

I nod to where the ball lies near his feet. "Psychometry," I say. "Just one of many talents a Timekeeper has at their disposal, it seems."

He cocks his head, pauses a beat, then nods as though my dad's choice to run suddenly makes sense. He was buying time to embed a message he hoped I'd someday find. And I did.

If there are any miracles here, it was that.

And as saddened as I am by the loss, I'm relieved to know my father was never the man I accused him of being. The opposite of the deadbeat dad I'd convinced myself that he was, my father was kind, smart, and loving. It wasn't his choice to desert us. My dad died a hero, doing right by both the Timekeepers and me.

Suddenly, it all makes sense. All those teachings—the tarot, numerology, the symbols, the art, the ancient philosophers—all of it was leading to this.

My father knew all along that this, right here, is what I was destined for.

Which means that time the Unraveling revealed his distress when my mom showed him the pregnancy test—it wasn't because he didn't want me. It was more that he was grieving the life I was destined to live. That it wouldn't be normal, happy, but instead burdened by the sort of destiny I never would've chosen for myself.

My father dedicated his last breath to trying to protect me, warn me, against the very person who now stands before me.

A boy I so recently kissed.

And to think I turned my back on Braxton for being a Timekeeper, only to discover that I'm a Timekeeper, too. The irony feels like a cruel joke played at my expense.

"I was a different person back then," Killian says, pulling me out of my reverie. "I was fourteen, full of cocky bravado, out to make my mark on the world."

"By killing my dad."

"By following Arthur's orders."

My blood runs ice-cold. "Arthur told you to kill him?" I hold my breath in my cheeks, wondering if it's even worse than I thought.

Killian hesitates, then shakes his head. "No," he finally says. "That one's on me, and it's a terrible mistake I regret to this day."

"A terrible mistake because you only got the decoy?"

He shakes his head, runs a hand through his hair. Eyes narrowed on mine, he says, "You still don't get it—do you?"

I glare at Killian, unsure what he's getting at.

"Only a Timekeeper can find the missing pieces," he says. "The decoys, the real ones—they're all enchanted."

I nod, sensing there's more. "And?" I tighten my grip on the hilt so hard, my knuckles turn white.

"And only a Timekeeper can carry the pieces through time," he tells me, confirming what my dad just told me.

"And I suppose that's the only reason I'm still alive?"

"No, Shiv." He shakes his head emphatically. "Everything I told you, my feelings for you—that's all real. You've got to believe me!"

"Believe you? How can I believe you when I *saw* you? I watched the whole thing as though I was there." I swallow past the lump in my throat and force myself to continue. "I saw you dump your cigarette ash onto my dad's face. I saw you—"

"Shiv, I—" Killian starts to protest, but I cut him right off.

"All this time, you pretended to be my friend, pretended you cared about me, when it was all just a lie—some sick attempt at getting revenge on Braxton for leaving you behind, when all he was really doing was protecting me from you!"

"You don't know that. You—"

"Oh, but that's where you're wrong. I know everything now, including your plan to rape me before you eventually kill me!"

The vision replays in my head. Killian, with a leer on his face, thrusting his hips back and forth as he brags about his plans to send me out with a bang. "I saw you, Killian. The *real* you. Not this charming, pretend version you show to the world."

"What you saw," he says, his voice weary, "was the fourteen-year-old version of me. I swear, I'm changed, I'm— "

"You *killed* my dad! Are you seriously going to try to deny that?"

Killian stands before me. In a quiet voice, he says, "I didn't know it was your dad. To me, he was just another Timekeeper. And he was hardly the first."

I think about the one he left for dead in Versailles, then wonder how many others there might've been before he got to my dad.

"But why are you killing them if you need them?" I ask.

Killian huffs out a breath. "We didn't know we needed them. Up until you, it was all trial and error. We were finding our way with no one to guide us."

"Until I came along." The truth leaves a harsh, bitter taste on my tongue.

"You've turned this whole thing around, Shiv. Made the dream possible."

"So, you work as Arthur's Timekeeper assassin?"

Killian shrugs, rubs his hands nervously together. "You can think what you want," he says. "But Arthur saved me, much like he saved everyone else on that rock. And I guess I felt like I owed him. And considering how I lived before, in a constant fight for survival, well, I found a way to make peace with it. But after a while, I realized it was taking a toll. So I asked if there was some way I might try to even out the karmic score."

"Let me guess," I say. "That's when you started saving people from witch hunts and the like."

He shrugs, rubs a hand against the back of his head. "It

made it easier to live with myself."

"Is any of this even true?" I ask. "I mean, you were fourteen when you got left behind, so just how many people could you have saved before then?"

"I'm not from your timeline, Shiv. There. You happy now that you've managed to get that truth out of me?" He shakes his head, rolls his knuckles across his browbone. "Life was brutal back in my day. Kids grew up fast. Childhood was nothing but a shortcut to get to adulthood. The first life I took, I was ten. I was about to hang when Arthur saved me. Since then, I've made a point of paying that forward. You've got to believe me when I say I've saved more lives than I've taken. That's gotta count for something. Shiv, don't you believe in redemption?"

"Sure," I say. "But don't look to me to grant that for you. Not after you took the one life that meant everything to me. Also, you lied to me—lied about nearly everything," I remind him.

"And what choice did I have? How was I supposed to tell the girl I'd fallen for that I'm the reason her father never returned? Tell me, Shiv—would you still have kissed me if you'd known?"

"Of course not," I say. "And I regret every moment I shared with you before then."

"Please don't say that." His tanned face turns suddenly pale, blunted by the agony, the futility, of a past he can't change. "Isn't there any way you can forgive me? Isn't there anything I can do?"

"Yeah," I say. "Go back in time and undo it."

"You know that's not possible," he says. "I can't enter the same river twice. And Shiv, it's already done."

"But maybe I can go back and stop you."

It's as though the lights in his eyes have switched off, and the way Killian looks at me, hollow and anxious, it's clear I've gotten to him.

Good. I want him to be worried. I want him to think I'm just angry enough to go back in time and erase his existence.

The thought is so tempting, maybe I will. But there's a long list of other things I need to do first.

"You have no idea what you've done," I grind out the words. "That one simple act had far-reaching effects. It shattered my mother. She was never the same, and she never recovered. And it shattered me, too. It led to a stream of horrible decisions that landed me at Gray Wolf."

There's a notable shift in Killian's mood. It's like all the candles were snuffed and the windows thrown open to let in the cold.

"But see, that's where you're wrong," he says, regarding me with a merciless gaze. "You were always headed for Gray Wolf. You've been on Arthur's radar for much longer than you realize. Why, you're the first female Timekeeper in history."

69

The words spin through my head, robbing me of breath. I saw that, too, but I guess I was so sidetracked by everything else that it didn't really land until now.

"Funny how I know more about you than you know about yourself," Killian says.

I press a hand to my belly, forcing the air to flow in and out. Slow, steady, easy, until I regain control of myself.

"Truth is, you were never *not* coming to Gray Wolf. Arthur needs you. You're the key to making his dream come true."

"His dream of remaking the world," I say, my voice as flat and empty as I'm feeling inside.

Killian shrugs. "Are you seriously going to argue that the world isn't in need of a makeover?"

I remember our conversation in the Hideaway Tavern. The question Killian raised when he asked: *What would you do if you were like Arthur—if you had the same sort of unlimited access to money and technology? Would you do whatever you could to make the world a better place for as many people as possible? Or would you leave it to the hand of fate?*

At the time, I refused to answer. But now I know that, as a Timekeeper, it's my destiny to stop Arthur from remaking the world. And if I know that, then clearly Killian knows that as well.

"Maybe the world is desperately in need of a little rehab," I say. "But why does Arthur get to decide how it unfolds? Why does he get to play God? I mean, isn't that essentially what Savonarola tried to do—remake the world according to his fanatical beliefs, his distorted perception, his own narrow vision?"

"Fuck Savonarola," Killian spits. "Arthur is nothing like him, and you know it. Seriously, Shiv, can you think of anyone who's better suited to remaking the world than Arthur?"

"I don't understand why you just accept this," I say. "Or why you continue to help him."

"Me?" Killian lifts his shoulder. "I'm just a cog in the wheel. We all are. I go where I'm told, do what I'm asked, and I'm well compensated for it. What's the harm?"

"*What's the harm?*" I scoff. "I'm sure you're familiar with the saying, 'Power corrupts, and absolute power corrupts absolutely.' No one person should ever have that much control over the way of things. Not even the legendary Arthur Blackstone."

"Be that as it may," Killian says. "But better Arthur than just about anyone else. Besides, there's no stopping him."

"You sure about that?" An idea begins to form in my mind. "Because if it's true what you say about me being the key, then it's up to me to decide whether or not to cooperate."

"Don't forget, he's supporting your mom. Not to mention your best friend, Mason."

And that's when it hits me. That's when I know that Mason's coming to Gray Wolf was never really because of the hair clip I inadvertently sent. This is all Arthur's doing. Mason's just collateral to ensure I continue to bring back the missing pieces so he can restore his precious Antikythera. Mason's just one more destiny Arthur has chosen to rule.

"Who sent the diamond clip to Mason?" I ask.

Killian raises his hands. "Clearly it wasn't me. I was in your custody. Wasn't it your boy who brought him to Gray Wolf?"

His gaze hardens on mine, but I'm careful to keep my

expression locked tight. I've got a plan. One he certainly won't like. And in order for it to work, I need to take him by surprise.

"So now you know the truth," Killian says. "Are we clear that Braxton's the one who left me behind?"

"With good reason." I frown.

"Maybe so." Killian shrugs. "But I don't give a fuck about him. The only thing I care about is you."

"Don't waste your energy," I say.

He glances at my knife. "You going to use that on me?"

I look between the blade and him. "I don't know—maybe. What do you think?"

"I don't think you're the killing type."

"Don't underestimate me." I scowl.

"Trust me," he says. "That's a compliment. Any fool can kill. It takes a wise person to know when to walk away. Look, I know you want to cut me, and while I definitely don't blame you, I also don't believe that you will. You're a good person, Shiv. You're not an asshole like me—or at least the younger version of me."

I stand before him, unsure how to end this. All I know is I need to get to Braxton, but I can't leave Killian to walk free.

"I know you won't believe me, but I really am sorry," he whispers. "I was young, stupid. I didn't know what I was doing—I didn't—"

Before he can finish, I lunge, the tip of my blade aiming straight for his neck.

70

To Killian's credit, he doesn't so much as flinch.

Doesn't make a single move to defend himself.

He just remains standing in place, ready to receive whatever punishment I decide to give.

Probably because he knows that he's right—unless I'm actively defending myself, I just don't have it in me to hurt anyone.

But that still leaves me with a load of other options.

"I need you to stop talking and sit." I hook my leg around a chair, slide it toward him, and watch as he obediently bends to my command.

Retrieving his muslin shirt from the floor where he dropped it, I tear the fabric into long strips and use them to tie Killian's wrists behind his back. Then, I use the rest to bind his ankles to the legs of the chair.

"You know this won't actually hold me, right?" His gaze tracks me as I pace about the room, trying to decide my next move. "You know the only reason you're getting away with this is because I've chosen to cooperate."

"Shut up," I say. "Or do you want me to put a gag in your mouth?" My mind flashes back to when I silenced the duke with his own lace cravat.

"Shiv," he says. "Please. Be reasonable. I'll do anything to make it up to you. Just name it, and I'll do it."

"But you can't," I tell him. "It's already done. Because of you, my dad is dead. Unless I decide to go back in time and get to you first."

Killian sighs, closes his eyes. When he opens them again, he says, "Look, the portal doesn't open until tomorrow. Which means you're not going anywhere now. And I really don't want to think about you traipsing around Bonfire of the Vanities day all on your own. I know we can work something out. I'm sure that—"

I roll my eyes and tune him out. Maybe our portal doesn't open until tomorrow, but there's another portal that Braxton came through. And considering how Cosimo knew where to send the coach to fetch us on our arrival, I'm betting they always use the same location. I only hope it's not too late. I've wasted so much time already.

"Shiv, please," Killian says. "I'm responsible for looking after you—and—I love you."

I watch in astonishment as the lie slides from his lips. What's even more shocking is the fact that he actually thinks that he means it.

Or maybe it's more accurate to say that by trying to convince himself that he means it, he thinks he can convince me.

But really, what could a boy like Killian, a boy who works as Arthur's Timekeeper assassin, know about love?

And what could I possibly know about it, either, seeing how I've treated Braxton—the boy I'd given my heart to.

Still, I look at Killian and say, "If that's true—if you really do love me—then you won't come after me, and you won't let on to Arthur that I know anything you told me today."

"So, you're going back to Gray Wolf?" There's a palpable relief in his voice.

"Where else would I go?" I ask. "It's not like I can stay here."

"Freya told me you were after the book, so I thought—"

Wait—Killian knows about the book?

And did he tell her about my going to Italy? Is that why Freya said buon viaggio just after she delivered my breakfast?

"You thought what?" I whirl on him. Crossing the space between us, I angle the tip of my dagger to his face. "Tell me, Killian. If you love me, you'll—"

He frowns. "No need to exploit my feelings," he says. "I'll tell you because I'm serious about trying to make it up to you. It's the least I can do. The book is hidden with my things in the trunk. Freya was going to give it to you at breakfast, but she said you copped an attitude, so—"

I make an impatient rolling motion with my hand. "What exactly does the book do?"

"It's a book of magick," he says. "The witches use it to time travel."

I look at him, unsure if he's telling the truth.

"Where do you think Song went? Anjou, too? It's an underground movement at Gray Wolf. Arthur's done his best to stop it, but some things slip past him. Do you really think he'd just let people go missing in time?"

"He didn't send anyone after you."

"Because Braxton convinced Arthur I was dead. It wasn't until you came along that he learned the truth. But Shiv, it's dangerous and unstable. You should at least let me come with you."

"Not a chance," I say. "But nice try."

I'm heading for our rooms when Killian calls, "You'll need to find the portal. I can show you."

I'm way ahead of you, I think, leaving Killian bound to the chair as I race toward a new plan.

71

I rush into our room, tear into the trunk, and after rifling through Killian's things, I find the small leather-bound book.

And right there on the cover is the mark I once mistook for a sigil but is actually an etching of a small red rose placed at the center of an infinity symbol.

If Killian told the truth about this, then does that mean he's told the truth about everything else?

Did Anjou and Song really choose to go?

And if so, why didn't Anjou tell Song?

And why didn't Song stick around long enough to tell me when she claimed she wanted to talk?

Is it because the conditions were just right, and they didn't want to miss their chance while they had it?

Hurriedly, I flip through the pages, seeing a blur of various moon phases and symbols that's impossible to make sense of.

There are long paragraphs devoted to intention, and the margins are scrawled with handwritten notes, including the date and time Anjou disappeared and, right beside it, a small question mark.

Did Song go in pursuit of Anjou?

And if she didn't disappear on a Trip, if she left of her own accord, then why does Arthur not relieve us of our worries and tell us as much?

But then my mind returns to what Leonardo said: *Poor is*

the pupil who does not surpass his master.

And right away, I know the answer.

Arthur doesn't want us to know there's a way to travel on our own. He wants us to rely solely on him.

Gray Wolf Island contains a natural portal. But where there's one, there must be others.

What was it Song said? *Magick has always been the currency of the oppressed?*

My God—this has the potential to change everything!

Knowing that once I leave this palazzo, if things go as I hope, I won't be returning, I shrug on another clean shirt and pull on a jacket, since the ones I was wearing are still lying on the dining room floor. Then, after stashing my dagger and the Moon into my pockets, I head back into the dining room to check on Killian, remembering what Elodie recently said:

...until you're crystal clear on exactly what your intention is, it's best to stay away from all that. Otherwise, you risk falling victim to one whose intentions are far stronger than yours.

Well, my intentions are crystal clear. I know exactly where I'm going, and the anticipation leaves me positively thrumming.

But first, I need to find Braxton.

By the time I return to the dining room, the chair is tipped on its side, and Killian is nowhere in sight.

72

Fueled by a mix of panic and adrenaline, I bolt from the villa and onto the street.

I need to find Braxton. Hopefully before Killian can reach him, but seeing as how he got a head start, it's not looking good.

There's also the matter of where to look first—the baptistery where I left him, or the portal he might try to return to. Either way, I need to act fast—choose a direction. And I'm just about to turn toward the famous red dome when I notice a strip of muslin anchored under a rock.

At first I start to ignore it, but then, I spot another bit of muslin. Then another. And I realize Killian has taken the fabric I used to bind him and dropped them like breadcrumbs. He wants me to find him.

And when I do, unfortunately, it's even worse than I feared.

Killian is waiting in the same spot where the portal left us, only he isn't alone.

My gaze darts between him and Braxton. And though I'm filled with relief to see Braxton's alive, it's quickly overshadowed by the blade Killian holds fast to his throat.

"We've been waiting on you," Killian says.

I suck in an unsteady breath, trying to keep my panic in check. "So much for your promise to make it up to me," I say, hoping to distract him as my hand creeps toward my dagger.

"I'd think twice about that, Shiv." Killian nods toward my weapon and prods the tip of his own blade deeper into Braxton's flesh.

My stomach reels at the sight. And when I see the stream of blood running down the side of Braxton's face that I'm guessing is from his earlier head wound, and the trickle of blood spilling from the spot where Killian just punctured his throat, it's all I can do to swallow down the scream rising inside me. *I need to keep my cool. I need to—*

"Stop." I raise both hands so Killian can see them, wanting him to know I'm not a threat, that I'll do anything to save Braxton. "Just—tell me what you want."

"I want the Moon, Shiv." With his free hand, Killian reaches toward me. "Hand it over so your boy and I can bring it back to Arthur. I trust you can survive on your own until the next portal appears or you decide to give your new plan a go."

"But you promised," I say. "You promised you'd—"

"And I intend to keep my promise," he says. "Just as I'll keep my promise to Arthur. But this tosser"—he scratches his blade up the side of Braxton's neck—"I owe him nothing."

"If you hurt him, I'll never forgive you," I say. "Are you really willing to risk that?"

"Oh, I'm afraid we're already there." Killian shrugs. "I killed your father, don't forget."

As if I could.

I glance between the two of them, trying to determine what to do next.

"So, I guess that was all just a bunch of talk back at the palazzo," I say. "The fact that you're doing this proves you're still the same cocky asshole you were at fourteen."

Killian's gaze narrows. "You ever hear the one about the

scorpion and the frog, Shiv?"

I remain standing before him. I have no idea where this is leading. But if Killian's talking, he's not hurting Braxton, and I give him my full attention.

"It goes like this: A scorpion asks a frog for a ride across a river. The frog refuses—he's worried about getting stung, and rightly so. But the scorpion convinces the frog he wouldn't dream of doing such a thing as it would only result in them both drowning. Seeing the logic in that, the frog agrees, allowing the scorpion to hop onto his back. They're barely halfway across the river when the scorpion stings the frog. 'Why the hell did you do that?' the frog asks as they're both going down. 'Because it's in my nature,' says the scorpion."

I stare at Killian. "Let me guess—you're the scorpion in this charming tale."

"Only you can stop this," Killian says. "Give me the Moon, and your boy lives. If not, you can watch him die before I drag you back with me." Killian jabs the blade deeper into his flesh, causing the blood to go from a slow trickle to a steady drip, and I can't stand another second of this. I can't—

"Don't!" I cry, my voice hoarse, my throat burning with fear. "Just—" With one hand raised, I use the other to slowly reach into my pocket. "I'll give you the Moon—just leave Braxton out of it."

"But it's like I told you," Killian says. "The Moon's no good without him. Only a Timekeeper can deliver it into the future."

Braxton's gaze fixes on mine. Another secret revealed. Only none of this is going the way that I'd hoped.

"Hand it over, please!" Killian says.

I look to Braxton, noting the subtle shake of his head.

Then I look to Killian, pull my hand from my pocket, and flash my empty palm.

"Forget it," I say. "You don't get to manipulate me." But Killian just laughs.

"Thing is, Shiv," he says. "If you don't give me the Moon, sometime within, oh, I don't know, the next minute or so, your boy Braxton here is about to cross his own timeline. And I think we all know what that means."

73

My gaze finds Braxton's. "Is that true?"

He takes a shallow breath and nods in return.

"Then why'd you come here? Why would you risk it?"

"Because I needed to find you," he says. "I needed to save you from"—he glares at Killian—"him."

The words knock me sideways, stealing the air clean out of my lungs. *Braxton risked his life to save me from Killian, while I…*

While I left him to bleed—left him at the mercy of Savonarola's zealots.

"As touching as this is," Killian says. "I assure you, it's about to get a lot less sexy when he crosses his timeline and you watch him disintegrate before your very eyes."

"You're a monster." I glare at Killian. "You don't know the first thing about being a human, never mind what it means to love."

"Maybe so," he says. "But I tell you this, Shiv—you're as close to love as I've ever known, and I'm loyal to a fault. I take care of those who take care of me. You had your chance to be included in that lot, but you made your choice. And while I've no interest in punishing you or seeking revenge, I promised Arthur I'd bring him the Moon, and that's exactly what I intend to do. Now, kindly hand it over, so Braxton and I can be on our way."

Braxton sighs, nodding for me to go along. But that's only

because he sees no other way out of this mess.

Luckily, I do.

I slip a hand in my pocket, folding my fingers around the object I seek.

"I'm going to toss it to you," I tell him, my gaze fixed hard on Killian's. "And you better catch it, because I'm not coming any closer, and there won't be any do-overs."

Killian thrusts a hand forward while the other continues to hold the blade fast to Braxton's neck. "Nice and easy does the trick," he sings, his eyes glinting on me.

Raising my fist, I arc my arm wide and pitch the object into the air, aiming it just over Killian's head.

I watch as his gaze lifts—

Watch as he turns, lifting off his heels in an effort to catch it—

Then I lunge.

My hands shoving hard into Killian's side, I push him clear of the portal and clasp Braxton's hand in mine.

"You should probably keep that," I say, delighting in the sight of Killian's outraged face as he grasps the small onyx shiv he once carved for me. "Just a little reminder of another Trip that went sideways."

A second later, Braxton hits his clicker, and the two of us soar five hundred years forward in time.

But the stars that marked our starting fall away.
We must go deeper into great pain,
for it is not permitted that we stay.
—Dante Alighieri, *Inferno*

74

To my surprise, it's Elodie who meets us on the launchpad. Considering all that went down, better her than Arthur. And yet, I'm the only one who's surprised. Braxton looks like he was expecting it, and Elodie's expression reads as triumphant.

"So it worked." Elodie's face eases into a self-satisfied grin that fades the second she takes note of the blood-soaked cloth wrapped around Braxton's head. "What the hell happened?" she cries, rushing to his side.

"It's nothing." Braxton brushes her away. But considering his battered, bloodied state, she clearly doesn't believe him.

"You need to get over to Medical," she says. "Now would be good."

"No." Braxton tears another swath of fabric from his shirt and presses it to his neck. "No one can know. I'm sure it's not as bad as it looks."

"Oh, so you're sure?" Elodie smirks. "Well, that's a relief." She shakes her head, shoots me a look as if to say, *can you fucking believe this guy?*

"Did anyone notice I was gone?" Braxton asks.

"Everything went exactly as planned," Elodie tells him.

"You planned this?" I glance between them, trying to imagine how that might've happened.

"He did." She jabs a thumb Braxton's way. "I just manned the control room. And I'd totally be up for celebrating if it wasn't for that—" She gestures toward Braxton's general sorry state. Then, looking to me, she says, "Can you at least try to talk some sense into him?"

"I'll try," I tell her. "But I'm not entirely sure I understand what's going on here." I glance between them, unnerved to think they've been conspiring again.

Elodie sighs. "Just consider this number six. As for everything else, I'll leave it for Brax to explain."

Brax. The nickname she gave him when they were together. But surely she's over him now that she seems to have such a good thing going with Jago and Nash?

"I feel like I owe you," I say. What I don't say is how uneasy that leaves me.

Elodie lifts a brow, twists her lips to the side. "Then I'll be sure to collect when the time is right. But for now, get him out of here. I can't have him bleeding all over the floor."

Since he refuses to go to Medical, Braxton and I head for his room, and the first thing I see when I walk through the door is that the painting of *The Nightmare* has claimed a spot just across from *Narcissus*. And I hope that once we've had a chance to talk, he'll no longer need to surround himself with paintings like that—unless it's an aesthetic choice, as opposed to yet another way to punish himself.

After leading him into the bathroom, I guide him to sit on the edge of the tub, then I gather some supplies so I can at least try to tend to his wounds.

"How'd you end up in Florence?" I ask, dabbing a wet cloth to his head.

"Arthur sent me on some bullshit errand to the Elizabethan era. When I returned, Elodie told me Arthur sent Killian with you in my place." He speaks between gritted teeth, watching me warily as I rinse his blood from the washcloth, wring out the excess water, then return to his wound. "She was worried about you being alone with him and—ouch."

"Sorry," I say. After wringing the cloth once again, I have a go at his neck.

"She helped me Trip." He shuts his eyes, flinching when I press the washcloth to the cut on his throat.

"I didn't realize Elodie knew how to work the control room."

Braxton shrugs. "She knows more than anyone else who might've been willing to help."

"Weren't you worried?" I ask. "I mean, she could've messed up so easily." I cringe to think of all the places he could've landed, never to find his way back.

"You're worth the risk," Braxton says, and the gravity of his words sends a flush of shame to my cheeks when I remember how easily I doubted him, rejected him, left him to bleed. "And it was a risk I couldn't afford not to take, seeing how Arthur's away—"

"Wait—what?" I cut in.

"He's gone on business—left not long after you. He'll be out a few days."

My mind reels with the news. *If that's true, then—*

I shake my head and focus on tending to Braxton's injuries, though this is way beyond my abilities. He needs to see a doctor. The sooner the better.

"You really should head over to Medical," I tell him. Reaching for a roll of gauze, I begin wrapping his head.

"Head wounds bleed a lot," he says. "I'm sure that's all it is."

"But what if you have a concussion? You went down pretty hard."

"I promise. I'm fine," he insists. "Surprisingly, Savonarola's zealots took pity on me. As for the rest…I take all the blame. I should've been straight with you from the start. That morning, on your first day here, when I found you caught in the middle of an Unraveling, I wanted to tell you everything then, and I'm sorry I didn't."

"You knew what was happening?" I stare at him, wide-eyed.

"I recognized the signs. And you looked so scared, it took all my will not to comfort you—tell you I knew exactly what you were going through. That I've experienced it myself."

"What stopped you?" I ask.

Braxton sighs. "This place can make you so paranoid, it's impossible to know who to trust."

"But you knew I was a Timekeeper?"

He nods. "From the moment I first read your file."

I take a moment to process all that. "And Killian? Were you aware he knew about you—that you're a Timekeeper, too?"

Braxton shrugs. "After his return to Gray Wolf, I suspected as much."

"And I'm the one who brought him back."

"You had no way of knowing," he says, quick to defend me.

But while it's nice of him to try to ease my guilt, there's no denying I bear some of the blame.

"And how long have you known?" I ask. "About your Timekeeper legacy." I wonder if, like me, he stumbled upon it along the way. Or if someone might've prepared him for the journey ahead.

"I've known since I was old enough to really know things," he says. "My tattoo, just like my training, is left unfinished. My father was killed long before he could teach me anything useful. Soon after, Arthur found me. I was living in Boston by then, and he brought me back here."

"So, if your training had finished, you'd bear a mark like my dad's?"

"Yes," he says. "It's the Flower of Life."

75

The moment Braxton says it, I'm flooded with the memory of my dad showing me the tattoo he had inked into the crook of his arm. A series of equally spaced, interlinking circles—a symbol, he explained, that's well over two thousand years old.

A symbol that can be found throughout the world—from Buddhist temples in India to stone carvings in Scotland.

A symbol that embodies so many designs that it's said to contain the secrets of the universe—the workings of time and space—a record of all living things.

I remember gazing at it and how, depending on the way I centered my focus, I'd see a field of flowers, a six-pointed star, the tree of life, and more.

But now I know what it really is—the Flower of Life is the mark of a Timekeeper.

THE FLOWER OF LIFE

"There was a man," I say. "When I was in Regency England. I'm pretty sure he was a Timekeeper, but it was obvious he didn't know I was one, too."

Braxton inhales a quick breath and waits for me to continue.

"He had a pocket watch," I say. "A—"

Before I can finish, Braxton closes his eyes and, in a quiet voice, says, "A golden pocket watch with the Flower of Life engraved on its back."

When he opens his eyes and his gaze catches on mine, it all clicks into place. The boy I saw in the vision when I held that timepiece—the happy, laughing young boy with flashing blue eyes—it was Braxton.

A much younger version of Braxton, but Braxton all the same.

And that's when I remember the man's surprise when I said Braxton's name. The look of shock on his face—the unmistakable shake in his voice when he asked: *What did you say?*

"So you met my father." Braxton's voice is hoarse, the words so choked he needs a moment to compose himself. "I used to play with that watch when I was a kid," he says, his thoughts, like his gaze, traveling back to a time long before this. "He promised one day it would be mine. But that day never came."

There's a tightening in my chest, a searing pain at the back of my throat, as my mind whirls with the unbelievable, regrettable truth.

I met Braxton's dad, and—

And I left him injured, sliced his wrist, shoved a blade deep into his knee, then stole the watch and left him to bleed.

"You're—you're not from this timeline," I gasp. Considering all the things I could've said—should've said—it strikes me as odd that I'd lead with this. But I guess it feels safer to put the focus on him until I can find a way to voice the apology I desperately owe him.

"No." Braxton shakes his head. "I'm not. Now you know."

Then, remembering something Killian said, I ask, "Is Braxton your real name?"

He smiles softly, which is something I didn't expect. And I'm glad to know he's still capable of that.

"It is now," he says. "Though I started as James. Braxton was my surname, and Huntley was my mother's maiden name. Choosing to go by those two surnames is my way of honoring my parents and ensuring I never forget where, when, and whom I came from."

It makes sense. But then I remember the vision I saw in Versailles—the boy who looked a lot like Braxton—and yet, the timing just doesn't add up, and I tell him as much.

"Must've been a distant relation," he says. "I come from a long line of Timekeepers, and blue eyes and a thick mane of brown hair are family trademarks."

I exhale a ragged breath, feeling terrible for all the times I doubted him—for all the lies we told each other, when all along, we're the same. Two Timekeepers living at Gray Wolf, tasked with doing a job that goes against everything our ancestors stood for.

"I'm sorry it's taken me so long to come clean," he says. "I guess I needed to be sure it was safe—needed to determine just how loyal you were to Arthur."

"Apparently not as loyal as I thought." I fix my gaze on Braxton's and add, "I brought back the pocket watch, and I didn't turn it in."

"You still have it?" Braxton's eyes widen with the faintest glimmer of hope.

I nod. "But Braxton, I..." I close my eyes, blow out a breath, then force myself to start again. "I'm afraid I..."

The words are all lined up, and though my mouth falls open, nothing comes out.

How can I possibly tell him what I did—the bloody, injured state I left his father in?

And yet, I know there's no choice. It's our lies that got us both here, and the fresh start I've longed for starts now, with me.

So, I swallow hard and try again.

"But in order to get it," I say, dreading the words still to come but continuing anyway. "I hurt him. I used the skills you taught me, along with a few I made up on the fly. But I didn't know he was your dad. I didn't even know I was a Timekeeper. So, I—" The words are coming too fast, but before I can finish, Braxton holds up a hand.

"But you left him alive?" There's a fresh trail of blood sliding along the curve of his neck, and when I start to press the washcloth to it, Braxton guides my hand back to my side.

"Yes," I tell him. "His injuries weren't fatal, but still..." I sigh, haunted by the memory of his dad staggering backward, faltering to the ground.

"But you didn't kill him." He grinds out the words. "Wish I could say the same about your dad."

I reach for his arm, my fingers pressing against the thin muslin of his shirt, insisting he look at me or, failing that, at least agree to hear me. "You have to stop," I say, hoping he'll grasp the urgency in my words. "You can't keep blaming yourself for something that wasn't your fault. I saw the whole thing. I know it was Killian who plunged that blade into my dad's heart."

Of course, the moment I say it, my mind fills with that horrible vision, so I turn my focus to the washcloth, when Braxton's surprisingly cold fingers lock on my wrist.

"Tasha," he says, his voice gone as weak as his grip. "As much as I dread telling you this, it *is* my fault. I was in that necropolis. And I did nothing to stop it. Didn't even step in to help."

I remember the mumbled words from his nightmares: *I didn't... I should've... Merde...* and I know all this time he's been dreaming of my dad and the guilt he carries for the part that he played.

"But you did try to help," I remind him. "I saw that, too. Only, by the time you reached him, it was too late."

Braxton lets go of my hand, rejecting my assurances as though he's undeserving of such kindness. "Killing him was never the plan," he says. "We were supposed to keep him alive so he could bring back the Sun. After that, I have no idea what Arthur had planned, but he wasn't supposed to die. And though I'm certain Killian had no idea I was a Timekeeper, Arthur must've known all along, or at least he suspected as much."

"But Arthur needs us," I say. "Which means we're both safe so long as we remain useful to him."

"And then what?" Braxton asks, a fresh trail of blood dripping from his neck and splashing onto his shirt. "What happens once the Antikythera is finally restored?"

"It's not going to be restored," I say.

"But what about the Moon? You brought it back, didn't you?"

I nod. "And I have every intention of giving it to him."

Braxton watches me with a troubled gaze, and I'm not sure if it's a reaction to what I just said, or if it's the result of his trying to suppress the pain he must be in.

"Why do I feel like you're planning something?" he says.

"Because I am. And while I haven't yet worked out the details, the good news is Arthur still has a way to go before he's anywhere close to fulfilling his dream. And that alone will buy us some time to stay under the radar until we figure it out."

"And Killian?" Braxton studies me. "He'll return as soon as the next portal appears."

"But I have the clicker." I hold up my hand, showing him the silver ring that Killian insisted on giving to me.

"And without the clicker, when the time on the portal runs out, so does the energy that created the passage." Braxton looks from the ring to me. "How did you know that?"

"I didn't." I shrug. "But I figured there had to be some kind of catch. Otherwise, anyone could wander into it and be flung forward in time. And though I do feel awful about leaving someone stranded in another century, when I think of what Killian did to my dad…" I shake my head, preferring not to dwell in that space. "Anyway, Killian's resourceful. Eventually, he'll find his way back. And yet, when he does, I don't think he'll pose a problem."

"How can you be so sure?" Braxton asks.

"Because he's loyal to Arthur," I say. "He's determined to help him restore the Antikythera. But he can't do it without us. Which is why I don't think he'll admit to what happened in Florence. It'll make him look bad, and he's smart enough not to risk that."

"But you know you can't trust him, right?" Braxton says.

"He killed my dad." I frown. "What more proof could I possibly need?"

"Tasha—" Braxton's expression is grim, his voice gone suddenly tight. "I hate asking you this, but since we're being honest, I need to know. Did something happen between you and Killian? I know you thought of him as a friend. I know you guys even hung out now and then."

I bite down on my lip, but Braxton just shrugs.

"And fine, I get it. You wanted to make up your own mind. But… What I need to know is, just how far did it go?"

76

Braxton sits before me, wounded, bleeding, and it's all because of me.

Because he risked his life—his very existence—to try to save me from an enemy I mistook for a friend.

The least I can do is tell him the truth.

I inhale an uneasy breath, remembering when Braxton learned I'd kissed Killian when I was caught in a Fade. How he assured me it was nothing to worry about. That as long as I return safely to Gray Wolf, to him, that's all that really matters. In the grand scheme of things, what happens in a Fade is a blip of no consequence.

But this time, when I made the choice to kiss Killian, my head was clear. I acted of my own free will—pursuing something that, at the time, I convinced myself I wanted to do.

And though I know it's the last thing Braxton wants to hear, if I'm serious about unraveling the web of lies we've both spun, then I need to resolve this one, too. After all, I owe him that much.

"Braxton, I—" I pause, already regretting the hurt I'm about to deliver. "Yes." I sigh. "Killian and I…we kissed. We…kinda made out. But only because my heart was broken. I thought you'd betrayed me, and I think I was just looking for comfort, or to reclaim some part of myself, or replace you with someone else, or… Honestly, I don't even know what got into me. But yeah, I'm not gonna lie. And though I almost let it go too far, in the end, it never amounted to anything more than the two of us kissing."

Braxton inhales a sharp breath. There's a flash of pain in his eyes that has nothing to do with his injuries. And the sight of it breaks me to pieces.

"But from the very start," I say, hoping he'll hear me, desperately needing him to believe me, "it was clear that Killian *isn't* you. He doesn't even come close." I pause, swallow past the sob in my throat. "And, well, what I need you to know is that despite how angry I felt, there was no denying that it wasn't Killian's kiss that I wanted."

Braxton drags in a breath, his gaze never once leaving mine.

"It was *your* kiss that I longed for." My throat squeezes tight, but I force the words past. "Even in my darkest moment, when I was sure you'd shattered my heart, there was still only you."

After a few silent beats, Braxton says, "Thank you for your honesty."

"Always," I tell him. "From here on out, I give you my promise if you'll do the same."

"You have my word." He nods. Then the two of us come together, sealing our vow with a kiss.

When I draw away, I say, "Do you ever wonder if Arthur is…I don't know, maybe somehow manipulating us, or…" My voice fades, unsure exactly where I'm going with this.

"You mean by sending Killian in my place when he promised it to me?" Braxton says, putting words to my unformed thoughts.

I shrug. "For starters, yeah."

"I wouldn't put it past him." He frowns. "I'm not sure it's in his best interest to have two Timekeepers working together. If you think about it, the whole culture at Gray Wolf is one of distrust and paranoia, which keeps us from—"

"Being honest, open, and truthful with one another." I shake my head sadly.

"At least we're past that," he says, planting a kiss on my forehead.

And I'm just about to return the kiss when I notice he's already soaked through the bandage I secured at his head. "You need to go to Medical," I say. "And I'm not taking no for an answer."

"On one condition." He pulls me back to him.

I press closer, gazing into his impossibly beautiful face.

"Whatever you're cooking up in your head, you won't act on it until I'm well enough to help you."

"What makes you think I'm cooking up anything?" I ask.

Braxton looks at me. "Because you have the world's worst poker face. So do you promise?"

I remember what Mason said about the *Salvator Mundi*, how those crossed fingers could be interpreted in multiple ways.

But when I cross mine, it only means one thing: I'm about to tell Braxton yet another lie. Only this time, I sincerely hope it's my last.

I nod, grin, then tip onto my toes and find his lips once again.

His kiss is sweet and warm, and I linger there much longer than I should, determined to memorize the feel of him, the taste of him, in hopes I can carry it with me where I plan to go next.

77

While Braxton is in Medical, I retrieve a few things from my room. By the time I return to get him, he has a handful of stitches at the back of his head, a fresh bandage on his neck, and, having been cleared of any risk of concussion, he's under strict orders to rest.

"Are you coming inside?" he asks, pressing his thumb to the keypad.

I shoot him a playful glance. "Pretty sure that's not what the doctor meant when she ordered you to bed."

He reaches for my hand, entwining his fingers with mine. "I'll rest a lot easier knowing you're by my side."

We head into his bedroom, where he strips down to a T-shirt and boxers. Then we crawl under the covers, and with my body curled around his, Braxton falls asleep within seconds.

Still, I wait a bit longer just to make sure, then I slip out of bed, go in search of some paper and a pen, then drop onto his soft leather couch and write him a note revealing the truth I've held back until now.

Because while I promised Braxton I'd wait until he was better to act on my plan, that was never my intention. And at the very least, he deserves an explanation.

Dear Braxton, I start.

I pause, tapping the pen against my chin as I try to think of the best way to explain why I need to make this next Trip on my own, and why I chose not to tell him even when he sensed something was up.

When you wake up and discover I'm gone, please don't worry about me.

And please try not to be mad. Or at least not for long.

I know I'm breaking my own promise, and believe me, I feel terrible about it. The only reason I didn't tell you before is because I didn't want you to try to talk me out of it—or worse, try to stop me. Not that either of those things would've worked. Because the truth is, this is something I need to do on my own.

Also, here's a few things I've been wanting to say and desperately need you to know:

I'm grateful for you.

I'm glad I met you at Arcana and that you brought me to Gray Wolf.

I like the person it's allowed me to become. And chances are, I never would've met that girl, if it wasn't for you.

What happened to my dad wasn't your fault, and I think it's time for us both to end our personal nightmares.

And, if we really are destined like you once said, then I guess we'll have to place our trust in the same moon and stars we once kissed under that everything will work out for the best—that no matter what divides us—oceans, continents, or even time itself—we will always find our way back to each other.

Speaking of the Moon—I've hidden it somewhere for you to find. I'm sure if you read this note carefully, you'll figure it out. And when you do find it, please make sure to give it to Arthur. It's all he really cares about, and as long as he has it, I'm sure he'll be willing to overlook any other transgressions he might become aware of. With me gone, he'll need you more than ever. Certainly, more than he needs Killian.

For now, I leave you with this:

I love you, Braxton.

There. I said it first. Who would've thought? ☺

And next time we're together, I'm going to say it to your face, so get ready.

In the meantime, please take care of yourself.

xoxo

Tasha

After signing my name, I'm about to slide the note under the golden pocket watch and leave it next to his coffeemaker so he'll see it when he wakes, but then I remember Leonardo's sketch, and I decide to leave that as well.

It's funny looking at it now that I'm back at Gray Wolf, just a handful of hours and five centuries from when the portrait was drawn. After everything that's happened and all that I've learned, it's like the lens has shifted into focus, and I can finally see why Leonardo wanted to sketch me.

It's all right there—everything he was perceptive enough to capture on this ancient scrap of parchment, well before I was even aware of my feelings.

In the drawing, my hair falls in long waves that spill past my shoulders, my brow is smooth, my chin held at an angle as my fingers reach for my talisman, but it's my gaze that I keep coming back to.

What I once mistook for a question held in my eyes is not at all what I expected to find.

Though my lids do appear slightly pinched, it's not so much a narrowed gaze or a questioning gaze as it is an incisive one, an astute one. The way the great master captured me as I stared across the table at Killian leaves me to wonder if Leonardo was portraying me as I was in that moment, or rather in a future moment that he knew would soon come.

Because in that sketch, there's no mistaking that the person I'm observing isn't some potential love interest I was conflicted about.

No, in that sketch, the person I'm looking at is clearly my enemy.

And of course, there, just beneath the artist's signature, is the sign of a Timekeeper.

Those interlinked circles he drew acting as another message of sorts that I also didn't understand until now.

Clearly, Leonardo recognized me for who I am, even when I didn't yet know it myself.

After leaving the note, the pocket watch, and the sketch in Braxton's kitchen, I slip quietly into his closet, where I hide the Moon in the toe of those old vomit- and blood-stained boots. Then I quietly let myself out and make my way to Elodie's door.

78

Elodie leans against the doorframe, scrubbing a hand over her face.

"I'm sorry I woke you," I say. Then, remembering she's not exactly single these days, I add, "Is Jago—?" I nod toward the general direction of the bed, but Elodie's quick to shake her head.

"Please." She rolls her eyes and ushers me inside. "As much as I enjoy having him visit my sheets, when it comes to sleeping, I prefer to go it alone."

I follow her into the room, watching as she drops onto the blue velvet settee as I sink onto the purple chair across from her.

"Should I call down for some coffee or tea, or maybe even a couple mimosas?" She starts to reach for her tablet, but it's not that kind of visit and I quickly wave it away. "So, what's this about?" She squints at the Renaissance-style clothes I'm still wearing.

"It's about this." I reach into one of the many hidden pockets, retrieve the small leather-bound book, and place it on the table between us.

Elodie glances from it to me and back again but makes no move to claim it.

"What about it?" she asks, which surprises me. I would've assumed her first question would be to inquire how I got my hands on it.

"Well," I say. "I was hoping you can tell me how it works."

Elodie tucks her legs underneath her and says, "Why me? Why not ask one of the Gray Wolf witches like Freya or Maisie or, hell, even Finn?"

"So, Finn really is a witch?" I say, remembering how I caught the scent of the Niki de Saint Phalle perfume on him.

"Hardly." Elodie laughs. "He and Oliver started to dabble, probably egged on by Song. But it didn't take long for Oliver to back off, and Finn quickly followed. Song, unfortunately, kept going. Magick can be addictive, and Song didn't know when to stop."

"So…you're confirming that Song left by choice?"

"Confirming?" She shakes her head. "No. Since I wasn't there, I can't say for sure. Though the evidence does seem to stack up." She shrugs, deciding to leave it at that. "Look," she says, "I know you think no one gives a shit that she's gone, but really, it's more like there's nothing anyone can do. Song and Anjou made their choices, and it's not my place to interfere."

"So why didn't anyone just tell me all this?"

Elodie crosses her legs and sinks deeper into her seat. "Well, I would've told you a lot earlier if you hadn't been so convinced that I'm solely to blame for every bad thing that ever happened to you." Her gaze narrows on mine; her mouth flattens into a thin, grim line. "Did it ever occur to you that your perception—or at least your perception of me—is totally warped?"

Her words stop me cold, reminding me of that day in art class when our teacher taught us about the vanishing point. The place where two parallel lines appear to converge, even when they don't. A phenomenon that occurs based on the perspective of the viewer.

I look at Elodie. I mean, really look at her. Maybe she's right. Maybe my perspective, at least where she's concerned, has been skewed all this time.

Either way, we've clearly reached a crossroads. Considering how many lies, or at least perceived lies, we hold between us, it's time to get to the bottom of them if we have any hope of moving forward as friends—or at least as close to friends as Elodie and I can become.

"So you're telling me you didn't try to purposely strand me in Versailles?" I say. "That you didn't mess with my mask so that I'd cross my own timeline and never find my way back?"

"That's exactly what I'm telling you," she says. "Question is whether or not you'll choose to believe me."

"But if it wasn't you, then who?"

"How the hell should I know?" She throws up her hands. "Glitches happen, Nat. Technology fails. Tripping is risky. You know all that, and yet you still prefer to blame me for every unlucky random event."

"And Mason?" I say, figuring now that we're here, I may as well work my way through the list. "Did you set him up?"

"Why the hell would I want Mason here?" she asks. "He hated me at school, and he barely tolerates me at Gray Wolf."

I lift my gaze to the chandelier that hangs over our heads, taking a few beats to process everything she just said. Considering how I still need something from her, I decide to put it all behind me, and say, "Fine. I believe you."

"No," she says, eyeing me warily. "You most certainly don't. But you're closer than you were before, so I guess it's a start." She holds my gaze for a long, steady beat. Then, retrieving the book from the table, she says, "So, tell me, Nat: *when* exactly is it you're so determined to visit?"

79

Elodie sits before me, shaking her head.

"No," she says after I've made my case. "No way am I helping you with that."

"Fine." I rise to my feet and snatch the book from her hands. "Then I'll go it alone."

I'm halfway to the door when she calls me back.

"I can't fucking believe I'm letting you play me like this." Her mouth tugs into a frown.

I meet her look straight on. "What do you say we count this as number seven?"

She rolls her eyes. "You know you can't enter the same river twice."

"Which is why I have no plans to cross my own timeline," I say. "I won't go anywhere near it."

"Then I don't understand—" Her brow creases, eyes narrow in confusion.

"You don't need to understand," I say. "You just need to show me how, and I'll take it from there."

"Does Braxton know what you're up to?"

I close my eyes. I was hoping she wouldn't ask. When I open them again, her gaze is lit with suspicion.

"I left him a note," I say. "He'll find it when he wakes, which is why I need to get out of here before that can happen."

"You do realize this is not going to go at all how you think."

Her voice is admonishing. "And you absolutely cannot risk changing a thing because—"

"Because of the butterfly effect, and the balance of the universe, and yeah, I know. But I'm not out to change anything. I just need—" I pause. "I just need some information."

"There's a whole library of info right here at Gray Wolf," she says. "Free for the taking."

"Why is it starting to seem like you're trying to stall me until Braxton wakes and the two of you can join forces against me?"

Elodie groans. "Fine." She relents. "You sure this is what you want?"

"Absolutely certain," I say.

"So, why the book? Why magick? Why not let me send you out the same way I did with Braxton?"

"Because I'm not sure how long it'll take. And if I miss that portal, then I need to know how to find my way back on my own."

"The thing with magick—" Elodie starts, but I'm quick to cut her off.

"I need to have a crystal clear intention, I know."

She shoots me an impatient look. "What I was going to say is the thing with magick is that while it is a process of bending reality to one's will, it can be really unstable."

"I'll take my chances," I tell her, but according to the hard set of her jaw, the slant of her brow, she's far from sold.

"You do realize that most people who use it never return?"

"Most is better than none," I reply. "Also, it's entirely possible you never see them again because they found what they wanted, no?"

"And what about you?" she asks. "Do you plan to come back?"

I nod. "Believe it or not, I like my life here."

"You swear?"

She looks vulnerable, even fearful, and it's the first time I've ever seen her that way. So I hold out my pinkie, which prompts her to laugh, but still she's quick to hook hers around it.

"Tell me," she says. "Is this actually binding? It's the first time I've ever done something like this." And the moment she reveals that, my heart breaks on her behalf.

Elodie was raised in an elevated space of great privilege, high culture, and art. She's traveled through history, ridden in gilded horse-drawn carriages, attended fancy balls where she's danced with princes, and, according to her, she even slept with the infamous King Henry VIII back when he was young and handsome and not yet prone to beheading his wives.

Elodie was raised in a world most would consider a marvel, and yet, she's never had a real friend, and so she has no idea how to be one.

Does that mean it's up to me to set the example and show her the way?

When my eyes meet hers, I break into a grin. "The pinkie swear is as good as a blood oath," I tell her. "Only a lot more hygienic."

"Next thing you know we'll be making each other friendship bracelets," she says, causing us both to laugh. Then, her mood turns serious again when she says, "So, if I do decide to help you with this—can we finally let go of our past?"

Her gaze holds steady on mine as I study her face. Her beautiful, angelic, deceptive face. And for a moment, I think of Killian's beautiful, deceptive face.

If I agree to this, does it mean I'm playing the frog to yet another scorpion?

Maybe.

Possibly.

I mean, this is the same girl who once framed me for a crime I didn't commit.

And yet, trusting her with this is a chance I'm willing to take.

"Of course," I say. "From this moment on, it's a clean slate."

Seemingly satisfied, she reaches for the book and says, "Okay, here's how it works."

80

Elodie was right.

When it comes to magick, intention really is everything.

Just like blending in is everything when you Trip.

Which is how we find ourselves down in wardrobe, combing through racks of clothing from the late 1990s.

"Did they really wear their jeans this low?" I frown at my image in the trifold mirror, trying to pull my T-shirt down to meet the waistband of my jeans, but it keeps rising up, displaying a sizeable slice of glaringly white belly.

"The trend didn't really hit the mainstream until a couple years later. But you, my friend, are an early adaptor." Elodie laughs.

"And what about my hair?" I ask. "How should I wear it?"

"A couple passes with the flat iron, and you're good to go." She speaks like she's some kind of expert, and it makes me wonder if she ever traveled to that timeline.

"How do you know all this?" I ask. "Did you Trip to the nineties?"

"Course not," she says. "Anything Arthur might've wanted back then was his for the taking, or at least for the purchasing. But I have seen *Friends* and a few episodes of *Sex and the City*." Looking at me, she adds, "I needed references. How do you think I was so quick to catch on to your *Pretty Woman* jokes back when I gave you that makeover?"

My mind flashes back to that time when Elodie gave me a whole new look just before she took me to Arcana and my entire life was altered forever.

"Is it wrong that this is fun?" she asks, and I watch as she chooses an outfit for herself. A black slip dress with a white baby tee worn underneath and chunky-soled boots.

"Since when do you equate having fun with doing something wrong?" I ask, marveling at how effortlessly she fits into every decade. "You're pretty much the biggest hedonist I know."

"While I'm flattered you think so, considering how hard I've worked for that honor, the truth is, I'm not used to going behind Arthur's back. And now this makes for twice in one day."

"It's normal for kids to rebel against their parents," I say. "It's part of growing up, forging your own identity apart from theirs, and all that."

"Maybe so." She reaches for the flat iron, checks to see that it's ready, then has a go at my hair. "But Arthur's no ordinary parent, and I hate the idea of disappointing him. I owe everything to him."

I wait. Wait for her to reveal something beyond how he rescued her from some sketchy children's home. But Elodie seems uninterested in sharing her history. Finishing up with my hair, she starts straightening hers.

"I mean it, Nat," she says, her voice edged with anxiety. "You have to return before he gets back."

"I *will*," I insist, even though there's really no way I can guarantee such a thing. It'll take as long as it takes, and there's still the issue of finding my way back.

"But if something were to happen, and he finds out that—"

"He'll never know you had a part in it," I say. "Unless you tell him, of course."

"Why would I do that?" she asks.

"Exactly." I grin.

When I'm dressed and my hair is hanging to my waist in a shiny flat sheet, Elodie hands me a tiny backpack and says, "Apparently, they were all the rage. Don't ask why, because there's just no explaining it. But you're definitely gonna need it, since those jeans allow no room for pockets, so whatever you're bringing with you, you'll need to stash it in there."

After I fill the backpack with the book, the unread letter from my mom, and a small wad of cash that Elodie gives me, I look at her and say, "To *The Magician*?"

She shakes her head. "No. The timing's all wrong. The waxing moon is still days away, and I'm pretty sure you don't want to wait."

"Then what the heck is all this for?" I ask, wondering if she intended to stall me so that Braxton could wake up and—

"I've decided to send you out the right way," she says. "The safe way. If nothing else, at least we can be sure you'll land in the right time and place."

I take a breath and nod. I can't argue with that.

With one final look in the mirror, I follow her to the control room, and just as I've always suspected, Elodie has access to parts of Gray Wolf that are strictly off-limits to the rest of us. And as I take my place on the launchpad, I'm secretly glad to be leaving this way. It really is safer. And, after her crash course on how the book works, I've got a pretty good grasp on how to find my way back should I need to.

"The portal will stay open for two hours," she says.

I turn on her then. "That's not nearly—"

She holds up a hand. "Then I'll send another every day for the next two days, until Arthur returns. After that, it's on you to find your way back."

I nod. "And the clicker?"

"Oh, shit." Elodie's eyes widen. "I can't believe I forgot. I'll be right back!"

The sight of her fleeing sets my belly to churning. Still, I've chosen to trust her, so I remain right in place, all the while hoping I'm not making a colossal mistake.

"Elodie?" I call when it's starting to feel like it's taking too long, or at least longer than my nerve-rattled brain tells me it should. "El—" I start to call out again, only to have my voice fade when I see someone else walking toward me instead.

Braxton.

With a bandage wrapped around his head and another taped to his neck, he looks so vulnerable my heart splits on his behalf. And when his blue eyes meet mine, I wonder if he'll ever be able to forgive me for this.

"Tasha?" He squints as though trying to make sense of what it is that he's seeing. "What are you doing—where are you trying to go?"

I gnaw the inside of my cheek. This is not at all how it was supposed to go down. "Did you get my note?" I look beyond him, desperately searching for Elodie, but she's nowhere in sight.

"What note?" he says. "Tasha, what's this about?"

My stomach drops to my knees, and my heart sumersaults. "You didn't get the note?" My voice pitches high, panicky.

Braxton shakes his head, clearly confused. But not nearly as confused as me.

"Then how did you know to come here?" I ask.

Just then, a light breath of wind begins to blow at my feet as Elodie crosses the room. Coming to stand beside Braxton, she says, "Because I told him."

81

Elodie tricked me—she—

The second she stands beside Braxton, their shoulders just a whisper apart, my heart crashes to the ground, shattering into a million unmendable shards.

I knew I couldn't trust her, and now…

My gaze locks on hers as I choke out the words, "How could you betray me like this?"

"*You're* the one who's betrayed?" Braxton shakes his head, but the cost of the movement is too great, and he winces in pain.

"I left you a note," I tell him. "It explains everything. Or, almost everything, and—"

"Tasha," he says. "Just tell me where it is that you're going."

"She's going to visit her dad." Elodie looks from me to him.

"But you can't!" Braxton whirls on me. "You can't stop what's already happened—"

"Believe me," Elodie says. "I tried to talk her out of it, but you know how she gets."

I glare at Elodie. "I can't believe you did this. I can't believe you told him."

"Someone had to," she says. "He deserves to know."

"I'm coming with you," Braxton starts, but Elodie puts a hand on his arm.

"In your condition? I don't think so. All you can do now is kiss your girl goodbye and wish her bon voyage."

"Dammit." Braxton tugs at his bandages. "Tasha, please, don't do this on your own."

"Make it quick," Elodie says. "The sooner she leaves, the sooner she gets back. Hopefully before Arthur returns."

I take a deep breath and step off the launchpad. "I'm sorry," I say. "But it's all in my note."

"Why not tell me now?" His shipwrecked gaze searches my face as I pull an uneasy breath, wishing I could tell him, but I can't. Not now. He's too mad, too hurt, and this is not at all how I wanted it to go.

So instead, I hug him tightly to me, my lips at his ear. "Please understand," I say. "I need to do this. You said it yourself—your training was cut short, and if we have any hope of succeeding, then we need to know more. Killian robbed me of precious time with my dad, so I'm going back to reclaim what I can. All I ask is that you try to understand."

"I do understand," he says, pulling away. "But Tasha, I—"

I press my lips to his for one last sweet kiss. When I withdraw, I pinch the talisman between my fingers and say, "I will always find my way back to you. I promise you that."

Then, before I can lose my nerve, I turn away and step onto the launchpad, only to find the wind is really starting to kick. Soon after, the lights begin to flicker, and the ground starts to shake.

Any second now, that dazzling white light will explode into the space. And once it collides with that gaseous cloud, the glimmering doorway will appear, and still, Elodie has yet to hand over the clicker I'll need to make my way back.

Trying to hide my panic, I thrust a hand toward her and say, "You have the clicker, right? Because now would be a really good time to hand it over."

Elodie's face lights up in a grin. "Actually," she says. "I've had it all along."

Wait—what?

My nostrils jam with the scent of sulfur.

Next, a thunderous buzz hums through the room.

I watch in terror as the glass wall begins to drop, knowing that soon, I'll be thrust right out of this timeline and back into another, with no viable way to return.

I'll be forced to rely on the book—and suddenly, I feel a lot less sure of my ability to make that work.

Never mind that I can no longer trust anything Elodie might've taught me.

"Elodie!" I raise my voice, trying to shout over the noise. But the buzzing is too loud, and it drowns me right out.

All I can see is the sight of Elodie's beautiful, laughing face.

She's mocking me.

Having the worst sort of fun at my expense.

"Elodie—*please*!" I shout, knowing it's futile. This is too far along. Too late for her to change her mind even if she wanted to.

The Trip is already in motion, and now it's up to me to find my way back. I only hope that it's possible.

With a sigh of resignation, I brace myself for the journey to come.

Only to be left gaping in astonishment when Elodie races past Braxton, leaps onto the launchpad beside me, and says, "Seriously, Nat. Would you stop being such a drama queen? It's been way too long since we last played hooky, and this is gonna be epic."

Before my mind has a chance to catch up, Elodie grabs hold of my hand, and the last thing I see before gravity fails, before the two of us lift high off our heels and we're rocketed straight out of the twenty-first century and back into another, is the look of utter heartbreak on Braxton's face as he watches us go.

End of Book Two

Turn the page for an exclusive look at one bonus scene from Braxton's point of view...

Braxton

The Moon Garden
Present Day

The second Tasha takes her turn before the *Bocca della Verità*, I'm overcome with regret.

I wanted this night to be special.

Wanted to surprise her with a private dinner, the earrings I brought back from Renaissance Italy, and the news I couldn't wait to share—that Arthur agreed to let us Trip together to Florence, preceded by a brief stop in Venice, where we'd finally be together.

But nothing about this night is going as planned.

Tasha's been cagey, hard to pin down. At times retreating into herself so deeply she seemed impossible to reach, and at others, giving herself so willingly, it required all my will not to haul her up against that stone wall and join with her in the way that I've longed for.

And now I worry she might've misread my hesitation as disinterest or worse. When the truth is, I've wanted her from the very first moment I saw her. I knew right then that there was something special about her—that she was the one.

Those wonderful nights spent with her in my arms are a gift

I know I don't deserve.

Still, I ache for this girl.

Hell, I *love* this girl.

And yes, I know it sounds implausible, ridiculous, like some hormonal fool who's mistaken lust for love at first sight. There was a time I would've thought the same thing. But that was before I met Tasha and my entire world was knocked on its side.

And though there's nothing I wouldn't do for her—as it turns out, the one thing I can't give her is the one thing she wants most: the truth.

The truth of what happened to Killian.

The truth of what I'm really doing here at Gray Wolf.

She knows I'm holding back. I saw it in her eyes this morning when I caught her in the grasp of a vision that left her on edge.

Is that what drove her to see Killian? Did she turn to him for the truth I've denied her?

Not that Killian's capable of telling the truth.

I should've dumped those boots long before Tasha could find them.

I should've ended Killian when I had the chance—locked him in that crypt along with old King Dagobert's bones and Tasha's poor dad.

But I'm nothing like Killian. Killing doesn't come easy to me.

Besides, who would've thought he'd ever return to Gray Wolf?

And who would've especially thought it would be Tasha who brought him back?

That night, when I returned with Mason only to find Killian sitting beside Tasha with his hand clasped on her knee, was one of the worst nights of my life. And ever since, there've been so many times when I wanted to unburden myself, tell her everything about what really happened in 1741 France.

But, if I tell her one part of that story, I'll have to cop to it all. And as long as we're at Gray Wolf, under Arthur's watch, I can't bring myself to go through with it.

There is more at stake than what happened in that necropolis.

But Italy will be different. Once we're in Venice, I'll lay it all on the line, then leave it to her to decide if she can forgive me.

Hell, I'm so desperate to confess, I nearly told her tonight. It's why I offered to take the first turn before the medieval lie detector. I was hoping she'd use the game to demand it of me. And there was a moment when I was sure that she would.

But in the end, she played softball. And while I won't pretend that I wasn't relieved, I can't help but mourn the missed opportunity.

And now that it's her turn, I can tell by the shake of her hand, the uncertain shift of her feet, that standing before that creepy stone frieze is the last place she wants to be. As though she truly believes that old marble slab is capable of removing her hand.

But all it really confirms is that Tasha has her own storehouse of secrets. One of which I'm guessing is that she spent much of the morning at the Hideaway Tavern with Killian.

It was Roxanne who told me. Not long after I returned from my Trip and turned over my Get. There was a glint in that glacier gaze when she casually mentioned it, like she enjoyed nothing more than being the bearer of what she was sure was bad news.

Of course, I brushed it off, pretended not to care. I refused to give her the satisfaction of knowing how easily she'd managed to steal the ground right out from under me.

I loathe the gossip that swirls around Gray Wolf. And I've never trusted Roxanne, probably because the two often go hand in hand.

Besides, I was sure Tasha would tell me herself. And though I gave her plenty of chances over dinner, she always found a way to maneuver around it.

Which can only mean that Tasha doesn't trust me enough to reveal her truth. And knowing that splits my heart right in two.

"Ready when you are," she says, the tremor in her voice betraying her fear.

And now it's all I can do to keep from rushing to her, clutching her tightly to my chest, and never, ever letting her go.

Together, we can shelter each other from this messed-up world Arthur built.

And, someday, hopefully soon, together we can burn it all down.

But for now, on this storm-ridden night, we find ourselves here, separated by lies, and I have no one to blame but myself.

Though I have no intention of asking about Killian, I do try to lighten the mood by teasing that I only play hardball. But when I see Tasha's green eyes widen in alarm, and her cheeks blanch paler than moonlight, my regret over this whole evening is only compounded.

I try to ease her worry, insisting there's nothing to fear. And while she clearly wants no part of this, she drags a deep inhale, shoves her hand inside that ragged maw, and visibly braces for the question to come.

Just as I voice it, a blast of thunder cracks overhead, soon followed by a bolt of lightning that threatens to burn up the sky.

When another earsplitting crack of thunder roars through the night, I know it's time to abandon this game.

I move toward her, so close I can see the finger-shaped bruises that mark her right arm. So close I can clearly make out the long scratch that spans the width of her neck.

What in God's name happened to her?

My mind travels back to that ancient necropolis, the disgusting thrust of Killian's hips, the grotesque dart of his tongue, when he demonstrated exactly what he'd do should he ever manage to find her.

If he's responsible for marking her, I will rip off his limbs, and—

Another crack of thunder smashes through the night sky, and my gaze returns to this beautiful girl—the only person I truly care about in the world. And I know it's my fault she continues to doubt me. What an absolute mess I've managed to make.

The sky cracks open, sending a torrent of rain slamming against the glass roof overhead. And this time, when I repeat my question, I watch as the tension whooshes right out of her.

Seems we both got off easy. Our lies have survived another night.

When it's over, I pull her into my arms, where I've wanted her all along. Then, after walking her back to her room, I decide right then to tell her.

I don't give a shit that Arthur might be listening. If it means mending this horrible breach, then I'll take the risk. This is my mess to fix.

But before I get a chance, Tasha tells me she's weary, eager for sleep. So I lock it all away for a few more days.

No matter, I console myself as I make for my room. Soon, it'll be just the two of us in Italy, where neither Arthur nor Killian can interfere.

Soon, I'll tell her everything—reveal every last detail.

And once it's done, once I've said my piece, I can only pray she'll find it in her heart to forgive me.

ACKNOWLEDGMENTS

Thank you to everyone who helped to make this book happen: my wonderful agent Elizabeth Bewley, and the amazing Entangled team: Liz Pelletier, Stacy Cantor Abrams, Meredith Johnson, Jessica Turner, Riki Cleveland, Heather Riccio, Katie Clapsadl, Bree Archer, Curtis Svehlak, Hannah Lindsey, and Hilary Shelby.

Also, thank you to Rebecca Mancini and Nicole Resciniti for ushering these books out into the world.

And of course, thank you to my incredible readers—your kindness, generosity, and enthusiasm inspire me in more ways than you know.

Ruling Destiny is a pulse-pounding, romantic time-traveling adventure with a satisfying happy ending. However, the story includes elements that might not be suitable for all readers. PTSD from a near-rape/sexual assault, violence, and discussions of a disappearing parent all appear in the novel. Readers who may be sensitive to these elements, please take note.

Some shadows protect you…others will kill you in this dazzling new fantasy series from award-winning author Abigail Owen.

Everything about my life is a lie. As a hidden twin princess, born second, I have only one purpose—to sacrifice my life for my sister if death comes for her. I've been living under the guise of a poor, obscure girl of no standing, slipping into the palace and into the role of the true princess when danger is present.

Now the queen is dead and the ageless King Eidolon has sent my sister a gift—an eerily familiar gift—and a proposal to wed. I don't trust him, so I do what I was born to do and secretly take her place on the eve of the coronation. Which is why, when a figure made of shadow kidnaps the new queen, he gets me by mistake.

As I try to escape, all the lies start to unravel. And not just my lies. The Shadowraith who took me has secrets of his own. He struggles to contain the shadows he wields—other faces, identities that threaten my very life.

Winter is at the walls. Darkness is looming. And the only way to save my sister and our dominion is to kill Eidolon…and the Shadowraith who has stolen my heart.

Let's be friends!

@EntangledTeen

@EntangledTeen

@EntangledTeen

@EntangledTeen

bit.ly/TeenNewsletter

entangled teen
an imprint of Entangled Publishing LLC